Before Ronin stood a version of the other. A strong, vibrant figure. His face, now scarless, had the nose of a hawk. The rest was Bujun flat. His fierce obsidian eyes blazed with power. His long, unbound hair trailed behind him like a tail.

His lips opened.

"Through all the centuries, I have returned. For the Kai-feng is come. I am here, therefore The Dolman is nigh."

His gaze turned to Ronin.

"The time is upon us. Even now the summoning of The Dolman has begun, but fear not, a chance for man still remains, for you are here.

"But now you must prepare yourself for your ultimate step. For I am come; I am ready. Do you trust yourself?"

Ronin opened his arms wide, said:

"Yes."

"Then now comes death—!"

By Eric V. Lustbader
Published by Fawcett Books:

The Sunset Warrior Cycle:
THE SUNSET WARRIOR
SHALLOWS OF NIGHT
DAI-SAN
BENEATH AN OPAL MOON

THE NINJA
SIRENS
BLACK HEART
THE MIKO
JIAN
SHAN
ZERO
FRENCH KISS
WHITE NINJA
ANGEL EYES

DAI-SAN

Book Three of
The Sunset Warrior Cycle

ERIC V.
LUSTBADER

FAWCETT CREST • NEW YORK

All of the characters in this book are fictitious, and any resemblance to actual persons, living or dead, is purely coincidental.

A Fawcett Crest Book
Published by Ballantine Books

ISBN 978-0-345-46675-4

This edition published by arrangement with Doubleday, a division of Bantam, Doubleday, Dell Publishing Group, Inc.

Manufactured in the United States of America

145038997

For the little boy who lived
down the lane—Welcome home.

Contents

As in the play, the man wears
a mask. Beneath the mask is
the myth. Behind the myth is
the image of God.

—*Bujun saying*

One

DROWNED

Sails

RONIN.

It floated in his mind like a scented jewel. An island; an oasis in a turbulent, flashing stream. Life in a shifting void where there should be no other presence.

Ronin.

Soft and sensual; dusky, alive with a meaning more than inflection. Crimson letters, a brand of fire written across the heavens of his mind.

Ronin sat up, peered into the darkness. The creakings of the ship cradled him; the gentle sighing of the endless sea. The squat brass lamp swung on its chain. Dimly, from above, he heard the watch bell chime.

Imperceptibly, the gloom softened.

"Moeru?"

Yes.

He got up. His eyes roamed the small cabin. Then, startled: "But you cannot speak. This is a dream."

I called you from sleep.

He turned slowly in a circle. The berths in the sloping bulkhead, the narrow shelves, the basin of water, a glint of the ocean's phosphorescence reflected through the porthole burnishing the brass compass. Splash of the creaming water.

"Where are you?"

Here.

He moved to the closed door. The tiny glow from the spangled night played along the muscles of his naked back.

In your mind.

He pulled open the door.

"Who are you?"

I—do not know.

And he went swiftly down the companionway, silently as a cat, to her cabin, to meet her.

By the time he came on deck, it was already midway through the dragonfly watch. He went up the aft companionway to the high poop, crossed to the stern rail. His dark green sea cloak whipped about his legs in the pre-dawn breeze. High aloft, the thick white canvas of the sails, faintly luminescent with incipient light, cracked; the yards creaked as the ship ran eastward. Behind them, the night shrank back as if in terror from the pearl light of the nascent sun. Their wake was black.

There was already some movement around the fo'c'sle hatch, but he ignored it, staring fixedly out to sea, contemplating the vastness upon which they rode.

"He spends precious time up there." The voice came from behind him.

"Hmmm?"

"Morning, Captain."

A tall, thickly muscled figure approached him. Deep hazel eyes flashed.

Ronin turned from the rolling sea.

"Are all navigators like you, Moichi? Sleepless and ever vigilant?"

The wide, thick-lipped mouth split in a grin, the white teeth made more startling by contrast with the rich cinnamon skin.

"Hah! There are none so fine as myself, Captain."

"You mean none so foolhardy as to venture out into uncharted waters."

The smile did not fade as the tall man brandished a sheet of rice paper.

"This Bonneduce, he gave me the chart when he hired me, Captain."

"Your *rutter* is thick with the details of all the lands to which you have sailed. Yet there is no mention of Ama-no-mori."

Moichi put his hands into the wide cloth sash banding his waist, looked down at his high shining sea boots.

"This Bonneduce, Captain, he is your friend, am I right?" His bearded head nodded. "Well, should he lie? This chart says there is an island called Ama-no-mori toward which"—here he made a swift sign across his chest—"the Oruborus willing—we sail." He glanced up. "I have sailed to many ports, Captain; seen things so strange that I tell them now as tall tales, sitting around a warm hearth in the public room of a tavern in some fly-blown port of call, half-drunk, while everyone laughs and compliments me on my imagination. Have faith, Captain—"

There came a soft cry from aloft as the lookouts changed with the watch. The rigging swung to the men's weight.

"Hey, you see that sight, Captain?" He pointed for'ard to the first pink crescent of the sun climbing over the flat horizon. The color floated to them, tiny scimitars on the sea's surface. "Long as I see that come cormorant, I know that all's right."

He made a sound not unlike an animal's bark but which Ronin had come to know as the navigator's laugh.

"Let me tell you a thing about Moichi Annai-Nin because I like you." He paused for a moment, scratching his long nose. "I knew you were no captain when first you set foot on board this ship. You love the sea, yes, very much, but your time upon it is short, am I right?" His dark head bobbed. "Yes, well there is no shame in it, you see. You are a man; I could see that too as soon as I saw you, and now, sixty-six days later, I know I was right."

The sun spilled its strange flat light over the expanse of the ocean, lending it a dazzling and illusory solidity. The topsails began to burn bright. He squinted into the pink rising sun.

"Now most navigators want one thing more than all else: silver. It makes no difference to them where they sail, nor who their masters are, but only if the cargo is valuable. For the dearer that is, the fatter their percentage when they make port." He slapped his broad chest. "I am different. Oh, I will not lie to you and say that I do not enjoy my silver for most certainly I do." The bright grin came again, ivory cast in dusky granite. "But I live to fill the *rutter* with facts and without new lands to sail to, it does not grow. I tell you truthfully, Captain, that when the Bonneduce showed me the chart, I cared not one whit for the *Kioku*'s cargo. 'Let the captain, whoever he may be, care for the cargo,' I said to myself. To sail a fast schooner to an unknown isle; to turn myth into reality; the chance of a lifetime!"

Moichi's wide-sleeved blouse rippled in the strengthening breeze, rolling wavelike across his broad chest. He put a hand on the silver pommel of his thick broadsword, which hung within a worn tattooed leather scabbard from his right hip. A pair of copper-handled dirks were thrust into his sash. He turned his head into the rising sun, and the light fired the tiny diamond set in the flesh of his right nostril.

"This gimpy knows what he is talking about, Captain. The chart is no fake, that I can tell you, for many a forgery has been sold to me in my youth. It is my great good fortune to take this beauty to a land long forgotten by man."

"Then it is your opinion that Ama-no-mori still exists."

"Yes, Captain, in my opinion it does." The deep-set eyes raked Ronin's face. "But do you not feel this already"—he slapped his chest—"here?"

Ronin's colorless eyes at last left the roiling sea before them, swung to study the angular face with its long hooked nose and hooded eyes. A depth of strength was alive within that visage as solid as a harsh rock promontory in a fierce gale, battered but victorious.

Ronin nodded and said slowly: "You are right, my friend, of course. But you must also understand that for me the search for this isle has been long, has forged my life into a shape totally unknown to me. Now it is almost too much to think that at last it will be over."

Moichi's cinnamon face softened and he gripped Ronin's shoulder momentarily.

"It is the truth, Captain. You live with an idea for so long a time that, after a while, it is just that which begins to have the reality. Be careful of that."

Ronin smiled, then cocked his head. There was a small silence.

"What was it that you said to me when you came up?"

The navigator turned his head, spat over the ship's rail.

"That first mate of yours, he spends too much time for'ard."

"Is there something wrong with that?"

"Mates rarely go before the mast, Captain, 'cept to call a man out and administer discipline. His place is aft."

"Then why is that one for'ard?"

Moichi shrugged his massive shoulders.

"Men at sea, they all have their particular reasons for being here. They are misfits, Captain, thus they avoid the land. No one asks questions aboard ship. As for the first"—he shrugged again—"perhaps there is something here he wishes to avoid."

"You do not know this crew?"

"Captain, navigators rarely meet the same sailor twice. This lot must come from the four corners of the continent of man. Nothing queer about that but I cannot vouchsafe even one of them." He crossed his arms across his chest. "Here, I can know only Moichi Annai-Nin. And by the Oruborus, he is the only one I care to know about"—his mouth twisted into a smile—"save yourself, Captain."

"I take that as quite a compliment."

"And well you might," said the navigator dryly, walking off.

Ronin turned his gaze for'ard, shading his eyes from the oblate sun now plastered onto the burning white sky like a hot rice paper lantern. Lances of light shot from the moving crests of the waves. The blue was very deep in the wide troughs. Men had begun to play out lines along the starboard side, fishing for breakfast. Scents climbed from the tarred deck as the sun heated the wood: the harsh, bitter stench of fish innards, the tang of caked salt, the aromatic spice of warm pitch and tar, the sour scent of stale sweat.

There came a hoarse shout and several men starboard dropped their lines to aid a sailor who was being dragged overboard by the weight at the end of his hook. They hauled on the line, in concert, singing, the quarter-rhythm coordinating their efforts, and gradually, the dripping line piled itself at their feet. Muscles jumped under sun-tanned skin and sweat broke out across their naked backs as they heaved.

A long gray-brown tentacle curled up over the starboard rail, then an amorphous lump perhaps twice the length of a man flopped onto the deck. The men, seeing it at last, stepped away from its writhing body. One shouted for Moichi, who turned from his chart and went across the main deck to where they stood. After a moment's argument, he brushed through the tight circle and, drawing his broadsword, slew the thing. Dull green blood spurted and a tentacle quivered about his high boots. Someone handed him a cloth and he wiped down his blade before sheathing it. Gingerly, as if with enormous distaste, the men heaved the bulk over the side. Reluctantly, they went back to their lines, talking among themselves in low tones.

Ronin leaned over the inside rail of the poop.

"What was it, Moichi?"

The cinnamon face peered up at him briefly.

"Devilfish, Captain," he said. "It is nothing. Nothing."

"But?"

"The men do not like it."

He went back to his charts.

For'ard, Ronin could make out the gaunt figure of the first mate, a black silhouette against the low sun. His hideously misshapen face shadowed, mercifully blank now. Ronin had seen him only from a distance, as he had seen most of the men, but he knew that the man had no lower jaw and that his cheeks were deeply scarred. An accident at sea, the story went, adrift in shark waters. And by the time he had been pulled to safety—It was a miracle that he was even alive, they said.

Ronin shrugged and turned away. If the first mate wished to keep to himself and spend his days before the mast, he had no objections. The man did his job, and as Moichi had said, no one asks questions at sea.

His concern now was Moeru. Who was she? After communicating with her for more than half a watch he still had no idea because neither did she.

He had picked her off the streets of Sha'angh'sei, sick and starving, and he had saved her. On impulse, out of instinct, call it what he might. The fact remained that, from that moment, their fates were joined. She became, in her convalescence at Tenchō, the guardian of the strange root which, according to the apothecary who had been its custodian, had been the catalyst in the creation of The Dolman many eons ago. The same root which Ronin had eaten in the pine forest north of Kamado, the yellow citadel, and in so doing had been reunited with Bonneduce the Last and his more than animal companion Hynd.

And she had followed him north from Sha'angh'sei in pursuit of the Makkon, to Kamado, to the forest of the Hart of Darkness, waiting patiently, mysteriously for him, riding with him across the burning continent of man, to the port of Khiyan while, behind them, the last battle of mankind raged before the high walls of Kamado. Dumb Moeru, who could not speak yet now could form words in his mind. She was not from Sha'angh'sei or its environs, her features had not the characteristic cast. And although he had discovered her among the refugees of the fighting in the north who daily streamed into the streets of Sha'angh'sei, she was hardly a peasant for her hands were delicate and uncallused.

She could tell him nothing for her memory had fled her, whether from a direct blow or from shock and extreme exposure or from something else entirely he had no way of knowing. She remembered only Tenchō, Kiri, Matsu—and Ronin. Who she was and where she had come from remained a mystery. Yet there seemed time now, while the *Kioku* plowed the vastness of the ocean in search of the isle of the fabulous Bujun, on this long voyage to the end of his quest, to discover Moeru's past.

It was an enigma he wished to unlock, yet, too, he longed to know the fate of those locked within the great stone citadel of Kamado; whether the forces of man were holding their own against the rising tide of the human and unhuman hordes of The Dolman. Had Kiri as yet returned from her mission in Sha'angh'sei to unite the feuding Greens and Reds? But, above all, had the four Makkon at last appeared on the continent of man. Two he already knew had been together. When all four united, they would summon The Dolman again to the world of man. Then surely Kamado would fall.

The bronze bell chimed the mid-watch and he was brought breakfast: strips of raw white fish, skinned and cleaned, and portion of dried seaweed.

He turned at a sound, saw Moeru reach the poop via the aft companionway. She wore wide cobalt blue silk pants and a quilted jacket, bottle green, embroidered with leaping fish. As she moved across the deck to join him, illumined by the morning sun, he marveled once more at her satin beauty. Her high cheekbones, accented by a rather sharp chin and large blue-green eyes, the color of a far-off soundless sea, almond-shaped and tilted, were veiled by her long dark hair as the salt breeze filmed it about her like a fine rain. She seemed strong and fit. How different she was now from the frail mud-soaked woman he had lifted from the rutted streets of Sha'angh'sei. As she stopped before him he saw that she wore the slender silver chain with its center flower—what was that blossom called?—which he had given her last night. A Bujun artifact that he had plucked from a dying man in a dismal alley in Sha'angh'sei, and which, later, amongst the Greens, had almost cost him his life. He was unaccountably pleased that she wore it.

"Hungry?"

Yes, came the sound in his mind and he started in spite of himself.

He called to a sailor who brought her a plate of food. For a time he watched her eat.

"Tell me again what happened," he said abruptly.

She lifted her golden face to him, her eyes catching the sun, turning white, then black as her hair caught up with the motion, shadowing her.

When I called to you in the night.

"Not before." He wondered if this was a question.

She drew a wisp of hair from in front of one eye with her first two fingers and he thought: Matsu, a wild uneasy cry in the night.

Moeru stared at him for a moment, a blank, curiously opaque look. Then she blinked as if she were trying to remember a stray thought that had just crossed her mind. She steadied herself against the roll and pitch of the ship.

What did you say?

"Not before."

No. Otherwise I would have called to you sooner. Surely.

"I expect so." Turning from her to throw the scraps of his meal over the side. He did not turn back but continued to stare into the glinting enigmatic face of the water.

Moeru went back to her breakfast but now her eyes studied him with some deliberation.

For'ard, the bosun ordered men into the shrouds to unfurl every centimeter of canvas to the stiffening wind. The sun went behind a cloud and the air turned abruptly chill. Then its white face emerged and the heat returned. Farther off, patches of shadow stained the sea, mirroring the passage of the clouds racing across the sky.

I cannot read your mind, if that is what you are thinking.

"I did not really—"

No. Of course not. She devoured the last slice of fish.

"All right. It *did* cross my mind."

I saw Moichi kill that thing that the men caught.

"The devilfish." Noted her change of subject.

He slit its belly, did you see? Because they are viviparous. He made certain that the babies died too.

"How would you know that?" He was genuinely curious.

I—I do not know.

"Have you ever been to sea?"

It seems that I have, yes.

"Perhaps then your people are sailors."

Oh no. I do not think so. She put the plate aside and, as she bent, her hair slid across her eyes, a swiftly flowing river of darkness. She stood up.

"What then?" He dissected her silence. "Try not to think. Watch the sea. What do you feel?"

Her eyes traced the endless movement of the waves hurling themselves against the hull of the ship far below them. Up here, in the protection of their eyrie. Leaning on the stern rail, her chin on the backs of her slender white hands, she sighed, a red and gold leaf in an autumn storm.

Perhaps merely a peasant from the north, a refugee of the war. As you first saw me.

"Now I must tell you no."

A tear glistened in the corner of one eye and she blinked. It rolled down her cheek. He put his arm around her and she came against his hard body, giving in at last.

I am adrift in the unknown and it terrifies me. Who am I, Ronin? What am I doing here? I feel as if I must not leave your side. I feel—a little like a corpse, drowned on a tide, thrown up onto an alien shore. I must—

"What?"

She threw her head, her hair flying, and wiped at her eyes.

Tell me what happened in the forest near Kamado. When you emerged, you were so white that I feared you had lost blood from a severe wound.

Ronin smiled bleakly.

"Wounded? No. At least not in the sense you mean." He held the warmth of her body against him like a cloak. "I encountered a bizarre creature and it had been much on my mind of late." He shook his head as if in disbelief. "It was a man, Moeru, a man with a hart's great head, black-furred, crowned by enormous treed antlers." His voice lowered and a hard edge crept into it. "I drew my sword but my fingers would not hold it. It came at me and my legs would not support me. It lifted a great black onyx sword over its head and then a strange thing occurred. It stared into my face and I saw within its very human eyes fear. We were locked together, neither able to act."

Aloft, the yards swung to and the canvas groaned as it caught the following wind, hurtling the schooner across the limitless sea. Muscles rippling, sailors sprang to the lines, securing the new set of the rigging. A man shouted, seeming far away, and Ronin heard the peculiar, dark voice of the first mate like hot pitch on a wound, recalling—

This Hart of Darkness. Her blue-green eyes moved. *Why does he disturb you so?*

"I—do not know. I faced him and felt as if—"

Patiently, she waited for him to finish.

"As if I was drowning."

And he? What do you suppose he felt?

He looked at her curiously.

"What an extraordinary thing to say. How would I know what he felt?"

She shrugged.

I thought you might know.

He shook his head.

What did you see in his face, Ronin?

The Hart of Darkness swam before him, that strange mixture of man and beast. He saw the sleekly furred snout, the wide, blunt herbivorous teeth, the black, flaring nostrils, quivering as they sampled scents, the oval, human eyes, and abruptly he felt a chill at the center of his being, heard the cool click of Bonneduce the Last's Bones, rolling over the patterned rug in the house in the City of Ten Thousand Paths so long ago. *You do not fear death,* the little man had said, *and that is good. Yet you fear—*

"Stop!" cried Ronin.

What is it? Moeru gripped his arm, the long fingers firm and supple.

He passed a hand across his eyes.

"Nothing. Just the ghost of a dream."

You know him, Ronin.

The fear rose inside him, unbidden.

"Now you speak nonsense."

A sky dark with vultures; the stiff rustle of their circling flight.

I see it in your eyes.

Irrationally, he turned on her, away from himself. *A stench worse than putrefaction.*

"Chill take you, bitch! Shut up! You—"

"Captain!"

Ronin swung away, saw Moichi racing up the aft companionway.

"What is it?"

Moeru moved away from him, her eyes bleak and as opaque as stones.

"Lookouts report sails to port." The big man approached them. He pointed. "Just visible now over the horizon."

"What manner of vessels?" Ronin asked, shading his eyes as he looked out over the water.

"Too far away as yet, Captain." His hazel eyes were chilled. "But this far out I would hardly expect them to be merchantmen."

"Very well. Swing away from them." Moichi nodded assent. "But mark you, I do not wish to waste valuable time.

A swift landfall at Ama-no-mori is imperative."

"Aye, Captain," said Moichi, already swinging away, calling to the bosun in his deep voice. The bosun, at midships, relayed the order to the first.

Slowly, the schooner heeled, beginning its wide arc to starboard. Spray flew up into their faces, rich and cool and fragrant with life.

And they began their run from the oncoming ships.

The seas rose as they plunged ahead, the men constantly in the shrouds now to take advantage of the shifting wind. The ocean turned a deep green, then a hard, flat gray as banks of rippling thunderheads climbed into the western skies.

"They are gaining on us," said Moichi, on the poop with Ronin and the helmsman. "The sails are tetrahedral, an unfamiliar configuration to me."

"Have they seen us?" asked Ronin.

"Seen us? I think," said the navigator, "that they have been searching for us."

"How could that be?"

His shoulders lifted, fell. "Captain, my expertise is in guiding ships like this to safe ports."

The rain began then a good distance away, a strange sight, the downpour a dark oblique brush flailing harshly at the sea with such furious intensity that it appeared as if the sea water were actually flowing upward.

"Hard to port!" called Moichi, and the *Kioku* returned eastward with the black rain and the odd sails in full pursuit.

Moeru left her spot at the aft rail and came and stood beside Ronin.

Who knows of your voyage?

Ronin watched the shrouds straining their lines. He had been thinking along a similar path. Futilely.

"To my knowledge, only Bonneduce the Last."

Moichi was too involved with the helmsman and the sails to question the seemingly one-sided conversation.

Still, another may know.

Perhaps he was only half-listening then. Certainly he did not understand her remark, part of their previous conversation.

Moichi left the helmsman, went across the deck, stood at the poop's port railing.

"Captain," he said. "I do not think that these are natural ships."

Ronin went to stand beside him, Moeru in his wake. He saw lines creasing the navigator's face.

"What do you mean?" Ronin asked.

"These ships, Captain. Well, look for yourself."

The trio peered into the west. The rain there had slackened, yet still the purple skies were dark. Out there, the sea was gray and white like the wings of a seagull. Purple-tinged.

Moeru's fingers gripped Moichi's arm.

"Yes."

Three ships, dark with high prows, their silhouettes slender and swift, sped toward them. They were still far away but now they were close enough to make out several important details.

Their sails were black and obviously not of conventional canvas, for they shone in the wan light of the dismal afternoon. Emblazoned across the center of each sail was the image of a grinning armored bird. They gleamed and flickered as if they were on fire.

"Look below," said Moichi deliberately.

They saw that the hulls of the ships were completely dry as they ran, keelless, across the sea, above the waves. Nevertheless, the sea furrowed beneath them and white spray flew in their wakes.

"You have sorcerous foes, Captain," said Moichi flatly. "The crew will not like that."

"They do not have to like it," answered Ronin. "They merely have to fight." He turned. "And what of you, Moichi. Where do you stand?"

"As I have said, Captain, I have beheld many strange sights, even as you have. There is nothing on land nor sea which frightens me." He slapped the port rail. "I have a good ship under my feet even if it is no match for those sorcerous ships out there." He shrugged. "There have ever been battles in my life."

"Then I have no cause for worry. Have the first mate break out the arms and prepare for boarding."

"Aye, Captain." The white teeth shone wolfishly. "A pleasure."

What of me?

"Get below."

But I wish to fight.

He turned to her and watched her eyes for a moment.

"Have the bosun get you a sword, then."

There is no choice but to fight.

He looked seaward.

"We cannot outrun them. Moichi understood that immediately. They mean to take us." His right hand had drifted unconsciously to the hilt of his blade and his left hand clenched inside the Makkon gauntlet. He felt the adrenalin surging through his chest and arms. He breathed deeply, oxygenating his system to help forestall muscle fatigue in the battle to come. He longed for battle now, the warrior within him aching for release. "And I—" he said thickly, "I wish to destroy them."

They were of obsidian, rough-hewn, sparking in the lowering sun, which peered out from behind jagged rents in the rippling clouds with a heavy light that was painful to the eyes. The high prows, sleek and sharp, still shattering the green water beneath them as they came on, were carved into grotesque faces, horned and beaked, resembling, uncannily, the Makkon.

The masts seemed to be carved from vast alien rubies, for they were translucent, shedding thin escarpments of bloody shadow across the narrow decks and into the sea before the ships.

"These craft are from another time," said Moichi with some professional awe. "I'd give an arm to pilot one."

Already they could discern movement along the enemy's decks. Through the crashing, creaming bow waves, they could make out bright flashes of high helms and short-bladed swords like shining, articulated insects within a teeming hive.

And now they saw that those who sailed the obsidian ships were not men at all. These beings were wide-shouldered, without the characteristic human slant. They were wasp-waisted with legs distinguished by bulging thighs and virtually no calfs. Their heads seemed stuck directly onto shoulders without benefit of neck or throat. They wore sweeping conical helms of ebon metal and their barrel chests were encased in dark armor.

Look at their faces.

Ronin stared. Above the nose they had the skull of man, but below, black nostrils were gouged directly into the flesh, as if plunged by some murderous scalpel, and lower, the massive bone was pushed out into a snout, making them appear as if they had been dropped on the backs of their heads as they had been born. Their eyes were not the ovals of man but were round and beaded, glossily obsidian, like those of birds of prey. Indeed, as the ships drew closer, he saw that the helms were in fact long glistening plumage, which covered the heads of these strange warriors from crown to the center of the back.

Ronin looked around the *Kioku*. All the men were armed and the first mate had fully half the complement along the port sheer-strake, preparing to repel the boarders.

And now the crash of the sea, as if the violent surf were striking a knife-toothed shore, and three obsidian effigies loomed over them, momentarily blotting out the fading light. In that instant the penumbra of the alien masts crisscrossed the *Kioku* in a bloody foreshadowing.

And now the air was filled with the whirring of the grappling hooks as they arced in the air like a rain of black lava, thick ropes snaking behind their flights. The *Kioku* shuddered, its prow lifting momentarily out of the water like a trapped animal, then crashed into an oncoming wave, the decks awash now with sea water as well as clambering creatures.

Drawing his sword, Ronin leapt from the high poop, hurtling himself into the oncoming wave of warriors. They shouted, high, piercing sounds, and parted like grain at his intrusion. They reared back, their short, heavy blades clashing into his longer one.

Within their midst, he swung two-handed at their bodies, but finding them too well protected by their ebon armor, he shifted his aim higher. In a blur, he sheared off a head in a welter of yellow bone, pink and gray matter. Feathers fluttered and blood fountained up, pumping from a dying heart, staining the air, filling it with an awful stench.

Again and again he swung, his long, double-edged blade a platinum swath amidst dark masses of scrambling warriors. His arteries swelled as he increased the depth of his breathing, compensating for the adrenalin's oxygen drain to his system. An exquisite sensation gripped him, his blade running with beaded blood and bits of brain, as if he were looking within an infinitude of mirrors and the strength of all his replicated selves layered him in an invulnerable mantle of strength and endurance.

Now the strange warriors attempted to scatter before his berserk attack, but using the *Kioku*'s rigging, he cut them off. Some continued to flee only to meet the ready edges of his sailors' blades.

At length, he turned to see Moichi still on the poop, defending his territory with his curving broadsword. A clutter of warriors blotted out his view, then, moments later, he spied

Moeru beside the navigator, cutting her way through the enemy with a preciseness and efficiency that surprised him.

There was little time to marvel, for a trio of blades came whistling at him in great rapidity. He slew these three warriors and hacked through another group, finding himself in a small clearing. He glanced around. The sailors appeared to be holding their own, but now the second and third ships were closing, their grappling hooks already spinning through the air. Soon their warriors would join the battle.

He began to fight his way starboard, hoping to sever the new lines and thus delay the arrival of the reinforcements. But the warriors divined his intent and converged to block his way. Still he fought on, soaked now in blood and marrow.

"Moichi!" he called over the din. "The lines to starboard!"

The navigator left the few remaining enemy in his area to Moeru and leaped to the main deck, his massive frame a battering ram of muscle and force of will.

Sheathing his sword, he kicked out at an advancing warrior and went into the ratlines and, above the battle, worked his way to midships where, drawing a copper-handled dirk, he went to work with tight arcs, snapping the lines. They whipped into the sea, but the ships came on and new lines snaked aboard.

Ronin dodged a blow meant to disembowel him and, ducking, ripped his sodden sea cloak from him; its weight had begun to hinder his movements. He smashed a two-handed blow into the seam along one side of the attacker's body armor. The warrior screamed and clutched at his side. Blood spurted. He went to his knees. Ronin swiveled as he swung, shearing off another warrior's snout. A flurry like heated snow.

Ronin made his laborious way toward Moichi, through forests of warriors. He thrust straight ahead and his blade shattered the breastplate of a warrior. He jerked it free and, in the same movement, arced it violently backward, severing the jugular of an advancing warrior to his rear. He slammed headlong into two more, scattering them in a flutter of feathers. He swung right, then left, his bulging arms sticky and running with moisture.

Before the mast he fought, as the decks were piled high with corpses and the footing became treacherously slippery. He was aware of a tall figure near him, hewing at the warriors, the man's long blade just visible on the far periphery of his vision, shearing through a plumed head. He swung again into a mass of avian warriors then he was on his knees, coughing and shaking his head. Lights danced in front of his eyes. He tried to focus and could not. Just the hint of a blurred shadow, blossoming. He tasted blood and gore, still warm and moving as if alive. He spat, attempting to rise, slipping in the slick muck on the deck. His vision cleared. Severed head of a plumed warrior staring at him accusingly from the deck. Hit me, he thought dazedly. Who threw it?

He blinked back the mingled sweat and blood running down his scalp. Looked up, stared into the twisted face of the first mate.

Indeed there was no lower jaw. White scars, livid and pulsing, were raised from the otherwise sunburned flesh like the hideous distended veins of the dead. They ran from the twisted upper lip across the gouged bridge of the nose onto an island of scar tissue pooled under the right eye.

The first mate laughed, a strange susurration, and slashed out with his boot. The plumed skull flew into Ronin's chest. And in that motion Ronin knew, saw the swift flash of white as the light caught the sheen of the artificial left eye, and abruptly he was hurtled back in time to twin feluccas flying across a vast, uncharted sea of ice, locked together, one now to the howling, chill wind, as two powerful figures fought, one for control, the other for freedom, darkness and light, a vicious battle. Ronin had fought Freidal then, had felled the Security Saardin of the Freehold with a brutal blow to his face.

He had thought Freidal dead, his sadistic torturings and murders of Ronin's old friends avenged at last as the two ships parted with only the Saardin's ever-present scribe left standing, immobile and mute, aboard the helmless vessel as he had cut it away.

Ronin twisted away so that Freidal's next kick only grazed his ribs instead of breaking them, as the Saardin had intended.

He regained his feet and lifted his sword.

"Come to me," hissed Freidal, his misshapen mouth giving his words a distorted, leaden quality. "Come and meet your death." He raised his own blade. But it was he who advanced on Ronin. Their swords clashed.

"And where is Borros? He too I must seek out and destroy."

The blades swung away, sliced through the air.

"Dead and buried long ago. Free at last of his terror and beyond your blade."

Freidal lunged, in and down, and Ronin turned, parrying.

"Do you expect me to believe that? Traitor! You have spat upon the Law of the Freehold and there is only one penalty for such a transgression."

"After seeing this world, you still cling to the Law of the Freehold?"

Swords flashing, the panting of hot breath, muscles locked and straining, eyes seeking an advantage.

"This world only validates the Law; if you were not such a fool, you would understand that. All is chaos here. War, death, and the dying lying broken in streets of mud and filth. We of the Freehold are beyond all that. The Law is our mistress; it is what sets us apart from this scum. We set the Law above all else, thus are we to remain men. But this is something that I do not expect you to understand. You had already reverted to the animalisms of the Surface world while in the Freehold. You were never one of us." He lunged again. "You flaunted the Law; now you must die." With a grunt, he swung hard into Ronin's side, twisting his blade in an attempt to evade Ronin's block. But Ronin felt the excess pressure and leaned away from it instead of fighting it and they were at a deadlock, their faces only centimeters apart.

"You thought me dead," whispered Freidal, "but I survived our last encounter, your traitorous blow. I clung to life, I would not die, for my mission was not yet complete. The strength of the righteous flowed through me and, as the cold days and nights passed, my scribe opened his veins to me. He knew his duty. He fed me the warmth and the life from his own body so that the Law might be served, so that I might seek you and Borros out, so that justice might be done."

Freidal broke away, feinted, then swept in the opposite direction, saying: "Law must ever be the victor against chaos!" He cut in under Ronin's defense and the edge of his blade sliced through cloth and skin. Then Ronin's blade was up, breaking the momentum of the blow and he would not retreat.

"Agh!" screamed the Saardin. "What sort of man are you? Coward! Why do you not attack?"

The whisper in his ear: a soft susurration with a core of steel. Ronin heard again the Salamander, his Senseii, talking to him as he took Ronin through Combat practice on one of the high Levels of the Freehold: "It is not just the strong arm, my dear boy, which wins in Combat. Let your eye judge your opponent. Stand your ground. Do not attack, yet neither do you retreat. Be the rock upon which your opponent throws himself, thus will you see his weaknesses. And then, dear boy, when his frustration turns inexorably to rage, his reactions will suffer and, if you are most clever, you will find the proper path to victory."

Thus he stood upon the unquiet deck, in the shadow of the looming obsidian ships, their strange avian sails dominating the sky, and repulsed all that Freidal threw at him. He parried the powerful horizontal strokes, he turned aside the vicious oblique cuts, he blocked the swift vertical strikes, all the while gauging the feints and false movements, the careful counterbalancing of Combat that made it such a complex art, that lifted its finest executors into a realm far above a mere warrior's. And in this Ronin recognized the truth within the distortions the Saardin mouthed: The Freehold's Combat system had made him a superior artist in weaponry. Knew too, on an instinctive level, just how dangerous Freidal was. His belief in his righteousness, in the iron fastness of the Law, could not be shaken. He was no mercenary, proficient but easily dealt with. His fanaticism was his power, would feed him deep reserves of strength and will. Thus at last did Ronin recognize his evil as the Freehold's.

Freidal feinted another blow, threw his sword at Ronin instead, and in the same motion, slammed his balled fists into Ronin's throat. His knee lifted and smashed into Ronin's stomach. Ronin fell against the starboard sheer-strake, his breath gone and his eyes watering. He gagged, willing his lungs to do their work. Freidal's good eye gleamed as he swung from the hips, slamming his fists alongside Ronin's head. He watched the other sink to his knees.

Freidal looked down and, grinning wolfishly, bent and picked up Ronin's fallen sword. Languidly, almost lovingly, he tested its weight and judged its balance. Ronin's head came up and the Saardin swiped at the face with the back of his hand.

Now he held Ronin's sword with both hands and slowly lifted it high above his head. It gleamed all along its length, a bolt of stiff lightning that too soon began its blurred descent.

Ronin tried to focus but all he could see was a dark shape looming over him, a streak of white light that hurt his eyes. The world drained of color: two polymorphous black entities, two shards of bitter ebon will, linked by a slashing line of white.

His fingers like lances, stiff as steel inside the Makkon

gauntlet, his body already moving without conscious volition as something bellowed darkly inside him, echoing on a torrent of wind filled with animal scents. Bright and unbidden, the Hart, stately, black, fearsomely atavistic, shook his antlers within a deep pine glade.

Something coalesced within him, with the motion. The rushing of the white blade, his forked fingers rising upward, Freidal's cruel gloating hideous face, confident of victory, upward and downward, the weapons crossed in an "x" pattern, the Saardin's incipient surprise as the fingers plunged into his eyes. Black and white; white and black. Whistle of the impotent sword blade, a dying insect beside his ear.

Freidal was screaming, a loathsome, shivering sound filled with pain and fear. His head drew back, instinctively seeking release. But the terrible weapon lanced forward, inexorable as metal, the alien hide inimical to human flesh. Impaling him. Then the fingers curled, ripping at the soft viscera, digging with enormous strength, and with a herculean jerking motion, they broke through the cheekbones, stripped the flesh from the Saardin's face.

The sounds came again, ceaseless, like waves of fire, an envelope of agony, a hot tomb closed by the final smash of the gauntleted fist into the center of the broken face, shattering the skull. Teeth sprayed like cracked nuts and the body collapsed, the stench overpowering as the sphincter muscle relaxed.

Never had death been so satisfying.

The din of the battle surrounding him came back gradually and at length he became aware that Moichi was calling his name. He turned his head, saw the navigator beset by plumed warriors who sought to stop him from severing the snaking lines from the other obsidian ships. He plucked his stolen sword from the nerveless fingers of the bloody Saardin lying at his feet and turned, grinning. Slammed his blade through the corselet of an oncoming warrior with such force that the armor flew from the creature's body. He swiftly decapitated it and, swinging his sword in great arcs, forced his way further aft, toward the navigator.

Hurling the plumed warriors from him, Ronin at last made Moichi's side and, together, back to back, they fought the oncoming tide. Clearing away the warriors momentarily, they began to work feverishly on the grappling lines which sang with tension as the sailors aboard the obsidian vessels heaved mightily and the black hulls, crystalline, repulsing the sea water, dancing above the waves, looming near to starboard.

They hacked at the ropes as Moeru, having cleared the poop of the enemy, worked her way down the aft companionway to the main deck, leading a complement of sailors across the port sheer-strake and onto the decks of the first obsidian ship.

Onward the plumed warriors came and Ronin left the cutting of the ropes to Moichi while he turned and met the attack, his sword a bright, bloody arc, reaping a red, hot harvest of flesh and bone.

Abruptly, he felt the trembling of the deck. The *Kioku* heaved in the water. More lines hissed over the starboard sheer-strake. He looked up as the deck rolled violently but the sky was filled with harmless, puffy clouds racing before the unsteady following wind. Mauve and gold, the world readied itself for sunset. Yet the ocean below them swelled and sucked as if a storm were raging.

Higher and higher the swells tossed them until, with a great rending, the lines binding the *Kioku* to the surrounding obsidian ships split and broke asunder. Like a great wild stallion, the *Kioku* raised her bow high above the troughs of the waves.

Free.

Ronin, clinging to the starboard sheer-strake, risked a glance overboard. All about them the seas were black and glossy, humped and agitated, as if in reaction to the ascension of a creature of incalculable size. The deep was alive with motion and potency.

The *Kioku* bucked forward on the inexorable tide of another enormous wave, which, cresting violently and unpredictably, capsized one of the obsidian ships. With a great roar, it disappeared beneath the heavy sea. Onward the *Kioku* was hurled by the churning swells and at last Ronin looked about the ship.

"Moichi!" he called. "Where is Moeru?"

The battle aboard the *Kioku* was all but finished. Still, Moichi fought the last of his foes, dispatching him with a ferocious thrust. He turned to Ronin, wiping at his sweating brow. Blood and gore streaked his arms and his shirt clung wetly to his caked chest.

"The last I saw of her, Captain, she was leading a detachment of men onto an enemy vessel."

Ronin raced along the deck, leaping the mounds of the corpses and the wounded, calling to her in his mind, thrusting aside clumps of still fighting sailors and plumed warriors, heedless of friend or foe. Until, at length, he was certain that she was not on board, not even among the piles of the dead or the coughing, spitting maimed. The silence in his mind echoed like a tomb.

He ran back to Moichi, who was calling to the men.

"We must turn the *Kioku* around," he cried. "She is still on one of the enemy ships."

Moichi turned to him, his hazel eyes grave and watchful.

"Whatever unnatural thing parted us from the obsidian ships saved our lives, Captain." He turned his gaze out across the starboard sheer-strake, across the high black water. "Look there, Captain. D'you see? We cannot return." The tetrahedral sails with their fiercely grinning avian insignia were fast dwindling aft. "Neither tide nor winds govern the *Kioku* now. A force from the deep hurls us onward and for the moment you must face the fact that, for as long as it may last, you are not captain and neither am I navigator."

"Moichi—"

"My friend"—a large hand gripped his shoulder; the hazel eyes noted the pain in his face—"use your eyes. Think with your head, not your heart. We are powerless."

Alive or dead, drowned beneath the tidal wave, captured by the plumed warriors, he had no way of knowing. Moichi's raised voice came to him: "Overboard, lads! Cast them all into the sea! Clear the decks of this mess!"

Ronin wiped down his bloody sword on a corpse and sheathed it. He went carefully across the humped deck, mounted the high poop. His hands gripped the stern sheer-strake, his arms as rigid as stone, watching the black sea foaming and geysering, laced with luminescence, the flora of the deep. He heard the heavy splashes behind him as the *Kioku*'s load was lightened, as the dead meat swirled and sank beneath the dark creaming waves.

They were far away now, those forbidding obsidian vessels, foundering above the unnatural seas, and all at once it seemed to him that the setting sun dimmed, though no cloud passed before its orange face and, straining his ears, he thought that he could hear a peculiar high keening, inconstant and thin, away and away and what is she to me anyway—?

"Captain."

Moichi called to him and he turned and went down the companionway to help tend to the remaining men.

Some of you are avenged now. Freidal's death will not bring you back, Stahlig; it will not shorten your journey,

Borros. But—he turned from the silver and blue-green face of the sea to watch Moichi's hawklike features, feeling again the pressure of the wide hand upon him, the warmth it conveyed —I must not decieve myself, whether or not the dead are past knowing, this revenge was for me. The big man moved away for a moment. Yet somewhere I suppose that I believe that they are not yet past caring. Farewell now, my friends.

Still for him, he knew that revenge was far from over. The hate which continued to burn within him like a raging fire would never be slaked until he faced the Salamander once more. For the pale perfect face of his sister K'reen, dead by his own unknowing hand, still haunted him and only his former mentor's blood would ease the torment he felt at the fiendish trap the shrewd hunter had set for him. Scarred but undefeated, having pried apart the serrated jaws of that trap, he now wished to stalk his hunter so that, one way or another, the last account should be settled.

The decks had already been cleared of the bulk of the carnage. Over half the ship's crew had died in the battle but, Moichi told him matter of factly, nearly one and half again the number of corpses of the plumed warriors had been cast into the sea. Now sailors were casting down wooden buckets into the cool green depths, hauling up sea water, spilling it along the wide decks until the scuppers ceased to shed the blood of man or beast.

The residue of the great black tide pushed them onward, almost due south, and was soon joined by a stiff following wind out of the eastern quarter. At first, they had tried to tack away from it but even furling the t'gallants had not slowed their flight and, in the end, Moichi had shrugged and said to Ronin: "We must be patient and ride it out. We cannot fight the elements." And Ronin, who had learned long ago to bend before forces which he could not control or understand, reluctantly agreed.

For a time he had stood quite still, with the salt wind whipping his stained sea cloak about his body, calling silently to her. Then he had cleared his mind of all thoughts, a waiting receptacle for communication.

Silence. Deep and unremitting.

For much of his life, death had settled all about him, enwrapping those closest to him, rending them from him. Yet he now found it difficult to reconcile himself to Moeru's passing. Her scent, her voice in his mind like a taste, refused to fade or blur. But survival, he knew, was impossible amidst the warriors of the obsidian ships, for they had shown no interest in the capture of Ronin and the crew of the *Kioku*. Death was their only objective.

At last he turned from the taffrail.

Better by far for the black, turbulent sea to have taken her.

The days and nights passed swiftly or slowly, depending on his mood. He spurned his cabin, pacing the decks in the warm starlight while the men lay awake in the stinking fo'c'sle, listening to the heavy tramp of his boots over the planking.

Some days he slept in the lee of the mizzenmast while the shadows and sunlight wheeled slowly about him. On others, he was up and about, carefully sharpening the double edges of his blade or climbing the shrouds, staring at the unbroken horizon for hours. He drank little, ate even less, and would not listen to Moichi, who did his best to engage him in conversation.

Gradually, the seas became greener, luminescing just after sunset. The sun grew stronger during the days so that the nights became warmer and almost as humid as the daylight hours.

They began to see flying fish, silvery and acrobatic, swooping alongside the ship's bow, pacing her course for entire mornings or afternoons on end only to disappear for long periods before resurfacing; or perhaps they were different schools each time. It was a good sign, Moichi said. Ronin ignored him, sunk deep within his black arcane thoughts.

Seven days after first sighting the flying fish they spied a column of water off the starboard side perhaps half a league ahead. A great black shape lifted itself with both a heaviness and a certain grace from beneath the waves like a shivering, glittering bridge. Enormous blue-black flukes waved in the air for long moments while time and gravity seemed suspended. Then the sea crashed over the last of the shape and it was gone in a bouquet of silvery spray.

Later that day, they sighted a bird, the first one they had spied since the morning they had sailed from the port of Khiyan, on the western shore of the continent of man, more than ninety days ago. It was a gull, quite large, its wings purple-gray and white. It circled twice about the mainmast t'gallants, wheeled and flew off into the east.

Moichi called to the helmsman to set course after it.

They came up on it during a night that was dense and black with racing clouds, obscuring all traces of the horned moon which had hung before them, the centerpiece in an immense, spangled sky. He was aware of it only because of Moichi's keen nose; the lookouts were blind.

Sometime later, those few still on deck could just make out the aching cries of the gulls as they wheeled over invisible cliffs.

Land!

Ronin stood beside Moichi in the closeness of the darkness and the heat.

"Is it Ama-no-mori?" The first words he had uttered in days.

"We have sailed in the right general direction, Captain. I have tried to correct as best I know how but—" He shrugged into the night.

"Then the chances are that it is not."

"What we have before us, Captain, is an uncharted island. Ama-no-mori is an uncharted island."

"That is hardly sound logic."

Again the massive shoulder lifted, fell.

"Unfortunately, my friend, that is all that is left us."

He gave the order to heave to.

At first light, with pink staining the flat sea behind them and all the topsails furled, they sailed in.

It was a humpbacked slice of land, shimmering emerald green, seemingly all jungle, dense and entangled. Great blue rocks jutted in a naked headland just to port over which spray of gulls wheeled and cried. Directly ahead, a wide beach swept away to starboard.

Ronin gazed in fascination. Could this crescent of verdant land rising from the ocean's depths be Ama-no-mori, home of the fabled Bujun? Could this be the journey's end at last?

The shore loomed up at them and Moichi called for the ship to lie to. Men raced through the shrouds. He ordered the first sounding.

The sea was mottled: now gray-green, now blue-white, and perhaps this is why the lookouts failed to give the alarm. In any event, the ship would not heave to; perhaps she was caught on a tide. They heard the crashing of the breakers abruptly close and Moichi yelled to the helmsman: "Hard aport!" It made no difference. The helmsman dragged at the wheel but the *Kioku,* following some more powerful tenant, leapt straight ahead. Ronin saw Moichi running toward the helmsman to help him but it was far too late.

A moment later, the *Kioku* careered madly onto the jagged, saw-toothed spine of the coral reef lying barely a fathom beneath the creaming waves. It reared up like an animal in pain as the living mass ripped away its keel and rent its hull. The vessel shivered and splintered with such suddenness and force that men scrambling to get out of the way were impaled by flying shards of wood and metal.

In the ensuing explosion, the restless sea engulfed them all. Men were flung headlong onto the cracked spine of the reef, their bodies ripped to shreds by the impact with the natural bulwark.

Ronin sank into the sea but as he did so he relaxed his body, willing himself limp despite the screaming in his brain. All about him were flailing lumps, dark and jagged, haloed by churning bubbles, but he forced his eyes to remain open, alert for debris which might pin him to the sea bottom by its weight, searching for the first sign of the spiked coral which would flay him alive.

His lungs full of air, he dived deep, kicking with the powerful muscles of his legs, and he sank down below the awful turmoil.

An infinity of blue, dappled and darting, all perspective gone. It became calm and he devoted himself to concentrating on the feel of the tidal flow against his body. Somewhere there must be a gap in the barrier; this tide could take him there. He knew he could not fight the sea. He swam with it.

Bubbles streamed from his sleek body. Already his lungs were beginning to ache and he yearned to cast his heavy sword from him. The blue became dense as luminosity drifted away on another tide, and shadows, magnified to titanic proportions by the lens of the water, played over his moving form. Abruptly, the dark red of the coral reef loomed at him, balking his way. And still he swam with the tide, feeling its febrile pull sucking at him. His lungs were on fire and he felt his throat constrict; he forced down an urge to open his mouth, suck in on air that was not there. Still—But now he felt the tide quicken about him, eddying, and then it squirted him forward. In absolute darkness all the air was gone. He groaned inwardly and his eyes bulged. Faster and faster. His lips pulled back from his clenched teeth.

Shimmering green bloomed before him, so far away above him. It blurred, pulsing on the tide, and with his last ounce of energy, he struck out with his arms, kicking his legs upward,

upward, until he climbed, bursting, into sunlight and the sweet air.

He gasped. A rumbling in his ears. He swallowed. A wave washed over him and he choked.

Tumbling.

Shooting his body upward again, the oxygen beginning to circulate in his system. He broke the skin of the sea, heard the thunder, felt the shudder of the breakers. He buoyed himself up and, waiting, launched himself on the rolling crest of a wave, riding it, allowing it to carry the weight of his body, making it do his work.

And the breakers rolled endlessly in, sounding like the birth of the world: a wild, frenetic explosion of energy that tumbled and twisted him, sucked at him.

And borne on this gravid, ageless salt tide, with the red sun rising at his back, exhausted and gaunt, he was thrown up onto the pink sand of this foreign beach, a pliant and unconscious bit of flotsam given grudgingly by the cool sea onto the curving, heated shore.

Heart of Stone

ALL the warm morning he lay as if dead, while the last edge of the tide washed him in its creamy surf. Seaweed, stranded, strung across his broad back, wreathing him in deep green, half-covering the long scars of another battle.

Within the wet world of the crashing sea, the fat buzz of flies, the quizzical call of swooping gulls and cormorants.

Then the slosh of boots in the wet sand, slashing obliquely through the surf, their cruel progress disturbing the natural symmetry of the scene. A shadow fell across his still form. The large figure loomed over him. It was quite still for a moment. Then it bent and a hand plucked the drying seaweed from his back.

They sat cross-legged on the expanse of pink sand, drying out above the straggling black flotsam ribbon marking the high tide line. A soft breeze brought them the stench of rotting fish and they saw, off to their left, along the sweep of the beach, the blue-green pulsing of a swarm of flies, iridescent, seemingly armor-plated, flashing in the sunlight, rising and settling on the remains of a small fish, swept up by the tide. Their rhythmic movement seemed to set the thing back to grisly life.

Closer at hand, horseshoe crabs, their black carapaces shining, trundled noiselessly along the sand at the waterline, their stiff tails writing the toil of their lentitudinous passage.

"I was lucky," Moichi was saying. "The poop acted something like a catapult. I was thrown over the reef into the relatively clear water of the lagoon out there." He looked toward the hidden reef. "That cursed coral! How I wish you had grown taller."

"And the others?" asked Ronin.

"Captain," he said, letting the hot sand drift through his fingers, "there are no others."

The verge came up on them suddenly, a rich, verdant carpet, moist, humid, smelling of loam and minerals and natural decay, a sharp contrast to the salt aridity of the sweeping crescent of pink sand behind them, baking in the afternoon heat.

He stepped into the jungle and was immediately engulfed by the steamy cool world, so different from anything else he had encountered before. Engulfed in the jade cathedral, a vast tapestry of leaves, vines, branches. Thick gray boles gave way to shooting slender trunks, deep brown trees, thick and gnarled, covered in carpets of moss. Green sunlight, dusty, barred, oblique light, crept cautiously floorward without any success. Shadows flitted high above; flash of color.

Moichi had brought several oval fruit with them from the last rise of the beach. Large and green and glossy, their fibrous husks fell away at the touch of his dirk's blade. Inside, they found a round, hairy sphere, brown with three spots on one end. Moichi handed him one, showed him how to puncture two of the spots. The milk was thin and sweet and when he cracked the shell, he found that the white firm flesh was sweetly delicious.

They moved due west, straight into the humped interior of the island. Through the massed underbrush of ferns, wild tangled flowers, giant and filled with enormous insects, brief outcroppings of rock wholly covered by gray fungus and green moss, patches of great, brown- and dark red-spotted mushrooms as yellow as butter crowding around the twisted, ancient roots of immensely tall, primordial trees. And as they made their circuitous way into the interior of the jungle, it seemed to Ronin that these leafy giants must have been born during the world's first cataclysmic upheavals, as the steaming land broke the writhing skin of the sluicing seas, the boiling tides slowly withdrawing their relentless dominion over all the planet; that they had, in their long, gleaming adolescence, been mute witness to the birth of the slender, glittering creatures slithering up from the deep to explore the new world of air and dry land.

Brush strokes of scarlet and saffron, emerald and sapphire, turquoise and coral floated and shot through the multiterraced world high above their heads, the calls and the flutterings of the luxuriantly plumed birds a constant background to their slow progress.

Often they heard the deep growl or snuffling grunt of some large predatory animal but they sighted nothing through the thick veils of foliage. Game, such as grouse and quail, pheasant and rabbit, was plentiful; food was obviously no problem.

Time slipped away from them, down a receding tunnel, a distant, unnatural concept, the immense clutter and space of the jade jungle gripping them with an almost surreal presence, seeping into their minds as well as their bodies until all other typography they had once known became an improbable fevered fantasy.

Where the ground was soft and marshy, they were careful to pull off the brown and black leeches, wedge-shaped and hideous, which clung tenaciously to their exposed flesh.

Where the jungle's floor rose along a series of winding ridges, the trees seemed somewhat sparser but jagged bits of volcanic rock studded the earth.

When they tired, they paused beneath the spread of a towering tree, plucking fruit from its lower branches, sitting with their backs against the smooth bole, watching large white termites burrow and crawl. Then they would stand and again be dwarfed into insignificance by the illimitable whirring jungle.

At night, with squealing bats swooping, tracing a brown lattice-work across the open spaces aloft, they built small, compact fires, roasting fresh meat, caught and skinned at the abrupt onset of a brief twilight.

However such was the impenetrability of the jungle that almost all gradations beyond day and night vanished. The hours were lost to them, for they could see neither the sun nor the moon through the high vault of the treetops. They learned to judge the march of the day by the species of animals which hunted and fled around them, for each had its own time governed by an internal clock that wound down only in death.

"The first mate was known to you, Captain," said Moichi across a crackling fire one evening.

"Yes. An old enemy," said Ronin. "He destroyed many of my friends back—home." Looking up, he saw the inconstant firelight illumine the red pinpoints of the bats' eyes, their leathery wings unfurled like the sailors of the damned.

"You are from the north, eh, Captain?" Moichi threw a small bone into the chittering blackness crawling beyond the glow of their fire. "A most persistent fellow." He shook his head.

"You were right." He smiled wryly, briefly. "He did spend too much time before the mast."

"Ah, we all have our evil secrets, my friend." Moichi broke the skin of a purple fruit. Juice ran down into his thick beard. Then: "How you hate home."

Ronin sat with his hands over his drawn-up knees.

"Home is an evil place for me, Moichi." He wiped the grease from his lips. "But that is all over now."

The navigator's eyes were a deep moss green as he watched Ronin from across the fire.

"My experience has been that it is never truly over. Home has a peculiar hold on us all."

"Only on those weak enough to want to return, I think."

Moichi shrugged.

"Perhaps." He twirled the fruit stem between two fingers as he scraped along his teeth with his fingernail. "But it is also true that potent forces are set in motion at the precise moment of our births, *because* of our births. But these forces are not so well defined as to affect only us; they touch those who are around us also." He spat out a piece of skin. "I do not mean just physically close."

Ronin's eyes were half-closed and Moichi was not even certain that he had been listening at the end. There was no more movement at fireside.

Aloft, the humid night shuddered with the flight of numberless wings.

Late the next day, as they climbed over a series of stiff, gray roots, spiralled and fibrous, which arched from the rich, loamy floor of the jungle like a line of miniature bridges, Moichi stopped in his tracks. Perfectly still, he said nothing and Ronin was on the point of asking him why he had paused when he saw the movement, sinuous and glittery, at the big man's feet. Rising, curling about his ankles, slithering above the tops of his muddy boots, was a serpent, glossy, diamonds of green and ocher along its length, its flat blunt head questing.

They stood, transformed into two more trees in the jungle. The serpent wound its way upward, silent and deadly, across Moichi's buttocks, along the ridged muscles of his back, until it wound itself along his left arm. Its forked tongue flickered in and out, searching, its eyes two sharp points of obsidian.

In a blur, Moichi's right hand leapt for its head, his thumb and forefinger digging into each side of its jaw, jamming the hinge. The mouth gaped open, long fangs, needle-sharp and hollow with venom, glistened. The body writhed, winding and unwinding. Moichi broke its jaw, then for the first time, he spoke:

"Get me a broad green leaf, will you, Captain."

Moichi knelt and placed the broken head upon the carpet of the leaf Ronin had found for him. Carefully he withdrew one copper-handled dirk and slit the top of the creature's head from snout to the beginning of its still twitching body. He pressed down on the exposed flesh, using the tips of two fingers. Through the hollow fangs oozed the venom, dark red and thin, until it had all pooled onto the leaf.

Moichi threw the serpent from him and, cutting green moss from the bole of an adjacent tree, let the venom be absorbed by the substance. He wrapped the wet moss in the leaf and stood.

"There, my friend. The world is not very often either black or white but only shades of gray." He put the packet into his sash, then replaced his drink. "You see, from the most deadly creature comes a liquid which would kill us if the serpent had bitten us. Yet now, drying within the organic matter, it becomes an antidote to the other poisons of this place."

"How come you to know of this creature?" said Ronin as they continued through the jungle.

"You are from the north, Captain, where the serpent cannot live. But I am from the south. Farther still than this island." They cut through a dense thicket of ferns. "It is a land, I am told, that was once part of the continent of man, many centuries ago, but as the crust of the planet resettled, it broke away."

"How came you then to the continent of man?" asked Ronin. "Are your people seamen?"

"The Iskamen?" Moichi smiled. "Ah no, Captain. We are tillers of the soil by tradition. But we are fishermen, also, and are greatly skilled at sailing close to shore." He bent to avoid a broken branch, thick and gnarled, teeming with red and black insects. "Too, my people are warriors, a vocation forced upon them by circumstance. We are fierce desert fighters grown used to hardship and denial; a proud desolate race rich in ancient tradition. Ours, Captain, is a history of slavery and eventual self-knowledge."

"Your land is distant from the continent of man?"

"From Khiyan? Yes, very. It is easier to sail from the eastern shore of the continent. In fact there is a trade route from Sha'angh'sei. Do you know the city?"

Ronin smiled.

"Yes. I have spent some little time there."

"I know it!" Moichi laughed. "By the Oruborus, we shall meet there one day in different times, and shake each other's hands and walk along the streets of that great enigmatic city, yes, Captain? For having lived there, you must know that it is a place unrivaled in all the known world for adventure and intrigue."

"I would look forward to such a time," Ronin said. "But tell me now of your land."

"In Iskael I have a brother," Moichi began, chewing on a mint leaf which he had just plucked. "We were born just moments apart yet we resemble each other so little that my father wondered if we were brothers at all."

"Surely you are exaggerating."

Moichi shook his head; the diamond in his nostril sparked momentarily. "My father was an intently devout man and his belief in the God of our fathers was unshakable; His strength, the cornerstone of his life. He suspected, I think, that God had planted one of us in my mother's womb."

"Toward what end?"

Moichi's great shoulders lifted, fell.

"Who can say? My father was an unfathomable man. Perhaps he longed to see the long-awaited prophet of my people appear within his own family." He spit out the dark residue of the chewed leaf, put another in his mouth. "My father was quite wealthy in his own way and when we were born he held dominion over a sizable piece of land." Screeching, a flurry of red and gold shot by above their heads. "But do not anticipate me, Captain, for this is no tale of the king's two heirs, one good and the other evil. I never wished for my father's land, just as I never craved to be a warrior. I wished only to travel, to find out what lay over the vast sea, to climb aboard the great ships with their white sails and carved figureheads, which appeared all at once over the flat horizon, bearing men from another world.

"But I was the elder son and my responsibility was great. Our land was immense and required much attention; my tutor rode with me wherever I went to manage my family's affairs. But ever I would reach a crest, I would turn my gaze to the shimmering sea, lying like spun silver in the sun, and wonder, as I wiped the sweat from my eyes, when I would ride those moving crests."

Adrift in a sea of jade, Ronin listened to Moichi's vibrant voice as he watched the slow parade of the mammoth trees, smelled the humid, fecund air. He bent and picked up a giant horned beetle, its blue-black carapace shining in the diffuse light like burnished metal. He carried it with him for a while before finally setting it down atop a low shelf of rock slanting out of the jungle's floor.

"One day I came across my brother fighting with the son of a neighboring farmer—a lord, you might say, though we have no word for that in our language save God. Now my brother was no coward but in that time neither was he a warrior though big and strong. His fists were like clubs and he was quick. Thus the table was turned on this boy who had sought a quick battle. Blood streamed from his nose as my brother hit him. He called for mercy and when my brother stopped, the boy pulled a hidden knife. My brother, being unfamiliar with weapons, would surely have died with the first thrust had I not intervened. I knocked my brother aside and grappled with the boy, who was strong and clever. We struggled. The boy died impaled upon his own blade."

Beyond, in the depths of the jade ocean, the buzz of fat flies was joined by the chirruping of cicadas, a foreshadow of the quick slash of dusk.

"My brother wished to stay. I did not. There was nought else to do, in any event. My father took me to the port city of Alara'at and with a bar of silver paid for my passage on the first ship sailing for the continent of man."

"How could your father let you—"

"Our laws are quite precise, Captain, and never more so than when it comes to murder. That farmer owned quite a piece of land—"

"But surely there was another way. Your brother—"

"Was leagues away, as far as anyone else knew. My father would not risk the both of us being involved. As I have told you, he was a pious man and our God is an unforgiving one. It was I who struggled with the boy when he died and in truth I cannot tell you whether it was my hand or his that guided the dagger's blade. But to my father it did not matter; my intervention caused the boy's death and it was my responsibility to take the consequences."

The calling of the birds, echoing softly through the high emerald gallery, haunted them as they moved, giving Moichi's tale a spectral background.

"And your brother—?"

They ignored the dry hiss of a giant constrictor sliding

along a vine linking two branches to their right. Soon it was behind them.

"My brother," said Moichi without inflection, "never said a word."

Night came with a rush of soft mauve and before the deep green had completely metamorphosed into black, they had built a sputtering fire and were roasting a brace of rabbits they had caught during the day.

Already the nocturnal birds could be heard over the soft crackling, the hissing of dripping fat, their cries deeper and less shrill than their diurnal counterparts; hoarse whispers rather than shouts. The buzz of insects had died to a high whine, laced with the song of the cicadas, the silences in between, creating white noise on eardrums already used to the soundwash of the jungle.

In the distance, the whooshing of leaves and an occasional yelp followed by a guttural growl bespoke the padding of stealthy predators. An owl hooted close by and in the reflected light of the fire, Ronin saw its wide head swivel, its great round eyes blinking slowly as it peered sagely down on them from its perch among the lower branches of the tree beside which they had built the fire.

They awoke at firstlight, adrift again within a jade jewel. It had begun to rain, as it did at least once every day, a fine oblique downpour that nevertheless seemed more like a heavy mist by the time it had filtered down to their level close to the jungle's floor.

Moichi scattered the white ashes of the cold fire among which one ember, uncovered, still glowed dismally. It hissed briefly, then died.

They began, almost immediately, to climb, the way suddenly more broken, strewn with thick rivulets of igneous rock, shiny and bright with embedded minerals. The ferns grew higher here, great rustling fans bending under the weight of the moisture and the darting insects.

The immense trees were draped with looping vines wherever they looked now and from these natural connectors swung brown monkeys with long tails and bright curious eyes. They chittered excitedly at first sight of the intruders and the pair could hear the echoes preceding their progress. But gradually, the creatures' indignation appeared to fade. Yet they continued to chatter among themselves, calling to each other, following the path of the two men.

Just past noon, they crested the hill whose slopes they had been climbing since early morning and by midafternoon they were aware that the character of the jungle had changed for good.

The air was denser although the light seemed to be stronger, less watery, and abruptly, they knew that the susurrus with which they had lived for so long, had altered subtlely.

They plunged onward and, quite without further warning, found themselves on the high bank of a wide, muddy river, its waters blue-green, streaked with gray.

There came a heavy splash off to their left and they saw a long scaly form heave itself into the water until only its slightly popped eyes protruded above the surface. But the creature's image stayed in Ronin's brain. He wondered why until, later, he saw one at closer range and recognized the ancient crocodile which Bonneduce the Last had described to him in explaining the origins of both Hynd and the little man's Bones.

Out into the heavy sea of moist air, down the slope to the shore, ribbons of earth, rich and black, trickled after them. The atmosphere was alive with the scent of life and decay.

The rain had ceased, at least for the moment. Above them, the sky was white and the sun, bloated and diffused by the haze, nevertheless blazed down upon them. The heat was appalling after so many days in the shadows of the jungle. The river dazzled in the sunlight and they shaded their eyes, half-closing them until they became accustomed to the high-intensity glare.

They squatted at the bank and drank cautiously, lifting their heads immediately as sudden ripples became a splashing near the center of the river. A great snout reared up, purple-gray, streamered with green and brown weed. The mouth gaped wide, revealing enormous blunt teeth and a mud-streaked pink interior. There came a snorting, as of air being blown through a huge bellows. Black eyes regarded them placidly and, with a roll, the head disappeared beneath the lapping wavelets.

"There is obviously no point in swimming it," said Ronin.

"No, but ford it we must." The big man turned, his cinnamon skin like burnished brass in the heat and light. "There are many slender trees on this bank, at the lip of the jungle. Have you ever built a raft?"

They spent the better part of that day cutting down the smaller trees above the embankment. In between, they collected lengths of the weeping vines which, as Moichi had predicted, were stronger than they looked. Every so often, Ronin found himself searching the terraced trees at the verge of the jungle for movement but no monkeys showed themselves. Perhaps they had a healthy fear of the river creatures or, more likely, did not care for the noise and destruction the two men were making.

When they judged they had enough trunks, they hacked off the tops to standardize the lengths roughly. Then they set about tying them together with the vines.

Evening fell with a tired sigh and still they worked on so that they would be ready to set out at dawn. The far shore, high, rocky, and bankless, held at its summit a continuation of the jungle. After almost an entire day in the full heat of the naked sun, Ronin found that he was grateful to be returning to the steamy protection of the vegetation.

The raft was completed before darkness fell and, after one last inspection for loose knots, they left it on the bank and climbed back into the jungle's chittering cover to build a fire for the night. They feasted on fish and baked tubers.

Before giving themselves to sleep, they hacked down two slender branches of resilient wood and fire-hardened their ends. "Poles against the current," Moichi said.

At dawn, they quit the bank and launched the raft, leaning on their poles, breaking from the shore, out onto the swirling current, the muddy water washing over the wood.

Insects buzzed, droning in the heated air. Water spiders skated across the surface of the river, black molecular dancers.

Two slothful crocodiles awoke and left the baking bank, squirming clumsily until they were far enough into the water to glide in silent concert toward the disturbance caused by the raft.

Their heads went under and Ronin called softly to Moichi, who moved from the port side, directly aft. Ronin lifted his pole out of the water, dropping it onto the raft.

He drew his blade.

With a powerful rush, the long scaled snout lifted from the depths, hinging open. The rows of razor teeth were awesome at close range.

"You'll have to stop their lunge," cautioned Moichi, "else their weight will capsize us."

The great jaws snapped shut centimeters from the edge of the raft, then the beast disappeared and for moments the water appeared still. Moichi continued to pole them across.

Then the snout broke the skin of the river, already gaping

wide, the short but powerful legs propelling it upward.

Ronin yelled and, planting his feet wide apart upon the rocking, unsteady surface, slashed an oblique stroke beginning up over his right shoulder. The edge of the sword bit into the oncoming head just behind the left eye, shearing through scales and flesh and bone in a yellow-white spray. The great body, balked in its upward rush, shuddered in the air, then falling, crashed heavily into the river. As it sank, the blood pumping out, a great boiling began just under the surface of the water as if the current were alive with a thousand darting predators. The river foamed.

On the slick deck of the raft, the long severed head grinned in ivory disarray.

They had saved a vine for the far shore. Making for an overhanging tree, Ronin steadied the raft while Moichi whipped the vine into the tangled foliage.

Ronin refused to relinquish his prize even on the laborious climb up the abrupt, rocky face of the far shore to the verge of the jungle high above them.

Once again enclosed within the jade shadows he bade Moichi sit while he pried at the jaws. Then, using the point of his dirk, he carefully set about extracting the crocodile's teeth.

It was quieter here and at once they missed the friendly chattering of the monkeys and the shrill cries of the bright plumed birds. They heard the monotonous drone of the insects and, occasionally, the flap of great wings swooping over their heads, yet these sounds served only to heighten the metamorphosed character of the jungle. They felt alone again, somehow abandoned, as if they had come to the last outpost of man and now, having pased through a forbidding barrier, stood on the brink of another world.

At length Ronin had collected all the teeth and, leaving the plundered skull behind, they plunged again due west, ever deeper into the island's hidden interior.

For a time it rained, the jungle whooshing around them with the weight of the pattering drops. Then, briefly, jade light spilled over them in complex patterns, warm and humid as honey, the temperature rising as the sun beat down out of the white crucible of the hidden sky.

It was raining again when Ronin heard Moichi's grunt and then his whispered: "Over here."

Just ahead of them, on a slight tangent from their intended path, was a carved stone obelisk.

It rose, chrysolitic, from the forest floor to just over the height of a man. It was somewhat tapered and all over its four sides were carved strange pictoglyphs, outlines of men in plumed headdresses, standing or sitting in profile. Invariably their features included a protruding forehead and a long curved nose. The obelisk was crowned by a careful carving, repeated on each of the monument's four sides, of a grinning skull.

By late afternoon they were certain.

They were by no means expert woodsmen but they had spent many days now encased within the jade sea and they were both warriors, trained in, among other arts, the keenness of perceptions.

They had seen no other object that seemed made by the hand of man. But as the day crept along on silent swaying feet they were at length quite certain that they were not alone traveling through the jungle. They caught no glimpse of whoever watched them, yet they were never without the feeling that the dense foliage hid some beings that paralleled their path.

Still they moved ceaselessly onward, through an endless emerald dream, hot and sticky, the steamy heat palpable, almost gluey now.

At night there was little relief from the heat and they slept fitfully, dozing for short periods sitting cross-legged before the fire, coming awake with a start and a swift pulse of the heart at the sound of stealthy padding beyond the perimeter of flickering lemon light.

Once or twice Ronin fired a handful of a reed which they had found would burn brightly despite the excessive humidity and went out perhaps a hundred meters from their camp. For a time he saw nothing, then, as he turned back to Moichi, his peripheral vision caught a quick spark of reflected light from his torch and, swinging back around, he thought he saw the pulse of red eyes, burning like heated embers in the night. But these glimpses were so brief that he could not be certain whether these lights were organic or inorganic in origin.

On a day when it rained steadily, turning the world about them a dismal pale gray-green, the pair climbed a heavily overgrown escarpment, an "s" shaped double-crescent and, just beyond it, found four stone stelae perhaps three times the size of the obelisk. These also were carved along all four of their faces from top to bottom. The pictoglyphs were similar to the obelisk's.

The grouping, had it a horizontal section across the top, would have constituted a gate.

They passed between the stelae while the jungle wept sorrowfully.

They could hear nothing now save the hiss and drip of the rain, which swept through the jungle in waves, for once unintimidated by the terraces of leaves and vines, raking the spongy floor. Visibility was extremely poor and they were forced to move forward cautiously.

Half a kilometer past the stelae the jungle ceased, its death so abrupt that they found themselves on the brink of cleared land before they had realized what had happened.

They stood very still and stared at the incredible expanse which swept majestically away before them.

The rain had all but stopped and, from above them, the sun shone, against the background of dark gray thunderheads, into the illimitable valley, casting into brilliant white complex stone buildings of immense size, a towering, pyramidal city linked by uncurving stone causeways edged by low stone causeways edged by low stone monuments.

The buildings were ornate, terrifyingly alien and hypnotically familiar at the same time, and none more so than that structure which dominated the entire valley city.

It was an enormous stepped pyramid in the stone city's center. It towered over all the other buildings, bizarre and compelling. It was four-sided, perhaps typical of this culture, with central stairs running up each face, set within the cyclopean steps. At its flat summit was a stone slab, an oval striated green and black. It looked like an altar.

"Ama-no-mori?" whispered Moichi.

An oval, thought Ronin, suddenly dizzy, on the verge now, parting from the leafy shadows of the jade sea, an enfolding talisman against the terrible stone city crouched watchfully.

Waiting.

"It appears deserted."

"Yet, a feeling—"

"I know."

"Where are the inhabitants?"

Everywhere he looked the great stone stelae and buildings were richly carved with strange scenes filled with myriad figures. Were these men or gods? Or perhaps both, mingled on the grounds of this site, for surely they saw depicted the abandoned, the defeated, the humbled, the sacrificed overshadowed by the fierce, the victorious, the revenged, ensplendored and revered in stone three times the size of man.

At the commencement of the central stone causeway, wide and perfectly flat, they passed between twin stone cats, giant jaws agape, stretched forepaws many meters in length, rippling shoulder muscles deeply etched, the mighty relief of the massive chests sweeping in sinuous curves up and away to the lifted rumps and quiescent tails.

Just beyond these mammoth stone guardians, two more stelae rose on either side of the causeway, immense, covered in such high relief and complex glyphs that it was impossible to count the number of their sides.

Passing between these they saw a great stepped plaza rising on their left. Pools on the stone steps, remnants of the day's heavy rain, glistened in the lowering sun. Here and there, as they moved, their angle of vision changing, these shallow pools broke into arcing pastel rainbows.

On either side of the plaza, to north and south, were high structures with windowless stone walls, vertical and sheer on their inner sides, sloping outward on their opposite walls. A lone doorway set in each vertical wall led onto the plaza.

"Strange," said Moichi as he halted before the first steps of the plaza. He gazed all about him. "The arch seems unknown to these people. You see, Ronin"—he pointed to the structures at either end of the plaza—"they use, instead, the corbel vault to support their taller buildings."

Ronin's gaze at length swung away from the plaza complex, west, along the flat causeway, and he called softly to his companion. Before the great stepped pyramid which rose above them a quarter of a kilometer away, he could make out three silhouetted figures, tall and black, featureless against the diffuse mauve and copper glare of the dying sun, slipping steadily into the highest reaches of the towering jungle beyond the stone valley.

"This way. Come on."

They were masked.

Two men and one woman with great feline mantles covering their entire heads. These were cunningly crafted, furred and spotted, with triangular ears, black muzzles with long, stiff whiskers, and cold, glittering eyes, the color of gold or light green jade, translucent, glassy, and somehow disturbing.

All three were extremely tall, fully two and a half meters, the men with deep chests and long, muscular legs. Their skin was the color of stained teak.

The two men were garbed in gold and black spotted fur cloths wound about their loins. They wore sandals of black leather. Along their arms were bands of gold of varying widths, beaten and carved with fantastic designs. Ronin could pick out a bizarre scene between several headdressed warriors and a multiheaded creature which he took to be a god.

The woman was fully as tall as the men, her great untangled mane of blue-black hair outlasting the length of her grotesque mask; it rode to the small of her back. She wore a short tunic of golden fur that reached from her heavy breasts to just past the juncture of her thighs. Her legs were long and beautifully formed. She wore no gold on her arms but rather a band of pink and white jade, not more than a centimeter across, carved into an intricate latticework design through which the rich copper of her skin could be seen.

The man on the left stepped forward one pace.

"Welcome," he said, his voice distant and strange through the grillwork of ivory fangs, "to Xich Chih, the great city of the Chacmool."

"Time," said Cabal Xiu.

He was the shorter of the two men.

"It has ever been our greatest concern."

A light breeze ruffled the fur of his mask.

"Thus our history is written in stone to survive the cataclysms of the ages."

To the north and south, low pillared edifices; to the east, the jungle shivered, a high, almost impenetrable barrier. On a stepped acropolis, facing west. Across the wide, stone causeway, another structure loomed, a stepped pyramid perhaps one third the size of the giant structure near the center of the stone city, made up of nine successively smaller terraces. At the top was an oblong building set on six thick columns, heavily carved and worked. A set of wide steps along the center of the near side of the edifice gave access to the top.

"We have waited—" Cabal Xiu paused as if debating his choice of words. "We are waiting—"

The absurdity of the situation, Ronin reflected uneasily as his gaze swung back to the three bizarrely disfigured creatures sitting before him, failed to impress itself upon him. There was a disturbing aspect to this trio that disallowed any but the most immediately self-involving thoughts.

"Waiting for what?" said Moichi. "The end?"

The feline mask which covered Cabal Xiu's head swiveled

in his direction. The oblate sun's dying rays fired his eyes.

"Oh no." A line of crimson light fired his whiskers and was gone. "That has already come."

In a hush, the sun left the land and the city of Xich Chih was engulfed in amethyst and lapis light. In reflection, the valley glowed, as if from a frozen spectral fire kilometers distant.

"See to the rushes, Kin Coba," said Cabal Xiu.

The woman rose from her alabaster stone seat, crossed the stone acropolis to the north building. Ronin watched the movement of her buttocks, the strength of her firm thighs.

She returned moments later with two reed torches, smokily lit, which she set into stone pillars on either side of the group.

"This is the Chacmool," said Uxmal Chac, the taller of the two men, speaking for the first time. He pointed to the low table between them. It's top was the back of a cat, stylized and perfectly flat. The stone from which it was carved was either stained red or was naturally ruddy. Into its sides and back had been sunk circles of green jade, representing spots. The table's top was strewn with fired clay bowls of dried white corn and a heavy milky drink, spiced and certainly alcoholic. "It is the Red Jaguar, which still roams this land. It is unique in all the worlds for the Chacmool never knows defeat until all life has fled from its body." His mask shook as he spoke; several strands of mixed teeth and claws and carved flint clicked against each other as they lay around his neck. "It is the fiercest and therefore the most feared of carnivores." His eyes were in deep shadow. "Among our people it was told sometimes that the Chacmool was a supernatural being; that it could, for short periods, assume the form of man."

"The Red Jaguar was the basis for many tales," said Kin Coba, her voice evenly modulated. "Quite natural since the creature was always extremely rare."

"In the end," said Cabal Xiu, "it was revered as a god."

Now the stars, glittery in close array, manifested themselves through the deep azure and magenta of evening's haze, the brilliantine light of frosted ice crystals scattered across the sky by cosmic breath.

The great stone city lay just beneath this eternal blanket, an unmoving, articulated expanse of planes and angles, mathematically precise, perfectly situated, abruptly in harmony, now that darkness had fallen, with the slow intense wheel of the heavens, stupefying in its chill, cruel calculation.

Uxmal Chac inclined his head. "Tell us—"

"I think," said Cabal Xiu, deliberately interrupting, "that our guests must be fatigued after their long journey through the jungle." He extended a long arm. "Kin Coba, please see that these men are comfortable. Uxmal Chac and I have much to discuss."

At their backs a green and gold bird fluttered across the cool geometric expanse of the acropolis before disappearing into the tangled maze of the black jungle.

Night.

They were narrow cubicles within the building at the north end of the acropolis. What little light fell across their lintels was the result of reed tapers set along the blank stone walls of the brown airless corridors. In his and in Moichi's thin straw bed without legs lay on the stucco floor. Next to each was a shallow earthen bowl filled with water and, in the opposite corner, a chamber pot.

The walls of the cubicles were frescoed. Strange beasts and fantastic warriors bedecked in plumed headdresses and animal skins, men with large hooked noses and flat craniums, long eyes and wide full lips; scenes painted in hues of soft maize and brick red, deep green and lustrous midnight blue (purple seemed an unknown color here, except in the sky).

"Is there anything that you require?" said Kin Coba. She addressed both of them as they stood in the corridor.

"Not for the moment," said Moichi.

"Well, then," she said in farewell.

They listened to the slap of her sandals against the hard floor diminishing as she went away from them.

Ronin signed to the big man and silently they followed her out of the building.

They watched her within the shadows of the doorway as she headed across the adamantine acropolis.

"Just as well we left the rooms," whispered Moichi. "I could hardly breathe in there."

"Too much dust in there to believe that anyone has slept there for a long time," said Ronin.

Kin Coba went swiftly down the steps and across the wide white causeway toward the pillared building atop the pyramid to the west.

"Who are these people?" Moichi asked himself as much as Ronin.

"Whoever they are, they seem singularly uncurious about who *we* are or how we came here."

Moichi nodded.

"As it makes no difference."

"What was it Cabal Xiu said—?"

Kin Coba had reached the foot of the pyramid. She began to climb the stone stairway along its near face.

"'We have been waiting'?"

"For what? Us?"

"Let us find out," said Ronin.

And they stepped from the dark shadows, following in Kin Coba's footsteps, across the acropolis, toward the bulk of the waiting pyramid.

"There can be only one answer," Uxmal Chac said in his deep voice. "Surely you need no reminder, o my 'brother'." He could not keep the scorn from his voice.

"I do not believe that it is so clear-cut," said Cabal Xiu. "There must be no error. We—"

"Can you have already forgotten that though I am commander of the Majapan, I was once, many *katun* ago, a priest like you?"

"How can one forget what has been seared into one's brain, Uxmal Chac? Even though the military is something with which I can have no sympathy, still I understand your position."

"I abhor your condescension," growled Uxmal Chac, turning his back on the other. Kin Coba stood between them, arms folded across her breasts, watching them both as a lizard would a pair of fighting cocks, with a mesmeric but rather detached fascination.

"Ah, at last it comes out." Cabal Xiu took a step forward, away from the brazier of fire, the sloping wall of hieroglyphs in high relief. Beyond, to either side, shadowed archways rose to low vaulted ceilings, blackened with the caked charcoal residue of many burning torches.

Uxmal Chac whirled around and his hands lifted menacingly. The short stone weapon which was neither a sword nor an ax, slapped heavily against his thigh.

"You will not lecture to *me*. I have studied the Book of Balam; I know it as well as do you." He pointed to the glyph wall behind the burning brazier. "The wording is quite precise; it cannot be twisted—by you or anyone else—"

"You forget, my 'brother,'" Cabal Xiu said calmly, "that there *are* no others but us. Yet."

"Oh yes. Not since the Sundering. Not since the ending of

the fourth age. Yes, my 'brother,' you, the devout one. With every beat of my heart there is pain for the Majapan who worshiped us, for without them the rebirth—"

"Enough blasphemy from you!" Cabal Xiu was trembling and stiff-legged he took another step forward. Uxmal Chac's left hand went to his right hip. His fingers closed over the cold stone of his weapon. Flesh jumped as his muscles tensed.

"Is there not something you must attend to?" Kin Coba said softly.

They were as still as statues for a moment.

Orange light licked and flickered across dark cool flesh and tawny fur.

Then Uxmal Chac turned his back on them and strode from the building. The clatter of his leather sandals down the stone steps echoed into the humid night.

Cabal Xiu sighed, his body relaxing.

"He may be right, you know," he said.

"Would that it were so."

He turned to the glyph wall and spoke, sounding, at times, as if he were reading:

"So many *katun* since the destruction of the Majapan, our beloved race, so many barren *katun*, with only the promise of the Book of Balam, keeping us here, waiting, waiting for the *katun* of Ce-Acatl to come again." He gestured and Kin Coba moved silently to stand beside him, staring up at the walls of glyphs. "It comes now. At midnight the *katun* of Ce-Acatl returns; the primary; the beginning of the sixth age; the time of the Majapan's return."

Within one arch's deep shadow Ronin gestured to Moichi to follow Uxmal Chac while he stayed to listen.

"He may return to see if we are in our rooms," he whispered in Moichi's ear. "We will meet in your chamber later tonight." He returned his attention to the pair in the light.

"The origins of the Majapan are steeped in mystery," Cabal Xiu continued. "They carried with them the knowledge and the power of an age before the birth of man. Then the Majapan lived in a land of heat and jungle bordered on all sides by a great fathomless sea filled with monstrous creatures. From their gods, they received great gifts and knowledge but they were cursed for they came into being at the end of the Old Time and, as the time of man grew nigh, vast upheavals of the earth and the sea and the sky occurred.

"And the priests, who foretold these cataclysms, for even then was the Book of Balam in existence, now went among the Majapan and, gathering them all upon an immense plain near the shores of the writhing seas, bade them construct ships, speaking to them thusly: 'Now you shall build strong ships to sail upon the seas for the land of our birth will soon be no more. If the Majapan shall survive, it will be in another land.'

"And the people were terrified, for they were not good sailors and had no love for the water and they milled about, contending amongst themselves. Thus the priests said unto them: 'Fear not the high seas nor the leviathans of the deep, for the true danger lies here. Now will our land turn red and black and belch smoke and sulphur and the blood of the earth shall pour forth. Then will our land split asunder and hurl itself into the fathomless caverns of the earth for all time and the seas will wash over it like two hands clasped together.'

"Thus spake the priests and the Majapan listened and set themselves to build the ships of their salvation. And they went then to their ships, gathering up their children and their food and leaving all other manner of possessions behind. And the priests took up their sacred scrolls and left and the great wealth of the Majapan was left behind.

"So the Majapan set out from their doomed land, which already burned at its heart with the ending of the Old Time, and they were divided by the priests. One quarter went to the north, one quarter to the south, one quarter to the east and one quarter to the west.

"Thus the Majapan came to this island, this vast jut of limestone ledge, thrusting up from the floor of the sea. And here they founded Xich Chih, the city of their forefathers, the true city.

"Only here were the Majapan not assimilated into the birthing cultures of man, who spawned upon the world like maggots. Only here the Majapan remained unadulterated. And when they saw the Chacmool, they knew it at once for what it was: the personification of Tzcatlipoca."

"And now," breathed Kin Coba, her voice rich and tremulous upon the thick air, "in the *katun* of Ce-Acatl, in the dawning of the sixth age, the first of the Majapan have returned to their sacred city, where this night Tzcatlipoca may be reborn to once again see His Xich Chih.

Here and there streaks of water, last remnants of the hard rain, passed to platinum in the moonlight. Each carved stone block was moved to eerie caligraphy by the swift interplay of light and shadow; a numinous history hewn into each surface. It is a city of the dead now, Ronin thought, as he followed the fleet figure of Kin Coba through the dappled city. Perhaps time and solitude have turned them mad, for these three, the keepers of Xich Chih, were apparently not Majapan. What were they, beneath the Chacmool masks, he wondered, as he moved from shadow to shadow, down the pyramid's side, along the bright stone causeway. Would they, naked, resemble the figures in the pictoglyphs which encrusted the architecture of Xich Chih?

A dreamscape it was. Great stone heads seemed to float in air, thrusting out as they did from shadowed walls, immense oblique plazas with sloping sides, crowned by crenellated tops, endlessly tiered buildings with walls made unsolid by the concentration of hieroglyphs.

He lost her in a shaft of deep shadow into which she disappeared. He went after her, cautiously, silently, the stones his enemy now, for they would echo his pursuit if he were not careful. The path she had been following ran beside three buildings, along a narrow defile for perhaps another hundred meters beyond the pocket of shadow within which he now stood.

He was still for a moment, watching and, perhaps even more acutely, listening for her muted footfalls. All about him the chronicles of the Majapan hulked mutely, savagely; a history in stone, waiting.

Moving slowly along the defile, he caught a glimpse of movement. But now he hesitated, unsure whether to follow or to return to the house on the acropolis. After a moment's deliberation, he moved onward, swifter now that he had reached a decision.

Down the defile and then sharply left, into a cleft of darkness, all sight gone for long moments.

Something had changed. Abruptly, the nature of the darkness had altered. It was at once thicker and more expansive and he realized that he was out from the buildings. He looked up but could see no stars, no moon.

He heard again the muffled sound in front of him and went on. There were trees now in patches of deeper darkness and as his eyes slowly adjusted to the werelight he saw that he loped through an outthrusting of the jungle which surrounded the city.

Now and again he thought he saw a glimmering ahead, as of some reflected light, but always it was rather close to the ground, certainly less than two meters from the floor of the forest. Who or what was he following? He had had an intuition that he had lost Kin Coba somewhere within the defile. Then why had he come here?

The jungle gave grudgingly onto a moon-dappled glade and he paused just outside the lip, drenched in shadow. He heard nothing but the whining of the nocturnal insects, the sighing of the trees.

He went swiftly down the aisle of the clearing, around an abrupt turning and saw, bathed in indifferent moonlight, the black and white edifice, strewn, collapsing, etched into the far side of the glade.

It was set off the ropy jungle floor by pillars in the shape of an undulating serpent in a repeating squared off "S" shape so that each wave of its body formed part of the foundation. It was the first time that he had seen this creature represented in the city. The building's central stairway had fallen away in several places.

The building itself had twelve doorways and over the thick lintel of each was carved the same serpent, with plumes or wings as if it were flying.

One entire side of the building was choked with the inevitable influx of the returning jungle. Green moss across the steps like an unkempt carpet.

Something flickered at the periphery of his vision and he went closer. The white spark came again and now he saw that before the building stood a statue under the shadow of an overhanging tree. As the wind swung the heavily laden branches, a sliver of moonlight caught the statue's top.

It was incomplete. Someone had deliberately hacked away the head. It towered over him, perhaps six and a half meters high.

It was a warrior.

With breastplate and high boots, thickly muscled arms. Two scabbards hung at its waist, one filled, the other empty. One arm was raised. That, too, had been vandalized. It ended in a severed wrist.

A cool wind fluttered the massed treetops some meters away; the night insects were calling to each other. No other sounds.

For long moments he stood staring in dumb fascination at the statue, hearing, perhaps, some dark, faraway call. He felt an unknown power seeping into his body as if from the glade itself or his proximity to the stone structures. Too, he became aware of an incipient urgency.

Then he turned slowly away, into the rustling, steamy shadows of the jungle.

He lifted his eyes for one last look.

Somewhere close, above his head, feathered wings spread and took off into the clear, calm night.

Outside, away from the overhanging foliage, the vast geometrical plain was lit below the black bowl of heaven by the full moon and the myriad dancing stars. Away to the east, far down near the horizon, the wide belt of thickly clustered stars stretched in an attenuated arc. Far, far away was fragrant Sha'angh'sei and the yellow citadel to the north, Kamado, where the Kai-feng had already commenced.

In the building on the north edge of the acropolis, Ronin closed his eyes, waiting for Moichi to return.

Angrily he stalks the corridors of a corroded, forgotten house. The way is narrow and dark so that he is continually forced to peer ahead in order to guide himself. Because of this, he has no time to look into the doorways which parade past him mockingly on either side, although this is what he wishes to do. Or perhaps not. But in any case, as he strides along, his anger grows, a deep, fierce, nonrational rage. He sees himself in a mirror then and recoils from his image, stumbling away.

He plunges onward, downward into blackness, along the corridor. There are no others. Soon the doorways end and solid walls rush by him as he begins to run, faster and faster, his boot soles echoing, echoing like drumbeats, a strange cadence to some long hidden song. This is not prudent, he thinks in the lightlessness. Chill take it! As the rage burns like a spreading fire. Out of control; a rush of doom like black, leathery wings. Faster he rushes down the narrow corridor.

Down and down all in a blur as he feels slightly vertiginous. And now he realizes that the ceiling had been lowering. Stooped and bent uncomfortably, he stumbles forward. Faster.

He trips, tumbling head over heels through the blackness. Fetched up suddenly, his arms flung over his head, his fingers gripping tightly.

He hangs, suspended in space, grasping a bar which is the nethermost lip of the corridor-tunnel-funnel, arcing downward like a spout, trying to spit him out. And down.

Hot and sweating, he holds desperately on while below him a space of incalculable depth and width. Yawning.

Great clashings and groanings issue forth from the deep. A dimly seen scaffolding somewhere below him, too far to drop, perspective dwindling it to the width of a sword tip.

Explosions, dull and booming, rising toward him, painful to the ears.

Still he peers downward, fascinated, terrified, unable to break his gaze away.

A writhing form appears, glutinous, tentacled, writhing upon a translucent ellipse. A great dark form materializes from out of the deep. Formless, it bends over the monstrous creature, encysting it within its corpus. The tentacles emerge with the thing's great head, shivering. Two eyes burn, lidless, their pupils jagged shards of obsidian.

Then, far too rapidly for him to comprehend, the face flickers with changing features, ten thousand within each instant until a single eye is formed long enough for him to be lashed to its baleful unblinking gaze, bound and broken and helpless.

Heat like a cry. His eyeballs seared, his struggling body cooked and blackened; burning, burning. And a stench, rising . . .

"I heard you cry out," she said, bending over him. He stared sightlessly at her great furred head, grotesque, distorted shadows racing across its pelt in the flickering, dim light of the reed torches in the corridor beyond his doorway.

Ronin rose to one elbow on his pallet, wiped the sweat from his face.

"Are you ill?"

"No. No," he said slowly, still far away. "A dream only." His voice sounded thick and furry.

"A dream."

"Yes."

Kin Coba knelt beside him.

He stared at the fresco on the wall in front of him. Men in plumed headdresses ran at each other across a rectangular field bordered along each long side by obliquely angled stone stands surmounting sheer walls. From each side wall, at the field's center, at a height of perhaps five meters, protruded a carved stone ring.

"What are they doing?"

Her head turned with a rustle.

"The Majapan play the sacred ball game."

The sloped stands rose on either end to form a clawing Chacmool.

"They were originally farmers," she said softly. "The Majapan loved the land, the huge harvests of maize and beans and fruits. But always there were other tribes, fierce, powerful, decadent in their religion. Thus the Majapan were forced to become warriors."

He watched the wan light caress her naked thigh.

"Yet they would have no part in war. Thus the priests devised the sacred ball game and the Majapan constructed the courts, and the tribes who would war upon them were forced to pick a team of their best warriors. Nineteen men, each side was allowed, and they played the sacred ball game upon the stone courts in complex and ritualistic patterns, using flat stone paddles. The object was to get the ball through the stone ring while effectively blocking the opposing team from doing the same."

His gaze swept back to the fresco.

"So there was no war."

"The Majapan way."

"And all the tribes abided by your rules."

"All feared—" She paused as if she had committed a transgression.

"Feared what?" He watched her face now, half in shadow, searching for some hint of emotion, some small betrayal, in the eyes behind the mask.

"A—god. A god we once worshiped." Her voice had turned somber. "But," she continued more brightly, "that was in the time-that-was; it is not important now for that—false god was banished from this land many *katun* ago."

An overgrown building, partially destroyed; a headless statue; a plumed serpent.

"Only the Chacmool had reigned in Xich Chih," she said. "His priests devised the sacred ball game—"

"So the Majapan avoided bloodshed by playing the game," said Ronin.

Her head swiveled and the light caught her eyes, shining, tawny, like perfect topazes.

"Whatever gave you that idea?" said Kin Coba, startled and indignant at the same time. "The heads of the losing team were delivered into the arms of their tribal chieftains as a warning against further aggression. Their steaming hearts were used to fertilize our crops. The Majapan were a very practical race."

There was a small silence while he digested this, then: "You mean the Majapan never lost a game?"

"No," she said. "Never."

A peculiar depression had descended upon him. In an effort to break it, he said: "What lies behind that Chacmool mask, Kin Coba?"

Her slender hands, which had been in her lap, rose into the still air, a silent explosion, more truthful than words could ever be.

"Do you wish," she said, "to possess me?"

He thought her choice of words curious.

"You mean make love."

"If that is what you desire."

He reached out, ran his finger tips up from her knee, along the inside of her thigh. Her eyes glittered.

"Not with that mask."

"Then you shall not have this."

Her strong fingers took his hand, lifted it higher. He felt her heat, steamy as the jungle at midday. Her other hand moved along his prone form.

"And you *do* want it."

She lifted herself up and pulled at his leggings, freeing him. Then she knelt over him, descending slowly, her eyes closing, the lids fluttering. She gasped. She lowered her torso and he felt the heat of her heavy breasts and the fluttering of her stomach. He put a hand up to her face but her firm fingers entwined in his and she pulled his hand down to the side of one breast. Her hips moved downward.

He grappled with her in the humid night, inhaling her strange, pungent musk, wondering what she looked like, the coupling like a great wrestling match as their bodies lacquered with sweat and saliva, in a rising cadence, while he felt again the rushing down a claustrophobically metamorphosing corridor-tunnel-funnel.

And at the precise moment when she cried out and her body trembled, he felt her cruelty wash over him like a fetid tide and he felt himself recoil, an image in a fleeting mirror. Her fingernails gouging at his flesh, the imprisoning grip of her powerful thighs, her torso arching up above him, her breasts swaying, the nipples long and hard.

Inside, in turmoil, he tried to grapple with the rancorous emotions that had begun to bellow loudly in his inner ear. He felt pleasure pool itself far away in his loins.

Her hips grinding in a circle, her breath loud and sensuous.

He lifted his hands and squeezed her breasts. She moaned. And thrust against him. And his hands went to the mask, lifted it from her shoulders and, even as he heard a deep growling, a harsh shout from outside, he stared upward, outward from the glowing gems of her eyes.

Impaled.

Deep in the spangled night, Moichi loped from shadow to shadow, his eyes intent on the tall figure of Uxmal Chac as he swept away from the low pyramid.

Unreasonably, Moichi had expected him to head for the great stepped pyramid to the west but, instead, Uxmal Chac turned right, off the causeway, toward the far side of the city.

Glittering, secretive, it stretched away from him, filled with the knowledge of the ages. There it crouched upon the plain, an incipient life hovering somewhere close.

In all of Xich Chih, there was only one round building, small and relatively unadorned, and it was to this that Uxmal Chac now went.

Moichi could see, as they approached, that the edifice was somewhat over one hundred meters high, a circular tower, resting on two terraces set one upon the other; the lower broader one was of grass, the higher, of stone. Stairways, centered on one side, led up to the tower, which had three doorways, set at precise though unequal distances from each other.

Beneath the lintel of a neighboring doorway, depicting a priest surrounded by hieroglyphs, Moichi watched intently as Uxmal Chac mounted the two stairways and stood directly in front of the tower's first doorway, at the extreme left, staring up into the night sky. After a time, he held something dark to his eye.

Moichi's gaze left him, clouded in moonlight, swept upward. Toward which constellation did he look? Moichi asked himself. The Seven Sisters? The Great Bear? And where was the Serpent, the enormous constellation which had guided him to many a safe port from out of the uncharted sea?

For a long time Uxmal Chac regarded the heavens and then, apparently finding the answer to his unvoiced question among the hard points of unreachable light, stepped inside the tower for a brief moment before re-emerging. He went down the stairway, across the grass terrace, down again, and plunged into shadow.

At once, Moichi left the darkness of the doorway, moving away from the building, after the tall figure.

He found himself quite near the edge of the thick, entangled jungle. Turning, he could just make out the top of the great, stepped pyramid to the west. He heard the soft slap of Uxmal Chac's sandals ahead of him and he went on. A series of low buildings stretched away from him.

Abruptly, a dark shape crossed his path, becoming visible as it loped from the dense shadows of the jungle. The platinum light was pellucid and he saw it clearly: the deep, unmistakable red of its glossy pelt, its bright yellow-green eyes cold and hard as flint, glowing as if from some internal energy source. Its long tail flickered at the humid air.

"Chacmool," he breathed.

It leapt at him, its great dark head extended, jaws beginning to open, the talons of its forepaws raking the night. It growled deep in its throat and Moichi shouted in reflex as he drew forth a copper-handled dirk. Then the beast was upon him.

The jaws gaped wide, the head reared back, as the forepaws commenced to slash at his flesh. Light gleamed wetly along the curved surfaces of the Chacmool's fangs. They dripped with saliva and something darker.

The beast lunged for his neck. He twisted aside and the teeth snapped together. He strove to free his right hand, to lift the long blade of his tightly gripped dirk into the Chacmool's belly. It growled in frustration and doubled up its hind legs, attempting to scrape its long talons across Moichi's exposed stomach and thighs.

There was dark movement behind and above him but he ignored it as he rolled on the white stones of Xich Chih enwrapped by the Chacmool. He strained and ground his teeth and, at last, he had freed his right arm. The opened jaws came at him again and he slammed his heavy copper wristlet against the fangs. The Chacmool screamed. He turned the blade of his dirk, silvered by the strong moonlight, and drove it toward the beast's heart. The thrust aborted; his wrist immobilized. His body thrashed against the weight of the thing, his nostrils filled with its powerful scent, and he twisted his head to see what—

The Chacmool sank its teeth into his neck.

Godgame

"TIME is the slayer."

A series of masks, replicated.

"Time is the healer. Time is the boundary. Time is the victor."

Stone Chacmool guarded its lower reaches with opened jaws.

"Our heads are bowed before your inevitable power."

Uxmal Chac's voice began as the last echoes of Cabal Xiu's litany died away:

"As it must be. As it was foretold in the Long Count, in the Book of Balam, of the Majapan." The note of triumph in his voice was unmistakable. "It is midnight. Now the *katun* of Ce-Acatl commences. It is the sixth age!"

Now they were maskless.

Uxmal Chac had a face that was long and thin. His nose was as the trunk of an elephant.

Cabal Xiu's jaw was snoutlike. His mouth was lipless, his nose all nostrils.

Kin Coba's eyes were triangular, their pupils feline slivers. Her ears, high up on her head, twitched at every sound.

The strange trio stood revealed on the nethermost step of the great pyramid which dominated the heart of Xich Chih. At their feet Ronin and Moichi lay, conscious but unmoving.

"Think!" cried Kin Coba, ecstatically, thrusting out her arms. "Remember! Do you feel it?" She whirled in the night. "Our lost power begins to return! The Majapan, who spawned us in the Old Time will, at dawn, return to us once more! After an age of barrenness comes an age of plenty!"

"These two shall return the Majapan to us!" cried Cabal Xiu. "For on these steps of the Sacred Pyramid of Tzcatlipoca will come death." The distant trees seemed to shudder and shake and the stone city vibrated as his voice filled with energy and power with every word he uttered. "And life; life for Xich Chih once more!"

"Now it begins!" Cabal Xiu called out into the changing night, as, black-robed, he mounted the central stairway of the pyramid. Uxmal Chac turned to follow him but Kin Coba grasped his arm, took him to the side. Ronin strained to hear their conversation even though he could not turn his head.

"He has seen it, Uxmal Chac, the forgotten shrine and the —the statue."

"What?" Uxmal Chac's eyes blazed. "The one who followed you saw the statue of Atsbilan?" He glanced at Ronin for a moment, then he shook his strange head. "It matters not. He-Who-Sets-The-Sun has been banished from this land for *katun* without end, just as his Father, whose name must not be uttered, was banished in the Sundering." He put a hand on Kin Coba's shoulder. "Long has Tzcatlipoca reigned in Xich Chih and thus will it be forevermore. Now must begin the sacrifice which will return Tzcatlipoca to Xich Chih and, with Him, the Majapan."

Kin Coba stared up into his face.

"Yet I am frightened, for he has been to the place and perhaps he is the One—"

Uxmal Chac's hand slammed into her face and she recoiled.

"Are you mad? We are what we are, yes, but see how shabby we have become during all the *katun* without the shadow of Tzcatlipoca to make us great!"

"I am Kin Coba," she said proudly, ignoring the blood which trickled down her cheek. "I do not need you to tell me what I am. But have you forgotten the rest of the Book of Balam's foretelling, Uxmal Chac?"

His head twisted from her words as if they were alive.

"Ah, wicked blasphemer!" Uxmal Chac spat.

Above them all, Cabal Xiu neared the flat summit of the Pyramid of Tzcatlipoca.

"How can you bow before one section of the Book while renouncing another?" Kin Coba's voice held a metallic thread. "Do you not see? It took me awhile to understand too. You know what Cabal Xiu means to do. What will become of us then, if all of the Book is true?"

"Leave those thoughts behind, Kin Coba. We have changed the Book of Balam, you know that." His hands gripped her arms. "Have you so soon forgotten how all of us fought Him and banished Him finally from the land of Xich Chih so that Tzcatlipoca might reign alone here for all time? Have you so soon forgotten our comrades lost in that titanic struggle?"

"No," she said sadly. "I am forever scarred by that battle. But it is again the year of Ce-Acatl. He was created in the year Ce-Acatl; He bore Atsbilan in the year Ce-Acatl; we defeated Him in the year Ce-Acatl; and the Book declares that He shall come again in the year Ce-Acatl." Her hair streamered back from her slanted face; her eyes were feral. "You know that His coming means the end of Tzcatlipoca's reign over Xich Chih. Without His protection, the balance we fear shall be restored and we shall perish!"

There came a cry from far above them and Ronin raised his eyes to the top of the stepped pyramid, saw the tall black-garbed figure of Cabal Xiu before the Temple of Tzcatlipoca, heard the deep booming voice as it echoed out over the waiting empty city:

"Oh, Itzamna, Lord of Heaven, son of Hunab Ku, creator of the world, Thou art no more, dethroned by Chac.

"Oh, Chac, Thou deserter of the true Majapan, friend of man, traitor to Tzcatlipoca, great was the power that sent you from us—"

It was a summoning of power and, as Cabal Xiu intoned, the Sacred Pyramid seemed to shine more brightly, as if the moon, hanging like a platinum teardrop in the black, spangled river of the heavens, had grown swollen with light and energy.

Ronin turned to the big man lying beside him.

"Moichi, can you move?"

The navigator shook his head. No.

"What have they done to us? The last I remember, the Chacmool—"

"They knew our movements from the first," said Ronin quietly. "Perhaps even before we reached the city. Those eyes in the jungle—"

"The Red Jaguars—?"

A dim crackling came from the Sacred Pyramid's summit and they lifted their eyes. Cold flames, white and blue, had begun to flicker, twisting in awesome splendor from the Temple of Tzcatlipoca, throwing the figure of Cabal Xiu into sharp silhouette.

"Oh, old and tired deities," the priest continued to intone, "thy time has ended, so the *katun* of the Long Count in the

Book of Balam has decreed. Thy power had faded and crumbled—"

The flames writhed higher: liquid, silvered, unnatural. Cabal Xiu lifted his arms to the waiting moon.

"The time is now come. It is once again the *katun* of Ce-Acatl. It is the dawning of the sixth age—"

Ronin blinked, for now it seemed that the black figure throbbed and grew.

"Come, Xaman Balam!"

The flames streamed at his back.

There came a grinding roar, as his corpus ballooned, blurred.

The night turned platinum.

Ronin and Moichi covered their eyes and when they could look once again toward the Sacred Pyramid's summit, there were four figures descending, eschewing the central stairs, striding across the immense steps of the structure.

"It is done," breathed Kin Coba, her slanted face even more alien in the unnatural light. "Xaman Balam lives again!" She turned to look at Ronin.

"Who is it?" he said.

"The One-Who-Is-Four," said Uxmal Chac. He took a step up the face of the Sacred Pyramid. "He who survived the cataclysms of the ages. They who held up the four corners of the world in the Old Time when the great flood came, reaching up, grasping the stars for support, lest they slip into the deep."

They were identical, these four, with long blazing eyes, neither of man nor beast, long noses like the trunks of elephants, narrow, tapering skulls gleaming in the frosted light, wide mouths with thick, curling lips. One was garbed all in red; one in white; one in yellow; one in black.

Simultaneously, the four mouths opened and four identical voices rolled eerily down to them, inundating them:

"I am come now, unstoppable: Xib, Sac, Kan, Ek. Xaman Balam speaks after lo these many *katun*." Moichi shivered at the sound of the voices.

The figures continued to descend, until they stood on the penultimate step nearest the ground.

"The summoning of Tzcatlipoca is at hand and when He comes He shall lead the Majapan back from the deep to the land of the Chacmool, to Xich Chih, most holy of cities!"

Pale green lightning crackled in the air and its sharp stench invaded them, borne from the place where Xaman Balam had been birthed.

"With the gathering of sides, the Sacred Sacrifice commences." They pointed to Ronin. "You will play against the forces of Tzcatlipoca, just as it was done in the Old Time, for without contention, without the spilling of blood, He cannot come. You will ascend to the fourth step." Ronin counted. There were nine steps in all. "The boundaries," they continued, "are contained across this face of the Sacred Pyramid—"

And abruptly, Ronin found himself able to move. Yet still not in control, he watched his legs take him up the central stairway to the fourth level.

"The skull," said Ek, the black aspect of Xaman Balam.

Xib, the red aspect, stood directly above Ronin on the seventh step. He wore a mask of a grinning skull.

"The vulture."

Sac, the white aspect, in a swooping bird's mask, stood on the sixth step, to the left of Ronin.

"The crocodile."

Kin Coba, in a mask that was all jutting jaws, stood also on the sixth step, but to Ronin's right.

"The monkey."

Kan, the yellow aspect, stood on the fifth step, on Ronin's far left.

"Flint."

Uxmal Chac, in a towering, angular mask, stood on the fifth step, on Ronin's far right.

"These are your adversaries," said black Ek, ascending to the Sacred Pyramid's top step. "As they are arrayed against you, they will attempt to force you downward, off the face of the pyramid. When they succeed in this, you and your companion will die and in so doing you shall be catalysts in the summoning of Tzcatlipoca. Your severed heads, your steaming hearts, shall bring Him once again to His beloved Xich Chih."

"And if I win?" said Ronin.

Ek smiled, his teeth pointed and black, shining with saliva. "If you should manage, by some miracle, to ascend to the summit of the Sacred Pyramid, then you and your companion shall be free to depart from there." The strange eyes bloomed like poisoned flowers. "But I tell you now that there is no hope. I know that you have seen the statue of Atsbilan, He-Who-Sets-The-Sun; I know that you have seen the vandalized temple of his defeated Father, whose name must not be mentioned. But they were driven out of Xich Chih and the memory of the Majapan at the time of the Sundering. The book of Balam has been rewritten and we have nothing to fear. The power of Tzcatlipoca is supreme in Xich Chih—!"

"If this is a game," called Ronin, "then there must be sides. Where are my forces?"

Ek laughed, his eyes like beacons: "Find them, mighty warrior!" And his deep voice resounded in the close valleys and stepped hills of the stone city, precise, geometric, deserted.

Now from above him, Kan, in the rippling brown monkey mask, advanced. He brandished a staff, hooked at one end, carved into the head of an animal.

Ronin drew his sword in time to parry a flicking jab of the long staff. Over and over, the monkey's weapon slashed at him, blurry, indistinct with speed, powered it seemed by the merest movement of the wrists. Again and again it slammed against him with explosive force.

Green and blue lightning ringed the theater of combat, emanating from the temple behind Ek at the summit of the Sacred Pyramid.

The monkey pressed his attack, the blows constant and unremitting and Ronin moved slowly backward under the intense assault along the length of the great stone step. He was still slightly dazed, his reflexes dull and unresponsive. His brain refused to think clearly.

Backward he was forced, far to his left, until he was directly below the vulture on the sixth level. In that moment, as the monkey held him in that position, the vulture stepped down to the fifth level.

Glancing up, Ronin began to perceive what was happening. Ek had not fully explained the rules of this game, just as he would not divulge the nature of Ronin's forces. He realized now that the monkey had deliberately forced him to retreat toward the left side of the pyramid's face in order to allow the vulture to descend. He knew now that he had to battle each opponent while staying away from each of their corresponding spaces on his step, else they were permitted to move against him simultaneously.

Feinting, he spun away from the monkey, willing his body to work for him, concentrating on clearing his mind of distractions. As he left the vulture's space on his level, he was gratified to see him freeze into immobility on the step just above him.

But the monkey was intent on his attack once more and he pressed forward, forcing Ronin down a step onto the third level. He attempted a fierce counterattack, but when even the complex *faes* failed against the monkey, he was certain that he would not be able to prevail using merely his sword. Somewhere lay the key. Where are my forces?

He spun away from the oncoming staff, trying desperately to think of the answer.

"You understand now the impossibility of victory, the inevitability of defeat," called Ek from far above, "for you battle not men but the last gods of the Majapan!"

His weapon was useless for the moment; he sheathed it. Sensing victory, the monkey lunged at him. The staff whistled through the dark, electric air and Ronin reached out for it. They struggled for endless moments, linked by the wooden weapon. The head of the staff was before his face and abruptly, intuitively, he bent his knees, exerted force. Muscles rippled along his mighty arms and tendons stood out like corded rope down the sides of his neck. He ground his teeth, grunted, finding renewed strength within himself, transmitting it up through his legs, muscles jumping with the strain, into his torso. His body twisted one way and, as the monkey began to compensate, to turn his body with the expected force. Ronin let go, reversed the momentum, whipping his shoulders and arms with explosive power in the opposite direction.

If one operates only with the conscious, one sees just what one wants to see. but the brain registers everything the eye picks up and in Combat training one learns to allow the subconscious to scan the entirety of the vision field, unraveling the frequently curious paths of victory by working out clues not readily available to the conscious.

The staff was his.

When the weapon was in front of his face, he had been concentrating on strength and balance with his conscious mind. But his subconscious had been working on survival and it had picked out from the myriad images within his vision field, the carven head of the monkey's weapon. He had been mistaken when he had thought it an animal. Or perhaps not. It was a man's head. The subconscious had worked on the problem and had found the solution.

He slammed the carved head into the monkey mask with enormous force. It shattered into a cloud of choking powder blossoming garishly into the humid night. Kan's headless body sank to the cold stone.

"The first move is completed," Ek intoned mechanically. "Man defeats monkey."

So there *is* a way, after all, thought Ronin as, peripherally, he caught a movement from just above and saw the vulture drop down to the fourth level. He reached up with the staff and the vulture, his arm ramrod stiff, cracked it in half. Ronin threw it from him. The pieces spun in the air, bouncing off the lowest step and onto the stone paving before the Sacred Pyramid.

And a different counter to each opponent. But how am I to know?

The vulture reached the third step.

Ronin had defeated the monkey but in so doing he had lost a step and now was one level closer to being driven off the face of the pyramid.

He concentrated on his second foe. The vulture carried no weapon but his arms were thin, brownish-yellow, scaled, and, as he lifted them, Ronin saw that they ended in four-fingered claws tipped with curved talons. These commenced to beat the air in front of the vulture as it came at him.

In a flurry, the talons flashed out and he jerked aside, hearing the hissing of their close passage. They came at him again, aiming for his cheek. He ducked and the other set of talons sank into his shoulder, ripping at his flesh. He groaned, staggering. The step became narrow and his boot went over the edge. He toppled over, taking the clutching vulture with him onto the second level.

He scrabbled at his belt for his dirk as the claw sank deeper into the muscles of his shoulder. At last he pulled it free and the flickering light licked along its blade as the edge scraped across the scales of one of the vulture's arms, but the claw refused to relinqulish its painful hold on him. Again the talons twisted in his flesh and fire seared through him. Gasping now, he hacked with the point of the blade. A shrill call came from within the vulture mask and he smelled an awful, sickly sweet stench: mummified remains, lying within moldy corridors of the ages; cement and limestone walls collapsing; rotting vegetation rising thickly; fetid swamps burbling their liquid call. . . .

Pain; the edge of the second step like a sword blade on his back as the vulture bore its weight down upon him. He was on his way down to the first level!

"Moichi!" someone cried. "Moichi!"

Up his throat.

And he called out again.

A rustling, a thud of boot soles.

His body tipped precariously while the vulture bore down even harder.

"Ah!"

A soft breeze behind him.

Talons gouged and he closed his mind against the pain.

The vulture heaved at his body.

Going over.

No! No!

He never reached the first step. His back fetched up against solid flesh, immobile, rocklike. He braced himself against the unexpected bulwark, feeling the hard thud of the heart against the ridged muscles of his back. He gained strength, backstopped. He reached up with both hands, dropping his useless dirk and, screaming, wrenched the convulsed claw from his shoulder.

He took a deep breath, his frame shuddering, and as his blood oxygenated, he felt a surge of adrenalin and now, lowering one wrist to act as a fulcrum, he slammed his balled fist into the claw. Sweat broke out along his forehead, rolled down his heaving sides, along his tensed legs. The vulture wailed as, with a splintering of bone and dry sinew, the wrist snapped. Shards of hollow bone punctured the rent skin and black blood ran in icy rivulets from the maimed member.

The vulture mask vibrated as if with hate and the good claw flailed, the questing talons making a dark melody as they swept through the air. Then the vulture leapt at him.

Gray blur blooming, deadly; heavy whiff of discarded centuries. And, without further thought, Ronin leapt upward and away.

On the third step, panting, he turned, looked downward. The broken body of the vulture knelt against the edifice of Moichi's body as if it had hit a stone wall instead of—

"The second move is completed," Ek intoned from the pyramid's summit. "House defeats vulture."

Already there was motion above him and Kin Coba, the crocodile, landed above him on the fourth step. The long jaws gaped, just centimeters from his face. He rolled away and she came after him, brandishing a short-hafted battle ax in her right hand.

He drew his blade once more and it clashed against her swing, the metal scraping together. She pivoted, swung again, and as he ducked away, leapt to the third step.

He recovered and slashed at her, bracing for the concussion as their weapons crashed together in a welter of sparks and noise.

Blood streamed from his shoulder where the vulture's talons had sunk. For the moment, the pumping adrenalin compensated for the energy drain, but all too soon—

He stood his ground, letting her come against him, over and over, gauging the manner of her combat.

She was a warrior. She swung from her widely planted bare feet, using her hips and upper torso to make up for her arms, which were more slender than a man's. And she was clever. Time and again she nearly got behind his guard for a killing blow. But perhaps more importantly she was tireless. Stunting, varying the angles of her attacks, carefully calculating each blow, she became a machine of destruction and, with pain and fatigue lapping at the periphery of his senses, the idea of defeat crept into his mind.

He shook his head, risked a glance toward Ek high above him. Was it his imagination or was the ebon-robed figure bent in concentration? With that, he knew that the thoughts of defeat were not his own and he returned his concentration to his battle on the third step. Once again, he knew that his sword alone could not prevail against the god. What then?

And out of the corner of his eye, a possible answer came crawling along the cold stone. A small lizard on the step perhaps a meter behind the crocodile, its bright eyes staring, its forked tongue flicking the air before it.

The clashing was hypnotic and he held his ground. The lizard seemed transfixed by the replicated movements of the battle. Ronin retreated and the lizard scuttled forward. Locked together, he allowed the crocodile to push him further back. This time the lizard scuttled further along the stone until it was just behind his foe.

Abruptly he pressed his attack, exerting great force, shoving the crocodile backward along the step. One bare foot struck the lizard, who squealed, terrified, and squirmed.

The crocodile stumbled for an instant.

It was all Ronin needed.

Slamming a mighty blow with the flat of his sword against the side of her face, he sent her flying. She cried out as she tumbled downward, her mask slipping off as she hit the top of one of the great stone Chacmools at the base of the Sacred Pyramid. A crack like thunder.

Ronin swung up onto the fourth step.

"The third move is complete," Ek cried from above. "Lizard defeats crocodile."

While he gained the fifth level.

Uxmal Chac: flint moving against him now; the light of the low platinum moon, which frosted the swaying tops of the massed trees in the west, shot dazzlingly from his adversary's high metallic mask.

The night was waning. Would the dawn bring Tzcatlipoca?

Jagged blue-green lightning banded the Sacred Pyramid; a distant growling had begun from the interior of the Temple of Tzcatlipoca at its summit.

Ronin felt the pain in his shoulder intensify as his sword met the crescent flint blade of Uxmal Chac. But he urged his body onward, his iron will forcing the agony down into insignificance.

It is my time now, he thought wildly and he yelled the battle cry of his unknown ancestors, a call of power and determination, of strength and perseverence.

Uxmal Chac appeared confused by the cry, his attack brought up short. His great arms lifted his weapon high over his head; as he began the massive downswing, he tried to change direction, perceiving the flight of Ronin's long blade. A blur, it was within his guard, slamming aside his vertical blow, and clove his high mask down the center.

Great yellow and blue sparks flew from the violent contact, and bearing down, Ronin drove the sword further, through bone, tissue, more bone, and the body of Uxmal Chac dissipated like smoke upon the air. A clapping, as of dry stones crashing.

He vaulted to the sixth level.

"Ah, no!" Ek's voice no longer recited toneless liturgy. And, from below, Ronin heard the desperate cry of Kin Coba as she pulled her broken body up the Sacred Pyramid's central stairway:

"It is true then. What was written in the Long Count, in the Book of Balam, cannot be changed—"

Got it!

"No!" cried Ronin, stalking the sixth level. "I was born in the *katun* Ce-Acatl. I was driven from Xich Chih with my Father in the *katun* Ce-Acatl. And, as the Long Count and the Book of Balam foretold, I have returned in the *katun* Ce-Acatl!"

"What?" Ek threw up his hands. "What madness is this? What do you know of Atsbilan, warrior?"

"All!" cried Ronin. "For I am He-Who-Sets-The-Sun!"

Ek screamed: "Impossible! It cannot be!"

Ronin raced along the stone step on the sixth level, his eyes intent on Xib, the skull, coming alive on the seventh step. A fresh breeze had sprung up and as it reached him he turned and in the east saw the horizon, entirely visible at this elevation over the distant treetops of the immense jungle, saw the faint edges of pink and pearl gray streaked there as if by an artist's brush, presaging dawn.

"Return!" cried Kin Coba. "Reassemble!"

Crouching, the skull advanced.

Ronin made the seventh step.

"Oh, Tzcatlipoca." Ek raised his arms toward the black heavens. "Master of the moon and the pole star and the deep of night, is this truly Atsbilan or is it some imposter?"

It was what frightened them. He used it.

"It is I, Ek! Atsbilan has returned! Who else but He-Who-Sets-the-Sun could prevail against the forces of Tzcatlipoca in the sacred game?"

He closed with the red aspect and, as he did so, the skull drew forth an ebon rapier, ivory-handled, its blade thin and flexible.

The two unequal blades flashed, crossing.

"Destroy him!" sobbed Kin Coba. "He must not reach the ninth step!" Her spine splintered, still she strove to crawl up the central staircase, a ruined jaguar, noble even in death.

He used both hands to maneuver his sword against the lightning-like rapier as the grinning skull in his red robes caused the air to whine with the complex patterns of thrust, feint, thrust.

All along the seventh level they fought like fiends, using every ounce of their strength, every trick in their cunning combat vocabulary, their deadly dance as precise, as coldly geometric as the silent stone city crouched far below them. They whirled and lunged, twisted and circled, stalking the one instant of hesitation, searching for the one flicker of an eyelid indicating a break in concentration that would signal the death of one combatant.

The breeze from the east stiffened, tugging at the skull's crimson robes, fluttering Ronin's long hair.

Ek's fevered cries rose again into the dying night:

"Tzcatlipoca, hear the call of Your children, we who have served You faithfully and tirelessly through the endless *katun* of Time. We must be victorious this night for Your time in Xich Chih has come again! Once again it shall be filled to overflowing with Your worshipers, who will walk with the prowling Chacmool; who will serve You. Aid us now against Your enemy!"

The green and blue lightning crackled and it seemed to Ronin that Ek's desperate cry was successful for surely now the skull's attack grew fiercer and he grew stronger with each new thrust of his blurred blade so that Ronin was forced back along the stone step. Back and back under the murderous assault, dizzying him, impossible to stop. The skull loomed out of the mother of pearl night, the rapier on a deadly trajectory that nothing could stop.

A calling, distant, sparked in his mind as the rapier came on, a comforting sound like the gentle chatter of a great rainfall and he felt a trembling in the core of his being. Inside him, red and yellow lightning-like bolts of thought, currents of energy multiplying through him in geometric progression.

He attempted no parry.

The rapier rushed at his heart.

But merely, dreamlike, lifting his long sword obliquely, higher, higher still, until, with a harmonious sigh like the profoundest of musical chords, echoing away and away into the infinitude of the heavens, it reached the proper angle.

The blade seemed to ripple in pleasure as the first rays of the leading edge of the rising red sun shot along its length, running like molten metal. Ronin felt the vibrations of energy and his entire being seemed to expand with strength.

The long beautiful blade swam with pink and an intense bolt of light exploded from its tip, an extension of the solar engine filling the eastern horizon, lancing out along the line of the blade, striking the skull at the juncture of his throat.

"Oh!"

Such a small, pathetic sound, coming from the lips of a god, lost now on the rising wind from the east. The mask ballooned out grotesquely, shattered like a glass goblet, and Xib's acephalous body went heavily down the immense steps of the structure, tumbling, tumbling, in a swirl of scarlet and gray.

While Ronin, alight with power, vaulted to the eighth level, rolling, hurtling upward again to stand, at last, on the ninth step, the summit of the Sacred Pyramid of Tzcatlipoca.

Ek towered before him, his ebon robes filmy and ethereal,

billowing about his lean body. He threw a crescent of flat stone at Ronin and it struck his sword so that it spun from his grasp, clanging against the stones of the pyramid's summit.

But Ronin, lunging to his right, scooped up the huge brass brazier, burning brightly, lifting it from its base and flinging it in a hail of blue flame and red coals into Ek's face.

With a peculiar dry popping, the face fired.

Ronin ran for his sword, sheathed it, and turning, beheld not the burning form of Ek but something else.

The body swayed as if, weightless, it was caught in the wind's gusting crosscurrents.

Ronin stared.

From the blackened, smoking pit between the wide shoulders, there came a gnashing as of huge jaws working convulsively. A weird, unhuman cry billowed out into night's swift close and the very air about the tall form wavered and shuddered so that, for an instant, Ronin could not clearly see what was occurring.

The air cleared. And Ek was gone.

Reunited, the four brothers from the Old Time had become the one: Xaman Balam, the Hand of dark Tzcatlipoca, forger of the Sundering, instigator of the rewritten Book of Balam, minister of the night.

Born in the west, where ever there was darkness, his robes were a black so deep that they absorbed light and his huge head, which crowned his wide, powerful shoulders, was the atavistic visage of the Chacmool, icon of his Master: red, ebon-spotted, pointed yellow fangs bristling from his avenging muzzle, his round yellow and black eyes fierce, unblinking.

And Ronin, with the groundswell of energy still coursing within him, yet knew that he could not hope to do battle with this nightmare god and emerge victorious. The power which confronted him now was awesome, his body shaking with the pulsing of its emanations.

For here stood death and now life was beyond all imagining.

Xaman Balam's great animal jaws hinged open and sound emerged that no mortal was ever meant to hear. It tore at his eardrums like flint knives.

Thus the last great god of Xich Chih spoke and Ronin shuddered, weak before the first intimations of a power beyond understanding and, as Xaman Balam strode toward him he drew his sword, preparing to fight, looking inward, setting his soul for death's dark journey.

And Xaman Balam came on, his arms jerking upward, the talons at the tips of his fingers curling into the palms. Ronin gripped his useless sword more tightly, tensing his muscles for one last impotent blow, raising the blade.

But the god had halted and it took Ronin several moments to realize that the god had abandoned his attack and was, in fact, in the act of supplication.

Ronin turned to face the rising sun.

It was the brightest of lights, coming from the east, as if a piece of the sun itself had broken away. Writhing in the air, it bloomed as it approached with incredible velocity.

Rippling.

And Ronin saw now that it was a great serpent, covered in enormous feathers of every color in existence. It headed directly for the summit of the sacred Pyramid of Tzcatlipoca. Xaman Balam stood immobile as if mortally stricken.

And from just below them, Ronin heard a voice:

"Oh Xaman Balam, here is our end! Atsbilan's return has brought his Father back, just as the Long Count foretold!" It was Kin Coba, her face filled with awe and pain, pale and beautiful and hideous.

"Kukulkan is come again to Xich Chih! We are destroyed!"

The great serpent's head, so like the broken stone carvings surmounting the lintels of the small temple with its headless statue, lowered above Xaman Balam, the enormous body in constant motion. The fluttering of its plumes were like a whirlwind.

And now its rippling coils lowered and wrapped the dark god in their feathered embrace, squeezing, squeezing, until the huge, fierce jaws gnashed and the Chacmool head arched back in agony and the feet were lifted from the cool stone of its beloved pyramid.

Xaman Balam cried out, a piercing howl that rent the skies.

Still Kukulkan drew his coils ever tighter above the terrifying figure.

Then Kukulkan spoke:

"Sheathe your sword, my son."

Ronin obeyed and, at the same instant he lifted forth his Makkon gauntlet, his hand outstretched, palm upward, as if in friendship.

It filled with ruby light, building, building, until the color was so deep that he could not look into its depth.

Only then did the light leap from his extended finger tips, splashing like acid into the round eyes of the Chacmool-headed god.

Heatflash.

Aviator

BLUE. White. Blue. Gray-white, mottled. A rushing in his ears; cool air against his body; a balm to his aches and lacerations.

Weightless.

His eyes closing in weariness. Mind floating.

His hands gripped the soft, trembling plumes. A vast fluttering. Fans of Tenchō, so far away. A great rippling.

His eyes opened by force of will. Day. Because it was still light. Time enough to sleep when darkness falls.

He stretched, peering downward. A break in the cloud layer, marble parting. Far, far below him the flat sea arced away from him, following the curvature of the world. The hot sun's reflected light, chopped up into pin points of dazzling whiteness, dancing along its surface, caused him to think of a cauldron of molten gold. Searching for a black speck, invisible within the gold. Where are you now, Moichi?

Thus Ronin rode Kukulkan, the Great Plumed Serpent, out from the crumbling limestone, the cracking wood of the humped island upon which was built the stone city of Xich Chih, gone now in a swift, fireless quake. The seething blue-green sea, rushing to claim new territory, extended its shifting, twilit domain.

Xich Chih was adrift now on the tides.

And above his head, the pearl gray undersides of clouds, forming and shredding in the winds aloft. Solid-seeming, cities in the heavens, they part at the coming of Kukulkan, a great articulated rainbow, rippling through the skies.

And Ronin, drunk now with the exhilaration of life, of this race, grips the pulsing sides, the tufted plumes warm against his skin, and spreads wide his arms in exultation, the blood singing in his veins, light pulsing behond his eyes, a part of this flying colossus, whom Kin Coba called the Creator of the Sun, before she died.

Crawling like a severed insect up the wide stone stairway. The sky lightening now, the moon, refusing to set in this latitude, nevertheless on the wane. For now it was the earth which darkened like the night as great clouds of black smoke poured from widening gaps between the buildings of Xich Chih.

Then the foundation of the island began to dissemble.

Atop the shuddering pyramid, Kin Coba averted her ashen face as Kukulkan spoke:

"Climb upon my back, my son."

Ronin gestured. "My friend. I will not leave him here."

The Great Plumed Serpent shook his head but said nothing.

Ronin turned and raced down the stairway of the pyramid. The blue and green lightning had ceased at the approach of Kukulkan.

"Come on!" he called to Moichi. "Come on!"

Dazedly, the big man began to climb.

Shards of stone flew through the air while larger chunks slid downward as if in slow motion, colliding, crackling. His nostrils filled with dust and he caught the pungent stench of newly released sulphur. He slipped as another tremor ripped through the valley. Jagged lines appeared along the breaking causeways. Faint red glow from the depths.

They fell against each other and, together, raced for the summit. Up the crumbling stairway, they leapt over the still form of Kin Coba. Her topaz eyes stared downward, hard as glass, away from the enemy of Tzcatlipoca, past remembering even the dark god whom she had served so well in this arcane city.

The wind was rising and now fully half the structures were obscured by smoke.

They were airborne in a great flutter, the ruined city dropping swiftly away from them, its precise geometry askew and disappearing until it was just another vast pile of stone and dust and bones.

And then the sea.

My life is nought but a dream filled with surprises, Ronin thought now, alone with the Creator of the Sun. There is no past. There is no future. There is only a present more compelling, more fearsome, more beautiful, than any vision I could imagine asleep or awake.

The ship awaited them, or so he had thought, but dipping

so low that they skimmed the tops of the creaming waves, Kukulkan said: "For the other, only. You rise with me, my son."

Thus Moichi and Ronin had parted.

"When next we meet—"

"I will know you." And Moichi dropped to the wooden deck.

Creaming coral reefs fell behind them as out across the jade deep they flew, where lurked the unknown, unfathomable wonders born at the dawning of the world, still alive in their dim world of perpetual shadow. Passing the violent trenches that still shudered from eon to eon, causing the seas to rear up, swallowing ships or islands, lying low on their basalt foundations. Past gorges immeasurably deep where no life or again the beginning of all life dwelled. Past vast shelves of layered granite worn smooth where myriad multicolored fish swam lazily in the sun-dappled waters, serene and uncaring.

The planet turned below them as they sped upon their way. Ronin dozing at last for, he suspected, night would soon be upon them.

Yet, though the sun dipped in its arc, heading downward, Kukulkan flew so high that they were, in fact, within a region where darkness could not engulf them. Here the sun, still resplendent in all its life and warmth, reigned supreme, where night had never, in all the countless millennia since the creation of Time itself, been even a brief visitor.

Thus Ronin slept, his body resting, his strength renewing itself from the terrible ordeal which had expended itself across the southern face of the Sacred Pyramid, defeated gods whose time had come and was now gone.

And Ronin dreamed.

Of a giant cat with the form of a woman, who purred to him, lulling him to sleep with her warm, susurrant body, her jutting breasts, her curving thighs, her soft lips. Who rocked against him with her hips, scraping her nipples against his chest. Whose eyes were like glowing stones. Whose cruelty was such that she desired pain instead of tenderness.

Of a headless statue, cracked and tilted in the silt of a swirling lagoon, encroached by weed and long eels, the glyphs along its base already worn smooth by the churning tides.

Peering down at the disappearing answer, Tell me, he cried in an explosion of white bubbles.

Tell me, crooned the feline woman as her legs drew him inward.

Of a shadow approaching now out of the deep green expanse of a forest filled with the sharp points of pine needles, starred weapons. A pungent animal smell in his nostrils. A deep whinnying, so familiar. A guttural snort, the blasting of cold air. Black antlers, rimed with frost, shaking the cluster of branches, heavy with snow. The sun behind a bank of lavender clouds. The fierce, human eyes. The fear—

Tell me now: two voices just out of synch.

He steps forward.

Into the dazzling splendor of the darkness.

Beneath him, mighty Kukulkan delights in his swift flight across the face of the world. Long has he waited for the day when he would feel the small weight of a body upon his undulating back. He feels the heat of the sun upon his fluttering feathers and rejoices in the energy.

"Wake up," he calls softly. "Wake up, my son."

Ronin opens his eyes, looks downward, through the marbled clouds, past the gyring gulls below him, to a distant shore of steep cliffs, rearing out of the jade sea.

"Behold," whispers Kukulkan. "Ama-no-mori."

Two

BEYOND THE MYTHS OF MORNING

Down the Kisokaido

THE lavender-and-lace dragonfly leapt into the air. The warm breeze sizzled with the quick beats of its double wings, spread like shining fans in the moonlight.

From budding twig to budding twig it went, its long, tubular body as straight as a blade. It hovered, alighted, the beating of its transparent wings never ceasing, then leapt heavenward again. At length, it came upon an opened flower with pink, belled petals, its cupped center damp and fragrant, and it headed downward.

Ronin moved.

The dragonfly froze, clinging to the blossom which swayed slightly from the tiny weight. Even its wings were at rest, like obliquely angled hands in a gesture of supplication.

The night beat on around them.

Far away and below him, he could hear the echoing crash and hiss of the breakers rushing endlessly at the base of the steep cliff. The chirruping of the insects surrounded him. An owl hooted close by. He remained still for some time. In the darkness, away from the cliff's edge, he could hear the croakings of frogs.

Reassured, the dragonfly came to life and resumed its darting, erratic flight amidst the thicket of flowers. Light from the sliver of horned moon low in the sky splashed over the blossoms in a chill, silver shower.

Ama-no-mori.

The name echoed in Ronin's mind for perhaps the hundredth time.

They had descended at last out of the golden sun-drenched realm, dipping earthward. Dusk, evening, then night rushed up to embrace them as they fell through the sky.

Rolling off the back as the great coils floated centimeters above the land, letting moist clods of soil run through his fingers, hearing only the echo of the voice as Kukulkan rose into the air with a silent flutter, a brief wind.

"Good-by, my son."

Ronin stared after him as he ascended toward the sun, hidden now below the horizon of the world.

Ronin sat in the meadow bordered, in the direction he was facing, by a hanger of maples. The night air was clean and mild. Soon, he knew, he would set off in search of the Bujun, the people of Ama-no-mori, of the great mage dor-Sefrith, whose enigmatic writing he still carried with him, sealed within the hollow hilt of his sword, writing that once translated could turn the destiny of all men. But for this brief moment in time, he savored the exquisite taste of victory, at last upon the soil of Ama-no-mori, his long, arduous quest at an end.

He lay back, watching the winking stars wheel high above him, dew seeping through his shirt, dampening the skin of his back. He thought of Kukulkan in his domain of sun. He thought of flying, the trembling of power, the emerald sea drifting by far below him. The rush of a warm wind against his face as the world spun beneath him. Soon.

He closed his eyes.

He awoke to the soft rustling of the grass about him. A night bird called, unseen, in a jeweled voice. The trilling returned; a brief clatter of busy wings.

Silence, save for the quiet chirruping, the distant soft croaking.

He stood up, hearing the sighs of the maples as their tops swayed in the wind off the water. His gaze swung left and he saw the intermittent crystalline spark of a small fire. He set off in that direction, stretching his sore muscles, glad of the easy exercise. He breathed slowly as he went across the meadow, consciously exhaling more than he inhaled so that his automatic reflexes took over and he was breathing deeply and naturally once more. His lungs filled with the perfumed air.

Away from the hanger, he passed a stand of tall, slender pines, lonely and spectacular, regal in their aloofness, on a ridge of land, the verge of a shallow drop to the interior of the island. The sickle moon rode their shivering tops.

Down the incline of brown earth and tangled roots, through a copse and into the reeds. To his right he could make out the black bulk of a forest, gaining dominance over the land as he moved obliquely into the interior.

Soon he heard the ripple of water and the rhythmic sing-song of the frogs filled the night. There came a soft splash and the croakings ceased momentarily before starting up again. Abruptly, the fire bloomed before him in a glow of oranges and saffrons.

He paused just within the circle of firelight. A figure, a chiaroscuro of black and orange, squatted before the fire, turning pieces of food skewered on a green sapling stick. The head turned and an oval face, flat and yellow, peered up at him with dark eyes. They took in his entire figure.

"Would you join me, warrior?" The voice was soft and musical and, while some of the vowels seemed distorted to his ear, he had no trouble understanding the man.

"Yes, I—" His sword felt heavy at his hip. "I *am* hungry."

"Well then." The head swiveled. "Come and sit down, by all means."

He hesitated.

"Are strangers always so welcome here?"

The man laughed, a silvery sound which mingled gently with the rich clatter of the river somewhere near on their right. "Would you slay me then for the mouthfuls of food which are already yours? Or perhaps you desire my fishing poles and bait." He laughed again. "Sit. Sit."

Ronin went and sat cross-legged near the man. The shining face peered at him, the wide cheeks, the flat nose, the almond eyes giving the face a humorous countenance even when the features were at rest. It was neither an old face nor a young one.

"Hoshi is my name, warrior." He handed Ronin a chunk of hot vegetable.

Ronin held it in his finger tips, watching the steam disappear into the night. The frogs' song was a steady reverberation.

"I am Ronin," he said. "I am not from this island."

"That is quite apparent from the cast of your face," said Hoshi. He selected a lump from the stick, popped it into his mouth, chewed slowly, almost reflectively. His black eyes never left Ronin's face.

"What—is the name of this place?" After so long, he could not hold back; his tongue almost caught on his teeth.

The oval face cocked at an angle, the wide lips licked the charcoal from the blunt finger tips.

"Ama-no-mori, Ronin. The Floating Kingdom."

Ronin's exhaled breath was yet another sigh borne upon the rustling night.

Hoshi looked down for a moment, offered him another piece of hot vegetable.

"Where are you bound?"

"I search for the Bujun."

"Ah." The fisherman nodded to himself. "I should have guessed." He ground the point of the bare stick into the white ash in the fire's center. "Well, my repairs are completed and I travel upriver at dawn. I can take you part of the way, at least, hm?"

"Part of the way where?"

"To Eido, of course."

Firstlight was surreal.

A pearl mist turned all the countryside into a pointillist painting. Tall brown reeds floated by them on either side as Hoshi poled the long thin boat. The trees along the high banks were pastel greens and faded browns and, farther off, the rounded hillsides and the forest were the gray wisps of a waking dream.

The air was cool and moist. Hoshi poled with rapid, powerful strokes in a rhythmic cadence. A crane blew out a bamboo break to their left as they passed, its blue body grayed and subdued in color. The wet clatter of its rising began a chain of calls by nearby frogs and upriver there was a brief silvery flash and a shivering of the ghostly reeds.

Hoshi stood amidst the slimy fruits of his work. The unskinned fish sloshing back and forth to the boat's movements in the few centimeters of water he had proved for them.

Ronin sat silently near the boat's bow, watching the land rising from the mist, trying to clear his mind of the thousand tumbling questions he wished to ask but was sure that the fisherman could not answer. He was not Bujun.

Surprisingly, the rising sun merely warmed the fog but could not burn it off and the world continued to float by him serenely with little or no signs of life. Insects buzzed in the mounting heat and, occasionally, the low-bowing branch of a weeping willow caused him to duck out of the way of its lacy embrace.

They paused under the shelter of a spreading maple just past midday. Hoshi sat on the aft bench, produced a knife with a curving, serrated blade, and proceeded to skin and filet a fish. He offered Ronin half. They chewed silently, enjoying the stillness, the peace. They shared the last of Hoshi's clear rice wine.

Just before dusk, Hoshi altered their course again and headed toward the right-hand shore. When they had moored the boat, Hoshi fileted another fish, wrapped it in oiled paper for Ronin.

"Your way lies to the east," he said, pointing. "Along the Kisokaido."

Ronin thanked him and set off along the indicated path. The mist was turning a pale lavender and the world glowed like a lovely amethyst held up to a light as he strode down the winding road. The forest had finally dropped away from them during the long afternoon and now the road led him through rolling grasslands, rich and fallow. He sniffed, smelling animals and looked around. He saw none nearby and the mist made a wider search impossible.

It grew cooler. He began to ascend, the road continually doubling back upon itself as the incline became steeper. Large outcroppings of rock became frequent and at several points he felt certain that the Kisokaido had been cut through solid granite.

Gradually, he rose above the mist as the road wound up the slopes of a mountain. He broke out of it into the cool clear night, the sky above cloudy and restless. He turned, looking at the tall pines and cedars whose lower halves were still wrapped in its moist embrace.

It began to rain, a cleansing, drenching downpour, refreshing and invigorating, pattering and hissing along the rocks and earth and scrub brush of the mountain road.

He went on and ahead he could see, within a stand of dancing pine, a small three-sided wooden shelter, the stark, clean beauty of its construction illuminated by a lone oiled paper lantern hanging within its interior. The torrent was already turning the narrow road to mud, as black soil washed downward and he was glad to find some sanctuary.

As he drew close, he saw that the lantern hung not from a beam of the shelter but rather from the side of a dappled mare which stood sleeping in one corner. By her side slumped a man in a wide straw hat, moisture beading its crown, rain still dropping off its brim.

Ronin entered the shelter. The horse's tail flicked at a fly, her flank muscles jumping reflexively. The man did not move.

Ronin hunkered down in an opposite corner, inhaling the mingled scents of the cedar structure and the matted coat of the animal. There seemed no smell of human sweat.

He looked about him. The building was superbly constructed: clean, angular lines, simple, as befitted a mountain station; somehow regal in its austerity.

It was warmer in here despite the openness of one side, the architecture keeping out the damp chill of the downpour. Ronin turned his attention to the crouched figure but his lowered sedge hat concealed his face.

The rain hammered against the sloped wooden roof, the drumming lulling, hypnotic. Outside, the dark was alive with the obliquely falling rain, streaks of bouncing energy, silvered where the light from the lantern hit it.

The man in the dripping sedge hat stirred but his head did not lift.

The beat of the rain.

Ronin slept.

The man crouched before him, staring into his just-opened eyes. He resisted the impulse to jump up and draw his sword. He had glimpsed the man's long blade as he had entered the shelter last night. Now he saw that he carried a shorter sword on his opposite hip. A warrior. Was he Bujun, then? He was dressed in a brown wrapped robe, embroidered with a green spoked wheel pattern, plain sandals. Lacquered reed greaves protected his legs from just under the knee to just above the ankle. On his back was strapped a small round shield, lacquered brown and green. His hair was shiny black, set in a queue. His features were flat. Ridges of muscle ran along the sides of his thick neck. Pouches of flesh hung beneath his eyes, which were almond-shaped but nevertheless rather peculiar. They reminded Ronin of someone else's but he could not think of who.

"Good morning to you, stranger." The man spoke softly. His eyes were unwavering.

"Good morning."

"If one may be excused so rude a question: where are you from?"

Ronin said nothing, observing the other.

The man's right hand drifted languidly to the slightly curved hilt of his long sword.

"There are no strangers come to Ama-no-mori for many many years," said the man even more quietly. "Excuse me again, but I see that you are a warrior. I would know why one such as yourself would come to this island and how he came here."

Ronin looked steadily into the black unfathomable eyes so close to his, keeping his gaze studiously away from the man's hands.

"I come to Ama-no-mori seeking the Bujun," he said slowly, "for I have been told by those who know that the Bujun, and only the Bujun, may aid me now." He allowed himself an unhurried breath. "It is on a quest of the greatest import that I have come to Ama-no-mori. I am here as a friend of the Bujun. I have spent much time and many lives have been lost so that I should be here now. A confrontation with you is the last thing I desire." His hands were motionless on his muscled thighs.

"How came you to Ama-no-mori?" said the man. "No ships were sighted."

Ronin did not ask him how he could know this.

"I did not come by ship," he said.

They were motionless. Outside, the rain had ceased sometime before dawn and the sun was already sparking along the granite and schist outcroppings. A rainbow arced in the air. Birds called sweetly from the high treetops behind them on the mountainslopes. Far away but quite clear in the still air, he heard the steady clop-clop of a horse's hoofs along the path, ascending. The sky was white. The cedars were very green.

"Someone comes," said Ronin.

The man grunted abruptly, a sound both incongruous and harmonious with the morning.

"You may accompany me to Eido, if that is your wish."

He stood up and turned away, went to his horse, and while the animal fed on dry grain, pulled a square tablet from his baggage.

"Eat if you desire. This morning is too fine to pass up. I will paint for a time. Then will the journey resume."

He strode to the edge of the enclosure, patting his mount's withers, then went out and across the Kisokaido, squatting in the dappled sunlight at the far edge of the highway. He began to draw with a black brush in short, arcing strokes, sure and precise.

Ronin unwrapped the oiled paper Hoshi had given him, chewed on a piece of raw fish. It was still juicy. Wiping his mouth, he went out onto the road.

The air was clear and bright, the trees whispering behind him. The horse's clop-clop was louder now and a small animal bounded out of the brush to his left, hopped down the road for several steps, then quickly disappeared behind a stand of thick cedars. The day was pungent with their fragrance.

The rider appeared, in sedge hat and deep gray riding cloak. He nodded to Ronin and, putting spurs to his steed's flanks, went around a turning to their right.

Ronin went across the highway, stood beside the man.

"What shall I call you?"

The man did not turn from his delicate, exacting work.

"My name is Okami, stranger."

Ronin squatted beside the man.

"Does it have a meaning?"

Okami's shoulders lifted, fell.

"All Bujun names have a meaning. Mine means 'snow-wolf' in the old tongue, though why my mother chose to call me that I cannot say. There were no okami within a hundred leagues of the village of my birth."

Ronin listened to the cicadas for a time, absorbed in Okami's drawing. Then he said: "Why is it, do you think, that we two, born in far distant lands, can yet speak to each other with little difficulty? One would think that—"

"Why we are both men, of course," Okami said reasonably.

"Are not the Bujun different?"

"Many ages ago," said the other, ignoring him, "or so it is said by our fathers' fathers, there were so many folk upon the face of the world, that they spoke a myriad of languages." He shrugged. "But that was a different time and it is known that these things change. When men spring from the same root, they can converse with one another without difficulty, though their birthplaces may differ." His hand moved deftly over the mulberry paper tablet. "Who knows, perhaps it is shared destiny which makes it so."

His skill was bringing to life the expanse of mountain, valley, and shelves of slopes which were before them. His rendering was delicate yet filled with a vitality proclaiming the vibrancy inherent in nature.

"What is your name?"

Ronin told him.

His head turned from the scene on his lap. It was a strong, purposeful visage, the eyes intelligent and full of understanding. His high cheekbones and the firmness of his jaw gave him a stern appearance yet the flatness of his features helped to soften this effect.

"Yes? Really." His eyes held a measure of surprise for only the briefest of instants. Then he returned to his painting. A swaying cedar blossomed under his brush point. "That is a Bujun word."

It was Ronin's turn to show surprise.

"But—that cannot be."

"It is, stranger. Did I not say that all men come from the same root—"

"But I am not Bujun."

"Well, you do not look Bujun—"

"My people have never heard of Ama-no-mori—"

"Is that so? In that case, how came you to know of this island?"

Ronin thought. The City of Ten Thousand Paths, where representatives of all lands had come together, dwelling beneath the surface of the world made uninhabitable by the sorcerous wars. Within that city had dwelt both his ancestors and the great Bujun mage, dor-Sefrith.

"Perhaps," said Ronin, "it is possible."

"Of course," said Okami, seemingly satisfied.

"What does it mean?"

"A masterless warrior."

Laughter burst forth from Ronin, and Okami turned, smiling quizzically, not understanding at all.

They left the station sometime before noon, ascending, then descending slightly as the will of the mountain road dictated. The gaunt crags slid by them in a solid wall on their right. Below them, to the left, the cliff fell gradually away, revealing tall copses of pine and, further down, flat wet fields of rice, shimmering in a heat haze.

"I am Bujun, yes," said Okami.

"Then you know of dor-Sefrith."

"Only myths survive from the old days, I am afraid."

"What can you tell me about him?"

"Very little." Okami put his arm long his horse's mane. "Why is dor-Sefrith so important to you?"

"I carry a piece of his writing that may save all of this world now."

"Ah," said Okami noncommittally. "Once the Bujun were the greatest warrior-mages in the history of this world and we lasted far into the new time, when virtually all other sorcery had vanished." He slapped the mare. "But that was many eons ago. Sorcery is no longer practiced here."

"But surely there are people here who can translate the old language."

"I am sure that in Eido we shall find such a one, Ronin." He smiled. "Until then, let us speak of pleasanter matters."

At length they came upon a break in the inimical rock face to their right and were thus allowed a glimpse of a narrow defile, green, leafily shadowed, which opened onto a sunlit gorge down which tumbled an icy waterfall. Splayed rainbows danced at its base.

"The day is hot," said Okami. "Shall we cool off in the water?"

"I would reach Eido as swiftly as possible. Who knows how—"

"You do not wish to reach the capital stinking like a simple farmer." He clapped Ronin on the back. "Come. One needs to break up any journey."

The coolness of the defile was like a soothing balm. Okami, leading them through, tethered his horse beside a copse of pungent cedars and immediately stripped off his dusty clothes, dove into the frothy pool at the foot of the waterfall. With a brief glance around the gorge, Ronin joined him.

The water was icy and clear beneath the surface turbulence. Silver and blue fish darted away from Ronin's arcing body. He turned upward before he hit bottom, breaking the skin of the pool and whipping his head around to clear his eyes of water. Then he bent his head and drank his fill, savoring the sweetness.

They dried off in the sun. The power of Okami's heavily muscled frame did not escape Ronin's notice.

"May I see your other paintings?"

"Certainly."

Okami wrapped his robe about his still damp body and drew his pad from his saddlebags.

Ronin turned the pages slowly, fascinated by the economy of line which portrayed so stunningly the richness of the countryside and its inhabitants.

"Each one is a station of the Kisokaido," said Okami.

Behind them, the water clattered busily down the roughhewn walls of the gorge.

Ronin handed him the pad, began to get dressed.

"Would you like to learn?" said Okami.

Ronin looked up into the other's face, perhaps to see if he were being mocked, but Okami's eyes were serious.

"Yes," he said, surprising himself. "I would like that very much."

Three gray plovers left cover at the far end of the gorge, gusting into the sky.

"Splendid! Let us return to the highway and we shall commence as we continue our journey." He turned to put the pad back into its case.

In that instant, Ronin heard the soft whistle and began to draw his sword. Apparently Okami heard it also, for he turned back. The arrow pierced his left shoulder.

Ronin's blade was out; he was in a semicrouch, his eyes raking the dense foliage along the walls of the gorge. Okami grasped the shaft of the arrow and jerked powerfully. He threw the thing from him, simultaneously drawing his own long sword.

Down from the rocks, from behind their emerald cover, leapt five men. Long, slightly curved swords held before them in two-handed grips, they landed lightly beside the pool and advanced on the pair.

"Resistance will be futile," said one, obviously the leader. "Surely you can see that you are outnumbered." The five moved closer, spreading out in a rough semicircle. They were dressed similarly to Okami, in dark-colored robes and leather sandals. One carried a wooden bow obliquely across his back. Ronin saw no shields. "Please be good enough to hand us your money and your horse." When they did not move, the man said, somewhat harshly: "Drop your weapons."

"What you want from us," said Okami carefully, "you will have to get for yourselves."

"So be it," said the man. He gestured. "You two, take the tall one with the strange eyes."

They leapt at once, howling, and he faced them with his right side, feeling the familiar jolt of power rush through him at the onset of combat. His blade was held obliquely before him. Rock steady he stood as they hurled themselves at him. A strong pulse danced along the side of his neck and his lips broke involuntarily into a feral grin.

"We take the other," called the leader as the remaining men advanced on Okami.

The two swung their swords high above them as they closed on Ronin and as they began their swift downward arcs, he bent his knees, feinted a slash to the right. The man on that side cut short his downswing to compensate for the expected attack. It did not come. Instead, Ronin veered his sword to the left and, having momentarily neutralized his first opponent, brought a vicious horizontal blow under the second man's vertical strike. He caught the man squarely across the chest, the force cutting through cloth, skin, flesh, and cracking the breastbone. The man wailed and fell to the ground in a gush of blood.

He withdrew his blade in time to parry the thrust from the first man.

In the periphery of his vision, Ronin had the briefest glimpse of Okami's long curving blade, a platinum blur, disemboweling one of his foes with a blow of enormous power and speed.

Ronin's remaining foe feinted twice and chopped at him. Their weapons shuddered with the force of the electric contact as he countered. He felt the longer blade slip from his and withdrew his extended right leg as the man sought to cripple him with a new downward sweep.

As they circled each other, Ronin felt respect for his opponent's combat skills. The man was obviously a professional, his ability and knowledge would have exceeded those of most Bladesmen from the Freehold.

Fierce blue sparks flew from the crashing of their blades as they fought across the gorge, skirting the verge of the bubbling pool.

Ronin extended his leg again for a swift lunge. His foe angled his blade, anticipating the attack, and Ronin swept in high instead of low, a powerful vertical strike which left him exposed for a fraction of an instant. But the other had only enough time for his eyes to open wide, registering shock, before his skull was split open like a fruit. His sword arm, responding to galvanic action, continued its sweep and Ronin stepped aside. The body toppled into the pool and Ronin whirled.

Okami had just dispatched the second man with an economic reverse thrust as the man ran at his exposed back. Now he confronted the leader of the group. Okami yelled, forcing the other man back until he was stopped by the rocks at the rear of the gorge. Desperately, the man sought an avenue past Okami's guard, to his neck, but with a fierce surge of strength, Okami broke through first. His curving blade was a white blur as it drove deep into his foe's shoulder and chest. The man jerked, his head thrown back. Only the whites of his eyes showed as the body danced in death.

Okami turned, bowed to Ronin.

"Well, it seems as if this small respite from the toils of our journey has been most beneficial."

He wiped his long blade on the dead man's robe and, slowly, sheathed his weapon.

"I do not like it."

"Why not?"

"It is clumsy compared to yours."

The Kisokaido had become a steeper road, the rocks crowding out for a time the lushness of the jade foliage. Yet even these grays and blues seemed austere rather than bleak. Already Okami's paintings had taught him that.

"Please, Ronin, do not attempt to compare those things which have separate lives."

"But I do not—"

"It is advice only. Compare, by all means. But I tell you this now: you will never be happy with it."

"I am not satisfied."

"Good!" Okami clapped his hands. "An artist is never satisfied—"

"But you just said—"

"Happiness and satisfaction are two very different feelings."

They sat just outside the wooden overhang of a white station high up within the mountains. It was chilly and a thin covering of crisp snow shimmered white and blue across the highway. It was virgin save for their footprints and those of Okami's mare.

"Look here, Okami—" He indicated a point on the sheet of mulberry paper in his lap.

"Yes, and so—?"

"The trees are too squat and here the copse is bunched up."

"Change them then."

"All right. Uhm. How is that? Better?"

"You tell me."

"Well." He paused, studying it. "Yes. I like it better."

"There, you see? You have it."

He smelled the sharp fragrance of the fire they had lit in the interior of the shelter, within the stone hearth.

The sun was sinking, a flat red oblate, magnified and distorted by the haze near the horizon, almost directly in front of their eyes. A towering, snow-capped peak shimmered pink and mauve in the lowering light. A man and two women in wide-brimmed sedge hats and wooden sandals walked beside a laden cart pulled by a lone ox. They came down the mountain, passed the pair, and disappeared around a turning to the far left.

"We teach ourselves, we who can paint," said Okami, after a time. "We begin to explore what we see before us, each to our own precepts. Trust no one who would claim to teach you that." He pulled at the lobe of one ear. "Oh, the mechanics can be taught. I have already showed you how to hold the brush in order to get the strokes you desire. But"—he shrugged lightly—"who knows? You may find a better way of getting what you want from the brush." He stared at the darkling mountain peak jutting through the horizontal landscape. "Painting, as with all great endeavors, comes from the soul of man. Each individual. None other may teach that thing which makes art unique."

Ronin's right hand ceased its movements across the sheet of paper. He looked at the other.

"You paint and fight."

Okami nodded. "All Bujun must learn delicacy and compassion as well as fierceness and precision. Naturally, it has always been easier to acquire the latter qualities. One must work most diligently to learn the former." A line of black ants crossed the ground between them, carrying bits of food twice their own length. "I myself had a choice. We all do of course because the Bujun have long understood that, in some things, at least, authority does not engender discipline." The ants began to disappear, one by one, into their hill. "Dancing was not the way for me, neither the Noh, and I confess to being a rather poor poet—"

"But painting—"

"Yes, that is something in which I show some little expertise."

"As you do with your sword."

"So."

"Have you been down the Kisokaido before?" said Ronin, turning a page, smoothing the new, blank sheet of mulberry paper.

"Oh yes, many times."

"Then you have bathed in that pool before."

"Certainly. It was most refreshing, do you not agree?" He twisted off a stem of grass, stuck it into the corner of his mouth.

"I imagine one must be careful, these days, wherever one travels."

A small smile spread across Okami's face. "Oh, most assuredly, but the prudent traveler soon learns to avoid those places along the highway most frequented by brigands."

"Such as the gorge."

"You must admit," Okami said happily, "that each of us now knows the other much better."

Ronin had to admire the man. Each had shown the other his worth without the embarrassment of prying questions or the wastefulness of a direct confrontation. He recalled the deviousness of his first clash aboard Tuolin's ship on his way to Sha'angh'sei. Those men, too, had wished to gain the measure of his strengths as a warrior. How crude and unnecessary their actions seemed now.

"And your shoulder," said Ronin, taking up his brush once more.

"A flesh wound, only." Okami sat very still, breathing deeply. "And I have had many of those."

"I will not forget this."

Okami nodded.

"A man never forgets."

Ronin gestured. Dusk was settling comfortably in.

"I would paint that peak that we have seen all afternoon."

"Yes. I thought you might."

Ronin dipped the brush into the ink and began to paint.

"What is its name?"

"Fujiwara." Okami sighed in contentment. "'The Friend of Man.'" For a time, he watched the strokes of his brush in the stranger's hand, thinking, His name does not fit him. Once, perhaps, but I have a feeling—and are we not taught to feel? —that he has outgrown it now. He sighed again, his keen eyes lifting to the beauty he saw before him. Home. He blinked. This man's arrival will disturb the tranquility which we have observed for so many years. Change has come again to Ama-no-mori. He shrugged inwardly. Is not change what life is all about?

"Tomorrow," he said quietly, so that his companion would hear yet not be disturbed from his work, "we begin our descent into Eido."

On Ronin's lap, Fujiwara was born again.

Sakura

WAITING, he stood just inside the vermilion and green wooden gate. Above his head, a great oiled paper lantern, lacquered in black angular characters, swung gently from its wire moorings.

He looked out across the wide stone courtyard at the two-story wooden structure, its vermilion walls and sloping roof made more startling as they jutted from the concealment of the stand of cherry trees. On the right, across the courtyard, beyond the main building, rose the layered construct of a pagoda.

The clear chime of bells came to him on the crystalline air.

Men in wide-shouldered robes and wooden sandals strolled in twos and threes toward the vermilion building. Behind them, women in long robes and quilted coats, their heads hidden by oiled paper umbrellas, followed, chatting among themselves.

Plovers clattered against the wind.

They had come down out of the cold clear mountain air at dawn, the highway declining serpentinely, with the sky pink and platinum. Birds fluttered in the early sunshine, calling to each other.

Eido was spread out before them, flat and variegated, sitting astride two rivers, the one, narrow and swift, the other wide, marshy, and sluggish, sprawling across a large plain bordered on its far side by the first gentle slopes of Fujiwara. Beyond them, the steep sides of the mountain itself rose, enormous and majestic against the lightening sky.

Thus they stood for many moments mute, transfixed, despite their exhaustion, their need to bathe, by this view at the southernmost end of the Kisokaido, which, perhaps, transcended all other views in Ama-no-mori.

They went directly to Okami's home, a flat, elegant house of paper and wood and some stone in a section of the city between the rivers. Lanterns swung from the wooden gate.

"The garden is behind the house," Okami said.

They were met at the door by two women in brown robes, who bowed as they entered, beautiful as flowers, their hair dark and shining, their skin very white. The women undressed them, taking the clothes stiff with dried sweat, whose colors had faded with the layers of dust, and led them to the bath: two square stone tubs, sunken into the slatted wooden boards of the floor. As hot water was poured over them and the women commenced to scrub their bodies, Ronin was once again reminded of the pleasures of Tenchō.

Scrubbed, he floated in the warm water, watching one of the women tend to Okami's wound, cleaning it carefully, then cauterizing it with a deft flick of her fingers. Afterward, she applied a small bandage.

Okami began to talk rapidly to the second woman, apparently giving her instructions. Ronin stood up and, dripping, reached for a towel. The woman who had mended Okami's shoulder rubbed him down, then wrapped a clean robe around his body. It was dark blue with the now familiar spoked wheel pattern embroidered in green.

He opened a soji and went out into the garden. The woman glanced at Okami but he made a brief sign to her and she remained inside.

He went through a high stand of whispering bamboo, heard the frogs' distant croaking. In the heat haze, with the droning of the insects and the whispering of the exquisitely sculpted rows of sighing flowers, pink and gold, saffron and orange, Ronin conjured the extraordinary temple in the heart of Sha'angh'sei; its magnificent garden. He thought of the languid fish, calmly floating in their liquid world, the august tranquility of the old man who sat by the side of the metal urn. The breath of Eternity. Here was the complete peace that seeped through his skin, balming his nerves.

Like coming home, not to birth, but to history.

"First the Yoshiwara," said Okami, pushing away his empty dish. They had dined on fresh raw fish, sweet rice, and spiced tea.

"And what will we find there?" Ronin drank the last of his tea.

Okami smiled enigmatically.

"Not what. Who." He stood up from the low polished wood table as the women came in to clear the remnants of the meal. They were as silent as deer. "Azuki-iro. Kunshin of the Bujun."

"Does he not have a court?"

"Oh yes, of course." Okami went across the room, slid open the paper soji. The late afternoon sun fell obliquely into the room. The green of the garden was tinged with orange and russet. "He has a most elaborate castle but, for the most part, he prefers the energy, the breadth of Eido." They went out into the burnished light. Billowing white clouds chased each other across the arch of the blue sky, causing myriad shadows to darken the foliage, the stone paths, as they flew across the face of the sun. "He enjoys people, you see, more than anything else."

Cicadas wailed, hard-edged, like copper being beaten.

"You must try to understand so much about us, Ronin, for we are a most complex people and we baffle those foreigners who have been exposed to us. We are traditionalists, but only in a certain sense, I think. We are not fools."

They strolled through high groves of fragrant camellias, glowing like ribbons of fire in the sunlight.

"In our long yesterdays, our rulers were emperors who, so our myths tell us, were descended from the sun itself. But, over time, the emperors' power weakened, so much so that factions of Bujun warred among themselves for land and wealth and, at last, we saw the emergence of the Sho-gun. The first of these mighty warlords rose up, defeating all the daimyos, consolidating his power, thence ruling Ama-no-mori, leaving the emperor as an impotent figurehead." Sunlight flickered in chance patterns across Okami's wide head, dappling his skin as if he were the subject of a series of paintings. "For some time, this worked well for us for we needed the iron discipline the Sho-gun enforced upon us. We grew strong and indomitable." They broke cover and for a time, they were without shade. Distant bamboo shivered. There was a constant rustling. "But the Sho-gun were, of course, first and foremost great martialists and the Bujun became militant, land hungry; they sought war, victory over their neighboring races."

They came to the deep pool, a stone octagon stocked with a multitude of fish, large, sleek, and silvery, pink and blue. They sat on the cool stone edge. A gentle breeze brushed their cheeks. "Thus the eventual defeat of the Sho-gun was assured. So were born the first of the warrior-mages, for it was a time then when sorcery was tolerated in the world and for many eons the Bujun were isolated and content.

"But eventually the sorcerous wars came and Ama-no-mori was not left unscathed." The fish nibbled at the algae along the stone sides of the pool, deep down, far away from the surface. "A number of Bujun became involved in the holocaust, lured by the riches of the kingdoms of man. Chagrined, dor-Sefrith, the greatest of the Bujun, pursued them and defeated them. Still, for the world of man, the damage was already done. Dor-Sefrith returned to Ama-no-mori and sadly retold his tale of death and destruction. The Bujun decided instantly and he caused the island to be moved away from the continent of man so that none might again be tempted to cause destruction. Then he said his farewells and left Ama-no-mori to pay his personal debt to man in the City of Ten Thousand Paths. Thus the Bujun sank into the mists of legend."

"Surely there is more that you can tell me about dor-Sefrith," said Ronin, thinking of The Dolman, not yet wishing to voice his thoughts.

"So." Okami shrugged. "Perhaps there are others in Eido who know more of him." He watched their dark reflections dance upon the surface of the water. "We are a people who learn from history and thus the Kunshin came into being. Not the Emperor of the Sun; not the Sho-gun, but perhaps a combination of both. He is a ruler without the layers of state for he is Bujun just as I am Bujun and this is something that he cannot forget."

"And we will find him at the Yoshiwara?"

A brown and orange butterfly came between them, questing.

"If he takes his pleasure," said Okami, "yes."

Down a perfectly straight street, the wooden two-story dwellings narrowing in perspective before them, came the shadows of two tall men, as if they floated on the misty amethyst of early evening. Women in swirling, patterned robes, white-faced, red-lipped, carrying delicate paper parasols over their shoulders, passed them in bunches, giggling, whispering, flicking sidelong glances in their direction without ever turning their heads. Perfume on the air, cherry blossoms and musk.

"Welcome to the Yoshiwara," said Okami as they went through the door of a building. Beautiful women peered down at them like unfurling, phototropic lilies from second-story balconies.

A plump woman with coifed, gleaming hair greeted them, bowing. She wore a robe of mauve and pink silk, patterned in triangles. A pair of ivory pins went through her hair. Her face, plain and flat, was dominated by wide, inquisitive eyes. She smiled as her head lifted. Okami introduced Ronin and they all bowed again.

She held out an arm and Okami removed his sandals, Ronin his boots. They went across the tatamis to a low wooden table, uncarved and unlacquered, sat cross-legged around it. Two robed women came with steaming, fragrant tea and rice cakes. Somewhere, perhaps from the second story of the place, tiny bells sounded, ice flakes glittering through frigid air.

To their left, a soji slid back and three women entered. They were very young with exquisite heart-shaped faces, black-maned, black-eyed, crimson lips like bows. They smiled. The whispering of their silken robes.

"Not now, Juku," said Okami somewhat wistfully.

She nodded and waved a hand. The women disappeared.

"How may I help you, then?" she said when they were alone.

"Has Azuki-iro been here this evening?"

Juku smiled and her soft hand reached out to cover Okami's for just a moment. "You sweet thing. Of all the houses in the Yoshiwara, it is here that you come to inquire after Azuki-iro." She laughed. "You must know the Kunshin well, Okami. Yes, he was here but much earlier, perhaps, oh, midafternoon. He did not say—but wait—" She held up a hand, called softly but distinctly: "Onjin!"

Almost immediately, a soji opened and a woman came to their table. She knelt beside Juku. She was fine-boned, her skin so delicate as to be almost translucent. Her almond eyes were large, her cheekbones high. Her silk robe was the color of swirled gray ash.

Juku took the woman's slender hands in hers, softly stroking their backs. "Tell me, Onjin, when the Kunshin was with you today, did he say where he was going when he left here?"

Onjin stared at the two men for a moment, then her sooty eyes locked with those of her mistress.

"The Kameido, lady, is a place he mentioned sometime—after."

"Ah," said Juku. "And no others?"

Onjin thought for a moment, her brow furrowing. Even those lines could not disrupt her enormous beauty. "No others, lady."

"All right." She put a hand to the woman's cheek. "You may go now."

Onjin rose in a graceful stir of silk and flesh, gliding effortlessly across the tatamis. When the soji slid shut behind her, Juku said, "Lovely, isn't she?"

Okami nodded. "If there is time tonight, we shall return to find out for ourselves." His eyes were glittery in the low light.

"That would make me most happy, Okami," said Juku.

"Thank you."

The woman bowed her head. "You honor this establishment by your presence."

Out in the bustling street, Okami took them right, then right again, into an area that was close and crowded with merchants. This gave way, abruptly, to a flat garden perhaps two hundred meters long, dominated by gnarled plum trees. There were two small, obliquely roofed teahouses, wall-less on their garden sides, which bordered the place to the south and the west. Sprinkled throughout the garden itself were wide wooden benches on which people sat. Most seemed to be writing.

"The Kameido is the garden of the literati of Eido," said Okami. "The poets, the playwrights, come here for inspiration from the wisdom of the ancient plum trees and the extraordinary quietude amidst the bustle of the city."

Okami spoke to the proprietor of the teahouse but he had just come to Kameido and the day people had already gone for the evening meal. He offered them tea.

They stood on the steps of the building, sipping tiny porcelain cups of tea. A young man approached them. He was tall and slender, his black eyes bright, his sensual mouth smiling.

"You are looking for Azuki-iro?" His voice had the ring of metal.

Okami nodded.

"Yes."

"Are you sasori?"

Okami seemed somewhat taken aback, perhaps by the directness of the question.

"Not at all."

"Then there is no reason to tell you."

"You approached us."

The man looked around as if puzzled.

"So I did. I thought you might like to hear a poem that I—"

"Listen you—"

But Ronin caught Okami's arm.

"I would like to hear the poem," he said. He relinquished his grip on Okami's arm only when he felt the muscles under his fingers relax.

"Ah, splendid." The man glanced down at a small tablet of

rice paper that he held. His head lifted. "'And morning comes. The raven wakes, still tired.' Well?" He stared at them.

"And I thought my poetry was bad," Okami muttered.

"What does it mean?" said Ronin.

"I am sasori," said the man. "Soon the sasori will fly at night, taking what is theirs. No longer will we be forced to live on this small, insufficient island. Soon there will be wealth enough for all on Ama-no-mori, Bujun and non-Bujun—"

"Enough!" cried Okami, and this time Ronin did not attempt to stop him. He grabbed the man by the front of his robe. The small tablet tumbled to the earth of the garden. "I will hear no more of this. If you know where the Kunshin is now, you would do well to tell me!"

The man looked at Ronin, who said: "I think he means it. Tell him and be done with it."

The man shifted his gaze to Okami, who pulled harder on his robe. The fabric began to rip.

"There is a Noh performance at the Asakusa tonight," he said softly. "Perhaps you will find him there."

The great oiled paper lantern groaned accusingly in the wind. The plovers had disappeared beyond the cherry trees. The top of the Asakusa was already obscured as night rolled in in velvet blues and violets.

The stone courtyard was all but deserted now as the last of the figures disappeared into the wide wooden doorways of the vermilion building.

Okami came up beside him.

"There is time."

They went across the courtyard, past the bowing cherry trees.

"The Asakusa is the most renowned Noh theater in all of Ama-no-mori."

"The Noh are plays," said Ronin.

"Of a sort."

Inside, the sweep of the polished wooden stage dominated the space. Before it, down three steps, was a coarse gravel strip perhaps three meters wide, after which began the low-walled polished wooden boxes housing the audience.

They went down the central aisle; Okami chose a box near the front. Within, they sat on the wood floor, cross-legged.

Okami leaned over, whispered to a man in a neighboring box, then said to Ronin:

"Tonight the Noh is *Hagoromo*."

"What does that mean?"

"The Feathered Cloak."

The theater was completely filled.

"Is he here?"

Okami twisted his head briefly.

"I cannot tell."

The thin, harsh notes of a flute heralded the beginning of the Noh. It was not a play but more like an articulated poem. The leading actor played a female part. He was dressed in complex ceremonial robes; he wore a coifed wig and a fabulously carved mask with delicate, chiseled features of such beauty that Ronin was reminded of Onjin. The second actor was maskless.

For a time, they sat on the stark polished wood of the stage, half-singing, half-chanting in a language that Ronin found incomprehensible, moving only their upper torsos, and yet, because of the actors' consummate skill, he was able to follow the story line.

A goddess, having lost her cloak of feathers, descends into the world of man to retrieve it. The cloak has been found by a common fisherman who nevertheless understood the garment to be unique and of high value. The goddess discovers that the fisherman has taken her cloak and she attempts to persuade him to return it to her, yet all her arguments fail to move the fisherman, who refuses to part with his prize.

At length, the two strike a bargain. The fisherman will consent to return the feathered cloak if the goddess consents to dance for him.

Thus the Noh's climax was entirely composed of movement, devoid of all speech.

The goddess's dance commences and it is so unearthly, an intricate gyring so filled with intense emotion, that none within the Asakusa can tear his eyes away from the actor. The dance builds until the very air is charged with a metallic tension born of a beauty beyond mortal understanding. A goddess has taken the stage and now dances desperately for the life of her cloak.

And it is, finally, in that exalted state, with the goddess at the pinnacle of her art with the walls of the Asakusa gone, with barriers of reality aflutter, with the encroachment of infinity pouring across his mind, that he hears there a stirring out of the immense silence:

Ronin.

The river flowed around them, beneath them, wide and blue. Along both banks, the reeds had been cut down and fat fish swam in idle contentment, nibbling at algae clinging to the submerged rocks. Fireflies danced in the shadows.

Across the river, the other half of the enormous inn spread itself down the embankment for many meters, a mirror image, symmetrical and precise, of the wooden sections, raised on stilts, which jutted out into the bubbling water from the edge of the banks.

Okami had had to pull him away, in the end. The crowd was too thick.

The mist still flung itself across Eido, obscuring the top of Fujiwara. Red paper lanterns hung from the oiled sojis which served to separate the groups of people sipping tea or rice wine while enjoying their food. The lanterns' crimson glow gave the vast inn a sense of intimacy it otherwise might not have.

Alive! Ronin thought. Alive!

The buzz of low conversation, the sighing of silk as men and women made their way to and from the wooden sections along the water, the brief call of a heron, white against the blue-black water, the surrealistic fire of the lanterns' light on the river. There was constant motion.

He had jumped up, turning. But the audience was alive with movement. A great rustling sea, indifferent to his anxiety as his eyes darted from person to person. Somewhere there—

"Rice wine?"

A young woman bent over them. Okami looked at Ronin.

"Yes," he said. "For both of us."

Ronin watched distractedly as she swept away from them, gliding between the moving people. Okami asked him a question but he did not hear. In the audience at the Asakusa, his mind opened by the electrifying Noh performance, he had heard her calling to him. It was a sound which he thought he would never hear again. Three men and a woman entered the inn and were making their winding way toward a wooden section on the water. Idly, his eyes took them in. He felt a jolt go through him.

"Ronin?"

He was standing, staring at the woman as she was seated.

"Chill take me!" He was sure. It was Moeru. Miraculously alive and here in Eido. But how?

"Ronin!" A hand on his arm.

He bent.

"That woman."

"Where?"

"In the pink and silver robe. With the tall man in midnight blue—"

"That is Nikumu. What—?"

"I know her, Okami."

"Know her? But that is imposs—"

Ronin was gone.

"Ronin, no! Not Nikumu! Wait—!"

Through the sultry night, Eido like a translucent gem-in-a-mist, lantern-lit, far away on some flat tide, the richly patterned robes nearby, charcoal fumes in the air, through the maze of bodies, smiling women with gleaming hair and white faces, their perfumes mingling, laughing men with long queues and stiff-shouldered robes, past serving women with small laquered trays on which were precisely positioned pots of tea and rice wine, plates of raw fish and vegetables, like miniature gardens.

On the water, a heron, phosphorescent in the night, skimmed the surface as it took off, its long legs trailing behind.

"Moeru," he called, coming. "Moeru."

A tightening in his chest.

Calmly, the bird climbed into the mist above Eido.

Her oval face, pale and beautiful, upturned at his arrival. Her eyes the color of the sea on a stormy day. The men at her table were in stiff-shouldered robes, two in charcoal gray with the familiar wheel pattern in dark blue, the other, the one Okami had called Nikumu, in the midnight blue robe with wheels of gray. Their faces turned to his.

Far away now, the heron was a white smudge diminished by distance and the swirling mist.

He stared at her.

"Moeru."

His mind a receiver, waiting.

"How—?"

Nikumu stood. He was a tall man. Thin, ascetic nose in the midst of a wide-cheeked face. His pinched mouth seemed full of tension.

"Do we know you?"

Her eyes a murky sea, blank.

Away and away, finished in the mist.

"Moeru?"

"Where are your manners?"

"I know this woman."

Her pale face, still upturned, the ghost of a lost smile on her lips. And what ghost of him swam in the blue-green depths of her eyes?

"It is quite apparent that she does not know you." Nikumu turned to her. "Do you know this man, my dear?"

A slight hesitation, then a quick negative jerk of her head, almost convulsive, as if someone had pulled a string.

"You must be mistaken, you see." The tone matter of fact, the conversation ended.

"No, I—" Ronin bent slightly. Something in her eyes, a cloudy essence, a struggle, perhaps.

Nikumu sat. A muscle along his jaw twitched.

"Ke'ema," he said quietly.

One of the men in charcoal gray rose and gripped Ronin's bicep.

Ronin continued to stare, an edge of panic rising within him. Nothing.

"You will leave us now," said the man at his side. His grip tightened.

The perfect oval of her face.

The man began to exert real pressure.

The glint of silver around her slender white neck—

Ronin was pushed back a step. He jabbed with his elbow, simultaneously positioning his left foot. He struck out with his right arm, straight and rigid as a board. A bright crack as bone shattered. The man's mouth opened in a silent scream as he toppled backward into the river.

Nikumu rose, his face drained of blood. The remaining man in charcoal gray stepped toward Ronin.

Then Okami was at his side, his voice low and penetrating, and he took Ronin swiftly away, through the turning, curious faces, away from the shouts and the commotion, into the deepening mists of evening.

"What madness made you do that?"

"I know her."

"I cannot believe that."

"You must believe it."

"She is Nikumu's wife."

"What? But that cannot be!"

"My friend, what is, is."

"Her name is Moeru."

"Yes." Okami's face furrowed in puzzlement. "That's correct." He shook his head. "Nikumu's wife! How—?"

"Okami, she wears the silver sakura that I gave her—"

There was a silence between them for a time while Okami's eyes, black as stone, searched his face for the answer to an unknown question. And Ronin knew that here was the true test of the friendship that had been forged along the Kisokaido, in a mountain station powdered white by snow, in a high gorge filled with falling water and metal and death.

Beyond the oiled rice paper soji, the tall bamboo swayed in the gathering wind. The bright camellias were black in the night. A frog called to its mate, a lonely sound.

Okami went through the opened soji, out into the glowing dark. Ronin followed him. The sky was so clear that the stars seemed to be burning the fabric of the sky just above their heads.

"The cherry blossom of Ama-no-mori," Okami said then. "How would you get a sakura?"

Ronin sighed, knew that this was all that was left him now. "On the continent of man," he said slowly, "in Sha'angh'sei, its great port city, I came upon a man being beaten in an alley. It was near to night and all I could see was that there were four or five against the one. I went to his aid but it was already too late. I slew two of them but the man was dead. In one hand he grasped a silver chain with the sakura. For some reason, I cannot say what, I took it from him."

They began to walk to the pool.

"He was Bujun, of course, though why he was so far from Ama-no-mori is a mystery."

"What has this to do with Moeru?"

"I found her in Sha'angh'sei. She had come in, sick and starving, with refugees from the north. She would have been left for dead had I not taken her to Tenchō, where I stayed, to be cared for. When I sailed from the continent of man in search of Ama-no-mori, she was with me and I gave her the sakura as a present. I thought her killed in an attack by warriors in strange obsidian ships which rode above the waves. How she came here I have no idea."

"Why should she not be here?" said Okami. "She is Bujun."

The pool was silent between them.

"You do not believe me?"

"Why should she leave Ama-no-mori?"

"Why should a Bujun be in Sha'angh'sei?"

"Because—" Okami's face was in deep shadow, the light spilling from the house, at his back. "Ronin, Nikumu is leader of the sasori."

The frog had ceased its croaking at their approach. Only the cicadas chattered on, unperturbed.

"He is also the most powerful member of the jogen soru, the council which advises the Kunshin on vital matters of state policy. It is only recently that the sasori have risen. They are martialists, Bujun not content to live on Ama-no-mori. They wish to invade the continent of man."

"So the Bujun in Sha'angh'sei was a spy."

Okami nodded. "Suggested by Nikumu, passed by the jogen soru, he was sent to inform us of the city's strengths and weaknesses."

"Not all Bujun wish this."

"No, of course not. Just a minority. But recently, they have become much more powerful. And now that Nikumu is their leader—"

"What does the Kunshin think of that?"

Okami shrugged pragmatically.

"He has done nothing to stop the affiliation."

"Okami, you must trust me. I know Moeru."

"All right. I concede there is a possibility that she too was sent to the continent of man."

"You do not understand, my friend. There is something very wrong."

"What do you mean?"

"She did not recognize me. There was nothing in her eyes. Nothing."

Whisper of the bamboo. A fish broke the surface of the pool, a pale wisp of phosphorescence.

Okami got up.

"Come with me," he said.

Inside the house, he called for food and their traveling cloaks.

"Where are we going?"

"Into the countryside. Away from Eido for a while."

"But the scroll—"

"Nikumu will send his men here looking for you. We must be gone before then."

"But there must be other—"

"He will find us in Eido," Okami said flatly.

"I will not run from him. I must get Moeru back."

Okami turned on him.

"Back? She is his wife, Ronin."

He felt again the edge of a peculiar kind of desperation. K'reen, Matsu, now—No! There was a chance.

"Okami, I know her. She is not herself." Okami donned his long cloak. "I will stay here alone then."

"You will not." The eyes blazed and the voice took on the tone of command. "You will come with me and do exactly as I say." He gripped Ronin's arms and his face softened. "Think, my friend! If there is to be any chance for you and for Moeru, we must both leave now." Behind him, one of Okami's women settled his cloak about his shoulders.

Outside, in the garden, the frog began its sad song again.

They went south, out along the wide Tokaido, a more traveled highway than the mountainous Kisokaido and soon the vast sprawl of the city was far behind them, the flat yellow light like an aurora within the mist.

To the west, it was already raining; here the air was damp and still and electric. Above them, the stars were rapidly disappearing behind rushing black clouds. They wrapped their traveling cloaks more tightly about them and secured their sloping sedge hats on their heads. They were on foot although Ronin had argued against this, but his impatience was forced to accede to Okami's common sense: on horseback, they would be far more conspicuous. Now they were merely two more travelers on the Tokaido.

The slanting rain, hissing through the night, hit them just as they left a forest of pine. They had reached the foot of a steep hill. Trees lined the Tokaido here, tall, slender bamboo, affording little shelter. On the road stood a huge boulder, like a marker on a page.

"This is Nissaka," said Okami through the downpour as they passed the rock. The brims of their hats overlapped. "The stone is said to have witnessed the struggle between a woman and a mountain bandit who attacked her when she refused his demands. The woman was pregnant and, although she died, her baby survived because the stone cried out, invoking the merciful goddess Kannon, who reared the infant." The hill stretched out before them as they climbed. It was very dark and visibility was sharply decreased by the storm. "The child was male and when he reached manhood, he sought out the bandit and avenged his mother's death."

There was only rain now, in all the world.

"Do you believe such fanciful tales?"

"Whether the facts of the myth are true or not makes little difference. It is the spirit of the tale which is important. It is something by which all Bujun live."

"You are a vengeful people," Ronin said, aware of the private irony of his statement.

Okami wiped the rain from his face.

"Revenge and honor are two separate matters, my friend. One cannot forfeit honor and live."

"What is the difference then?"

"In the manner of the death. The truth of the life must never be clouded."

It was a hard road to travel here, especially in the bleak weather, and they were glad, at length, to reach the crest. Then around a turning, they could just make out a smudge of saffron light, a beckoning hand in the wretched darkness.

The small inn was perched on the high, steep slope of a hill. They were welcomed, and leaving their soaked cloaks to dry in front of a crackling fire of thick maple logs, Okami asked that hot tea be brought to them out on the balcony. The proprietress made no comment, despite the inclemency of the weather, merely bowed and ushered them through the inn's warm rooms.

Out on the roofed balcony, which ran along the far side of the inn and which overlooked a thickly forested valley devoid of all civilization or cultivation, they heard the woman calling for their tea.

Lanterns were still lit and by their glowing light they watched the silvered rain pour out of the sky. Far away, thunder rumbled like a bumbling giant. They unstrapped their hats and sat, the liquid beating of the rain on the roof of the inn soothing. The tea came, highly spiced and steaming, and as they drank, Ronin told Okami all he knew of the Makkon, the coming of The Dolman and the Kai-feng, which had already commenced at Kamado. More tea came. It was drained, then replaced far into the night until even the proprietress came to them, yawning, excusing herself to go to bed, leaving only two serving girls in the kitchen in the event they wished for food or more drink.

"If what you say is true, then the Kunshin must be made aware of the circumstances," said Okami when Ronin had finished his tale. "There is surely an obligation which must be met."

"The Bujun never forget."

Okami smiled with his lips but his eyes were grave.

"Never."

"And what of Nikumu, he who wishes the annexation of Ama-no-mori?"

Okami's eyes mirrored the rain.

"I know him as all Bujun know him save the Kunshin. He is a complex man who spends much time in his castle in Haneda. He is a great intellect, one of the foremost patrons of the Noh, as is the Kunshin. When I first heard that he led the sasori I could not believe it. A year ago, they were laughed at."

A moth had come in from the rain, attracted by the lanterns' light. It darted erratically about the warm oiled paper.

"And now?"

Okami shivered.

"It is like the old days," he whispered.

Ronin watched the moth as it rose, circling closer to the open top of the lantern where the light was stronger.

"Why then does the Kunshin do nothing to stop it?"

The other shrugged.

"Perhaps we see only part of it. Certainly Nikumu is not a monster, though it seems to me that he has changed much recently."

Caught in the hot downdraft, the moth fell into the flame at the center of the lantern. Ronin did not even hear a pop.

Rain continued to splatter against the bamboo roof above their heads, just as it battered the leaves on the maples in the valley below them.

"Time is at an end, Okami. For man, the eons have run their course unless The Dolman can be stopped, unless someone here can decipher this scroll of dor-Sefrith's." He gestured outward, to the valley. "All this beauty gone, as if it had never existed." Then, in a softer voice: "Where is Haneda, Okami?"

The face did not turn.

"To the south."

His heart leapt: they traveled south from Eido.

"How far?"

"A day," said Okami. "Just a day away."

By the time they reached the foot of the Yahagi Bridge, the landscape had changed drastically.

In the early afternoon, they had come upon a winding river and the highway had commenced to follow it through the countryside. Now the near bank was thick with high, swaying reeds and the far side disintegrated into wet marshland interspersed with flat glittering fields of rice. Mountains, blue in hazy distance, strung themselves along the far horizon, gaunt, unforgiving sentinels.

They set out across the long arcing span of the wood and stone bridge, feeling naked and exposed. Below them, white herons stalked the marsh, occasionally climbing the stark face of a small granite outcropping on their left.

On the far bank, they struck out to the left toward a distant copse of high cryptomeria trees, a cluster, an asymmetrical forest, a dark island on the marsh.

Far away, to the east, they spied the tall white sails of several fishing boats heading out to sea. Overhead, a flock of geese circled the cryptomeria and wheeled away to the south calling to each other in lonely concert.

They trod a soggy, winding path through the fields, deserted and still. Water spiders skimmed the taut surface of the marsh like bright fingernails scoring a fine bolt of silk.

At length, they reached a thick copse of bamboo from which they peered ahead and for the first time Ronin was able to distinguish a square blue arch and, beyond, the angled roofs of Nikumu's castle. Haneda.

"Perhaps he is still in Eido," said Ronin.

"Hardly likely. He was in Eido for the Noh."

"He will be searching for us in the city."

"No, his men will be carrying out that order." He continued to stare ahead. "See there?" He pointed. "No, further to the left. Horses. He has returned all right and Moeru with him. He would not dare to leave her in Eido now."

The white sails had vanished and now nothing broke the flat expanse save the castle of Haneda within the cryptomeria. The air was still damp and dense from the previous night's heavy rain. Gray clouds scudded to the west, ragged and retreating warriors. Behind them, the immense sky was aglow with streaks of bronze and russet. The sun had already gone. Night was falling fast.

There was movement within the grounds of Haneda.

"From this point on," whispered Okami, "until we reach the wood, we use hand signals only, for the marsh will carry even the tiniest sound." He pulled at his cloak. "Now watch me." He reversed the heavy garment and Ronin saw that it was lined with a dull black material. Ronin followed suit. Then they smeared their faces and the backs of their hands with mud.

Darkness came.

Startled, a goose flapped its wings and shot into the air. It was a relatively small sound yet, as Okami had foretold, in the quietude of the marsh the clatter magnified out of proportion, a dream sound.

They froze near the bole of a tall maple. Off to the left, Ronin saw an end to the rice fields. There, in the east, rolling grasslands, studded with low bushes and stands of thick maple, led to the line of high mountains, so far away that they looked like a painted backdrop, two dimensional and lifeless.

In the unraveling stillness, he heard the slosh of boots on the pathway through the marsh. He controlled his breathing, heard the thudding of his heart in his ears.

Four men in dark gray with the blue wheel pattern went by them perhaps twelve paces away. They were armed with swords and carried long bamboo pikes with metal tips. There was no talking. They were vigilant and extremely careful.

The minute rustlings of their passage faded but still neither he nor Okami moved. Time crawled forward and he longed to stretch his muscles. The water at his feet stirred. A long snake, black and sinuous, poked its head above the surface. Gnats hummed in the reeds, dancing above the mirrored surface of the marsh. The moon was rising, its pale light blanching the tops of the cryptomeria. A frog croaked tentatively and was answered.

At length they risked movement and slowly peered out from behind the trunk of the tree. Before them, the deep blue arch leading to Haneda. Light from the castle was diffused through the heavily foliaged trees.

They began to circle cautiously to the left, keeping to the reeds as much as possible in order to approach the castle from the flank. Keeping their eyes away from the moon and the marsh to avoid the possibility of reflection off the whites of their eyes.

Very near, the first of the cryptomeria where darkness hung like a shroud.

The frogs ceased their singing and they froze, crouched. Ronin's hand was on the hilt of his dagger. His eyes searched the intense shadow of the wood but he discerned no movement. They waited, the sweat breaking out along their upper lips, at their hairlines. A heron called across the marsh.

Okami signaled and they went into the cover of the first line of cryptomeria.

Within the wood the dazzle of lanterns' light was plain enough high up through the twisted branches. Crouched against the trunk of a tree, they were about to move again when they heard a sound. It was slight but sharp: the snapping of a twig along the ground.

Okami signaled for Ronin to move to his right and, as he set out, he saw the other head left. Ronin drew his dagger, holding it before him, point higher than hilt.

He caught the movement before him, as the man searched

the wood, and he came in swiftly, silently, his body and his arm moving in concert, the bright blade slashing in a short arc through the man's side, piercing a lung. There was no sound. He caught the body as it collapsed, pulling it into the underbrush.

He moved on, his course taking him obliquely toward the castle and Okami.

Two men passed in front of him. He let them go because silence was essential and he could not be certain of killing them both before one cried out.

There was a crackling overhead. Bats swooped and soared in the crowded, tangled sky enclosed by the cryptomeria. And he was turning, his left elbow jutting, as the figure leapt at him. Powerful hands went to his throat, the thumbs pressing inward, attempting to crush his windpipe. He jammed backward with his elbow, smashing it into the man just below his armpit. There was a grunt but the man held on tenaciously. They rolled on the ground and Ronin brought both his arms together in front of him within the other's lock. Using the heel of his hand like a battering ram, he smashed into the other's nose, hit again from the other side. Cartilage broke and the skin burst in a hail of blood. Still the thumbs pressed inward and he was running out of air.

But he was on top now, if for only a moment, and he lowered his right arm, closing his fingers, stiffening them, lashing out against the man's diaphragm just below the sternum. The fingers pierced skin and flesh like a blade and he jammed his hand upward. The man was dead before his mouth could open.

Ronin rolled away and moved off and, at length, he came upon Okami standing above a corpse. Together, they went toward the castle.

The walls were of stone and very high. Too high. They crouched within its hulking shadow.

"Both of us cannot get over," Ronin whispered.

"I know, but if you leap from my shoulders, you should make the top."

Ronin was about to say something but Okami silenced him: "There is no other way."

He dropped to the ground and silently crept toward the main building of the castle. The way seemed clear but still he clung to the ebon shadows of the trees. The wood rustled in the night wind. Near the side of the structure, he paused for a moment, then coiled his body and leapt for a thick branch overhead. He hung by his hands for a moment, then began to swing, using the weight of his body to overcome inertia and start his momentum. He swung, drawing his knees up to his chest, and he was sitting on the branch. Feeling his way carefully, he climbed into the upper reaches of the cryptomeria, then along another branch, and cautiously onto the tiled roof of the castle.

For some meters, he crawled along the sloping roof until he came to a window below. He lay on his stomach with his ears as close to the opening as he could reach. He was quite still for long moments. Bats flapped above his head. There was no sound from inside. And no light.

He dropped down and inward, silent as a raven.

The room was sparsely furnished. Dark wood. Tatamis covered the floor. A lambent shaft of moonlight illuminated a painted screen in pale greens and browns: two robed women with white faces, red lips, coifed hair, fans unfurled, hid nothing, save a bolt of mother-of-pearl silk thrown over the back of a low chair.

He crossed to the wooden door without even a whisper of sound, put one ear to it. With infinite slowness, he opened it a crack. A sliver of hallway appeared, lit by reed torches. Almost directly across from him, a fluted wood railing.

The crackling of the burning reeds.

He risked another centimeter, then cautiously crept out into the hall. The railing ran away from him to left and right, the entire length of the hall, which was, he saw now, a kind of inner balcony onto which the doorways of the rooms on this level opened.

To his left was a wide stairway leading down to the ground level. He heard, drifting up to him, muted footfalls echoing away. The brief clatter of metal pots, an angry voice. Nearer to him, the reeds expending themselves.

To his right, the balcony's inner edge twisted upon itself in a corkscrew flight of stone steps. From above, a deep saffron light unfurled, amorphous, seemingly as solid as molten metal.

He stood very still for long moments, listening to the minute sounds of the castle as they blended together, allowing the pattern to form within his ears, against his flesh, sink in, take hold, so that any substantial alteration would automatically be picked up, even if his concentration was elsewhere.

Then he headed toward the purling light.

He passed two doorways other than the one he had come through. Cautiously he climbed the stairs, deliberately lifting his feet high, placing the ball of each foot on the stone before the heel. He ascended slowly, pausing every few steps, alert for sounds from above and below. And as he climbed, the light grew brighter and denser, coloring him, cascading over him until he felt awash on some fantastic sea. He stopped. Voices. They were indistinct yet they carried the tone of conversation. He moved upward.

At length, he came upon an alcove. This gave out on a great circular chamber with high sloping conical walls which thrust upward, toward the night sky. The height of the wall was irregular and beyond a low section, he could see the swaying tops of the cryptomeria, thick and somehow remote, the finality of earth's domain.

In the center of the chamber a fire burned in an enormous oval hearth made of glazed brick which held no trace of charcoal or soot. It was solely from this fire that the liquid light emanated. The flames rearing above the bricks were yellow, with no trace of orange or blue. They were pure, elemental.

A door opened along the curving wall and Ronin flattened himself within the concealing shadows of the tiny alcove. The tall figure of Nikumu came into view. His skin seemed yellowed, patinaed like ancient ivory. His long almond eyes glittered in the reflected light of the fire, turning opaque, and for an instant, Ronin found himself back in the alley in Sha'angh'sei, kneeling over the dead body of the defeated Bujun. Then another image superimposed itself upon his conscious, recalling his first meeting with Borros, deep inside the Freehold. These symbols of sickness and death blurred his vision for a moment. He blinked, curious.

Nikumu, garbed in a long silk robe of midnight blue with the repeating wheel pattern of charcoal gray, strode across the room, stood a moment before the rising flames. Ronin wondered where the chamber's other occupant was. Nikumu had not been talking to himself.

The tall man seemed lost in thought and when he moved it was almost as if he floated above the floor. From a cabinet with a fluted façade he produced a rice paper scroll.

Across the room, Ronin caught a flicker of movement. A shadow struck the stone hearth, fell across the stone floor. Long and lean, it seemed almost to be Nikumu's shadow, as if it had somehow been dislodged from his person. Then a figure glided into view. His back was to Ronin but he could see that the man had a long narrow skull, wide shoulders made more impressive by the stiff-shouldered robe he wore. His waist was narrow, as were his hips. His black robe was belted and from each hip hung a scabbarded sword. The one on his left hip was so long that it scraped the floor when he moved.

"You cannot mean to go through with it," he said.

Nikumu did not move, his head did not lift as his eyes continued to study the scroll. Only a pulse beating fast along the side of his neck indicated that he had heard the other.

"There are forces set in motion, you must know that," continued the dark figure. "The man at—"

"What would you have me do?" cried Nikumu, whirling toward the other, his face made hard and lined by the chiaroscuro of the firelight.

"I? What would *I* have you do?" The other shook his head. "You are Bujun. Your soul knows what must be done, just as hers does. Will she be stopped because she cannot speak? She will find a way, Nikumu, if she has not already."

"That is why she must be chained, just as I am."

"The man will come, Nikumu—"

"Then I will kill him!"

"Fool! If you could see what that thing has done to you. Do you not understand that when he comes, you will have to kill them both."

"No!" said Nikumu, but already his eyes were dead. "No."

Ronin went silently down the stairs, away from the flowing river of light, away from the disturbing confrontation. Much of the dialogue made no sense to him but this much he had learned: Moeru was indeed here and she was being held prisoner.

On the balcony overlooking the main floor, he paused to allow his eyes to adjust to the dimmer light. He heard a clatter on the lower staircase, at the opposite end of the balcony, and he retreated into the dense shadows behind the circular stairs.

Two armed men, one carrying a tray of food and drink, emerged onto his level. They came toward him and, for a moment, he thought that they were going to climb the corkscrew stairs, but instead they turned the other way and unlocked one of the doors along the outer wall.

He peered out, past their retreating backs, into the dimly lit room. It was densely furnished, chairs and piles of rolled rugs scattered at random as if the accumulation of years of living had been thrust into that small area.

On a chair in front of high curtained windows, near the

wan light of a flickering oil lamp, sat a slender figure. Sliver of white oval face, like a new crescent moon, long sweep of dark hair. Flash of the sea as her eyes shifted at their approach.

And Ronin was already leaping from his hiding place and, swinging his left arm in a vicious arc, slammed his balled fist into the side of the first man's neck. The jaws gaped open as the hide of the Makkon gauntlet tore through muscles and tendons. The teeth dashed together, severing the man's tongue tip. A hail of blood. And he was already past, as the corpse began to fold in upon itself, drawing his sword as he sprang at the second man. The tray of food and drink went flying and the eyes had just opened with shock when the head tumbled to the floor, went rolling until it struck one of her feet.

She said nothing.

She turned her exquisite face upward to him but her features were quiescent. She gazed into his colorless eyes with a distant curiosity. He knelt before her nakedness.

"Moeru," he said urgently. "Do you recognize me? Surely—"

Outside the cicadas orchestrated the passage of the moon. Wind rattled branches of a nearby cryptomeria against the closed window behind them.

He felt, for an instant, the keen edge of panic, a knife blade at his throat.

Then he closed his eyes and listened to the nothingness.

"Moeru." His lips barely moved.

Blackness, pearling.

"Moeru."

An endless sky littered with the pale mauve clouds of sunset.

"Moeru."

A zigzag line of geese flying above the blue and gold marsh, calling, calling plaintively toward the vast low horizon.

Abruptly a wind caught his cry, tore it from his lips, wheeling it away, away beneath the dark vault of the heavens, and he was in pitch blackness, beyond the sunset, far past the last edge of his world.

Touch was all that was left him.

He used it, following the tingling at his finger tips straight ahead until it lessened. Turn to the right. No. Turn to the left. Increasing. Onward, not walking, not running. Moving.

Tingling racing up his arms until his hands are numb. Ears

blocked. Shoulder sockets vibrating. Forward. And he hears it now. Music. A terrible liquid music at violent decibels that violate his eardrums. His teeth clatter and his body feels chilled. The music fills his world, his chest flying apart with the force. His head lifts now and his eyes blink of their own accord. He is absolutely motionless in the kinetic world, through the bass's brown booming, past the heavily stringed chords.

Staring.

Before him black peaks, shining like obsidian, thrust upward into a black sky filled with black stars. There is no horizon.

He sees Moeru in bondage, chained to the black peaks. Or rather it is her essence, he realizes, her crying out in torment: the savage singing. The music of pain and despair.

Her eyes widen as she sees him and she calls to him. The terrible music intensifies and his body shudders. She heaves herself upon the rough-hewn peaks.

The sky billows like a sea shroud. Three black suns rise in funereal procession. The crags move as if breathing. Here, naked before him, in her unimaginable torment, he sees the recognition lighting her eyes. The music drives through him like pikes, drenching him. His muscles jump in protest. He wills his legs to work.

She howls in agony. Her skin gleams with sweat. The ebon chains hold her fast, spread-eagled in the center of her world.

He raises his sword, the long blade a bright arc, and as it comes abreast of her white body, the music lessens, the sound somehow deflecting off its honed edges, away from him in a spiraling crescent of dark energy. His numbed mind begins to clear.

And now he comes for her.

At the verge of the black peaks, writhing now, less shiny obsidian, more scaly hide. The thing grasps her tightly. Black and monstrous, it seeks his death, but he is berserk now, the love a living pulse within him, feeding his muscles, the fear an added inducement, and he strikes again and again, his long blade a white blur singing past her white body, two spots of reflection in the blackness of this pit. And the song is death.

The peaks shear away, the air trembles, a shower of hot, sticky slime, she climbs into his arms, and still the sword wields destruction—

Ronin, come—

Black cormorants wheel into the black suns. Black stars burst by then—

—away, now. Oh, Ronin—

A wetness against his cheek, and the blade crying with a life of its own, demanding vengeance, a hot wind turns chill and a frost comes as the three black suns converge, trembling on implosion—

Now, now, now—

And with a mighty leap, Ronin carries her away into green mist, into the light of the sea shining behind her eyes, into the heavy air of Haneda.

Within his powerful arms, she pants heavily as his lips search for hers. His eyes open and he covers her naked body in his night-black cloak. She wrenches her mouth away from his, gasps:

"Quickly. He knows and is coming. Take me away."

Sheathing his sword, he raced with her to the window, but the shutters were locked. He grasped her hand and then they ran from the room. Down the dim balcony. Above them, he heard a sharp exclamation and a muffled crash. Nikumu's deep voice. Past closed doors. The pounding of boots. Into the doorway through which he had first come. Noise of pursuit, increasing.

Across the dimly lighted room to the window gaping open. Gulp of fresh night air, an intoxicating elixir. Thrusting her out into the embracing branches of the spreading cryptomeria. Then turning back into the room.

Nikumu burst through the doorway, sword drawn, eyes blazing.

"Where is she?" he cried.

"Perhaps you begin to understand now," said the voice of the other from the inner balcony. He had not yet come through the doorway.

"Who summoned you!" Nikumu snarled.

"Why," the voice said, equably, "you did, of course."

This seemed to enrage Nikumu further and he ran at Ronin. "I will kill you for this. She is mine!"

And the tall man, lifting his long Bujun blade above his head, ran at Ronin. He was very swift but he was not reckless and Ronin saw this at the last instant, recognized the enormous danger, dodging the blow and, in the same motion, swept both legs beyond the window sash. Wood splintered behind him and he twisted his body in the opposite direction. Another blow fell across the window frame and stone shattered in a cloud of dust just as he leapt along the thick horizontal branch of the cryptomeria, then scrambled down the gnarled trunk, joining Moeru on the ground.

He peered up through the gloom of the night. Nikumu's tall dark figure seemed bounded by two shadows. His silk robe whipped about him as if he were some spectral creature.

"I will hunt you down like animals!" he called wildly. He swung his sword in a great arc. Chips of stone and wood flew at them with explosive force.

"You are dead now!" he cried. "Dead!"

And a sound swept after them as they ran through the cryptomeria wood and Ronin could not tell whether it was the booming of laughter or the echoing of anguished sobs.

"There is only one place now," he said quietly, "for us to go."

"Yes. It is not really a difficult problem." His voice was filled with fatigue.

"So?" The face registered surprise.

"The castle of the Kunshin."

They sat on the covered terrace of a quiet inn set high up on purple cliffs which dove headlong, as if suicidal, into the churning combers far below them. The cool light of the horned moon broke the froth of the surf into bright diamond shards, the spindrift into platinum lace.

Above them and to the right, dark pines swayed in the breeze coming in off the sea like drowsing sentinels. To the left, the cliffs ran downward somewhat, covered in a thick matting of scrub and gorse.

Somewhere high up, a snow owl hooted in the pines, then fell silent.

On the tiled terrace, covered in tatamis, tea steamed before them on a low lacquered table. Rice cakes lay on a tiny plate beside their half-filled cups. Okami, his wide round face serene, sat cross-legged, facing Ronin. Within the inn, Moeru lay in exhausted sleep.

"This adventure was a mistake, I fear," Okami said. "Nikumu is now your enemy and a more deadly, implacable foe in all of Eido would be hard to find."

"He was holding her against her will. If you had seen—"

"She is his wife, after all, Ronin—"

"Does that absolve her of her rights to live her own life? Is this the wondrous Bujun way?"

Rushing clouds obscured the moon for a moment. When its marbled light returned, Okami said:

"My friend, I understand—"

"Excuse me for my bluntness this time, Okami, but I must tell you that there is no way that you *could* understand this situation. In some as yet unfathomable way, Moeru and I are bound together." After a moment, he said: "She can speak to me."

Okami stared out to sea, then he carefully poured tea for Ronin and himself. He lifted his porcelain cup with his finger tips and slowly sipped at the hot liquid.

"There is no use moaning about events which have already transpired," he said quietly. "Forgive me, my friend. For good or ill, she is here now with us. It is our karma."

"And what of the Kunshin?"

Okami's tone became more businesslike. "First, he is the only Bujun on Ama-no-mori powerful enough to repulse Nikumu's vengeful efforts—"

"But Nikumu is his friend."

"Let me finish, please. It is the scroll of dor-Sefrith which may save us all now for, you see, Azuki-iro, it is said, still retains some of the lost knowledge of the warrior-mages of Ama-no-mori's past. If it is as important as you say, then he will have no choice but to hold Nikumu at bay until he can make some determination."

"And then?"

Okami shrugged.

"When he has seen what you have brought, perhaps then he will come to realize the evil that lies so close to him, that has already begun to eat into Ama-no-mori. The sasori must be destroyed. If Nikumu is now their leader, then he must be the first to die."

Long after Okami had retired to the interior of the inn, Ronin sat cross-legged on the tatamied terrace, listening to the relentless pounding of the surf against the purple cliffs. A gray mist hung in the branches of the pines like the spun web of an enormous spider. The stars were no longer visible. The moon had gone down some time before.

He stared outward into the mist, inward into the core of his soul. And he made a vow. No one would stop him. Not Nikumu. Not the Makkon. Not even The Dolman. He would finish what he came here to do, for he too had a karma and its power was too strong to deny. He had no clear idea as yet what would be required of him. No matter. He knew in his heart that the fate of the entire world would not, *could* not, be decided by either Nikumu or the Kunshin. It could be no one element. Just as one's life was determined by a multiplicity of factors, so was history governed. The battle lines of his life had been drawn long ago, forged in blood and pain and loss. And he could not forget. Chill take Nikumu! And the Kunshin, if he decided against him. Yet one thing he had come to understand this night: he was surely close to the vortex of events toward which he had been journeying all his life.

And what of Moeru?

Her cool fingers along his neck.

She sat down next to him.

"Free." Her voice was soft against his ears.

"Did you hear me thinking about you?"

She threw her head back and laughed joyously.

"It is like being born again," she said.

The strong lines of her face were etched softly in the glowing light of an opalescent dawn breaking in a thin brushstroke beyond the towering summit of Fujiwara. Gray-green and smoke. Her dark hair swept over one eye and she lifted a slim hand to take it away. He stopped her. Their fingers twined.

"How?" he said.

"Come with me."

They got up, went across the tatamis to the railing of the terrace. She stood with her hands flat against the wooden railing. Their shoulders and hips brushed.

"We were separated when I left the *Kioku* during the attack. There was a storm that was not a storm." She turned to him, her long hair blown behind her by the wind. "What was it?"

"I do not know," he said, but he was not certain that that was the truth. A stirring in his mind.

"Look," she pointed delightedly. "The dawn."

Lonely pines, black against a pink, war-torn horizon. Majestic Fujiwara. The skyline of Ama-no-mori.

Her face was a pale rose in the early morning mist. Her swirling silk robe, which Okami had bought for her in the inn, was in sharp contrast with her black hair. One hand rose to her throat, caressed the tiny silver flower on its chain, lying the hollow.

"I returned here because of the sakura you gave me." The dawn wind whipped at her hair and he saw her now through a shifting latticework crisscrossing her cheeks and full lips. "I was overjoyed when I saw them coming. The great waves had already taken the *Kioku* far from me. We fought on but the sailors were outnumbered. One by one they died."

Their heads turned at a cry in the distance. Above the creaming waves, the first flock of gulls were already sweeping low over the burnished brass sea, searching for breakfast. The white of their plumage was stained pink by the rising sun.

"It was Nikumu who made the sakura, you see, and he gave it special properties. When the decision was made to send a Bujun to the continent of man, the Kunshin requested that some form of check be used. Nikumu devised the sakura. He knew that the Bujun would not part with it while he was alive, thus if he met some resistance, those on Ama-no-mori would know. What was not known was who had possession of the sakura after the Bujun perished. But this person, Nikumu reasoned, was surely involved in the Bujun's death. Thus he came for me."

In the crying dawn, Ronin thought back, remembered the brief darkening of the sun above the obsidian ship which carried Moeru, said:

"He flew then."

She turned to him, her eyes startled for an instant.

"Yes, but how did you know?"

"I saw—something, very far away."

"The steeds of ancient Ama-no-mori bore him and three of his men."

"And the four of them defeated a shipload of warriors?"

"They are Bujun, are they not?"

"You still wear the sakura. Surely he will know where you are."

"No, its power to act as a beacon ceased when I returned to Ama-no-mori."

"Why do you still wear it?"

"Because you gave it to me."

"Are you his wife?"

She did not even blink.

"I am sure that Okami already told you that."

"I want to hear it from you."

"I am Nikumu's wife."

"Then what were you doing on the continent of man?"

She turned her back on the light spreading itself over the far face of Fujiwara. Her slim body trembled against his.

"How did you free me?"

A whisper, a caress, a warmth. What was behind that question?

"Why should your husband imprison you?"

"Husbands can be as good or evil as anyone else."

Her sea eyes like whirlpools spinning him down.

"Which is Nikumu?"

The eyes closed for an instant, a universe blotted out. When she opened them again, they were wet.

"Neither. Both."

"Riddles."

He watched the slow path of the tears over her high cheekbones. Just the touch of a hand, reaching out. But he would not, now.

"He is afraid."

"Afraid of what?"

Reaching the crest, they held for a moment, quivering with her emotion, then they dropped silently to the tatamis.

"He is no longer Nikumu. Something—"

"Why is he leader of the sasori?"

She shook her head.

"I do not know. Something happened to him while I was away, something dreadful."

"Then he is as evil as Okami believes."

"No, no." She gripped his arms. "He has changed. Sometimes—sometimes he is as he was before and then, at other times, he is like a madman."

By their cries, he judged that the gulls had found food. Small clouds of them skimmed the water in tight arcs. Their calling was incessant now.

"Ronin, I fear that he is possessed."

"By what?"

"There is someone with him always now."

"Yes, I have seen him. But he has no control over Nikumu."

"You must do something."

"I?" He felt like laughing in her face. "Frost, Moeru, the man wants me dead! Now you ask me to help him?"

"Only you can."

"What nonsense is that?"

Her face hovered near his, her lashes long and wet.

"How did you free me?"

"I did not think about it."

"No, of course not. If you had to, you would not have done it. Nikumu would have slain you."

"Something evil lurks within Haneda, Moeru."

"Yes, but it is not Nikumu. He is a human being, not a monster."

"But what he did to you—"

"Ronin, you must help him!"

"But I am in no position to—"

"Only you were able to free me—"

"What you ask is madness, Moeru—"

"Only your power—"

"Chill take him—"

"He made me mute—"

"—no!"

"—so that I would not communicate with you."

Even through the hissing mist of the downpour hurtling from out of the red, fulminating sky, he could see how enormous the pine was. Many tiered, spreading outward like the limbs of heaven, constantly in motion from the gusting of the wind and the torrential rain, it arched out majestically, dwarfing even the rooftops of the Kunshin's sprawling stone castle.

They stood in drenched cloaks wrapped tight and dripping sedge hats. The wood and earth bridge lay before them, arcing over the moat which separated the domain of the leader of all the Bujun from the rest of Ama-no-mori.

Behind them rose the far eastern outskirts of Eido, blurred and indistinct, a painting in the rain. Beyond the last maple, where the road described a wide turning, an old woman sold tea to weary travelers from the inadequate shelter of a tiny wood station.

"How can we be sure that he is here?" said Ronin.

"He is not in Eido," said Okami.

"Why not the mountains, then?"

"He is here, my friend."

They stepped upon the eastern bridge, muddied now by the rain, and the world of Eido slipped away from them. Thunder rolled ominously from a long way off. The surface of the water spanned by the bridge's arc was goose-fleshed.

The Kunshin's guards met them as they stepped off the span and they were taken directly into the castle.

They were led into a small antechamber where a tiny robed woman took Moeru into an adjoining chamber after indicating their fresh clothes and the hot water in basins with which they could wash away the mud and dirt of their travels.

Moeru rejoined them. They all wore robes embroidered

with the spoked wheel pattern of the daimyos. They were Okami's colors.

Two armed Bujun in wide-shouldered robes woven with cloth-of-gold entered the chamber and led them up a flight of wide stone steps, past innumerable armed Bujun, down a vast hallway fully as large as a gallery, and at length, through double wooden doors, dark and highly polished. Brass glyphs surrounded by a circle were set in the center of either door.

As they entered the room, they heard again the hissing of the rain and Ronin looked to the large windows, open onto the storm. The brawny lower branches of the giant pine swayed and dipped. Rain ran along the window glass like cool tears, pattered onto the tatamis.

They were in a chamber of moderate size, not at all what Ronin had imagined the Kunshin's quarters to be like. There were no chairs, just a functional stool, which stood in front of a large wooden desk along the far wall. Low lacquered tables were set on the tatamis in an informal grouping in the center of the room. The Bujun left them.

Ronin watched the storm outside.

They removed their sandals.

"He reminds me of someone," said a deep voice. Ronin looked up, into the face of Azuki-iro. He was not sure to whom the Kunshin spoke. "That is significant."

He was a man with a functional head, as if his features had been carefully and lovingly crafted, each for a specific purpose. He had not one centimeter of superfluous flesh. His face was rather flat, like Okami's, yellow-skinned with long almond eyes and a wide, blunt nose. His thick black hair gleamed, bound in a queue. He had a wide neck and a barrel chest and he stood with his feet firmly planted on the floor. A warrior's stance: confident, not arrogant. Beneath his cloth-of-gold robe could be seen the hard curve of his muscles.

"A foreigner, yes?" said Azuki-iro. He cocked his head to one side for a moment, as if trying to decide a momentous issue. "I am not so certain." His eyes never left Ronin. "Where did you pick him up?" Only his tone of voice told of his shifting direction.

"On the Kisokaido," Okami said.

"Who are you?" Ronin turned. "Have you lied to me?"

Okami's face was placid. There was no hint of deceit in his clear eyes.

"I told you only those things which you needed to know. I betrayed no trust. You are here now, before the Kunshin. Is this not why you came to Ama-no-mori? Why look beyond your own needs?"

"I wish to know the truth."

"History shall record the truth," said Azuki-iro.

Ronin stepped back a pace, withdrew his sword. A laconic whisper, a deadly snake shedding its dry lifeless skin.

"The time is forever past when I will take only what is given me. I would have the answers I seek and I would have them now."

Azuki-iro's eyes narrowed and his muscles tensed.

"Hold!"

It was Moeru's voice and for the first time the Kunshin's face registered a hint of strong feeling: surprise.

"Moeru," he whispered. "What—?"

"It was Ronin."

The Kunshin's eyes shifted.

"It was," he said. Then the cloth-of-gold swirled as he held out a strong hand. "The scroll. May I see it?"

The sword point poised, restive. Something swam in Okami's eyes, half-hidden, unrealized. What? For this moment, Ronin had journeyed farther than any man on the face of his world. He had fought so many battles against foes familiar and strange. Had lost so many friends. Had seen the slow beginnings of the ultimate evil. Had felt the dark encroachment of terrifying forces. Yet now he hesitated. Here, at journey's end, unsure. Just beyond the point of his sword lay the open palm of Azuki-iro. Where should his trust lie? From Okami's eyes to Moeru's. He found nothing there, had known that even before he looked. Reflex. The forebrain trying to protect the organism. The answer was not within any of them.

Staring into Azuki-iro's eyes, he reversed his sword, unscrewing the hilt, withdrawing the scroll of dor-Sefrith. He handed it into the firm grasp of the Kunshin.

Without a word, Azuki-iro strode to the light of the open window. The rain had ceased momentarily but the great pine still wept its tears. A nightingale trilled sweetly, abruptly filling the room with song.

For endless moments, the Kunshin studied the scroll, his forehead furrowed in concentration, until at length he returned to where they waited. It seemed to Ronin that he had not drawn a single breath since Azuki-iro had begun to read the scroll. At last, an ending. At last, salvation for man.

The Kunshin addressed them all.

"It is indeed the time." There was a sharp inhalation of

breath from Okami. "The mind of dor-Sefrith reaches out through time, through space, past the ceasing that is death. For he returns now on the wheel of universal force."

The Kunshin's eyes focused on the warrior before him.

"Ronin, I know not where you come from nor how far you have traveled. But these are irrelevancies now. With the return of this scroll to Ama-no-mori, a cycle ends for the Bujun as well as for all men. A new age commences. What it may bring none may say with any degree of certainty, save that the world, as we now know it, has passed from us.

"Those of us who are able shall survive to see the dawn of this new age but I fear that for many that time shall not come." He shrugged. "That is their karma. The Kai-feng is upon us and no one on this world may remain neutral for it is the Last Battle. Death is as nothing to the Bujun. It is but the manner of our death which concerns us. Thus shall history remember us all. As heroes and as men."

Azuki-iro handed the scroll of dor-Sefrith back to Ronin, and with his fingers still holding it, he said: "I charge you now with the final part of your journey, Ronin. And you must understand that it is the most perilous part, for you know what will occur should you fail." His black eyes blazed. "Take the scroll of dor-Sefrith." His hand dropped to his side. "Take it and give it into the hands of the one man who can fully decipher it, the only man who can implement dor-Sefrith's instructions.

"Take the scroll to Nikumu."

Bujun

NIGHT crept over the marsh with a furtive deliberation. A ragged line of geese, brown and white against the red and ocher sky, disappearing toward the distant, rising peak of Fujiwara. To the east, the wide veldt rustled in the soft breeze, the calmness after the violence of the evening's squall.

Here and there, frogs began once again to croak after being startled into silence by the storm. Fireflies darted in amongst the high reeds, cautiously remaining on the verge of the marsh.

A salamander snaked just beneath the skin of the fecund water, crawled onto the tiny green island of a lily pad. It stared at the erratic flight of the fireflies, mesmerized by the patterns of cold, winking lights.

To the west, stillness reigned at Haneda.

Even the cicadas were quiescent. A blackbird flapped its wings, lifting off from the canopy of the cryptomeria wood. It circled high in the red sky, passing over the rice fields, then swept eastward toward the open veldt.

"There is nothing I can do," he had said, when they were alone.

"But you are the Kunshin—"

"I am Bujun first. That is the essential issue. I would not listen if the situation were reversed, and if he were foolish enough to ask me, I would kill him."

"But he is your strongest ally."

"You must understand, Ronin, that if he needed to ask me, he would have lost all value, to Eido, to Ama-no-mori, as well as to me."

"It has nothing to do with position then."

"Nothing whatsoever."

"What then?"

"History," Azuki-iro had said. "The code by which we live

our lives is our most unshakable bond; nothing may stand against it. We will die by our own hands rather than lose it." The reflection of the rain which had begun again with far less intensity, dappled his round face as they stood near the open window. "What Nikumu decides now, he must decide alone. What he has been doing in Haneda recently, I cannot tell you, nor could any Bujun, I think. The magus within him has gained in power, thus he rescued Moeru where none other on Ama-no-mori could."

"What of the sasori?"

"They are all under surveillance. We have nothing to fear from their virulence. It is Nikumu's involvement which has my curiosity."

"Why?"

"It is unlike him, and it is a clumsy manifestation of evil."

"This is too ironic."

"Ronin, you have journeyed long to deliver the scroll of dor-Sefrith into the rightful hands. Can you say why you did this? Would you forsake the obligation you took on so long ago? You do not fear him, of that I am certain. Still, it is entirely up to you, for you are free to leave this isle, as always you have been. The Bujun do not hold prisoners—"

"But Nikumu—"

"Precisely my point. What has Nikumu become?"

Outside, the great pine shivered in the last gustings of the passing squall, the thick branches scraping against the castle's outer wall. Moeru's voice came darkly to him: *He is possessed.*

"Who is Okami?"

"One of my daimyos." He lifted a hand. "Do not be concerned. I sent him to find you."

"How did you know of my coming?"

They went away from the glistening window, the Kunshin's arm around his shoulders.

"In the mythology of the Bujun," he said, "the tiger rules the land." They sat in the center of the room and he poured tea. "The heavens are ruled by the dragon."

"You know of Kukulkan."

"Oh yes. By another name. But it is he."

"I must go," said Ronin, staring out past the bulk of Azuki-iro, at the nightingale wrapping in his dripping bower, just past the open window.

"Yes, it is your karma. In these matters, there is no choice. One learns acceptance of certain basic life patterns and forces.

The Bujun understand this even before they are born, I think. We accept and live in peace with ourselves. The rest falls into place of its own accord."

"Would you accept then the coming of The Dolman?" Ronin said angrily. "Will you lie down and die in front of his might?"

"Now you deliberately misunderstand me," said Azuki-iro softly. "We are not fatalists, merely realists. What is, is, and we train ourselves to live within that framework. That does not mean that we do not continually strive for those things we want." His round face was abruptly eclipsed by the shadows of the room. "We learned well from the agonies of our ancestors. In the end, our sorcery was inimical to us."

"Yet sorcery seems to be man's only hope now."

The Kunshin's dark eyes glittered from out of the darkness. "Of sorcery The Dolman was born. His death can only spring from the same source. It is necessary, not desirable." He took a small sip of tea. "No matter what transpires here, the Bujun shall join the Kai-feng. It is our karma."

Ronin stood up. The Kunshin set his teacup carefully down on the top of a lacquered table.

"Why was Moeru sent to the continent of man?"

"She went for a purpose unknown to me," said Azuki-iro. "You must ask her husband, for it was he who sent her."

He had a hatchet jaw that in anyone else would have been a mark of considerable comment. Here it was but another bit of the unusual background terrain upon which the network of angular white scars was embossed, a mere hillside to the neighboring dells of his sunken cheeks.

He looked like the walking dead.

The web of scar tissue ran upward along his neck, criss-crossing his square jaw, zigzagging obliquely across his high cheekbones with such completeness that there seemed to be no normal skin in that area. His left eye, an earthen green that was nevertheless hard and cold, was pulled down at the outer corner by the last outpost of these minute wounds. His right eyelid never opened.

He stood squarely in a thick bar of light slanting obliquely through a high open window in Haneda's west wall. Beyond the white casement, brown sparrows chased each other through the twisting maze of the cryptomeria. Higher up came the leathery sound of the restless bats.

"The waiting is at an end now."

Nikumu slid a sheaf of rice paper across his long wooden table.

"There is still some little time." Then more softly. "There must be." A muscle spasm seemed to grip his face. He grimaced. The other looked on placidly. Then he shook his head and the scars danced in the light like a thousand fireflies.

"Have you not had enough of illusion?"

Nikumu spun about, his hands flat and deadly, the fingers stiff.

"It is agony, pure agony!"

"Yes, I know. Do not forget—"

"Oh, I do not think for a moment that you would ever let me forget!"

"It is what I have to give you."

"Give me?" hissed Nikumu. "You would be nothing—nothing without me!"

"History has already passed judgment upon me. Your struggle—"

"But you were not content with that."

"Nor were you," the scarred man pointed out equably.

Nikumu's features twisted. "I do not remember asking you to be my conscience when I brought you—"

"Do you mean to say that there was a certain understanding between us? Nonsense!" His tone abruptly changed, chilling the chamber. "Beyond the summoning, events will happen as they will."

"Of course," cried Nikumu, "and that is why he keeps you like this!" With a furious lunge, his clawed fingers shot forward toward the other's throat.

Within the deep shadows of the alcove near the spiral staircase, Ronin's muscles tensed. Then, stunned, he pressed himself back against the cool stone wall. He stifled the hiss of an indrawn breath. Nikumu's outflung hand had passed through the flesh of the scarred man as if it were made of smoke.

"Childish."

The other stepped back a pace. Nikumu did not follow. His arm fell to his side and he clutched at the table as if his legs would not support him.

"He is too powerful," Nikumu whispered like a frightened child.

"He has that which you will him, Nikumu."

"I am not as strong as you were. I do not think that I can win."

The scarred man looked away, as if deeply disappointed.

Then his head snapped up and for long moments he appeared to be listening for or perhaps to something. Nikumu, his face full of pain, took no notice.

Abruptly, as if coming to a decision, the other strode across the stone floor of the chamber, opened a copper-bound glass case. He withdrew three masks, one at a time. Ronin wondered at this. Was the man truly insubstantial or had Nikumu's attack been an illusion, some trick of the light.

"It is time for the Noh, Nikumu. You know which play."

The scarred man donned one mask. He now had the countenance of an elderly man, kind and avuncular.

"Toshi, the priest," he announced, carrying the second mask to Nikumu. He held it out at arm's length.

Nikumu took it, settled it slowly on his head.

"Reisho, the warrior," said Toshi.

One mask remained lying atop the copper and glass case and as Ronin stared at its glistening face, he understood that the scarred man had heard him somehow. He also knew for whom the last mask had been left.

As the scarred man drew Nikumu, now Reisho, across the chamber, away from the case, Ronin went silently across the stone floor and donned the mask. He turned.

"Look!" cried Toshi. "My lord Reisho, look who comes behind you!"

Reisho whirled.

"Tsuchigumo!"

The utterance, from within the mask, was alive with overtones and the acoustics of the open chamber acted like an amphitheater, causing his voice to reverberate without excessive volume.

Now they were all within the Noh.

"I warned you!" Toshi called, pointing at Tsuchigumo. "The strange illness which incapacitates you is caused by him!" His body described the beautiful ritualistic turns.

"No," said Reisho, his voice hollow. "The failing lies within me."

"No, sire, you must be mistaken," said Toshi, bowing before Reisho. "Look again, it is Tsuchigumo, the great spider. Can even one so grand as yourself prevail against so powerful an evil?"

"I do not know, priest, but your words give me hope, for perhaps in defeating Tsuchigumo, I can prevail over myself." Thus Reisho danced slowly, drawing his great sword. He bent his knees, holding the blade vertically, a line cutting his face into two halves. And Tsuchigumo saw that the left half of his mask had differing features from the right half, as if he were a man at war with himself.

"This battle, my lord, are you wise to fight it?" said Toshi, his tone wheedling.

"What do you mean, priest?" Reisho paused in his advance. "This is a struggle to the death."

"Yes, to the death, lord," said Toshi, dancing around Reisho. "And to what end? Tsuchigumo is powerful and you are weak now. It will only serve *his* purpose to battle you now."

"Yes, perhaps you are right."

"Certainly, lord."

The sword lifted. "But I am Reisho, the warrior. I am Bujun. I must do battle!"

Tsuchigumo moved forward, into the strong light of the fire.

"Ah!" cried Toshi, raising a fist within which he held a curved blade. "Now I have the power to destroy you!" The blade began its descent, toward Reisho's side. "For so long have I served Tsuchigumo, all for this one instant of power!"

Reisho whirled, his blade flashing up.

"Traitor!" he cried.

His blade pierced Toshi's heart.

And Reisho, within the same movement, turned and rushed at his hated foe, Tsuchigumo, who, standing his ground, withdrew his own blade, taking the warrior's initial blow along its long length.

Wordlessly, with small gruntings and harsh exhalations of breath, sounds made strange by filtration through the masks, they matched blow for blow, feint for feint.

They were masters, both.

There was little actual movement around the chamber; a fixed space of perhaps three meters on each side was all that either required to attack or make his defense.

Each a superb warrior, they fought as mirror images, almost as if they were aspects of the same person. So evenly matched were they that the combat appeared eerily to be more of a complexly choreographed dance and Ronin was reminded of the ending of the Noh he had witnessed at Asakusa. As that actor, playing the goddess, had filled his stage with his consummate skill, so now these two actors, these two warriors, filled the stage at Haneda with the culmination of their craft.

The metallic clangor became their music, the harsh exhalations of their breath, the percussives to which they matched their oblique movements. Muscles jumped and sweat oiled their bodies. Eyes gauged and compensated, nerves fired, triggering swift move after move, blurred counter after counter.

And the air was now unclear, white and shiny with the precise whirling of the blades, so that the pair seemed encased in lethal glass, a bloody womb from which only one would emerge.

Within, Tsuchigumo saw that his path was set. Yet it would not have been the one he would have chosen. Still, he *had* chosen it and was now locked within the combat within the Noh. Somehow, he must get through before the bloodshed began. Where was the scarred man? He had understood Ronin's presence at Haneda, had even chosen his role in the Noh: Tsuchigumo, the title figure.

And Tsuchigumo must initiate the action. But what?

Reisho pressed his attack, his white blade moving faster than ever, but Tsuchigumo refused to move and his defense was awesome. Reversing, he went on the attack, a ferocious barrage of blows culminating with the difficult *solenge*. Tsuchigumo saw the startled eyes behind Reisho's frozen visage and he was but a centimeter from being through the guard when Reisho executed the proper defense, the only defense, with blurring speed.

"Enough!"

The Reisho mask trembled and Nikumu stripped it from his head. Ronin removed the mask of Tsuchigumo.

"How does a foreigner fight in the manner of the Bujun?" Nikumu cried.

"I cannot answer that, Nikumu, but before our quarrel resumes, let something more important speak to you."

He reversed his sword, unscrewed the hilt.

"No!" cried Nikumu. His blade flashed up and now was the moment of his destiny. The honed tip quivered centimeters from Ronin's naked throat. He stood his ground, a warrior still, and watched Nikumu's flashing eyes, ignoring the blade below.

"You are my enemy!" Nikumu's lips were thin and bloodless in his fury. "You have taken my wife!"

Ronin spoke slowly, softly: "No, Nikumu, I freed her. She left Haneda with me because it was her wish—"

"Liar!" He restrained himself from jamming his blade into Ronin's flesh. "You plotted against me, poisoned her mind. She loves me!"

"She fears for you," said Ronin without emotion. "You are no longer someone she knows. What have you become, Nikumu? What has your sorcery made you?"

The tall man before him jerked as if he were a marionette. A muscle spasm at the side of his right eye ticked off the seconds like some monstrous clock.

"Where are you?" His eyes flicked about the chamber. "Where have you gone?"

"We are alone here, Nikumu," said Ronin. "Just the two of us now."

The ghost of a horrific smile creased Nikumu's mouth for an instant. "Never alone, now. Never."

"The scarred man has gone."

"Not him, you fool! Can you not feel the presence?"

"I see only you."

The blade dangerously close and he began to judge distances and reflexive times. No chance.

"It is within me that you must look!"

"I—"

"You did it with Moeru!"

The muscles tensed, the nerves on their fevered edge. He would be dead before he took one step.

"She wanted me to help you." Perhaps this was it.

"Then do it!"

Had the point moved fractionally toward him? What arcane struggle raged within Nikumu? Only one chance now because the tension was building far too rapidly. Nikumu was losing the battle and when that happened, he would lunge forward and his blade would pierce Ronin's heart. Odds were outrageously high but he had no choice now. Karma.

"I will do nothing to help you." He fed emotion into his voice. "You are pitiable. You call yourself Bujun but it is as false as the mask you wore. You are a coward, Nikumu! Yes! Kill me. That will surely bring you solace! Oh, false warrior, your sorcery has made you weak and frightened. It has let in the gods of death and their power has made you less than a man. Look not to the other or to me for support. There is no succor for you this night, for history writes itself here. The last chapter reverberates within these stone walls and there can be only one writer."

The eyes before him were feral. Shadows shifted in their dark depths as he spoke, figures fleeing across a barren, unstable landscape, the pursuer and the pursued.

Slowly, while still he stared within those eyes, his hands resumed their work on the hilt of his sword.

He drew out the scroll of dor-Sefrith.

With its release, Nikumu's gaze broke with his and the tall man looked down. Ronin put the scroll in his hands. His sword clattered to the floor and his legs appeared to fail him. He sank to his knees. Ronin stood perfectly still. Above their heads, a bat clattered about, confused by the light, then it raced upward into the dark of night.

Sweat rolled down Nikumu's face, dripped onto the stone floor. It bathed his forehead, stung his eyes. He blinked. His mouth gaped open and he gasped. He reached out with trembling fingers and grasped the lip of the table. His fingers slipped and he groaned but, as if with enormous effort, he raised his arm again and held onto the table. His knuckles turned white with the pressure he exerted. He seemed a drowning man.

With his other hand he opened the scroll of dor-Sefrith. His fingers shook as if with palsy.

His head jerked again, this way and that, but at last he forced his eyes to the writing on the scroll.

High above them, the horned moon soared over the tops of the cryptomeria, pouring down its platinum light into the high chamber at Haneda.

Nikumu's lips began to move and as their litany began, the liquid light from the fire seemed to fade, become insubstantial, turning them into shades.

Then the moonlight flooded the room completely, cold and clear. Every shape became sharply defined.

Nikumu continued to recite the glyph pattern which dor-Sefrith had written so many eons ago, his voice slowly becoming more confident, less ambiguous. He stood up.

And now it seemed to Ronin that Nikumu was altering form. Surely the outline of his body became translucent, pulsing out of focus for a brief instant. Surely now he towered over Ronin, shoulders wide and sharp in the traditional Bujun robe.

Within the blink of an eye, the outline contracted and Ronin thought he heard Nikumu cry out. Yet it was not a sound that could have been made by a human larynx. Nikumu's body shuddered and swayed, his lips pulled back in a grimace of pain, his white fists flailing the air.

Yet the litany continued.

Then from the depths of his chest came a burgeoning sound

like a distant roll of thunder and the outline of his form expanded. The thunder came again, traveling over a summer field, arid and dry, rolling again, coming closer and closer, bringing its fertile promise, until it washed over the chamber and its occupants like an unstoppable tidal wave, lifting them up upon great spread wings, all gravity nullified, and they were as free as two soaring eagles.

Then he was staggering across the floor of the chamber, staring as the face of Nikumu shattered like a Noh mask.

Before Ronin stood a version of the other. Younger. A strong, vibrant figure. His face, now scarless, had the nose of a hawk. The rest was Bujun flat. His fierce obsidian eyes blazed with power. His long, unbound hair trailed behind him like a tail.

Swept his long arms above him, stretching his body as if to embrace the entire vast spangled night.

His lips opened.

"At last!"

His voice was the rumble of a summer storm.

"Through all the centuries, I have returned. For the Kai-feng is come. I am here, therefore The Dolman is nigh."

His gaze turned to Ronin.

"And here is the champion of all man. Welcome, Ronin, to the forge of Ama-no-mori, to the anvil of Haneda. Welcome to the end of your journey."

His arms whirled about him and blue sparks lit the air, crackling into the night. The stars went out.

"The time is upon us. Even now the summoning of The Dolman has begun, but fear not, a chance for man still remains, for you are here. Nikumu has taken his final step, fought his last battle, and won. Thus shall history remember him for all time. Once again the Bujun triumph.

"But now you must prepare yourself for your ultimate step. For I am come; I am ready. Do you trust yourself?"

Ronin opened his arms wide, said:

"Yes."

"Then now comes death—!"

There was a clap of thunder that blotted out all sound.

"Thus sayeth dor-Sefrith!"

Everything turned white.

Deathshed

TWO elements existed within the whiteness: his essence and the voice.

He knew that he was Outside even before the voice told him.

Time was a multicolored pinwheel whirring far below him.

This is the end.

For Ronin, yes.

And for me?

The death of a myth. The concept shone on the theater of his unconsciousness like a castle cleared of mist.

And—

Life beyond life.

He laughed, placid bubbles, white on white.

Perhaps in time past I would have thought that a riddle.

And now?

Tell me something. You knew Nikumu. Why did he send Moeru to the continent of man?

Because I asked him to.

For what purpose?

His or mine?

Both.

Backup for his brother, who, under the influence, he sent into Sha'angh'sei to spy for the sasori. For myself, she was there to seek out someone, just as Bonneduce the Last and Hynd were sent to find you.

Who?

Setsoru.

The Hart of Darkness.

As men would call him.

I have met him.

Yes. It seemed inconceivable to me that that confrontation should ever take place on the continent of man. Hynd did not fail his master.

He could not. His love for Bonneduce the Last exceeds all else in his world.

Yes. That is quite correct.

You wished to locate the Hart—

Just as I wished to locate you.

Where is my body?

Shed. It is yours no longer. You belong to life; it to death.

And what am I to become?

Through sorcery and ancient surgery, through the last surviving knowledge of the Bujun warrior-mages, through methods that were old even in my time you shall become the last myth of mankind: the Sunset Warrior.

The eye of Time grew faint, then disappeared altogether. All color ceased.

He tumbled forward into nothingness. Not fields or mountains, rivers or marshlands. Not valleys or forests, deserts or seas. Neither mist nor cloud barred his way and his speed increased. He neither walked nor ran. Neither did he fly. Once he thought he felt the gargantuan undulations of Kukulkan, but then he thought that he must be mistaken.

Then, in the absence of color, he felt the darkness stealing over him, a relentless, restive sea, cold and deep and mysterious. And now a shrill wind took up around him, whining and moaning.

Before him a slowly turning vortex.

Light and shadow, blurred and distorted, an intense sense of vertigo and he was within a forest. Below him, boles and limbs and foliage, all in black and white. Perspective inverted as he plunged into the darkness of the wood, through leafy bowers and ridged escarpments, above verdant underbrush, below swaying branches.

Something at the core of his being constricted as an intimation of what rushed at him dawned. He remembered another day in another lifetime within a house deep in the bowels of the world. Climbing the stairs, hearing the deep, sonorous ticking and the bright clicking from the second-floor room where Bonneduce the Last crouched on a carpet of intricate design, rolling the Bones, foretelling his future. There had been terror then and, as the chord at the center of his being was plucked again by chill fingers, he felt anew that strange unknown emotion. *You are not afraid to die*, Bonneduce the Last had said. *What then?*

It was coming now or he to it.

The trees parted.

Then faded away to nothing.

He faced Setsoru.

Once again those terrible human eyes in the black-furred stag's head stared into his own. The great treed antlers quivered.

"Where am I?" cried the Hart. Then: "I sent the ships for you. Ah, no!" He screamed. "Stop this!" His head shook. His eyes darted, rolling in their sockets. "You can stop this. You must!"

Silence.

And if there was anyone else in their black and white world, he gave no tangible sign of his presence.

Foam flecked Setsoru's black animal lips and he gave a high whinnying whine. His horned hands reached for his black onyx sword but he was naked.

"Where are you?" called the Hart. His horned fingers went to his head, beating at it as if it were a mask he wished to smash.

"Enough!" His voice edged in hysteria, rising. "I have had enough of this jest!" Backing away from the being in front of him. "I have served you faithfully. I have destroyed so much life in your name. What have you done to me now?" His horned fingers grasped his antlers. His black lips trembled and he began a terrible laughter. "Power. Oh, power, where is it now? Deliver me from this hell—!"

There are no gods here, Setsoru, came his voice, filled with a peculiar vibration. The Hart jerked as if stung.

For the first time, Setsoru peered at the shape in front of him.

"Who are you, that you should fill me with such fear?"

I cannot answer that, for I do not know yet. I know only what I once was, a long time ago. Yet your fear is my fear.

"Truly?" The Hart held his ground, his great head craning forward. "The light is dim. I cannot see you clearly."

He moved closer.

"Ah!" Setsoru exclaimed. "I know now, I can feel it. From the forest. You stalked me like an animal—"

Not you. Another.

"He told me you were dead."

I am here.

"I said you searched for me in the forest. That while you lived, I would have no peace. You would hound me—"

He also said that I was dead.

"He would not lie to me."

He already has.

"What do you want of me?"

They were closer together now, though neither appeared to have moved on his own.

What do we want of each other?

The head jerked and the wide nostrils dilated, snorting. "I want nothing more than to be returned to the forest at Kamado."

In time, perhaps.

"He was right. You wish me dead!" The eyes were beserk.

I will not harm you. And thinks, Why not?

Setsoru laughed.

"You cannot!"

They came together and the battle was joined, an endless, deathless struggle. He realized this instantly, knew it was a puzzle he had to solve else they would be locked in combat, beyond the reach of Time itself.

He was terrified and as the panic rose within him, he blocked it, forcing it down, away from him. Tried to think. Mind a blank. The enormous furred face flailing back and forth before him.

"I fear nothing. I destroy!" The hysteria returning to the Hart, seizing him, squeezing. Never letting go. Never.

A kind of night was falling, deep and dense. Starless and endless. A blanket. To sleep. A shroud—

Into the shrouds. Upward. Sea birds calling. Toward the warm sun. Gone, now. Gone.

Think!

No sky. No horizon. No land.

Engulfed in the blackness.

Tumbling over and over, they fought. The panic deleted his strength. He had to overcome it.

Concentrate. Existence narrowing until—

He felt another touch of fear. A different kind now and he knew that something was coming. And he knew what it was.

Something beyond death.

The end.

No!

Unbound, the panic welled up, a vast, tidal wave of emotion and he relaxed now, feeling its thunderous, deafening approach. In the shallows now, holding his ground.

Into the deep.

And suddenly he knew and the knowledge, flowing through him like a dancing bolt of light, dazzled him with its energy.

You cannot harm me, he said.

Watching Setsoru's eyes.

Coming.

Airless.

You understand, he said. Tell me who you are.

"What do you mean?"

You know.

A constriction of the blackness.

"You are mad!"

A rushing of foul wings.

It will all be over unless you tell me.

Setsoru felt it too, now.

I know therefore you must know.

"I am afraid—"

That is all he has left.

It was there.

Tell me.

"I am," said Setsoru, "you."

The hiss of wind and it was gone from them.

Beneath them, as they spun, slithered the being at the center of the world, perhaps acephalous, indeed an endless landscape, turning and glistening and undulating, never the same, eternally constant.

Borne upward to them, a salt tide on the air. Color seeping.

The Hart's body was wracked with sobs as they held each other, drenched in salt sweat, and then they were together, inside each other, bound, and he felt at last for Setsoru another emotion which he could not identify.

They merged.

Energy raced through them and he/they/he saw the infinite fanfare of living thunder, heard the colored sky glowing from pink to white to blue to periwinkle to gray and brown to gold and orange and flame and rust, felt the push and pull of muscle as the working wings of vast flocks of geese and plovers hurtled eastward, living streamers, the parade's own celebrative bunting.

One.

An instant's flash of cold, pure gray.

Green semiconsciousness.

Warmth.

As something swam through the caverns of the sea, at the foundations of the world. And it seemed familiar, as if at some great time past, this something had been here. Or dreamed of it being here.

Amongst the towering basalt and granite at the base of the world he swam. And grew, developing a head and torso; arms and legs; hands and feet. And the features began to define themselves as he reached out and touched the immense, sloping side of the Aegir, rolling, undulating, endless.

Architecture built itself around him and he grew as he spun slowly on his axis, stroking the rough hide of the immeasurable being. He was sliced open, slit lengthwise down his arms, the blood pouring forth in black billowing clouds, the dust of another life. Swiftly the skin drew itself together in different configurations, colored and wealed, tattooed, a living hieroglyph upon which perhaps was written the history of all mankind.

Bones broke, as the skin pulled apart once again, shattering their calcium and phosphorous into drifting powder. But the shifting sea was rich in these minerals and others and it poured them back into the broken body. New bones constructed themselves in seeming odd lengths, joined and knitted with supreme cunning and skill.

Thus he passed from consciousness knowing only that he was changing, forming, shifting like the sea itself which held him in its dark and pressured embrace. And while he slept greater changes occurred. Merciful unconsciousness.

His face broke into ten thousand fragments, shards dissolving on the tides, re-forming, soft as putty, molded in unseen hands, shaped most delicately and carefully into a singular visage in all the world.

The body broadened and elongated and now the muscles hardened, stretching themselves upon the framework of the new limbs and torso, growing, layer upon layer, defining themselves in ridged plateaus.

And all the while he dreamed.

A panoply of images raced through his mind, people and places and events cascading in a roaring torrent. Of some other person's past or pasts. Ribboning like wind-swept clouds racing in pursuit of a westering sun.

Drifting downward to the earth.

On the bank of an ancient pond, kneeling. Across the green water, another form.

The stillness of the pond was so absolute that he was moved to tears. A frog leapt into the water and ripples rolled out in an everwidening ellipse.

He watched the water, patiently awaiting his reflection.

Now not even a furrow disturbed the hard dazzle of the pond. Perhaps a hint of a breeze floated above the surface, silent and vigilant.

He did not know what to expect.

But even so—

He awoke to find Haneda altered.

Nikumu's high, open room was a litter of stone and wood. A holocaust had descended from the heavens. Or a titanic battle. Rage laced the room, a fine venomous dust hanging in the air. And a hate so strong that it beat on into the night. Haneda was a shambles.

He was alone.

All the castle, sheared and ruined, echoed to his heavy footfalls. Small fires danced where torches had been flung, guttering in the welter of powdered stone and mortar.

Naked, he descended what was left of the staircase, leaping the last four meters into the midst of the cryptomeria wood.

There were none to see him. Not a sparrow, not an owl. Not this night. Even the bats had fled in terror.

Through the fragrant, silent wood and out across the wide marsh. Above him, geese rode before the silver horns of the moon. The sky's glittering face seemed to pulse.

The long reeds rustled, their pale stalks illuminated by the fitful light of fireflies. The cicadas wailed shrilly.

He began to run, eastward, broaching at length the verge of the veldt. He lengthened his strides, exulting in his indefatigable strength, and he crossed the plain, leaving the sensation of time behind him.

To the deep blue slopes of the mountain.

Fujiwara.

He commenced to climb and as he did a painting grew in his mind, a work of great design and harmonious colors.

The clear air turned chill. The stars signaled their ancestral message as he went up the face of Fujiwara.

His coming was as silent as an animal's passage across the floor of a jungle and, as he neared the rim of heaven, he could see the stars in the east fade and wink out. A rush of wind. A storm was coming.

At last he reached the cold purple summit of Fujiwara, crunched through the pale lavender snow.

It began to rain, despite the cold, the clouds roiling, seeming so close to his head that he was almost within their wreath.

He lifted his long arms as if to grab handfuls of moisture and at that instant the sky opened itself to him. Rain like platinum lances whipped his face and body.

And he lived now a moment that had come to him many times within his mind, in another lifetime, when he had been someone else.

Pink lightning gyred in the sky, an unearthly bridge and he began to laugh as the power surged through him and had his heart been an entirely human organ, it would have been split apart by the enormous force which rang through him. But Ronin was no more and he who stood atop Mount Fujiwara, the center of this startling storm, just below the billowing black and crimson clouds, ghostly ships shifting on a restless sea, was no longer truly human.

I am the Sunset Warrior, he thought ecstatically, marveling at the jump of his massive muscles, which stretched over his altered form with electric energy. I am come: let The Dolman beware.

Through the corrugate corridors of Time, he heard music from an age long destroyed or again not yet formed. Thick, wailing voices, replicated, mirrored, supported by instruments that seemed as if they created energy. The music skirled and thundered, aligning itself to his heartbeat. Crash like an exploding hillside.

Lightning crackled around his glistening shoulders.

Dor-Sefrith? He called silently.

But only the hissing of the rain pelting the mountain's summit and the cracked rumble of the echoing thunder answered him. And he stood, immobile, realizing at last that he must now make his own answers. He was now only partly Ronin the seeker, was as much Setsoru, the founder.

What else waited for him?

He shrugged.

He was the Sunset Warrior.

With that realization, he willed his mind to relax, and as he let go of the comforting poles linking him to the physical world, his power was unleashed and his consciousness whirled inward to the core of his existence, where Ronin had feared to look, and he found at last the glittering axis of his power, the still center in the rushing vortex of constant energy. He reached out calm hands to embrace it.

Eternity.

Three

KAI-FENG

Horse Latitudes

THE shimmering gray ice had crept southward during the long, agonizing time of the Kai-feng. As the three Makkon became stronger with the imminent arrival of their liege, as The Dolman swept toward the world from which he had once been banished, bent on a hideous vengeance, so the deathshead warriors burst from the confines of their spreading encampment. Led by great beasts with faceted eyes and shining blue-green carapaces, these warriors hurled themselves across the littered plain and against the high stone walls of Kamado, the last citadel of man.

Behind the deathshead warriors came the creaking and trundling of immense machines of war, designed to eject threescore pikes at a burst in a trajectory that would take them over the highest fortress wall, or hurtle liters of scalding liquid metal at oncoming warriors. There were towering scaffoldings housing immense horizontal pendulums sheathed in thick metal at one end. And more. Pulled by the dissolute and bedraggled hordes of the northern hill tribes, inveigled into The Dolman's employ by promises of power. So the world of man shuddered on its axis as if it knew by the quaking movement of these vast machines of war the impending doom rushing headlong to its curving hazed surface.

The fourth Makkon was about to arrive upon the continent of man.

And the last allies of The Dolman were called forth, those who had waited in secret for the time of the Kai-feng. Arming themselves, they traveled across frozen, bitter land, turbulent, violent seas, by means neither human nor readily understandable.

The Aegir, adrift in the deep, was preoccupied with more important matters. It did not hinder their progress yet it was aware of them, since all karma is intertwined. It was content to be the protector of its murderer.

With the coming of The Dolman's last allies to the flaming continent of man, the penultimate step had been taken to ensure the defeat of mankind. They watched with baleful, emotionless eyes, the torn, scarred face of the land, smoldering, ashen, blasted, a ribboning triptych through which they traveled, thinking only of their destination, a forest's verge, blind to the piles of rotting corpses alive with gorging rats and nervous wolves. They were deaf to the pitiable cries of the old, the infirm, and the very young wretched creatures who had somehow escaped the slaughter. They rode onward. Assembling, the vultures began their spiraling descent.

As the last allies of The Dolman made their arcane way across the continent of man, Kiri, the Empress of Sha'angh'sei, was returning northward to Kamado. She rode at the head of a vast column of warriors more than a kilometer in length. On either side of her rode two contrasting figures, though both were powerful leaders. On her right was an enormously fat man with keen, intelligent eyes and a forbidding manner. He was Du-Sing, taipan of Sha'angh'sei's Greens. On her left was a small, slightly built individual with a flat nose and flowing wispy beard trailing from his strong chin. He was Lui Wu, taipan of the Reds, who held sway in Sha'angh'sei's outlying northern districts. Now, after countless centuries as mortal enemies, the taipans of the Ching Pang and the Hung Pang rode together as did their men behind them. Kiri, who had united them in the common battle, dug her boot heels into the sweating flanks of her saffron luma, as if eager for the stench of Kamado, the clangor of the Kaifeng. Du-Sing took off after her, leaning forward in his saddle, the tourmaline which hung around his neck like a miniature sun, spinning with the motion. And Lui Wu, signaling to the trailing column to pick up the pace, rattled his reins, talking softly to his mount, urging him over the last rise toward Kamado.

Upon gaining the high ground that led to the great pine forest, one of the last allies of The Dolman broke away from the others, sought out the three Makkon.

Past tall, gaunt deathshead warriors with the deadly spiked globes swinging from worn leather braces tied about their narrow hips, past creatures with elongated skulls topped by plumes which flowed down to the center of their backs, past short, squat warriors with close-set eyes as dull as death, past beings who looked more like gargantuan insects than they did men.

He found these most powerful of all creatures save The Dolman himself in the frigid forest's center, waiting for their last brother. A chill wind swept sheets of snow high into the air like giant wraiths.

The Makkon's alien orange eyes, so terrifying, raked the shivering, snow-laden pines for a tangible sign of his arrival, for with it would begin the Summoning, when at last The Dolman would stand again upon the world of man.

"I am here," said the ally.

One hideous, beaked head turned slowly in his direction. The slitted pupils pulsed. The great tail snapped back and forth. He inhaled their stench.

The gray beak opened and a shrill screaming, inimical to human ears, came forth. But he had been trained, thus he heard:

"Yes. We know. We brought you on His instruction."

"Is he coming?"

"Would you doubt, fool? It has been promised, thus it shall be. Even Time may not interfere now." The orange eyes glowed. "You are held to your vow." The outlines of the Makkon pulsed in and out of focus. "You know the penalty if you fail—"

"You need not—"

The screaming increased to an unbearable level.

"You shall pray for death!"

"There are too many centuries of planning. I shall not fail. And then—"

The alien head swiveled away from him for a moment and it was as if a great weight had been lifted from him.

"Our brother comes now. Leave us at once. Go to the southern verge of the wood. You shall command the central strike force at the time of the Master's choosing. There will be direct communication with further orders. Now go, for no mortal may witness what is about to take place."

"But I am not—"

"Go!"

And he went away from them, through the maze of the forest, at length rejoining the others, leading them southward into the vast, seething camp of the legions of The Dolman. And, using a smooth voice born to command, he set about deploying the warriors in his command for the coming conflagration. And all the while, he chuckled to himself, hugging the horde of his secret knowledge tightly to his mailed breast.

There came a screaming from the forest of pines north of Kamado. In its center stood the four Makkon, joined at last. Their outlines pulsed irregularly, then beat more swiftly as their curved beaks worked against the air as if it were a substance inimical to them.

As one, they called out again and again, setting a rhythm.

Cold fire streaked downward from somewhere past the heavens.

Within the high yellow walls of Kamado, the forces of man rejoiced at the coming of the Greens and the Reds and the safe return of Kiri. And that gray, snow-filled night, the oil lamps burned bright and long, flickering against the gathering gloom, as the rikkagin and taipan met to decide upon their strategies for repulsing the dawn attack.

Later, with the low ruffling skies turned red by a chill unnatural sleet, Kiri climbed the ramparts of the citadel. Her footsteps were hushed in the snow covering the stone.

Rikkagin T'ien, whom she called Tuolin, met her along the northern rampart and there they sat beneath a sharply angled overhang, listening to the harsh rattle of the sleet, looking out at the wood where the enemy was encamped.

Kiri was reminded of another night when she had sat atop the same ramparts with Ronin, knowing that she had lost him forever to the unknown quest which drove him.

When Matsu had been slain by the Makkon in Sha'angh'sei, part of her had died. It could not have been otherwise. Without Matsu, she was but half a person. Both had known the perils of such a life—and the fierce, intense joys—and thus had they each guarded the other most closely and carefully. But the Makkon had destroyed all that when it ripped Matsu's soft white throat from the tendons of her neck. Because of Ronin. For it was searching madly for him.

Yet as she stared now into the dense wood alive with the minions of death and destruction, she felt only an overwhelming desire for him. She could sleep with other men, suffer being separated from him for long periods of time, and would, she knew, betray even her own people for him. Because beyond all else she wanted him. Other emotions, curious and hateful to her now, swam within the dark depths of her being, yet she would not touch them or even acknowledge their existence. Thus she numbed herself with the suffering of her losses for she sensed for the first time that her ultimate undoing would come only if she allowed herself to feel deeply.

After a time, she pulled forth from her heavy robe a long pipe and filled it carefully from a small leather pouch. She lit it from a small covered oil lamp.

She inhaled deeply, holding the smoke for long moments, reluctantly letting it go, her breath hissing in the night, a brief white mist dissipating upon the wet, frigid air. She heard the sound of distant voices and did not care, past knowing even whether they were her own creation.

Idly, she considered taking a long puff and never exhaling. An endless ecstasy-filled corridor. She wished to do this for she sensed dimly yet deeply the incipience of a personal tragedy infinitely more terrifying than the Kai-feng, to which she was now as indifferent as all the other outside elements of life. But, bitterly, she knew that her body would betray her and that with the soft furry smoke filling up all her lungs and all her body, entering her bloodstream, with consciousness failing, her automatic reflexes would take over and she would exhale without conscious volition. The organism, at least, wished to survive.

Beside her, Tuolin stared at her beautiful profile, pale in the red light of the sleet storm. Far way, across the blood-drenched field, in the deep shadows of the pine forest, something was happening. He felt the ground shudder. Still, his thoughts centered on her. What was she thinking?

He had known Kiri for a long time, for as long as he had been in Sha'angh'sei, for as long as he had been waging war, longer than he cared to remember. He knew her as the owner of Sha'angh'sei's finest house of pleasure. She was also the city's Empress. But, being a military man, this meant little to him. Titles were for figureheads. He was impressed only by deeds; talk was for those who were weak, afraid to act.

The best-known tale concerning him was told constantly throughout his company of warriors until it had taken on the patina of legend. Tuolin had overheard one of his men boasting about his exploits on the battlefield and, without comment, he had sliced off the man's head. This one superb action was more eloquent, more precise in its fierce and uncompromising statement than anything he could have said to admonish his men for that abuse of the warrior's power. It was also infinitely more effective.

He leaned over and quietly watched the last of the sweet smoke drift from the black split between her immobile lips. Her large violet eyes were glazed as she peered inward at the mystery of her self.

Gently, he opened her robe and eased her down into the snow. Slowly, her white arms came around him and drew him down to her waiting loins. His mouth opened, pressed her cool lips.

He wrapped the corners of her robe around their moving bodies.

Their terrible voices raised louder and the trees around them burst into frigid flames. The pulsing of the Makkon's bodies became more rapid and now explosions burst within the forest, splitting the trunks of the ancient pines.

Through their chants, they felt the vibrations begin, rolling outward from the epicenter at the forest's heart. All about them, the pines were aflame.

They redoubled their efforts.

A howling, from far away, from the throat of neither man nor beast.

They stood linked by their cruel talons, in the center of the flaming forest, hearing the sizzle of the sleet as it hit the cold fire, hearing the grinding of shifting rock, hearing the shriek of their own voices.

Their hideous cries echoed through the burning wood, the pale chill fire arcane and terrifying, and at last, all air was banished from the vicinity. Then all color. Then all light.

A darkness deeper than night, deeper than sleep, vaster than death, stretched itself upon the flaming skeleton of the dying pine forest, bending, lapping, flowing. Growing.

The Dolman.

Perhaps it was the lightning and thunder talking to him that ultimately led him, like a blind man, downward to a great ledge on the eastern face of Fujiwara, still quite near the snow summit.

Set upon the ledge was a wooden house with an obliquely sloping roof and a long terrace overlooking the sheer side of the mountain and the mist-shrouded valley at its feet.

At the rear of the house, the rock face had been cleared

away to make room for an enormous glazed chimney of green brick. Before it had been built a great forge.

Red sparks leapt upward into the roiling darkness in concert with the echoing sounds of violent hammering.

He approached the terraced side of the house and, mounting several wide slatted wood stairs, entered the house.

Three robed women met him. They appeared tiny beside his great frame. They seemed unconcerned by his nakedness. Their dark brown robes swirled as they bowed to him, ushering him down a dark hall and into the bath. It was only when he had climbed into the tub and they turned away from him for a moment that he saw the interlaced ellipses embroidered on the backs of their robes, soft green fans.

They dried him carefully and he donned a robe they held out for him, woven of swirling colors so cleverly constructed that he could not tell where one left off and another began.

They led him through the interior of the house. It was sparsely and simply furnished with tatamis upon the wooden floor and small lacquered tables. Upon the walls were prints of travelers upon two roads, one mountainous, the other winding by the sea.

At length, they reached the rear, where sparks flew and the heat was intense. They left him there and he went slowly down the steps. The high chimney loomed over his head.

Bellows moved.

Hammer hit upon the flat anvil and pink and yellow sparks shot into the air like fireworks.

A figure, bare to the waist, wearing black silk pants, faced away from him, working before the forge. Long black hair with deep blue highlights flowed down like an animal's mane. The shoulders were wide, the waist narrow, a scabbard sword hung from one hip—

The figure turned to him. Her bare breasts glistened. Her dark candid eyes stared up at him. Her wide lips curved into a smile. She lifted the great glowing hammer.

"Almost finished," she said in a rich musical voice, and he started, believing for a moment that he knew her. "You came not a moment too soon." She pointed to a rough-hewn wooden table to her right. "The short one's ready."

He went to the table, picked up the scabbarded sword, and slowly withdrew it. The long, slightly curving blade reflected the forge's glow, spangling the charged air.

He strapped the scabbard about his hip, spread his legs,

made several flashing cuts in the night. He felt its weight and balance, satisfied. Then sheathed it.

He was about to turn away when a shadow on the table top caught his eye and he reached out wonderingly. It was another Makkon gauntlet, seemingly the mate to the one on his left hand.

"By all means, put it on," said the smithy. "He left it here for you, after all."

They stared at each other for a moment.

"You know," she said, "you look different than I had imagined. Almost unfinished—" She shrugged.

"And you," he said, drawing on the second gauntlet, walking toward her, "you seem so familiar that I—"

"Here, look at this."

He stood behind her, watched her work, because it was what she wanted. She held in her hands a sword over one third again as long as the one he now wore, which she had called "the short one." The metal of its blade was blue-green down its center, but a glowing lavender along the honed double edges. The guard had been lovingly crafted of a carved piece of lapis lazuli reinforced by an inner core of metal. The hilt was constructed of a black metal center surrounded by sea-green jade, beveled and polished to a high gloss.

With a hiss and a turbulent cloud of white steam, the smithy doused the blade in a barrel of water. She wiped it with a chamois cloth before locking it onto the anvil. From a lacquered iron box near the forge, she withdrew an implement somewhat akin to a knife, using it to scrape down the length of each edge of the blade. Next, she produced a long file which she used to further refine the keen edges. When she was satisfied, she unstrapped the sword and took it a short distance to a wooden framework within which rested a gleaming stone. Mirrored chips danced in the light. By using her foot on a pedal, she caused the stone to revolve at a remarkably high speed. Carefully, she drew the blade across the surface of the stone.

Sparks flew like hot snow.

Again and again and again.

He became dizzy with the watching and he turned away, lifting up his eyes to the towering summit of Fujiwara high above his head. The clouds had rolled away on a high dry wind and he could once again see the glittering spray of stars, blue-white and terribly clear in the thin air. Perhaps they held a message for him. But he was certain now that they contained no answers, for as long as man reigned here, there would be mysteries.

At length, the smithy turned the edges of the blade to an oiled stone for polishing and, finally, she returned to the anvil, strapping it down again, rubbing its entire length with composed flakes.

She bent over and engraved her signature on the tang, then burnished the entire blade with a polishing needle.

She turned, handed it to him.

He took it, the weight an ecstasy to him, and as he held it up, he saw for the first time, within the shining face of his newly forged blade, his image.

His eyes were the palest lavender, speckled with gold around the rims of the large irises. They were long and almond-shaped. His angular forehead gave way to a mane of silky black hair, which fell unbound down to his shoulders. His skin was tawny. His cheekbones high and hard. But beyond these features, he could not understand the strange configuration of his face and he looked abruptly away, into the eyes of the blacksmith, dark as olives.

She stared at him placidly but, whirling into their depths, he beheld a ferocious force bound, quivering, in check. A dark, febrile force which he recognized.

Vengeance.

And what else did they share?

"Who are you?" he said.

"Are you pleased with your new weapons?"

"Yes, very much."

"Good," she said, laughing, her breasts shaking provocatively, and she led him back into the house.

The robed women stripped off her pants and it was then that he saw that they were held in place by an oval lapis pin.

And as she climbed into the steaming, fragrant, polished wooden tub, the memory surfaced in a rainbow flash, a flying fish breaking the roll of a stormy sea, an instant's sharp vision from another's lifetime.

"No," he said. "It cannot be. It cannot."

Her body seemed smaller now, pale and firm, the sweat washed from its gleaming surface, glowing with the stimulation of the rough sponges of her servants.

"I saw you die—felt the ribbons of your flesh and blood all—"

She held out her arms and called to him:

"Enough, now. I am the blacksmith; you are the sorcerer."

They took his robe from him and she gasped at his strange form, her dark eyes glowing.

"I do not understand," he whispered. "Dor-Sefrith is the sorcerer."

He climbed into the bath with her.

She kissed his strange lips, crying out as they touched, put her mouth against his ear.

"But he is no more." A breath as soft as dawn.

Her strong fingers exploring such a singular terrain.

His hands moved down her back, caressing her spine. Her eyes closed. They kissed again, their bodies sinking down into the slapping water. The turbulence increased.

Kneeling, the robed women wiped at the gathering moisture with new sponges.

He slept in her enormous bed while time stood still, while his body adjusted itself, completed the last of its healing, while she finished her exquisite, arduous task.

And when at length he awoke, the armor was ready for him.

He was dressed in black lacquer breastplate banded in lapis lazuli and sea-green jade. The scabbard for his great sword was of silver and streaked malachite in alternating bands. He was weaponed now on each hip, the shorter sword on his right, the great blade on his left.

The blacksmith placed the high curving helm of red jade and burnished copper upon his head. And all at once, he was eager to depart, to descend the mountain, to leave Ama-no-mori. The urgency of the Kai-feng swept over him like a tide. He was aware too that much more than a confrontation with The Dolman lay before him. He knew that without him the last remaining might of man would perish in the Kai-feng, yet he understood also that at every step he must be aware of his actions and of those about him—the very acuteness of his power necessitated that—for in his regained newness had come the knowledge of the complexity of life. Just as no one was forged by one event so no one was created for solely one purpose, not even the Sunset Warrior.

Fully garbed, he stood waiting.

The smithy dropped her arms to her side.

She shook her head, her long, dark hair waving like an undersea fan.

And she made a movement. Just a blur. Swift and threatening, she lunged at him with her sword.

Nerves willed muscles to instantaneous motion while the brain still mused. Thought drifted behind like a scarlet streamer, unwillingly forgotten, as his arm, his hand, his fingers, thus his blade turned to a platinum blur.

His eyes caught the dazzle of sunlight upon a choppy sea, just behind her, as the superbly honed sword shot through her body.

Red strung the air between them, as startling as the vermilion in the snow print upon her wall.

It splashed hotly onto his face, into his eyes, and he plummeted downward with a sharp sense of vertigo, crying, plunging at last into the deep, deep green of the sea.

Once again he found himself at the foundations of the world. They were still enormous yet now so too was he and he swam lazily through the colossal edifices, searching.

At length, he found the Aegir, the limitless landscape of its gently curving side, pulsing slightly with the breath of life, the rough hide rippling, and he swam along its length with great powerful strokes which seemed to carry him leagues with each kick.

He knew the way now even though the path seemed endless. Twisting through the foundations of the world, following the sinuous route, he went deeper and deeper, across shale shelves, below barrier reefs, past the black trenches, mysterious doorways, to the core of the world.

In time he gazed upon the head of the Aegir, so huge that he could not even make out the end of its snout. He was filled with infinite sadness and a great exhilaration as he lifted the great blade over his high helm. He struck downward, into the Aegir's brain with a mighty blow.

The body writhed, the head flew apart, smashing into him in great severing hunks. He gasped, no longer able to breathe, and swallowed convulsively. Water filled him.

Whole, she stood before him, smiling.

He looked from her to the long blue-green blade, dripping blood upon her tatamis. He was drenched in sea water.

"So now it is named and is truly yours," she said. "A soul of steel."

Still he stared at the shimmering blade.

"What is its name?"

"*Aka-i-tsuchi*," he said, not looking up.

Her head bowed before the weapon.

"I pity your enemies."

* * *

"Can she be of aid to us?" said Rikkagin Aerent.

"Now that The Dolman has come, I doubt if anyone can be of help." Tuolin stared out at the last of the cold flames.

"You know—"

"Yes, brother, I am aware that is not what you meant." The pine forest was but smoking charcoal now. "These are dismal days. We are all in ill humor." He turned from the scene to the north and his outstretched arm swept across the buildings of Kamado, whose inner porticoes were pillared with the images of the ancient gods of war. "They can no longer aid us and I fear that the weapons of man will not be enough to prevail over these sorcerous creatures." Still his eyes darted back and forth, met his brother's steady gaze only fleetingly. "You have seen as well as I have what those deathshead warriors can do to our men. They do not bleed and their strength is inhuman. If we but had a defense that would stop them."

Rikkagin Aerent put his strong arm about his brother's sinewy shoulders. Both men were tall and muscular. Tuolin, with his close-cropped blond hair was obviously the younger, for Rikkagin Aerent was already graying; his strong face with its curving nose and full beard bore the seams and scars of many campaigns. He turned Tuolin away from the darkness of the buildings, away from the somber streets of Kamado with their pin points of yellow and orange light.

"Tuolin, it is time we forgot the intervention of gods and sorcery. All of that belongs to another age, when other men, far different from ourselves, walked the world—"

"I do not think that they were so different from us except that they wielded more power."

"Oh no, they were as different from us as we are from the deathshead warriors out there. They were bound to serve, Tuolin. Our lot is not to throw ourselves upon the hard earth and grovel before a carved figure nor to mumble incantations from some rotting scroll. The world has changed. Our Laws will no longer tolerate sorcery's proliferation."

"Then what of The Dolman?"

"The end of a life long past its time. The Dolman was created in a forgotten age. He could not be birthed now. We shall destroy him and his legions." But Rikkagin Aerent's voice seemed brittle and hollow on this sorcerous night, even to himself.

After a time, he followed Tuolin down the wide stairway to the high ramparts, into the dark streets.

"Tell me," he said gently, "why she troubles you."

Tuolin sighed.

"Her soul has died. Or at least something important inside her."

"What happened?"

"Someone was killed. A woman, very close to her." He turned his head away, the small ivory bar run through the lobe of his ear flashing in the torchlight for a moment. "I knew them both"—he laughed bitterly—"I was about to say 'well,' but it is not the truth. I knew them a long time, that was all. I never bothered to understand their relationship clearly—"

"What of the other one?"

"Matsu?" Tuolin shrugged awkwardly. "I should have suspected that night when I first took Ronin to Tenchō. Matsu gave him a strangely patterned robe and then he asked for Kiri. What a fool, I thought. But she took him—"

"Why?"

"I do not know but I think that Matsu signaled her. They are linked, the three of them, in some curious way—"

"But Matsu was slain, you said."

"And now she will not talk about it." He meant Kiri. "Perhaps they were sisters."

"Why does it matter?"

A dog barked angrily. A smithy's hammer sounded, an echoing wail in the dense night.

"I feel like I am choking. This weather is unnatural."

"About Kiri," Rikkagin Aerent prompted.

"Why are you so interested in her?" said Tuolin, turning toward him. Rikkagin Aerent noted the gaunt cheeks, the hollowness around the eyes. His gaze took in the slight rise of the right shoulder and he wondered if his brother's wounds were healing satisfactorily.

"I care about you, that is all. I wish to know the cause of your melancholy. If you desire Kiri now, you need but ask. Once she was untouchable. She gives you—"

"Her body. There is nothing left but the shell—"

"She gives you what she can," Rikkagin Aerent said relentlessly.

"Not enough," Tuolin breathed. "It is the ghost of a half-remembered past only."

Rikkagin Aerent heard the bitter tone of his brother's voice and silently he mourned for him.

"I have nothing," Tuolin whispered. "Nothing."

"Yet she lives." Rikkagin Aerent gripped his brother's

arms. "She breathes, her heart pumps, she thinks. Find the way—"

But Tuolin was already shaking his head.

"It has died within her."

"Fool not to see what is directly before you!"

The clang of a bell came between them. The solid tramp of booted feet, somewhat muffled. The watch changed.

Rikkagin Aerent ran a hand through his hair and in a softer tone said, "Tuolin, I wish you would speak to her—"

"About what?"

"Ronin. She was closest to him, you said so yourself. Nothing has been heard of him since he was seen leaving the eastern edge of the forest. That was many moons ago. Perhaps he went for reinforcements after he slew the Hart. Perhaps she knows—"

Tuolin shoved his brother aside.

"Why do you not ask her yourself?" His angry voice drifted off dully into the fogbound night.

She kissed him tenderly and he closed his lids to his reflection in her eyes. Her lips were incredibly soft. His long arms went about her body.

His mouth broke away for something more important. To say it.

"How can I leave you?"

She took his arm and they went out onto the long balcony, staring out at the calmness, the last frosted shreds of the long night. They felt, rather than saw, the vast bulk of Fujiwara looming over them on their left.

Space.

They floated, a pair of powerful eagles, in the thin, charged air.

Her slender hands roamed his body, exploring still. She was a delighted child. And he, transported by the knowledge of her.

"Did he do this to you?" he said. "Dor-Sefrith?"

Did her head nod imperceptively?

"But how? And why?"

"You already know the way." She held him close to her. "As for the how—" She shrugged. "There is no telling, really."

"But I—he saw you—"

She turned to him. "And I see you now." Her fingers stroked his arms. "Would you have me ask who you are?" She shook her head. "You are no longer Ronin. You are—more complete. But Ronin is still there, his essence did not perish with his body. He is but a part now. So too with me."

"But what are you a part of?"

She climbed his body, kissed him again.

He felt a wetness on his cheeks.

His strong, strange fingers twined in her long hair. He searched her eyes.

"How can I leave you?" he said again.

"Soon," she whispered. "Soon."

It was but half a cry.

He had made but a third of the circuit around the vast citadel's ramparts when he saw her. She was leaning against the chill stone, her back to the cold conflagration of the pine forest. Her deep purple cloak was wrapped tightly about her body.

"Tuolin said that I might find you here."

Her head turned but her eyes did not move. They observed him impassively.

"I am always here at night," she said softly.

Below them, Kamado was still quiet, despite the first predawn stirrings of the cooks and grooms. Farther away, the snortings and stampings of the horses caused him to think momentarily of her extraordinary mount: a saffron luma. He had long wished to own such a steed. He had never even ridden one.

"He has changed so much in so little time." He sat beside her, so close that her hair, caught by the damp wind, brushed his face. "I hardly recognize him."

Kiri laughed humorlessly and he shivered at the sound.

"I can hardly recognize myself. We have all changed. The Kai-feng—"

"My brother has lived with war all his life, Kiri. The Kai-feng is but the last. It is not battle that makes him sad." And then after a moment: "He loves you."

"Yes. I know." Her voice so low, he barely heard her.

"You will destroy him."

"I am not an evil person," she said, almost to herself.

"It is not you," said Rikkagin Aerent. "The circumstances—" But he broke off, for he did not believe those words himself.

"But it *is* me! You must understand. *He* must understand. You must tell him. I am useless now, worse than useless for I no longer care—about anything, not the Kai-feng, not my people, not Tuolin—"

He watched the silent tears running down her cheeks. Even then she appeared beautiful.

"I fear for him." His voice clogged with emotion. "He thinks of you only. In the morning, when we go out to battle, he must be clear of mind. Only that and his skill as a warrior will keep him alive. He is my whole family—" Too late, he remembered and stopped awkwardly.

She did not wipe at the tears. Nor did she look at him.

"Leave him be," he said, not unkindly.

Her eyes closed, the long lashes jeweled in the damp night.

"What power I once had has been stripped from me," she whispered. "He will do what he must."

"Will you bring him down with you?"

She lurched to her feet, spun away from the wall where he still sat. Her head whipped at him and he felt the splattering of hot tears on his face.

"What do you want of me?"

Abruptly, he was fed up with her self-pity. He stood up, his tall frame seeming to explode with energy. She paused, a frightened doe mesmerized by bright torchlight.

"Be a woman, not a terrified child! If you wish to die, take a knife and plunge it into your own belly. At least, if you wish to live, have the decency not to destroy those around you—!"

"I wish only for time to reverse itself, for Matsu to be here with me, for Ronin to—" She turned away from him. Her hands gripped the icy stone of the parapet like claws.

He came up behind her and she winced at the force of his words, as if he were beating her physically.

"You disgust me! How many more miracles would you like? He fights here for the future of all man and you pray to your private gods to return your dead sister—!"

"She was not my sister!" And she turned on him, her fists beating against his chest. She was strong and her violence startled him. He stumbled backward against the assault, for she was a warrior also, and now she was unleashed, a ferocious, deadly animal, pounding him as he fell, straddling him, beating him, her violet eyes ablaze with anger and frustration and despair.

But the mauling was a small price to pay, he felt, for what he was learning.

"Bastard!" she cried. "Bastard! She was me! She was me!"

His nose cracked from a sharp blow and the skin along one

cheek ripped as her knuckles skidded along it. Still he put up only token defense. She split his lower lip, screaming at him, and, at last, she collapsed on his chest, gasping and sobbing, her hair wet with perspiration.

He said nothing, lay there feeling the blood seeping down his neck, onto his robe, under his breastplate. He breathed through his mouth, his puffed and swollen lips open wide.

She sat up.

"Do you understand now?" he said softly.

She sat very straight, her eyes closed.

"What is false and what is true?"

"I no longer know who I am."

He got up from under her.

She opened her eyes, gasped at her handiwork.

"Oh!"

"Where did Ronin go, Kiri?"

She reached down for a handful of snow, applied it to his nose. It turned pink.

"Far, far away, I think. I do not know where. But I am certain of one thing." She applied ice to his split lip. "He will return."

It was only then that she wiped the drying tears from her cheeks.

At first snow swirled about him, pearled and soft in the pink glow of dawn. But as he descended, he found himself immersed in clouds where all was diffuse and misty.

Soon, she had said. *Soon*. What was behind those eyes as dark as olives?

Lost in the clouds, he thought of the Aegir, who had aided him for so long when he was Ronin. He had recognized, even as he had slain it—the first blood, anointing his long blue-green blade, which she had engraved with the name *Aka-i-tsu-chi*, the ancient Bujun words meaning: Red Tidings—the being billowing darkly in the water far below his battered felucca, as he had made his unknowing way to Sha'angh'sei. He knew also that it had been the Aegir who had saved Ronin from the sorcerous sailors of The Dolman sent by Setsoru to destroy him before he found Ama-no-mori. The creature had heaved its great coils, causing the unnatural tidal waves which had swept his ship from the enemy vessels over the sea to the distant reefs of Xich Chih.

And he had slain the Aegir.

Why?

Inwardly, he shrugged, letting it go, relaxing, circling inward to the glowing core of his being.

Out of the steamy clouds, their vast undersides lit with green lightning, and onto the lower reaches of the mountain, where the shivering turquoise pines spoke to him in restless sibilants. Down the treelined slopes of Fujiwara he went until the path became abruptly less steep and his speed increased.

In full armor, he went easily down the lower reaches of the mountain, treading his way through the thickening pines, inhaling their pungent mask, hearing the distant cries of the flying geese, the diurnal insects chirruping, all the minute quotidian sounds of the waking world.

And they were there, waiting for him, as he stepped from Fujiwara's last majestic pines: Moeru, Okami, and Azuki-iro.

They stared upward at him as he approached and he saw Okami and Azuki-iro lower their eyes, not in awe but in respect for the last myth of their people, alive and standing before them.

"It is he who stops the darkness," whispered Okami. "It is the Sunset Warrior."

"Nikumu succeeded," said Azuki-iro, "as I knew he must. He was Bujun, our traditions were too deeply embedded within him, Karma. Now history shall honor him."

"Haneda is gone," said the Sunset Warrior. "Some vast, terrible struggle took place there while I was being born."

"Both Ronin and Nikumu have been buried beneath the warm ashes at Haneda," said Moeru quietly. "There a shrine will be built in the time to come."

"To dor-Sefrith," said the Sunset Warrior.

"To all the Bujun," said the Kunshin.

Silently, Moeru took a step forward, her gaze never leaving the strange countenance of the Sunset Warrior.

Azuki-iro turned to Okami.

"Come, my friend, it is time you and I rode for Eido. The daimyos are standing by and I must see to them." He took a small ivory oblong from the folds of his robe, handed it to Okami. "Take my chop and use it at the harbor master's. Instruct him in my name to prepare the ships. The Bujun join the Kai-feng now that the Sunset Warrior is come." He looked briefly upward to the amethyst slopes of Fujiwara high above them. "Truly the mountain has proved worthy of its name: 'Friend of Man.'"

They went without another word across the small field to where their horses stood tethered, chopping the sweet grass.

They mounted, swinging their steeds around, slapping their heels against the animals' flanks.

As they rode off across the wide undulating veldt, the Sunset Warrior turned his piercing gaze on the face of Moeru as if seeing it for the first time.

Morning had already broken and the oblique light bathed her face in pink and ocher. She turned away from his gaze and he watched her proud profile, the sweep of her neck as her hair fell away from her face, blown by the stiffening east wind. The tall pines stirred.

A rush of gray plovers took off over her shoulder, wheeling in the white sky. A mist was rising from the land.

"Why do you stare at me?" Moera said. "By rights it is I who should stare at you."

"You have been important to Ronin ever since he met you. Therefore you are important to me. I wish to know why."

She looked off into the distance, at the disappearing plovers.

"What happened to Nikumu?"

"He was the last of dor-Sefrith's line," said the Sunset Warrior. "Surely you knew that he was a warrior-mage, as the ancient Bujun used to be."

"He had used sorcery very little until quite recently."

"Yes. Of course dor-Sefrith knew of The Dolman, just as he knew that the Kai-feng would come. He was not immortal yet he knew that to ensure the safety of the Bujun and all man, he must somehow cheat death. Thus he worked his magic, thus each member of his family knew of his secrets, from generation to generation, and because he knew that his enemies were powerful and immortal, dor-Sefrith made plans within plans. I do not know them all. I know only what he told me."

Above them, the sky brightened, and the sun, clearing the forest's height, filled the morning with warmth. They began to walk toward two horses tethered some way across the field.

"Nikumu sensed the coming of the Kai-feng and thus it fell to him to summon dor-Sefrith. However, The Dolman was already more powerful than he anticipated and he was caught midway within the spell. While his concentration was taken up wholly by the difficult summoning, The Dolman invaded him." Moeru shivered involuntarily, put her arms about herself. "It was something of a deadlock. Dor-Sefrith became locked in insubstantial form—"

"The shade! It was he who I feared—"

"Yes, mistakenly. But you could not know of The Dolman. He was within Nikumu, attempting to exert his will, and dor-Sefrith, though he could speak, was powerless to aid Nikumu."

"But Ronin helped him, did he not?"

"Perhaps. In any event, you were right to urge him back to Haneda. He became the catalyst but, in the end, Azuki-iro was correct, it was Nikumu's battle. He had lost ground, assuming the leadership of the sasori, imprisoning you. You see, dor-Sefrith had counseled him to send you to the continent of man to find the Hart of Darkness—"

"Who?"

"Setsoru."

"Oh yes. I was close, finally, but I became embroiled in a battle with the Reds in the north. I slew three before I was knocked off my feet. Then the boot—"

"You were kicked in the head—"

"My memory. Setsoru?"

"I found him in the forest—Ronin—"

"Yes, you were so white— Where is he now?"

"We are together, Moeru. That is why Nikumu imprisoned you. First by taking your voice from you, then, in Haneda, binding you. The Dolman feared that Ronin would become this—" He tapped his chest.

"But what did that have to do with me?" said Moeru.

"Perhaps that is something that we both have to discover."

They reached the horses and mounted. The saddle was too small for him and he was obliged to fold his legs up so that his feet would take the stirrups.

"You were right, Moeru. Nikumu was a complex man. And a brave one. He could have killed Ronin and lived but the shame of that deed would not let him. He battled The Dolman with such ferocity that it allowed dor-Sefrith to return to life in his body—"

"But what happened at Haneda? The destruction—"

"It could only have been The Dolman. Perhaps he and dor-Sefrith fought while Ronin was dying."

"In that event—"

"Yes, I know. What was the outcome? Dor-Sefrith is no more."

Unaccountably, he thought then of another lifetime and the time he had shared with her. He debated asking her if she had loved Ronin but the question and thus the answer seemed as remote as yesterday's rain.

"No matter," he called to her, pulling on his reins. His mount trembled and reared. "I am here now. The Sunset Warrior is come to Ama-no-mori. For us, the Kai-feng!" Their horses leapt forward.

The wind shifted and he could smell, from a distant wooden edifice lying low on the veldt, the pungent fragrance of steaming tea.

In the great copper pot, rice was boiling. The flames licked lovingly at its blackened bottom. Steam rose up through the opened flue, into the massive chimney.

The cook wiped his hands on his greasy apron, turning away from the stacks of rough-hewn shallow wooden bowls stacked beside the high pile of firewood.

It was still early and the great room was empty. A yellow and gray dog wandered in from the narrow street, his nose close to the wooden floor, searching for food.

The cook yelled halfheartedly and, when the animal made no move, kicked out. The dog yelped as the toe of the cook's boot caught him in the ribs. His jagged claws skittered over the floor as the cook lashed out again, cursing. He went out onto the porch and sat, licking his bruised side.

Kiri came into the room from the street and the cook poured her some tea before he shuffled off into a corner near the fire to sleep before the breakfast rush.

She stood before the fire, feeling the heat but blind to its light. She sipped her tea mechanically.

When she had drained her cup, she took a bowl from the pile and, using a great black metal ladle, served herself a portion of the sticky rice. She went to a long table and sat, her bowl in front of her. She made no move to eat.

Someone came into the room, stood watching her back for a time, then came across the room, sat beside her.

Toulin poured himself some tea.

She felt her heart thudding beneath her robe as her pulse increased. She wanted to say something, but the unknown words stuck in her throat like cracked bones.

He would not look at her, nor would he speak, and thus they sat, as the great room began to teem with warriors who ate sitting or standing up, talking among themselves while the cook hastened to refill their bowls, knowing that they ate the first meal of a long day.

After a while, she got up, threaded her way through the throng.

Toulin reached out and touched her bowl of cold rice.

Standing in the prow of the Bujun flagship, *Shoju*, the Sunset Warrior gazed out onto the reaches of the glittering sea. The hot noon sun left a dazzling gilt path outward, eastward, behind him.

He faced west toward the continent of man and the Kai-feng.

He burned with anticipation.

Beside him stood Moeru, armored in breastplate of burnished metal banded with sea-green jade and mother-of-pearl. Her long black hair was tucked into her high copper helm. Two Bujun swords, one longer than the other, hung from her hips.

All about them was frantic motion, carefully coordinated and precise as the movements in the climax of a Noh play, as Bujun worked to set the vast armada's rigging.

Azuki-iro signed to him and Moeru murmured, "We are ready."

There came a shout, repeated endlessly, like the crying of the wheeling gulls circling their masts.

A rhythmic singing began as Bujun bowed over the great flat windlasses on their ships and with creaks and groans the wheels turned, bringing up the heavy chains of the anchors from the harbor's floor.

The Bujun's song, exciting and melodic, filled the air, already rich with salt and phosphorus.

The last of the mooring lines were cast off and made fast.

Bujun raced through the rigging.

The water was black with the bulk of the armada, stretching away and away, westward.

He looked to port and starboard, at the fifty score Bujun ships, cast off now from Ama-no-mori, rocking gently off the coast of Eido.

"It will take too long," Moeru said. "How will we ever reach the continent of man in time?"

"Nichiren," he said.

He left her, the sunlight spinning madly off her ebon armor, white plumes shooting from his high helm.

He braced himself against the base of the bowsprit of the *Shoju*.

He drew forth his blue-green blade, *Aka-i-tsuchi*, pale lavender running down its long double edges. With both hands, he reached it forth, over the sea.

He closed his eyes.

And the last legacy of his beastly protector flowed up from the dark depths, called by *Aka-i-tsuchi*, by his mind.

In the east, clouds formed along the horizon, building steep and purple. Yet where the ships rocked gently in the water, the sun shone hotly.

It grew quite calm, not a breath of air stirring.

The clouds writhed out of the east, rushing at the fleet.

The first hint of a wind from the east.

"Break out all sail!" called the Kunshin.

The east wind began to rise, cool, alive with electric intimations, filling all who felt its touch with a peculiar exhilaration.

The darkening clouds now raced across all the skies for as far as they could see. Pink lightning crackled, thunder wailed, echoing across the sea.

The wind tore at the armada.

With that, the Kunshin gave the last sign and the ships rushed out to meet the storm.

The seas heaved and the wind howled through the rigging, straining the sails to their limit, and the vast Bujun fleet leapt westward across the storm-tossed ocean of periwinkle and deep lavender, racing faster than any ships made by the hands of man.

Moeru stood in the bow of the *Shoju*, just behind the tall figure standing athwart the base of the bowsprit, watching the unnatural light undulate along the great blue-green blade, and what thoughts at that moment ran through her mind, none could say, not even the Sunset Warrior.

Nemesis

THERE was a man within the teeming camp of The Dolman who stayed close to certain people even though they were relative newcomers to the army. Obviously, they were leaders. And they did not stink like the other generals. In fact, as far as the man could tell, they were human.

The man was tall and thin, his muscles hard and ropy. His face, with its long, drooping mustache, was gaunt and haunted. Deep within, he mourned for his people and that aching frustration was built until it became an emotion so bitter that he could not bear to live with it. In desperate self-defense he had turned it outward, into implacable hatred so that at least he could wake each morning and not plunge a short sword into his lower belly.

Po had long ago aligned himself with the Reds of the northern provinces for he detested the fat hongs and eager rikkagin who held sway within the walls of Sha'angh'sei.

As a trader, he made frequent journeys to the continent of man's richest city, was even welcome within the houses of many of its wealthiest and most influential citizens, high up in the walled city district. He forced himself to fall neatly into the guise of a successful trader from the north, burying his hate by looking to the future—the future that was now—remaining sharp-tongued but carefully concealing his true feelings.

Yet, as the time of the Kai-feng drew nigh, as his time in the north revealed to him the true nature of the burgeoning battle, while those seemingly secure in their palatial homes in Sah'angh'sei grew fat and complacent, his temper writhed upon its tight leash, burning bright. Thus, when he had been insulted—or rather, when his taut nerves had caused him to believe he had been insulted—he had lashed out, spilling his guts, insulting in kind the people assembled at Llowan's dinner party. And so he had forever been banned from Llowan's home. He had castigated himself for days for his foolish lack of control. In disgust, he slew three Greens on the northern outskirts of the city. Then he vowed that never again would his emotions betray him.

Now, as he picked his teeth after a satisfying meal over a fragrant pine fire, he knew that it no longer mattered. At last the war for liberation was here and soon the rebel army, as he chose to call it, would break through Kamado's defenses. All Sha'angh'sei stood before him, waiting like a fat jewel to be plundered. These aliens, he knew, had no interest in either silver or the poppy, had not, he suspected, even the intelligence to understand the concept of wealth. No, these peculiar creatures lived only to kill and when they had sated themselves on the blood and the gore they would return to whatever hellholes out of which they had first crawled. He shuddered. Oh, how they stank! Then he thought of the wealth that would soon be his. With it he would assume control of the war-torn city, establish a new line for his people. They would stream in from the hills in the west, becoming proud and powerful within the confines of the new Sha'angh'sei. And the fat hongs would be the first to die under his regime. This was why he had resigned himself now to follow.

Confident, he strode through the vast stinking encampment, alive with the discord of alien languages, foreign dialects, winding his way through the teeming, bristling bodies. Twice he spied the black, beetling heads of the insect-eyed generals and he gave them a wide berth.

At length, he came to the tent of the fat man. He was a great general, Po knew, perhaps second only to the disgusting Makkon. That was why he had picked out the man when first he rode into camp on the ebon animal that was hard to look at for more than a few seconds. The fat man had come from the heart of the pine forest, from where Makkon were, and Po knew.

He went past the guards and, ducking, stepped through the tent flaps into the covered pavilion beyond.

"You sent for me," he said, bowing his head.

Three of the deathshead warriors passed in front of him and, stooping, went out through the back of the pavilion.

The fat man looked up from his charts.

"Yes," he said. "Come here."

A Makkon stood by his side, its hideous beaked head swiveling. Its thick tail flicked at the air, which was heavy with its stench. Po averted his eyes, clamped down on his surprise at seeing the being outside the forest. What is happening? His thoughts darted like unquiet fish.

"We wish," said the fat man silkily, "for you to do us a service."

"As you request," said Po, his head still bowed.

"Good," said the fat man. "Tonight you will infiltrate Kamado."

Po concealed his surprise once again, said: "I am, as you are no doubt aware, a prime master of jhindo."

"Concealment and assassination," said the fat man. "Yes, we know well. That is why we chose you, Po."

The Makkon opened its hooked beak and screamed, its gray tongue flailing at the scaled roof of its mouth. Po shuddered and closed his eyes momentarily, nauseated.

"There is someone we wish slain," said the fat man, seeming to translate the Makkon's request. "We wish it done silently and mysteriously to increase the terror." Then he gave Po a description.

"That could fit many people, sir." Still he was sickened by this weak, subservient pose. Yet he knew within its docility lay his ultimate strength to outlast and thus defeat these pompous generals and stinking aliens. "What is the name?"

The Makkon howled again and Po felt tears start at the corners of his eyes. His ears hurt.

"Her name," said the fat man quietly, "is Moeru."

They had gone on, leaving him alone in Sha'angh'sei. Behind Tenchō, in the palace of the Empress.

In his high gleaming helm, in his black lacquered armor ribbed in sea-green jade and lapis lazuli, he strode through the cool marble halls, hearing only the echoes of his footsteps.

He stood for a moment peering down a wide gallery, past flecked marble columns. Beaten brass lamps hung from long chains.

The palace was deserted.

The air was still, hanging dusty, like folded sheets, waiting for the occupants to return from some summer sojourn on another continent where the sun shone and it never rained.

For a moment, he thought he detected a presence high up at the other end of the vast gallery: an inquisitive voyeur, perhaps the gyring beat of primitive music. But the air was thick and the light dim and the shimmering was most likely some refraction of flames off his armor.

He shook his head, as if trying to remember a snippet of another's memory, and failing, strode from the palace, wondering what had led him to return here when events and time pressed for him to make all speed northward to Kamado.

He came out onto the jeweled garden, lush still in the ending of the year. The day was bright and cold, as brittle as porcelain. High cirrus clouds scoured the cerulian sky. The trees were red and orange, as shiny as copper or brass.

With his gauntleted hands on the bridle of his mount, he paused, his head turning back toward the hidden entrance to the Empress' palace, certain now that he had forgotten something there.

Then he shrugged, leapt upon his steed, and without another backward glance, galloped out of the open gates, through the maze on tumbled streets and black back alleys, for Sha'angh'sei, strange in their emptiness, northward to catch the column of Bujun on the march to Kamado.

Behind him, a great wind came into the palace as if seeking someone or something. It batted at the brass lamps as if in frustration of finding no one. They fell to the floor. Cold flame ran along the marble and the building shuddered as from a great, angry fist.

It was Bonneduce the Last who saw him first, at the head of the long column, and it was he who gave the order for the great postern gates of Kamado to be opened.

The little man's face was alight with pleasure as the Sunset Warrior reined in and dismounted. Amid the dust and clatter of the marching Bujun, he grasped Bonneduce the Last and picked him up in the air.

"Old friend," he said over and over. "Old friend."

"It is good to see you," said the little man, giving vent to his joy. "At last."

At their feet, Hynd, the singular mutant who was more than animal, growled in his throat, his round tail whipping the air.

The Sunset Warrior bent to stroke his furred head and Hynd coughed, his thin lips pulled back from his wicked teeth. He nuzzled the Sunset Warrior's leg.

Moeru reined in her horse and, bending, kissed the little man.

Out of the corner of his eye, the Sunset Warrior saw Kiri running toward him, then abruptly halt and stare as if stricken.

He watched her face as she moved backward, away from them, her eyes never leaving his.

"There have been changes since you embarked on your journey. It is not for you to help Kiri now," said Bonneduce the Last.

"I could not aid her before," he said, turning away. "Accompany us to the stables, old friend, and then we shall speak of many things."

"I will do better than that," said the little man, leading the way down Kamado's narrow streets.

Within the stables, they left their horses to be cared for by the grooms. But before they left, Bonneduce the Last took the Sunset Warrior to the far end of the stalls. There was Ronin's dark red luma.

The creature snorted as the Sunset Warrior stroked its neck.

"Ah, thank you, old friend."

Bonneduce the Last turned away, limped back down the aisle of stalls to where Moeru waited.

For long hours through the remainder of the day and into the brusque twilight, while skirmishes continued unabated without the walls, the rikkagin of men met with the Sunset Warrior, Bonneduce the Last, the taipan of Sha'angh'sei, the Kunshin and his daimyos.

"Each day," said Rikkagin Aerent, "the enemy attacks with more men. Each day our forces grow more depleted."

"As you know," Tuolin said, "the deathshead warriors can be destroyed by sword, but their number never seems to diminish. Now they are led by black creatures with the faceted eyes of insects. None of these have ever been killed or wounded. Our men are demoralized."

"And the rikkagin?" said the Sunset Warrior, looking about the smoky room. "The men but feel what they see in their leaders and emulate it. A more doom-filled group I cannot imagine. If you are downcast and hopeless, then expect only the same of them." His mailed fist struck the table around which they all sat. "Now we are all together, the last forces of mankind. The Bujun are come. They are the greatest warriors on the face of the world. We are at the peak of our strength. I will not wait here within these walls only to be beaten down by attrition. This is not the way of the warrior." He saw, in the periphery of his vision, Azuki-iro regarding him placidly, smiling. "At dawn tomorrow we will go out onto the plain, cross the river, attack the enemy. All of us. And by day's end, we shall know whether man shall live or die in the time to come." He signaled to Rikkagin Aerent, who spread out a detailed topographical map of the district. Upon it had been marked in various colored inks, the deployment of The Dolman's forces.

After a time, the Kunshin leaned over and stabbed with his forefinger.

"Here," he said. "And here."

Then they got down on it.

"It is good to have you back," said Rikkagin Aerent.

The Sunset Warrior laughed.

"Am I so unchanged then?"

"No." Rikkagin Aerent looked away for a moment, then his clear eyes returned to the strange visage before him. "Not at all. You are like no other I have ever seen before but even so"—he grasped a long arm for a moment—"even so, I could not mistake you." He paused to allow two warriors passage down the cramped, dark hall. They stood between smoking tapers, half-shadowed.

"What happened?" he said. "Or is that an indelicate question?"

"Karma," said the Sunset Warrior. "I went to meet my destiny and found it on Ama-no-mori."

"The fabled isle exists, then?" said Rikkagin Aerent. "Then the Bujun really come from there and not another part of the continent of man. There had been rumors—"

"It exists," said the Sunset Warrior. "It is my home now."

"And the woman warrior who accompanies you?"

"Moeru? What of her?"

"Who is she to you?"

"Why is it important?"

"For Tuolin perhaps it is essential. He loves Kiri and she—"

"Still loves me? No, Aerent, she loved Ronin and even then there was nothing he could give her."

"Perhaps then—"

"Yes. All right. I would not hurt Tuolin—"

"They will survive—"

"As may we all, Aerent."

Tattered banners fluttered from the ramparts of Kamado, borne on a tired wind.

He stood in the icy cold, surveying the burned and blackened pine forest, thinking of his first terrifying encounter with himself, knowing that now, within that twisted tangle, pulsed The Dolman, come at last to the world of man.

Dawn would see them face to face, the culmination of his life, the last burning page of the history of this dying age within which they all lived and felt joy and suffered.

Would they see the dawning of the new age?

He did not know but he felt sure that if they did not, no one, no thing, would.

And as he thought of The Dolman and his coming personal struggle, which would decide the outcome of the Kai-feng, a bright shard of Ronin's memory spun dazzlingly upward, from out of the swirling deep.

The Salamander.

Somewhere on this world, the Senseii of Ronin's Freehold still lived, the man who had set Ronin's sister K'reen against him so that Ronin was at last forced to kill her. The master warrior who had chosen Ronin for his Combat Class, who had, in effect, begun Ronin's long, hard struggle to become, ultimately, the Sunset Warrior.

After The Dolman—

"How different you appear," she said softly from behind him.

He did not have to turn around to recognize Kiri's voice.

"Yet I could not mistake you if ten thousand centuries had grown over us both."

He turned at last, staring down at her with his strange lavender eyes, and she gasped. She drew her hand from her mouth and reached slowly, hesitantly, out to touch him.

"He is gone, Kiri. His body is buried on Ama-no-mori."

"No," she said, her heart already broken, crushed to white ash. "How can it possibly be? You must—" Her warm hand stroked the odd planes of his cheek. Then: "How you must miss Matsu!" But he knew exactly what she meant.

She sobbed against his chest and, feeling the soft whisper of her unbound hair against his face, visions played, unbidden, across his mind: the stirrings of a fierce, sexual woman whose warm lips kissed his as he slashed her breast to ribbons; a gentle, pale oval face half obscured by long night-black hair as it fell over one eye, her red blood and hot gore spattering his face and hands as the Makkon calmly, deliberately, tore out her throat, a last impotent breath bubbling liquidly from between her already blue lips.

The Dolman and then certainly the Salamander.

They were all that existed for him now. Kiri was as the stone of the ramparts to him and, as an understanding of that filled her, she pushed away from him and, turning, left to him the view of the dark, smoking forest and the high frozen wastes of Kamado.

They had already secured the rope and he slipped into the chill, rushing water. He felt the steep bank drop away from his feet almost immediately.

Despite the depth of the river and the white water bubbling about his body, he felt quite safe as, hand over hand, he pulled himself across. A thin reed tube extended upward from between his closed lips, breaching the turbulent surface of the river.

He was garbed entirely in black. Even his face, where the flesh was exposed, away from the tight hood, had been blackened by charcoal, then greased to keep the water from washing it away. Gaining the far shore, he knelt unmoving, breathing silently, surveying the darkness of the night.

Racing clouds obscured the moon and a wind from the east rustled the leaves of the poplars, the needles of the pines. Behind him, the rushing of the water.

He scuttled into the underbrush and settled himself to dry. While he waited, he carefully wiped away the grease on his face and reapplied the charcoal powder until he was content that the flat matte finish would reflect no torchlight.

Stealthily, keeping to the deep shadows of the trees and the low foliage, he moved in an erratic, zigzag route toward the towering walls of Kamado.

He heard low voices and he froze, the hilt of his black dagger already in his right fist, point lifted slightly.

The voices swept nearer, borne on the wind, and as they came up on his position, he struck in two swift, silent cuts, ramming the dark blade through the soft skin under their chins, across their palates, into the base of their brains. The two warriors did not even have time to cry out.

Now he could have donned the clothes of either of the slain men and thus gained entrance to Kamado but this was not the way of the jhindo master.

He pulled them into a tangled clump of brush and continued on his stealthy way until, at length, he was at the foot of the stone walls of the citadel. He pulled several small black metal objects from within his tight ebon clothing and silently he began to climb the wall, hacking efficiently at the mortar used to join the great stones together.

Swiftly now, as he gained the rhythm, soaring into the dense, starless night.

He stroked Hynd's long, plaited back. The horny scales rippled in pleasure.

"It is wonderful to see the Bujun again," said Bonneduce the Last.

"You never told Ronin—"

The little man shrugged.

"There are many things which you may now be told. Before—" His shoulders lifted again.

"Can you tell me who you are?"

"Yes." He rubbed his short leg, stretched out before him. "It has been told before, you know."

"Indeed. To whom?"

"G'fand."

"What? But why?"

"He wished to know." Bonneduce the Last reached over and touched him with one finger. "Listen, my friend, the Bones told me that he would die shortly in the City of Ten Thousand Paths. There was nothing I could do about it. Karma. It was but another death I had to suffer knowing. It was a gift. He asked me and I told him."

"Do you think that he believed you?"

"I cannot say. Does it matter very much?"

There was silence for a time, while the fire crackled cheerily in the stone hearth. He strained, hearing again the sonorous ticking which accompanied the little man wherever he went. He was on the point of asking about the sound when Bonneduce the Last continued:

"My race is long gone, at least as it was known in its day. I alone have been preserved to see the Kai-feng and thus atone for the transgressions of my liege."

He got up, went to put another log on the fire. He stirred the glowing coals with the tip of his sword.

"Hynd and I live Outside time, as you have no doubt guessed by now. This was imperative if we were to survive the ravages of the millennia. For I am of the folk whose lord found the root in the forest glade, a part of which you ate—"

"The legend of the great warrior told to me by the old apothecary in Sha'angh'sei, the one who had the root—"

"Yes. He was Bujun—"

"And the garden—the temple in Sha'angh'sei—"

Bonneduce the Last nodded. "That, too."

What am I missing? thought the Sunset Warrior.

The little man limped back to his chair, his hand reaching down again to stroke Hynd's back.

"Because of his burning desire to rule over all the world," said the little man, returning to his story, "he was led into the forest glade where grew the root."

"Led by whom?"

"By God."

"Which god?"

"There is only one, my friend."

Behind the grate, a log cracked down its length and, with a soft crash, fell to the ashen bottom of the hearth. Orange flames leapt up with renewed vigor.

"In eating it, he became the most powerful warrior in the world and thus his thirst for conquest was slaked—"

He paused at the sight of the Sunset Warrior's raised hand.

Within the new mind had flashed the image of a huge man with cinnamon skin and hazel eyes. Unaccountably, he wished to see Moichi again, wished at the very least to know where he was. Upon the vast salt seas, riding the high poop of some heavily laden ship flying full sail to catch the wind and ride the tide, heading for some foreign port, hidden by the curve of a lush headland, his *rutter* thickened by new entries. Now what had made him think of Moichi at just this moment? He reviewed the conversation. *There is only one, my friend.* His lavender eyes opened, gold sparking around the irises.

"Go on," he said softly.

"In eating the root," the little man said, "he also caused to be created The Dolman. For as it was then, there was nothing on the world that could match his power and our Laws could not tolerate such an imbalance.

"Thus The Dolman was born, birthed to do battle with my liege. The Dolman was victorious but, in the process, he was severely injured and was forced from the world of man. Yet for centuries unending, he nurtured a growing obsession to return, to wreak his vengeance upon all of man, for his one lust is extinction."

"And now he waits within the forest to the north. For me."

"Yes," said Bonneduce the Last. "And my long mission over the ages has been accomplished."

The Sunset Warrior reached one gauntleted hand into the folds of his robe, beneath his armor, drew forth several small shapes, off-white in color. They gleamed in the firelight.

"Once," he said, "you gave a gift to Ronin. I still wear that gift. I still value its protection. Now here is my gift to you." He reached out a hand. "You told Ronin in Khiyan that the Bones were no longer useful. Perhaps that was because they belong to another time, a forgotten age. Here, my friend. From the jaws of a crocodile of today."

Into Bonneduce the Last's cupped palm, he dropped the teeth Ronin had gathered in the jungles outside of Xich Chih.

No one saw him; no one even heard his approach.

He was like the night wind, blowing in across the high ramparts.

His jhindo senseii would have been content.

In the dark, dank streets of Kamado, with the proliferation of noise and movement, he became but another flickering shadow thrown by the inconstant light of the swinging oil lamps.

Within the herds of whinnying, snorting horses, sweating, swearing soldiers, packs of lean yellow dogs, coats filthy and matted, past the precision of the changing of the guard at watch's end, he flitted through the crowds of the stone citadel, unchallenged and unnoticed, wrapped securely in his cloak of invisibility that was the soul of jhindo.

At various times he paused within deep shadows, overhearing snatches of conversations, making his way, at length, to a certain wood and stone house. Its long, quiet porch was identical to those of all the other barracks within Kamado. Yet this one was different, he knew.

He went around to the side, edging into the pitch blackness of a narrow alley littered with refuse. Squealing, rats skittered from underfoot. He stood still until they quieted and when at length he chose to move again, they made no sound.

Through a small window where lemon light did not thrust back the deep shadows, he hoisted himself lithely. Into the blackness of the building's interior.

Opening a wooden door just a crack, he peered out at two warriors talking at the far end of a long, narrow hall which was lit at intervals by oiled reed torches. His door was almost midway between the lights. It was the best placement he could hope for.

Carefully, he tested the hinges of the door.

Quickly now, he opened the door without a sound, his

hands already a blur. Two black metal stars sang through the air, buried themselves in the warriors' necks.

The man in black moved silently away, an articulated shadow.

"All doubts should have been swept away."

"Nonsense."

"No, old friend, I am a leader now. I feel the weight of all mankind."

"Are you unsure then of what you can do?"

"No, not that. More of who I am."

The hearth was carpeted with white ash. The logs, consumed by the fire, had all collapsed downward, shattering. Small flames still leapt and danced, scattered among the ashes.

"All of us are composed of pieces."

"I would feel easier knowing the outcome of the battle at Haneda."

"Perhaps the answer lies somewhere inside you. None else can know. Once I could have rolled the Bones, read the answer on their etched faces. Now—" He sighed deeply. "I am tired."

And for the first time, as he looked at him, the Sunset Warrior recognized a trace of mortality in the little man.

He smiled.

"I am here now." His voice whispered across the semidarkness. The sonorous ticking was a contrapuntal rhythm to their voices. "You have completed your task. The guilt of your liege has been expiated—"

Bonneduce the Last shook his head sadly.

"No. There has been altogether too much blood spilled. Man is not a wheat field waving in a summer wind, to be cut down, a harvest for sorcerous creatures. They have no right. They must pay. Some Laws stand for all time."

"Then The Dolman will be defeated."

The clear gray eyes stared at him, rents in the fabric of time.

"Will he? It was through my liege's insatiable greed that The Dolman was conceived. Perhaps it is man who must now pay the ultimate price." His shoulders lifted, fell with the finality of a death sentence. "None can say at this moment."

"Soon, old friend."

He got up, stood near the dying fire.

"Yes, soon an end to all the suffering I have borne witness to."

He limped across the room to a low chair over which he had thrown his worn leather shoulder bags and reached within their depths. Abruptly, the ticking became louder and he turned, walking back to the Sunset Warrior.

Bonneduce the Last held in front of him a small object of brown onyx and red jade. It was trapezoidal, glassed on one side. Within the structure could be seen a sphere of fire opal, revolving back and forth to the rhythmic sound.

"The Rhyalann," he said. "This is what keeps Hynd and me Outside, what has allowed us the breadth of eons."

"Ronin often wondered what caused the ticking that accompanies you wherever you go. I too."

Bonneduce the Last nodded. "I know. I show it to you now because you never asked to see it. Beyond a certain few, no one must even know of its existence, for with each person who sees it, its power decreases."

"Put it away," said the Sunset Warrior. "Put it away."

He heard the little man's limping step over the wooden floorboards.

Tuolin groaned.

He lifted a trembling hand. It cost him a great deal of energy.

I cannot, he thought.

Then he caught himself and began the deep breathing that was an essential part of his training. Back to basics.

His chest was sticky, warm and wet, but the pain was minimal there. The fierce grinding of flesh against bone was further up, at his shoulder socket.

The reaction had been entirely reflexive.

His arm like lead moving slowly upward. He gritted his teeth, forcing his muscles to work. His nerves screamed and he fought back the shout of pain that bubbled in his throat. He grunted.

The shadow had been thrown across the far periphery of his vision. Somewhere in his brain, it had registered.

At length, he reached far enough and without hesitation pulled it from his rent flesh. He almost passed out with the pain but he returned to the deep breathing, oxygenating his blood against the shock, pulling himself back from the brink of unconsciousness.

Oh, you fool, he thought. Get up!

So it was his training that had saved him. It was why he had been moving, even before he heard the harsh hissing coming toward him, why his body had already begun its turn away from the threat. It was why he was alive now while one of his men lay dead beside him.

Looking at the weapon in his hand, a metallic star, five-pointed, its edges serrated. And he cursed himself again, for he knew the evil that was now inside the walls of Kamado.

He lurched to his feet, staggered against the corridor's wall. Sweat broke out on his face, along his sides, under his arms.

A jhindo master within Kamado. His mind raced as he followed the path of the moving shadow. Even if he had not seen the direction of the wraith as he was falling—with superreal clarity because the intense concentration helped to block the pain and shock to the nervous system while the organism tried to adjust to the invasion of its flesh—he would have known which way to go. There was only one target that made sense in this barracks: the Sunset Warrior.

There were two guards in front of the door.

He stood quite still in the flickering shadows of the corridor. He was reasonably certain of his destination. Still, he wished to leave nothing at all to chance. Therefore, he determined that one would have to live, if only for the few moments it would take for the confirmation.

He launched himself, silently and swiftly, a human dart, his right hand snaking out in a blur, the ridged muscles, heavily calloused, a knife, breaking the sternum of the right-hand guard.

Even before the man fell, choking on his own blood as it poured into his lungs, the jhindo had broken the collarbones of the second guard with a fierce chop of each hand. He grabbed the man as he began to slide down the wall.

For the briefest moment, there was a whispered dialogue, then the jhindo slit the guard's throat with a hidden blade.

Crouching low, he threw open the door, rolling inside.

Onward, his stomach heaving, trying to force its contents up his throat.

Around the near turning, the corridor leapt up before his eyes as if pulled by strings controlled by a madman. He leaned against a wall, panting, pressing his forehead against the cool stone, urging himself onward, his soldier's instinct screaming. His tongue licked his dry lips. He knew he was dehydrating, the combination of shock, the loss of blood, and the sweat of his efforts.

He concentrated on the hate, cold and efficient, and with it came the release of adrenalin, bolstering his system. He willed his thoughts away from his crooked left arm and the warm blood leaking out of his shoulder.

The sight of the two sprawled bodies brought him up short. The door behind them was slightly ajar and though his nerves were screaming for immediate action, frantic at the time lost, he willed himself to stand perfectly still and close his eyes, because inside the room, it was darker than the dimness of the corridor and he would not go in there blind. Just an instant's blindness while he adjusted and the jhindo master could kill him six different ways. He knew enough about the secret art not to underestimate its practitioners.

He went in with a rush, crouching and rolling across the floor as soon as he had crossed the threshold. Away from the leakage of the lethal light.

Platinum glow from a rising moon, briefly freed from its dense cloud cover, splashed into the chamber through high, narrow windows whose shutters had been opened to the compound outside. Shimmering bars of some liquid prison.

His sword drawn, Tuolin's eyes swept the room, taking in the corner first, then the deepest shadows thrown by the placement of furniture.

He found them together on the wide cream-colored bed, locked in silent struggle.

The jhindo and Moeru.

He was above her, a dark, humped shape, and her legs were locked across his back as if they were in the act of making love. But her powerful thigh muscles were corded as they strained across his kidneys, her heels locked at the small of his back, pressing inward, seeking purchase to break his spine.

The jhindo's hands were at her throat, the thumbs searching for the soft flesh just beneath her jaw, directly below her ears.

The jhindo grunted as Moeru jerked her legs, digging her heels in. But he had found the spot now and he jabbed. Moeru gagged, tears of pain welling in her eyes, spilling down across her high cheeks.

She coughed, brought her left hand up in a swift arc, the edge stiff, slamming it into the jhindo's head just behind his ear. His head snapped up and his eyes seemed to glow with a feral hunger as he applied more pressure.

Moeru cried out.

Tuolin broke out of his stupor and, rushing to the bed, smashed the hilt of his sword into the jhindo's rib cage with enormous force. The man grunted, his body twisted, and he released Moeru as he leapt at Tuolin.

The deadly hands were a blur, sweeping the rikkagin's blade from his grasp and at the same time describing a mysterious blurred pass.

In the next instant, the jhindo planted his feet and swung from his shoulder. Tuolin saw him wince, then he was struck in the face.

Flesh ripped away and he felt a searing pain. He looked down. A row of black metal spikes covered the jhindo's knuckles, shiny now with blood.

Tuolin circled to his left, toward the jhindo's hurt side. He wiped the blood from his face. His cheekbone was not broken as it most surely would have been if the jhindo had not been injured, thus preventing the blow from landing with full force. Tuolin counted himself lucky and moved in.

In dimness, one learns to memorize outlines and shapes and when those change, the body moves and thinks later. Tuolin sank to the floor, his mind racing to recall the instant before the action, tracing in slow motion what his eyes had seen to trigger the instinctive response.

It was the jhindo's face. An added line, silvered by the light of the thin shafts of moonlight. He heard the whirring above him as he hit the floor and rolled away into deep shadow. His mind retained the latent image of the outward puffing of the jhindo's cheeks as he prepared to fire the poisoned dart.

The jhindo spit and Tuolin heard the tiny clatter of the concealed blowgun.

He ran straight at his foe, his arms locking about his waist. He grimaced with the pain.

He slammed his balled fists against the rib cage, heard several sharp cracks.

The jhindo's eyes rolled whitely and Tuolin almost missed the puckering of the lips. Then he saw the glint of the blowgun still within the jhindo's mouth. Despairingly, he cursed himself for falling for the ruse.

He increased his grip as he heard the soft phit through the

air and at the same instant he saw the hand descending in a blur.

Slim fingers pressed inward at the base of the jhindo's neck. The eyes rolled up and his lips went slack. Air, withheld, abruptly sighed out of his mouth, the blowgun dropped. The jhindo fell to the floor.

"I do not want him to know yet."

Her blue-green eyes stared into his.

She finished bandaging him.

"Do you understand?"

His eyes were still filled with the pain of his burning shoulder. His neck ached. He could not lift his arm.

"Not really. No."

Her gaze left him and swung to the unconscious ebon figure spread-eagled on the bed. His hands and feet were bound securely to the four metal corners. An obsidian star, like one of his own weapons.

"He came for me, Tuolin, do you realize that?"

"But I thought—"

"Naturally. You assumed that he had come to kill the Sunset Warrior and found me here instead." She shook her head, dark hair floating. "There was no mistake, of that I am certain. He attacked me, Tuolin. He was searching for no other."

Tuolin turned.

"We must tell the Sunset Warrior—"

Her hand on his good arm stopped him.

"Do you know what he would do," she said quietly, "if he were to come in here now?"

"And *you* will not kill him?"

She laughed, her voice a cool nocturnal whisper. "Oh yes, rikkagin. I shall kill him, but not now and not soon. Not before he tells me what I wish to know."

Tuolin moved his left arm into a more comfortable position. Already blood was darkening the bandage. His hand was numb.

"I too am curious about how our enemies knew of you but, Moeru, he is jhindo. He will die rather than say one word."

"Still," she said, staring at the cloaked figure, "I must know who sent him here."

"You will get nothing from him."

Her eyes glittered in the pale moonlight.

"Watch."

She moved silently to the bed and, reaching out, slapped the jhindo sharply across the face. Again.

She waited patiently until he was fully conscious, until the eyes were no longer glassy, before she tore off his ebon mask.

His dark eyes locked onto hers.

"Who sent you?"

She said it quietly, making sure that he could see her lips forming each word.

He stared at her unblinkingly.

She reached down, seeming only to press gently against his body. The jhindo's eyes opened wide. His face went white as blood drained from it. After a while, he opened his mouth to scream but nothing came out.

She repeated the process, talk and movement, and gradually Tuolin became aware that she had set a rhythm that somehow intensified the effect of her actions.

The air in the room grew heated even though the night was chill. The smell of sweat and something else hung heavily.

Tuolin went to a pitcher on a plain plank table, drank the cool water.

Every so often, the jhindo passed out. During one of these times, Tuolin said:

"Is this truly necessary? We waste time here. This man will not talk."

"I do not think you understand."

"What can it matter who sent him: Kill him and be done with it."

"He will tell me, eventually."

"I do not like this."

Her eyes never left the white face beneath her.

"Can a rikkagin be so squeamish?" Then she said: "Perhaps I frighten you."

He laughed hollowly.

"You begin to fear that I enjoy this work."

"No, I—" He came nearer to her. "Well, it could be true."

"What if it is—?"

"You are with him always—"

She turned her head to him now, still crouched over the sweating body.

"Look, I did not mean—" He paused, conscious of her clear eyes raking his face. "You saved my life. You are Bujun, an exceptional warrior, but I—"

"What?"

"I do not understand you."

"What you mean," she said simply, "is that you cannot equate good and evil within one person."

He stepped back a pace.

"I do not think that you—"

"Oh, I understand you well enough, Tuolin." At precise intervals she kept glancing back at the gleaming, drawn face beneath her.

"So you think of yourself as a good person, hmm?"

He thought of Kiri.

"Yes."

"Then it is not possible for you to harbor any ill feelings, any hate? You cannot destroy."

"I am a soldier," he said warily. "My business is to destroy."

"So it is your profession; you chose it."

"Yes. Certainly."

The jhindo groaned. His eyelids began to flutter as he rose again toward consciousness.

She put a hand on the waxen chest, monitoring respiration and pulse at the same time.

Now Tuolin bristled somewhat.

"I *am* a professional. What would you have done if I had not—"

"And that is the extent of it."

He checked his discourse.

"Yes."

"Fool! Have you never looked inside yourself? Have you been so busy going about your efficient, professional killing that you have failed to recognize your totality?"

She turned her attention back to the jhindo and, when she was certain that he was fully conscious, commenced to work on the nerves high up on the inside of his thighs. Sweat broke out anew on his forehead and his chest fluttered. His eyes rolled up, going white as he went into a trance, but she reached her fingers across his body, manipulating, pulling him out of it. His eyes snapped open, focusing, and for the first time, some emotion swam there.

She leaned over the trembling body, whispered:

"The thing is, that you will not die after all this. Because I will not let you. You know now that I have that power. If you do not tell me who sent you, I will bind your hands and feet and throw you back across the river. What will happen then, when they know? What will your masters do to you when they find out you have failed?" She paused for just the right amount of time, allowing grudging seconds to pile up before she continued. "And were captured?"

Her slender, powerful fingers dug in once more. His body arched and his mouth stretched soundlessly. He passed out.

"So I am an evil woman, Tuolin. Why listen to what I have to say? I will only lie."

"No," he said heavily, "I do not think that." He sat down on the bed, as if he were infinitely weary. "What is the truth, then?"

Her eyes left him, for a moment, flicking across the haggard visage of the jhindo.

"The truth lies within yourself, rikkagin. There are no easy answers. Words of wisdom from the sages are a part of myth. Life is rarely that simple." She checked again. "Have faith in yourself. Do not fear the bestial side of you. Accept it. You cannot live without doing that."

"What have I been doing up until now?"

"You have survived."

She palpated the jhindo's chest, bringing him out of it prematurely. His eyes sprang open, slightly glazed. They focused. She reached down and now, for the first time, Tuolin saw clearly what she did. With infinite slowness.

"Tell me."

Tighter.

And he was drenched in sweat. He tried to vomit but she depressed his windpipe and his body would not let him strangle on his own fluids; his jhindo control was finite.

"Tell me."

The violent cramping of his body began at last and she pressed the advantage, bringing the threshold of pain into the realm of the unbearable. His eyelids fluttered and his breathing became irregular. He gasped but already one spreading palm was across his mouth, forcing him to breathe through his nose. The oxygen intake was insufficient to maintain the system in his present state and she knew now that it was a matter of time.

She maintained the pain level, marveling at his fortitude, saddened still that it would end, how it would terminate itself.

The lack of oxygen was now acute, intensifying the pain, and it was not the fear of death which obsessed him now but the knowledge that when he retained consciousness, the process would begin anew.

She brought him to the edge.

"Tell me—"

And in twilight, he did.

His brain half numbed, his training stripped from him for precious moments, he uttered two words. Her thumbs went in all the way and blood gouted, a viscous cloud.

Drenched, she quit the bed and, turning to Tuolin, helped him to a low couch across the room. He seemed feverish, his shoulder swollen. She peered beneath the bandage, then fed him some water. She looked at him.

"Now who," she said, "is the Salamander?"

Frozen Tears

"ARE you certain now?"

"Perfectly. There was never a question."

"How long?"

"Long enough."

"Um. Tell me again. Everything."

She repeated the story.

He listened, looking for a moment at the white, anguished face of Po, the bitter trader who had loved his people above all other things and who had betrayed mankind for them. He was a mess now.

The Sunset Warrior turned away, knowing what she had done and understanding it.

"How did they know about me?"

"There is another question of far more import which needs be answered."

He looked at her oval face, pale and exquisite in the dancing lamplight: at the forest of her hair, the long sweep of her neck, the full arch of her lips, the crimson of her lacquered nails, gleaming with light flecks. A dark, glittering drop of blood lay on her collarbone.

Something inexplicable stirred within him. Ronin had loved her, he knew, yet there was about their strange relationship an abstractness, an implicitness rather than an explicitness, which resolved itself in a striving for something further. Now he knew that it went beyond love, far beyond, into territory new and mysterious. He trembled in anticipation.

"Ronin knew that man."

"The jhindo?"

"Another wasted life—"

"He knew the Salamander too—"

The Sunset Warrior laughed but his eyes were quite cold. It

seemed quite logical now and he wondered why he had not been able to predict this moment.

"Your voice still seems strange to me." He walked to the high windows. It was pitch black outside save for the pin points of the small lamps visible here and there along the narrow street. He peered up at the thick cloud cover, feeling its oppressive weight.

Shall we speak this way? she said in his mind.

The moon is down now, I think. It reminds me—

He did not finish the thought and she did not press him. And perhaps she caught a hint of a picture, an image that she understood better than he might expect.

She went across the room, unself-consciously opening the sash of her robe, caked with dried blood and flecks of viscera, watching the lamplight firing across the strange, fierce planes of his arcane face. She poured water into a bowl, cupped her hands.

"You are less alien to me now, do you know that?"

He turned from the window, closing the shutters behind him.

Her long lithe legs, the narrow waist, the flaring hips, her firm breasts gleamed now with spilled water.

"I thought I loved my husband." Hair, dark and jeweled with moisture, flung itself across her shoulders. "For a time I fought my feelings. I *would* not let myself care. After all Ronin was not Bujun, even though he fought like one." She pulled a large cloth from the back of a couch, toweled her body dry. "But then I found you." *Like this*. Her voice in his mind, a caress.

"And then—?"

And then you found me.

Her hair cascaded over her face momentarily as she moved. She brought a hand up to move it aside.

His eyes watched hers, then broke away.

"What of Tuolin?"

Dropping the cloth, she stood quite naked before him. Then, stooping, she belted a fresh robe around her.

"I will get Kiri—"

"Let one of the men—"

"No."

"The security—"

"Is adequate. I wish—"

"The blowgun missed him." As if he was just now beginning to understand.

"Yes, but the suriken that wounded him was also poisoned. His left arm is already paralyzed."

"There is nothing—"

"I will fetch her."

For a long moment, she kissed him.

Kiri shuddered and stopped in the midst of refilling her long, thin pipe. For just a moment, she thought she heard Matsu crying out as if she were still alive somewhere. She shook her head. She knew too well the effects of the poppy. It was why she smoked now. Matsu used to smoke, she knew, but the feeling now was far different. Her fingers automatically filled the small bowl while she thought. But what if Matsu *were* alive? Impossible! She castigated herself again with the frightful images: the beautiful white body pooled in steaming blood, her head attached to the torso only by a thin stretch of wet skin; the Makkon's talons gripping her throat and the base of her brain.

She fought down the gorge rising in her own throat at the remembrance of death's cold grasp. Even once removed—She felt again the hilt of the straight-bladed knife lying comfortingly against her belly in its ceremonial scabbard. Waiting patiently, she knew, for the hand that would push its cold, white blade into her entrails.

She closed her eyelids against the wetness welling there. And for the thousandth time since the murder she thought: I am dying without her.

"Kiri."

She opened her eyes. Moeru crouched before her.

"Kiri, listen to me. How much have you smoked?"

Mutely, Kiri shook her head. She had a terrible intimation, pulled from the other woman's eyes.

"A jhindo infiltrated Kamado. He was sent to assassinate me. Tuolin fought with him and was injured."

"How bad?"

"I think you should see him."

She felt the cold stone against her cheek. She closed her eyes.

"Fine," he said. "I feel fine."

The skin of his forehead was hot and dry.

She felt his hand softly stroking her face. So gently. There was something unrecognizable in his eyes.

"I love you," he said softly.

And she could not hold it back any longer. The stoic within her relented, the tears rolling down her cheeks, and at last she let go, all the hurt and anguish flowing out of her in great sobs while Tuolin held her in his arms, rocking her, stroking her hair. She clung to him as if she were a child in desperate need, unself-conscious and, now, not alone.

"It has been a long night," he said to her.

"Surprise," said Du-Sing.

"Yes," said Azuki-iro. "Most definitely. By the thrust of our main force, so will the Makkon guide the counterattack."

"Deployment is the key," said Rikkagin Aerent.

"Yes. *Our* deployment," said Lui Wu. "Perhaps we should already have crossed the river *here*"—his long finger stabbed at the mulberry paper map—"where it is most fordable when they counter."

"I do not think that would be wise," and Azuki-iro. "The Bujun, being an island people, have much experience with warfare near water and I tell you now that if we overextend ourselves and they begin to overrun us, we shall be backed up like a swollen sewer and the ensuing confusion will utterly destroy us."

"What then do you propose?" said Rikkagin Aerent.

"*Feint* a river crossing but give them ample warning," said the Kunshin. "They will come out to cut us off and when they hit the water, we attack. Use the soldiers to cover the archers, then let them come forward as the enemy founders in the mud."

"Sound strategy," said Rikkagin Aerent.

"We shall need every device, every bit of cunning this day," said Bonneduce the Last.

"We are terribly outnumbered," said Rikkagin Aerent.

"What happens when The Dolman enters the battle?" said an older rikkagin. "What chance have we then?"

"Leave The Dolman to me," said the Sunset Warrior. "Everyone must concentrate on his section of the battle, else they will surely overrun us."

"I would feel much more secure," said Rikkagin Aerent, "if we had a clearer idea of their current deployment. Many changes may have taken place beneath this night's concealing darkness. But we dare not waste the manpower. Those who we have sent out on previous nights have not returned."

There was a small silence, then the Sunset Warrior said: "That, too, is something I can take care of."

"What are you doing?" she cried.

"There is a job to be done."

"You must know how ill he is!"

"It is his choice, Kiri."

She knelt before Tuolin's half-reclining figure.

"What are you doing?"

"I am a soldier," he said.

"Must you obey every order?"

"No one ordered me to do this. It is something I want—I *must* do."

She lifted her head and her eyes flashed.

"What did you say to him?"

The Sunset Warrior looked down at her without expression. Behind him, Moeru stood with her back against the door opening onto the narrow corridor of the barracks building.

"I said only that I needed his help—"

"His help?" Her tone was scornful. "You know it will kill him."

"Tuolin must do as he sees fit."

She turned.

"Moeru, please talk to them."

"Kiri, a decision has been made, surely you see that."

"I see only that another life is being thrown away for some nocturnal foray—whose idea was this anyway? Which bright rikkagin schemed this? Let *him* go!"

"No one knows the terrain as well as Tuolin. If the mission is to succeed—"

"Curse the mission!"

Tuolin got up, the pain showing on his face. He gripped Kiri, stood holding her. He turned to them.

"Let me talk to her for a moment."

They went out of the chamber. Moeru closed the door behind them. They stood in the hall, waiting.

It was quite still.

After a time, they heard Kiri's muffled: "No!"

Then Tuolin came out, alone. Together, he and the Sunset Warrior went down the hall away from the quiet room.

* * *

A whippoorwill sounded in the dead of night.

They crouched in the dense shadow of a stand of poplars. In the distance, they could hear the rushing of the river. The moon had gone down and the night was still starless, dense with climbing cloud. Mist hung in the treetops like a spider's ghostly web.

Tuolin pointed off to their left. Through the longer, lower branches of the trees, they could see movement, black against black.

Cautiously, they moved within the stand of trees until they could hear the muffled chink of metal against metal, the harsh, guttural whispers of the enemy.

The pair moved closer, flitting among the deep shadows of the tree trunks. They were clothed in black. Each carried a pair of long-bladed stilettos, scabbardless, tucked into their wide sashes.

Now they could clearly make out fully a score of the squat warriors hard at work on one of the huge war machines. They had posted guards at intervals around the work perimeter.

Snow covered the ground and with the temperature still falling, it had become brittle, forming a thin but solid crust. The hazard now was sound, not sight.

Crept through the close copse of poplars, their tops already hidden in the descending mist, carefully through the crunching snow, and they were rolling, into a kicked up, silent blizzard, as the long bodies dropped out of the trees, giant black bats, piling into the pair.

It began to snow. The night turned gray.

White plumes of their breath clouding the chill air, they grappled with their foes.

These are new, thought the Sunset Warrior, and I know why they were standing guard at night.

They had eyes like owls, large and round and light brown. Quick, missing nothing. Their heads moved on their stubby necks in the same manner as birds, as if their eyes could not move in their sockets. Nose and mouth ran together, a hooked cartilaginous mass that was, nevertheless, not quite a beak. Hands beating winglike with fingers long and thin, sinewy as rope.

They made no sound.

Their eyes were bright beacons.

The Sunset Warrior used his Makkon gauntlets, his fists like heavy hammers as he sought the sockets, junctures of bone against bone, against which he applied great force.

Desiccated. Fleshless, they seemed to have been baked in hot desert winds for eons. They were implacable warriors. They gave no quarter.

Tuolin struggled to pull a stiletto from his sash, feeling the oblique strikes against him. He twisted his left shoulder away. Reached up. Slashed the weapon into the breast of one of the creatures. Heard a sharp crack, unnaturally distinct in the cold, damp air. The blade stuck, as if wedged into a seam in the bone.

He used his forearms as a defense against the ferocious strikes, acutely aware of the numbness which gripped his left arm. Used his legs finally, seeking purchase, finding a humped ridge of ice and earth, kicking outward from that base, his boot tip sinking into the juncture of the thighs.

A grunt and the creature rolling off him, only to be replaced by two others.

The Sunset Warrior crossed his wrists and twisted. With a dry snap, a creature's neck snapped, canted at an impossible angle.

Hands like boards, still and deadly, blurring through the dense, smoke-filled night, smashing bone and cartilage.

He crouched, breathing deeply; the center of a low mound of corpses.

Tuolin feinted with his useless left arm, broke through a creature's defense with a lightning strike of his right elbow. Broke the cartilaginous were-beak, gouged into the wide cold eyes. While other hands, clawlike, at his throat, throttling his windpipe. Stars dancing before his eyes, lungs burning for air. Arms pinned, he doubled his legs, broke upward, his boots describing a precisely measured arc, tearing through the leather corselet just below the avian rib cage. Flurry of sticky blood. Snow a pink hail and he averted his face, rolling away across the sharp frozen ground. Stopped by the strong hands of the Sunset Warrior.

"Let us away from here," he whispered, sucking in lungfuls of air. "Quickly now."

Later, in the deep darkness:

"I have heard of a place. Three Reds were killed while on patrol. I was with Greens. They killed two outright before I could stop them. The third—" A snow owl hooted forlornly in the branches of the copse of trees to their left. "The third I took care of and he talked before I allowed him to die. I thought then that he spoke in delirium, but now I think we should check his story." The snow fell on all about them, their friend now, deadening sound. Breath clouding the air in front of their faces. "A cave, it is said, where things—are born."

"What things?"

"I do not know."

"What of the location?"

"This way—" Pointing off to the left. "Somewhere beyond the trees." He started up.

The Sunset Warrior put a gauntleted hand on his arm.

"Have you the strength?"

"We must go now."

The Sunset Warrior handed him one of his stilettos but Tuolin shook his head, saying softly: "I can only use one at a time now."

They raced across the open field and into the tangled cover of the trees, moving cautiously now, lifting their boots high in order to avoid the invisible outthrusts of roots. Not far away, they could hear the rush of the river. The sound increased until they broke cover and found themselves on the reed-lined bank.

"The water is sufficiently shallow to cross here," said Tuolin.

They slipped past the reeds and into the freezing water. Black boulders strewn near the banks of the river here caused the racing current to slow, eddy, and whorl back upon itself so that the long passage was made somewhat easier. In mid-river, the current was still swift and once or twice Tuolin lost his balance.

They reached the far bank without any untoward incident, scrambling up the brush-filled shore and racing for a stand of scrubby firs.

They sat and listened. Tuolin shivered slightly.

Far off a bell, muffled and somehow sad, seemed to be tolling. Then nothing but the quiet hiss of the snowfall. Surreptitiously. Tuolin felt along his left side, down across his ribs. Numb.

"This way," he whispered, moving off.

Past the trees, they came to a series of dells, as if the land here was serrated, and now they took great care for they were heading deeper into the territory of The Dolman. Secretly, the Sunset Warrior perhaps hoped to come across the path of one of the Makkon, for he still remembered what one had done to those close to Ronin, but the night was quite still and they saw no Makkon.

Increasingly, the dells became more rocky, until by the fourth one, there seemed no earth whatsoever.

They crouched on the high verge, peering through the snow, two black boulders among the many.

Both saw it at once.

A brief flicker of orange.

Using the rocks as cover they crept down into the dell, careful that their boots did not dislodge any loose stones.

The snow fluttered down, increasing in intensity, softly numbing.

They had an anxious moment crossing a small patch of open ground before clinging to the sloping sides of the ice-encrusted rocks but the visibility was down now.

Slowly they wove their way through the maze of stone until they could observe the tiny clearing.

Around the fire sat a pair of the dark, insect-eyed generals. Past them, slightly to the right, several squat warriors were going in and out of a cave entrance, blacker than the night.

They drew back for a moment.

"You have no idea what is inside?" said the Sunset Warrior.

Tuolin shook his head.

"All right, there is only one way that I can see that we will have any success. I will engage the creatures while you explore the cave."

"There seems to be no light in there."

"Yes, I know. You will have to use a torch from the fire."

The Sunset Warrior withdrew *Aka-i-tsuchi*. The long, blue-green blade seemed to glow in the night, the snowflakes whispering against its angry metal skin, turning to watered tears.

With a great leap, the Sunset Warrior bounded into the clearing and, with two great sweeps of his sword, slew three of the squat warriors before they could make a move against him.

The insect-eyed generals rose and withdrew their weapons, great serrated sickles as thick as cleavers, purple-black, single-edged.

He rushed them and their blades clashed together, beginning the heavily percussive music of combat.

While behind the broad back of the Sunset Warrior, Tuolin raced for the fire, scooping up a burning brand and rushing headlong down the ebon throat of the tunnel.

Out of their unhuman eyes, the black creatures spied the blur of Tuolin's back and moved to follow him. The Sunset Warrior blocked their path.

Aka-i-tsuchi screamed in the air as it battered the generals in a swift series of oblique strikes.

Now that he was close to them, the Sunset Warrior saw that their faces were triangular, composed entirely of sharp angles. They had tiny mouths and no noses, merely slits in the hard, shell-like flesh of their faces. From their cheeks, protruded curving, hornlike tusks like those of the stag beetle.

Aka-i-tsuchi slashed downward, through the guard of one of the creatures, cleaving its head from its body. Viscous black blood spurted, congealing almost instantly in the cold.

The second creature reared up and attacked with a ferocity bordering almost on desperation. It seemed intent on following Tuolin down the black hole of the cave mouth.

The Sunset Warrior stepped aside and with an ill-aimed swipe it was by him, loping for the underground entrance. *Aka-i-tsuchi* flashed outward, the dense air crying with its swift passage, and the creature collapsed to the snow.

The Sunset Warrior heard a cry from within the cave and he sprinted over the white ground, disappearing into blackness.

Ahead he saw a fitful, feral glow. There came, echoing down the cave's long corridor, the clash of metal, then a brief cry, choked off.

He went downward, feeling the chill dissipating until it grew quite warm.

Around a turning, he found Tuolin back up against the cave's wall, slimy with humidity. Two squat warriors lay dead at his feet. Wordlessly, he pointed ahead.

Before them, the cave ended in a cul-de-sac. Piled up. Within its warm confines, were perhaps ten score spheroids, glossy, iridescent. As they watched, a crack zigzagged its way across the shining shell of one of the spheroids.

It broke open.

Bathed in slime, a tiny creature pulled itself out. It grew before their eyes and, as he saw the formation of the two glossy black insect eyes in its head, the Sunset Warrior lifted his sword and slew the infant.

"Eggs," he whispered. "Sorcerous eggs."

And now cracks were appearing in more of the shells. Too many for him to slay, and turning, he grabbed the burning torch from Tuolin's hand and fired the dead creature. With a pop the thing blazed up and now he fired the eggs as they split until the small fires were so numerous that they rushed together, covered all the splitting mound.

Noxious gases bloomed from the blaze and thick oily smoke filled the underground chamber.

The Sunset Warrior threw the torch into the flames, and coughing, they made their way upward to the surface of the world.

Out of the clearing they raced, hearing distant calls of alarms drawing nearer. Over the dells, they ran, conscious that little cover lay ahead until they reached the copse of firs just this side of the river.

Numbness had reached his hip and now Tuolin stumbled over a rock hidden by the thick carpet of snow. He sprawled on the ground, tried to pick himself up. The Sunset Warrior reached down, pulled, and they went on, hearing the cries gaining in intensity. There came the fierce barking of dogs.

The trees were in sight now but the numbness was traveling swiftly down Tuolin's leg and he could no longer feel the ground with his left foot.

The Sunset Warrior was otherwise occupied. He peered ahead through the fog and the swirling snow at the stand of firs, certain now that their configuration had altered somewhat. He called to Tuolin and unsheathed *Aka-i-tsuchi*. Their haven was alive with the enemy.

The squat warriors had set up a line of defense and now, before the swaying firs, they came together. *Aka-i-tsuchi* sang through the night. Tuolin jabbed with his stiletto, his body concentrating on the efforts of combat while his mind composed a poem.

He slew two of the squat warriors with his weapon before he was felled by a blow through his stomach. Still, he killed the attacker before he collapsed to the cold earth.

They were through the line but the air was alive now with the deadly whisper of black arrows as their pursuers closed in. The howling of the dogs grew in intensity.

The Sunset Warrior knelt beside him, about to carry him off.

"Wait." His voice like a sigh on the night. "My friend. I will not last the river crossing."

"We have accomplished what we came here for," said the Sunset Warrior.

"That was my line," said Tuolin, smiling thinly. His blood blackened the snow around him. With his cupped hands the Sunset Warrior attempted to keep Tuolin's organs within his rent flesh.

"Oh, my Sha'angh'sei," Tuolin said, his breath a whisper.

"I will never see your crimson skyline again." He paused for a moment as if to gather strength. The dogs were howling hysterically, nearer now. "I think she understood, in the end."

"I am sure she did."

"I could not stay there in that yellow hole to die. I am a warrior. I am happy now." The rustle of the snow, powdering his upturned face, whiter than white. The Sunset Warrior wiped the sweat from his eyes. "I love her, you know."

"Yes."

"I told her."

"I know."

The arrows had ceased. The warriors must be very close.

"That was so important."

"And what did she say?"

"She loved me."

"She understood, my friend. She is a warrior also."

"She loved me. That was why she cried out 'No!' when I told her." His eyes were glazing. "I know. You must go."

"I will not leave you."

"No, it is I who must leave." A rustling beyond the firs' branches laden with snow. Foot soldiers. Barking, sharp and insistent. He grasped the Sunset Warrior's arm with his right hand. Those fingers were the only part of his body not numb. "Now listen," he whispered thickly, "listen to me:

On a journey, ill,
Over endless, withered fields
dreams go wandering, still."

His eyes closed as if in dream.

The Sunset Warrior could hear the animals' panting, the harsh scrape of metal, the creak of leather.

He bore Tuolin up in his arms, ducking his head, went into the stand of firs.

Out the far side of the stand and down the brush, into the black swirling water. The snow hid them and in any event the river washed away their scent. The pursuers would not cross the water this night.

On the far bank, he waded through the reeds and climbed onto the humped earth.

Now he took his time, picking a space away from Kamado's hulking walls, away from the field of battle.

Silently, he buried Tuolin.

He lay his stilettos across the rikkagin's chest at an oblique angle.

Then the earth bore him away.

"It is beautiful."

"Yes."

"You told her, of course."

"Everything."

"Good. It will help, I think."

The windows were open. It was quite still outside in Kamado in the last several hours before dawn. Mist hung like smoke.

"Do you think there are more?"

He watched the burnished light on the soft planes of her face. Her skin shone like silk.

"The caves?" He shrugged. "Who can say?"

Outside, boots crunched in the snow, climbed down wooden steps. A door closed.

"What will you find, do you think, at journey's end?" Her blue-green eyes caught the light for a moment as she turned her head. They flashed white, then black, as shadows stole over her head.

"Vengeance," said the Sunset Warrior.

"For your friends who are long dead?"

"For all mankind, Moeru."

"And what of us? You and I? You said once that we were bound."

"There is no time now to think of that."

"It is important—"

"Yes," he said. "It is."

"Because both our dreams are wandering still—"

In the streets of Kamado even the dogs were silent as if aware of the coming of this last dawn and of its portent.

On the vast plain, the tattered banners are waving.

War horses snort and stamp nervously, nostrils dilated, producing plumes of smoke.

The numerous ranks of foot soldiers deploy themselves under the direction of their rikkagin. Men still march out from Kamado, a long, brave line, toward the flanks of the army of man.

Dawn had come but the smeary light was thin and watery, as if the pale sun was at last too spent to shine. Pink light spilled across the plain, vaporous and unnatural.

The chink of metal against metal.

The clash of dented armor.

Battle standards of the various Bujun daimyos waving slightly, rising above the flashing helms of the mounted warriors.

Dogs running free, barking.

A sneeze.

Then the harsh ram's horn sounding and the ranks of cavalry prancing down the slight incline and across the plain, past the stand of poplars, toward the dull water of the wide river. They stared curiously at the rent war machine, destroyed just before dawn by a raiding party led by the Sunset Warrior and Rikkagin Aerent.

As the cavalry drew closer, a kinetic wave undulating over the earth, the riders saw the far shore black and teeming with the legions of The Dolman.

Just behind the cavalry, as the council of war had planned, marched the archers, bows already strung taut, dense forests of arrows across their backs in quivers. They loped after the cavalry, crouched, expectant.

Rikkagin Aerent led the cavalry charge and gradually he speeded the wave of horsemen forward until they were galloping over the undulating turf.

A flock of blackbirds quit the high grass at their thunderous approach, flung themselves into the cloud-laden skies.

The plain shook to the music of half a million hoofs. Clods of brown and white earth and snow flew upward in their wake.

There was shouting from the far shore, flung across the turbulent gray water, and as the cavalry approached, the enemy hurled themselves down the bank and into the water, moving out to meet the charge.

Rikkagin Aerent could see the black, insect-eyed generals calling to their soldiers, fearful that they were spreading themselves out in too ragged a line.

At the last moment, Rikkagin Aerent flung up his right arm and the horsemen jerked on their reins, parting down the center, their horses wheeling toward the army's flanks. Thus the archers were revealed. In the first line, each man sank to one knee and, drawing forth arrows, let fly with a thick volley into the midst of the wading enemy.

The air was momentarily black with metal rain as the deadly cloud passed over the heads of the passing cavalry. The heavy air hummed and soldiers midway across the river died clutching at throats and chests, sinking beneath the waves, drowning in great numbers.

But now over the soldiers' backs leapt the deathshead warriors, tall and gaunt, almost skeletal, who bled not blood but a fine gray powder in a mist, whose snapping jaws could sever a man's leg.

The battery of archers on the near shore fired again—the second line, then the third, behind it—and again the air grew dark across the river. Yet the deathshead warriors were unaffected. They swatted at the arrows which had buried themselves in their bodies as if they were insects, snapping the hafts, ignoring the buried points. Coming on in a pale tide, dripping and invulnerable.

And now the air was filled with the harsh hiss of their fanged globes which they swung above their heads by metal chains. Rearing up from the heavy silt, they crashed into the first line of archers and the crunching of bones was a constant noise on the plain.

Rikkagin Aerent had jerked the reins of his mount and was already calling his cavalry inward from the flanks. They attacked the deathshead warriors from two sides.

Behind him he saw the foot soldiers sweeping across the undulating plain, down the bank of the river, as they began to engage the enemy along either flank.

He drew his sword as his horse broke through the enemy lines. He swung in economical arcs. His blade clove through a gaunt skull and gray dust puffed like the breath from a tomb in the humid air.

The archers were caught, dying by the score under the onslaught of the hissing globes, but now Rikkagin Aerent's cavalry had closed its ranks, pressing inward with a rush, and the deathshead warriors turned from the center outward to meet the attack. The remaining archers scrambled up the near bank, retreating.

The wan light of the sun had disappeared altogether as burnt billowing clouds tumbled across the sky, close and hanging like incipient tears. An icy sleet began, oblique and gray, adding to the din of the battle.

Banners flew back and forth across the field as small forays and skirmishes were won and lost. The bright, sharp standards of the Bujun could be seen advancing, always advancing.

Drawing his great blue-green blade, *Aka-i-tsuchi*, the Sunset Warrior urged his crimson luma down the near shore, wading into the thick of the battle at the great river crossing.

Aka-i-tsuchi carved a wide swath through the enemy warriors. It seemed to sing in the air, delighted in the carnage it was wreaking. The peculiar metal, forged for so long and with such love by the smithy high on the snowbound slopes of Fujiwara, appeared to glow a deeper blue-green and the desiccated flesh of the deathshead warriors sizzled where it cut through to the white bones.

Inhuman jaws with their pointed fangs clashed upward at him and the luma reared to take him out of danger. The hissing of the globes increased until it sounded like the onset of a swarm of famished locusts as the enemy jammed about him, trying to bring him down.

Moeru and Bonneduce the Last, both mounted, were fighting their way across the plain and now they grabbed their reins, kicking into their steeds' flanks, racing for the river crossing.

The sleet increased to a driving, pelting rush as hard as hail. It rattled off the armor and weapons of the warriors. And now even the shouts of the victorious and the screams of the dying were but muted background sounds to the clashing of metal upon metal and the hideous drum of the chilling sleet.

The banks of the river, muddy with alluvial soil at the beginning of the battle, ran red and the bodies of the fallen, dead or not, were ground into the earth by hoof and boot alike until the combatants fought on a higher level, battling across an expanse of shifting, crunching soil without dirt or grass.

Already strike forces, composed of the combined Greens and Reds, who were more familiar with the terrain, had been dispatched by their taipan to disable the great war machines of The Dolman. Certainly, it was unlikely that they would be used once the armies came fully together but the rikkagin felt it incumbent upon them to destroy the machines' effectiveness.

Moeru narrowly missed being decapitated by crashing jaws, slammed her blade down the center line of the forehead, and the deathshead skull splintered, blinding her momentarily with shards of bone and marrow and bits of brain. She felt a searing pain along her left arm and spun away as the acephalous body swung again reflexively, the fanged globe dark in the torrential downpour.

She slipped along a smooth piece of armor underfoot as she dismounted, the way clogged with bodies and her horse bleeding from a dozen wounds. She cracked a skull with her boot. Off balance, she swung, correcting her weight, her sword shearing through the torso of another warrior. This time, she ducked as the globe hissed in the air where her head had been. Then she raised her sword and slew her horse.

Waving to Bonneduce the Last, she waded through the soldiers and swung up upon his steed, just behind him. They went forward.

Adrenalin and something more soared through the Sunset Warrior's huge frame as he moved further into the enemy's ranks. His immense blade swung like a blurred scythe, so swiftly that his very outline dimmed. It ripped through four warriors on the forward strike, three as he reversed the momentum, swung the other way.

At his back, the foot soldiers, fresh from Kamado's gates, broke like a wedge into the midst of the deathshead warriors.

As Rikkagin Aerent saw the Sunset Warrior wade into the central attack, he wheeled his mount and signaled to his remaining cavalry to move out onto the army's right flank where the defense appeared weakest. Strange crested creatures were now directly behind the wave of deathshead warriors, commanded by the insect-eyed rikkagin.

He spurred his horse along the foaming banks of the river, the water a high silver spray in the hissing sleet. He heard the ram's horn sounding the charge. He leaned forward in his saddle, lashing at the enemy warriors who climbed out of the turbulent water. Here they were short muscular men with no necks and broad backs. They carried long black metal pikes and thick-bladed single-edged swords scabbarded at their hips.

Rikkagin Aerent turned in his saddle, shouting to be heard above the roar about him, attempting to deploy his men along the near bank, for the defense was weaker here than he had at first thought.

A blade flashed over one ear and the haft of a pike splintered and fell across the pommel of his saddle. He turned back, cursing, decapitating the warrior who had tried to impale him. He lifted his streaming blade to the soldier who had saved his life, then spurred his steed onward.

The squat warriors and the plumed soldiers poured up from the river crossing in great numbers now and Rikkagin Aerent sent two of his men back up the field for reinforcements.

The foot soldiers were falling back under the intense assault of the pikemen, giving ground grudgingly as the wave forced them from the near shore up onto the field.

"Into the river!" called Rikkagin Aerent, and his horsemen plunged into the pink water in an attempt to outflank the emerging warriors. He used his men as a wedge, surging horses bodies and flashing horny hoofs against the solid wall of the pikemen, forcing them in upon themselves.

His arm grew weary as he lofted his sword, striking downward over and over, as the squat soldiers fell beneath his assault.

Seeing the effectiveness of the cavalry, the foot soldiers rallied themselves under the cries of their rikkagin, standing their ground, then gradually beginning to advance upon their foes.

Then over the deafening tumult of the battle, Rikkagin Aerent heard a muted shout and he saw a squad of warriors streaming across the river crossing directly at him. In their midst, riding an ebon creature that was difficult to look at, he saw the rikkagin of the central forces of The Dolman.

He was an immense bulk of a man, with obsidian eyes. Long dark hair swept back from his temples like the wings of some predatory bird. Above him and just behind arced two banners, fresh and whipping in the sleet storm. Straining, Rikkagin Aerent made out the ensign of silk: an ebon field with a writhing lizard as crimson as the flames which danced at its feet.

The Sunset Warrior felt it before anyone else. Deep within the tangle of metal and flesh, bone and blood and gore, he tensed. The pressure of numbers which had occupied him all the morning was mysteriously giving way.

He looked up. Still the deathshead warriors streamed across the river crossing, mixing with the plumed warriors and the pikemen. But now they came in two lines and their shouts echoed through the din of battle. They called to each other and pointed off to their right.

Putting a gauntleted hand to his forehead, he peered into the distance, downriver. And now he saw a dark shape, emerging from the sleeting mist. He began to fight his way to his left, to get nearer to it.

It plunged into the river where the water was very deep and quite swift, perhaps two hundred meters downriver from him, directly across from a jutting headland on the near shore.

He saw clearly the cold orange eyes pulsing through the snow, heard now its hideous cry echoing across the rampaging water.

The Makkon.

But he was a long way from that part of the river and

though he swung his great blade to and fro, though he lurched through the heaving sea of writhing, flailing bodies, he could make little headway, so packed was the near bank.

The Makkon came on, swinging its wickedly curved talons. Its beaked mouth opened and closed spasmodically, revealing its stubby, gray tongue. Its call was an ululation, hitting the water flatly and rebounding like a skipped stone.

Kiri, riding her saffron luma, raised her head from the slaughter about her and, jerking her mount's reins, spurred it along the near bank and out onto the promontory.

Upon this narrow spit of land Kiri now rushed, her flashing blade and the hoofs of her luma throwing aside the deathshead warriors and squat pikemen from in front of her.

Her eyes were wild, the pupils dilated with excitement and fear. With a swipe of her sword, she cut a foe in two. Her heart pounding, she stared into the baleful gaze of the Makkon midway across the river.

She was at the edge of the land now, her luma rearing, the idea burning in her mind.

"I am Kiri," she seemed to speak to the river. "Empress of Sha'angh'sei. I call you now to your task, for vengeance must be ours and you must heed my call!"

She drew the short knife in its ceremonial scabbard from the warm place at the base of her stomach and threw it behind her. Then, leaping from the saddle, her body arched in a long dive, cleaving the surface of the choppy water.

The Sunset Warrior, making his slow way toward the Makkon, saw Kiri, heard her words over the din of battle, and reaching down for another bright shard of someone's memory, knew what was coming.

Out in the river with the white sleet slanting down and the wind rising, the waters before the oncoming Makkon began to boil. The Sunset Warrior saw Kiri's head and arms as she broke the skin of the water, as she swam toward the waiting Makkon.

Into the boiling water.

Her head went down suddenly as if something below the surface had sucked her below. For only a brief moment, her white fist remained above the churning waves, a hard, defiant gesture, then it too disappeared into the midst of a dark stain spreading itself directly in the path of the Makkon. Where the water churned madly.

The Sunset Warrior bellowed his war cry and his great sword became a blur. He was a killing machine. Berserk and lethal, he advanced upon the enemy along the near bank. And now even the deathshead warriors, who knew no fear, fell back under his fierce assault, fleeing from the death that came at them on an inexorable tide.

In the river, the Makkon slapped the unquiet waters with the flat of its great hands. A funneling waterspout rose before it, whirling moisture into its beaked face. And its head raised to the top of the spout, black with its living center, and its inhuman orange eyes gazed upon the face of the Lamiae, Kay-Iro De, half goddess, half sea serpent, the protectress of Sha'angh'sei.

Now Kay-Iro De rose from the top of the spout, the great scaled serpent's body surmounted by the female head with dead-white skin and dripping seaweed hair.

Now the head of the Lamiae turned and her eyes locked with the Sunset Warrior and even though he was prepared, still he felt a shock travel through him.

What he saw was Kiri's face, fierce and serene. A languid smile spread across the lips as the graceful head turned back and with a writhing of her coils, Kay-Iro De twined herself about the muscular, pulsing form of the Makkon.

Tighter and tighter the slick body wrapped about the creature, squeezing while the thing screamed and flailed at the water. Its powerful arms were pinioned to its side by the spiraling coils and it used its cruel beak to bite into the enwrapping serpent. Water creamed upward and outward, in a frantic froth.

The Makkon screamed again, calling, calling, and at last out from the fog-bound shadows of the far shore another hulking shape loomed.

The Sunset Warrior clove through the ranks of the enemy like a deadly whirlwind, preceded by the sounds of crunching bones, in his wake the moans of the dying.

Out in the writhing river, the Lamiae's coils slid upward, wrapping about the Makkon's sturdy thick neck. Its eyes bulged and the beak ripped at the scaled hide. But Kay-Iro De's eyes blazed like living lightning and her lips drew back, half-snarl, half-laugh. The Makkon began to choke.

The Sunset Warrior cut through the last of the enemy line foaming in the shallows of the riverbank as he saw the bulk of the second Makkon wading out into the water almost directly across the river from him. Between them, the struggle.

The Makkon, entwined, gave a great heave but the Lamiae's coil wound even tighter. There came a sharp snap, as distinct as a crack of thunder on a wind-swept day, and the Makkon's head lurched to one side.

A great cry of triumph trumpeted from the Lamiae as she shot upward, bleeding profusely. Then she sank beneath the gray waves of the river.

The dim, close skies cracked with lightning and the sleet became tinged with silver, so that it had the appearance of metal. The day grew dark and oppressive, dense with cold and pressure.

The strange, plumed warriors poured across the river crossing, directed by the immense rikkagin under the billowing lizard banner, sprinting upriver where the defenses of the army of man seemed weakest.

Okami, at the head of one of the Bujun divisions, met with three other daimyos in order to revise their coordinated strategy.

Slowly, they began to work their divisions down the plain in a pincer movement, in order to destroy the vanguard of the deathshead warriors who were threatening to breach the first line of the army's defense.

The far shore still teemed with soldiers waiting to ford the river, for in all other places it was far too deep for them to cross.

Moeru and Bonneduce the Last galloped along the near bank into the conflagration upriver, rallying the forces of man. She ducked the thrust of pike and, off balance, slid from the horse. She waved for the little man to go on without her and he raced off as she began to lead a group of foot soldiers out into the water.

The Sunset Warrior stalked the second Makkon, moving with the current to his left, away from Kamado. Downriver, the creature had not yet seen him and he intended that it should remain that way until he was ready.

The thing's outline pulsed darkly through the fog and the pink sleet and even at mid-river he could smell the stench. He swam effortlessly, hindered neither by the swift current nor the weight of his armor and weapons.

He moved cautiously into the shallows, using a stand of high reeds to cover his movements until he had gained the far shore.

The plain stretched away from him, littered with the detritus of half a million soldiers.

The camp of the enemy.

And but a half kilometer further back he could make out the hazy outline of the great pine forest, black, charred beyond restoration, where lurked The Dolman.

Up the far bank he ran, slipping in the mud that the sleet had washed into the churning brown and gray waters of the river.

Coming up on it in a rush.

Visions of Ronin's battle in the City of Ten Thousand Paths, or G'fand's screaming face, his dead, bulging eyes. The weredawn at Tenchō when Ronin had burst into Matsu's room, the thing's baleful, uncurious eyes staring into Ronin's as it deliberately tore out her throat, shredding it in a spray of blood and viscera.

And the power of the Hart, at his core, white-hot, atavistic, inexhaustible, crying its rage, swept through him and he screamed, a holocaust, and the Makkon turned its cold orange eyes like beacons probing his. And he wondered if this was the one, for while he knew now that they were all linked in some unfathomable way still he hoped for the body which had caused the suffering and death.

His great sword whispered in the air and the head snapped back, the beak opening soundlessly. It batted at the sword, then howled in pain and rage. It had never before been afraid of metal. But this was *Aka-i-tsuchi* and immediately it grew wary, dodging the swift strikes, attempting to move in for the deadly blows of its talon-tipped claws. Its thick tail whipped back and forth.

It lunged at him abruptly in an effort to get within his defense but the Sunset Warrior reversed the sword in his two-handed grip, using *Aka-i-tsuchi* as if it were an enormous dagger. With explosive force, the blue-green blade penetrated the Makkon's chest and he drove it swiftly downward into the creature's bowels.

Then he was spun off his feet by a tremendous blow. He saw the Makkon staggering, its heavy legs trembling, its claws scrabbling to pull the sword from its innards, howling as its hide burned from the contact. It sank to its knees, began to topple over and for the first time he saw a Makkon bleed, a sticky black viscous fluid flowing over the ragged wound.

Darkness fell over him.

A third Makkon.

The creature smiled a secret smile as it bent over him. It reached down, its talons outstretched. He rolled but the straddle of its legs prevented his escape.

Then he became aware that he did not feel the numbing cold which Ronin had struggled against in his two battles with the Makkon. He recalled Bonneduce the Last's words to Ronin in Khiyan just before he set sail in the *Kioku* in search for Ama-no-mori: *You cannot yet defeat the Makkon.* But Ronin was no more. His Hart cried out again, bellowing, and with this came the knowledge that at last he was on equal terms with the Makkon.

He yelled, batting away the reaching talons, stiffening his fingers inside his Makkon-hide gauntlets, and slammed them into the creature's unprotected throat.

The Makkon howled, an ululation, and he ducked a powerful strike from its talons.

With an enormous blow, he smashed the Makkon to the earth beside him.

He pounded at its face, the memory of Matsu filling him like a perfume, a mist in his eyes. He paid not the slightest attention to the snaking of its arms as the powerful claws reached up and closed about his throat.

He continued to pummel the Makkon, staring into the wicked eyes with their slit pupils of ebon and with great satisfaction heard the sharp crack as its beak split.

He smashed his gauntleted fists down again and the beak shattered, splintering fragments of keratin into his face. Matsu's hot blood and flesh in a nauseating spatter across Ronin's eyes. The hideous head whipped from side to side.

But now the thing's talons had gripped his throat, gaining control, squeezing all at once. His lungs were filled with air and he lifted his fists again, smashing them into the pulpy wound. He ripped off the last remaining shard of beak, the black blood flying, cold and wet, and drew its jagged edge across the Makkon's eyes. The serrations ripped into the eyeballs.

Briefly, he felt the sting of the points of the talons as they sank into his flesh, trying to rip out his throat, but he bent his body lower, bringing pressure to bear, maintaining his leverage.

He dug in deeper with the beak, slashing through hide and viscera. Flesh came away in long, raw strips. The talons were digging deeper and the Makkon began a series of jerking motions with its arms.

With one last titanic effort, even as he felt the fierce pull at the flesh of his throat, he rammed the jagged shard deep behind the Makkon's right eye up into the brain, pounding it home as if it were a spike.

The huge body jerked under him and blood and bits of pink and dusky yellow spurted upward. He choked and wiped at his face with his corded arms, leaning the weight of his whole frame behind the strike.

Beneath him, the Makkon shuddered, a brown liquid gurgled from the thing's mouth and the talons fell away from him.

On his knees, straddling the Makkon's corpse, he slammed his fist one more time into the ruined face of the Makkon. Then he stood, strode to where his sword rose like a grave marker above the body of the second Makkon. He ripped it from its flesh, sheathed it, turned away, loping to the river, feeling the chill water cleansing him of the caked filth which covered him. He ducked his head, came up snorting.

On the point of returning to the far bank, he heard, over the din of battle, screaming from upriver. The sleet had lessened momentarily and the sounds came to him clearly, funneled along the acoustic channel of the river.

Across the water, the enemy had broken through the lines of defense. He squinted into the afternoon gloom, saw the whipping banners as the forefront of the enormous wedge of warriors breaking out from their foothold on the bank, sweeping upward onto the field before Kamado's towering walls.

Crimson lizard on an ebon field and, his heart pounding, he struck out across the river with long, powerful strokes.

Whatever is happening downriver where the Bujun fight, we are losing the battle here, thought Rikkagin Aerent. He wheeled his horse about. The glistening hide was flecked with foam, blood, and gore. It trampled several wounded men as he drove it up a short rise.

He surveyed the scene, sickened by the monumental devastation. So many deaths and the day is but half gone.

The plain was a vast noisome sea of flailing flesh and ground bone, gouting gray dust and spurting blood. The field itself seemed to have undergone basic geological changes since the morning. Where once it had been a softly undulating expanse, it had now metamorphosed into a series of humpbacked hillocks by the carnage of the day's fighting. Immense mounds of the dead and wounded rolled away from him for as far as he could see. The constant sleet, pouring down from the angry skies, melting in the bloodheat, turned the whole into a grisly morass as it mingled with the spilled fluids of the fallen combatants.

He hacked at a squat warrior who ran at him, taking off the weapon arm at its socket. He pulled on the reins of his mount and it stamped on the falling body, its hard hoofs cracking the skull above the eyes.

Not for the first time, he thought about sending one of his men back up the field for the Bujun. He had witnessed their brilliant, fierce pincer attack, saw how it had wiped out the attacking deathshead warriors. Now they fought downriver and he turned to take in the extent of his remaining forces. They were so depleted that he could not afford to send a courier. Besides, the chances of one man surviving the long passage across the field were quite slim. He would just have to hold on here until help arrived.

Curse that rikkagin, whoever he was! thought Rikkagin Aerent. The lizard banners had haunted his cavalry all the day, matching him strategy for strategy, and all the while the sheer force of the enemy's numbers was slowly overpowering his line of defense.

He felt angry and helpless, as if caught in an immense and unmoving vise from which he seemed unable to extricate himself and his men.

Rikkagin Aerent knew his duty and now he felt that he was failing to perform it. He had had but one thought as he rode out onto the plain at the dawning of this unnatural day: to win. Now he felt that goal slipping away from him as the unseen sun dragged itself like a wounded dragon across the unquiet heavens.

Abruptly the tide of the battle brought Moeru close to him. She was mounted on some dead soldier's horse. Through the slime and muck of the jammed field she came toward him.

"I have been pinned for too long by that bastard lizard rikkagin!" he shouted to her. "Moeru, can you take command of the cavalry? I must penetrate to the rikkagin's standards and destroy him before his forces totally overrun this position."

Moeru nodded and spurred her blood-soaked steed toward the last beleaguered remnants of Rikkagin Aerent's cavalry. No officers were left alive.

She called to the riders and peeled off with ten of them, wheeling them in a tight arc, spinning them into a flank attack on the squat pikemen. They used their mounts' hoofs as battering rams.

Satisfied that he had made the correct decision, Rikkagin

Aerent jerked on his reins. His horse's head came about, snorting, and it reared into the air.

Now we go, he said to himself.

With a leap he rushed across the field of battle, up steep ridges of cracked armor and pink, flecked bones, toward a high picket line of pikes formed by fallen warriors. Onward, avoiding forests of pikes, hacking at marauding bands of plumed warriors, ducking the hissing, deadly globes of the deathshead warriors.

He plunged forward in a furious burst of killing breaking through the enemy guard line, the way black with their beetling bodies. Ahead lay the pike line and beyond the billowing banners of the rampant ebon lizard. Down a tunnel bristling with pikes and brandished swords he galloped, over rise after rise of mounded bodies, squirming and dank, splashing through puddles of blood, bogs of entrails, crunching skulls and spines, always the black banners flapping in the wind like expectant vultures, above him, just over the next rise of bodies, and he plunged onward with iron determination as the squat warriors screamed and seized at him with torn and bloody fingers, long nails twisted and peeling painfully away as they scraped along his mount's flanks and withers, grasping greasily at his boots, flailing their short swords, slipping in the mire that was the remnants of their fallen comrades.

His sword arm lifted and fell, over and over, endlessly, replicating death and destruction as he plowed through the quicksand of the battle, the sleet in his eyes, rimming his beard and eyebrows with pink frost. Blood and spittle flew at him. Limbs and heads were sheared away, fingers split, weapons spinning slowly in the thick, frosted air, the grim meatgrinder of his passage. And still the ebon and crimson banners flew triumphantly before him, seeming to mock his efforts, just ahead now, past another ten score warriors. Almost there.

And at length a rent opened up in the line and Rikkagin Aerent galloped madly through.

Bonneduce the Last, fighting quite near the lizard banners, saw the rikkagin hit the enemy position and squirt through. He spurred his luma forward, leaning low in the saddle and striking along his left flank, making considerable headway toward the black banners.

Now he saw Rikkagin Aerent nearing the huge figure riding atop the strange black beast and, as Bonneduce too broke through the line in a ferocious attack, his gaze swung toward the Salamander.

He gasped, uttering a name borne away on the tidal noise of the battle.

Now he whispered to his luma, urging it forward, through the twisting bodies, and as he topped a rise he found himself quite close to the lizard banners and he stared at the proud face, the cold, obsidian eyes, the wind-swept hair, the layers of fat added to disguise the characteristic shape of the high cheekbones and thought, So this is what has happened. Oh, I am happy that he is not here to witness this ultimate shame.

Now Bonneduce the Last turned once again to the mundane, numbing business of killing, using his luma to do some of the work, guiding it so that it plunged ahead, kicking out with its forelegs, battering helm and breastplate, cracking pike haft, as he slashed to left and right.

Over the slimy ridge and into the last dell.

Above his head the twin lizards crawled in their beds of flame.

He saw the Salamander's head come up and swing around as shouts from his guard presaged Rikkagin Aerent's swift approach. Staying the pike of one of his guards, he drew forth from the folds of his ebon robes two stubby sticks made of polished wood linked by a short length of black metal chain. Almost casually he gripped the sticks.

Rikkagin Aerent thrust his sword high in the air, screaming his battle cry, decapitating a squat warrior.

Bonneduce the Last spurred his luma forward, calling out a warning to the charging rikkagin. But even if his words had not been lost in the din of the conflagration, it would have been too late.

The Salamander had wheeled his mount, and with a deceptive flick of his left wrist, he tossed the weapon.

Rikkagin Aerent saw only a whirling blur. He tried to duck but he was too close and the thing was upon him almost before reflexive action could occur. The heavy, weighted wood slammed into his collarbone, the doubled iron chain whipping at him an instant later. The force of the dual blow threw him from his saddle. He was knocked sideways, twisting, and as he fell one boot was trapped in his stirrup.

Panicked, his mount leapt forward, dragging the rikkagin across the lumped ground. His body fetched up against the line of pikes over which the lizard banners flew and a bone splintered in his leg. His boot flew from the stirrup and he lay as if dead atop a mass of bleeding corpses over which clouds of flies had begun to settle.

The Salamander had already turned away from him, directing his foot soldiers into a small breach in the defenses of the army of many. The squat warriors leapt to do his bidding.

Bonneduce the Last urged his luma across the shallow valley, passing the twisted form of Rikkagin Aerent.

He made directly for the Salamander.

The thunder of his steed's hoofs echoed in his ears. He thought of Hynd, pacing restlessly, safe behind the walls of Kamado, reluctant to leave his side but knowing his duty nonetheless. Too, he thought of the Rhyalann ticking within the folds of his worn leather bags in the barracks house in Kamado. He had left it there on purpose, knowing full well the consequences of his action. At last he understood completely the meaning of his long miserable quest over the eons, beyond Time itself.

He brandished his nicked sword, black with blood, shards of white bone clinging to its long length.

"Tokagé!" he called. "Here I am! Is it not I for whom you have sought all this morning?"

With infinite slowness, the immense head, the pads of thick fat guarding his features, turned in his direction. The onyx eyes, lusterless as granite, glared at him, and the thick-lipped, pouting mouth curved gently upward.

"Fool to have come to me," said the Salamander, his voice rolling sonorously over the confused din of the raging conflict. "But I knew you would."

Bonneduce reined in his luma. It pranced nervously upon the insecure footing, disliking the tight rein. Eager to run again, it danced over the cracked skulls of the dead.

"How you escaped death I cannot imagine," said the little man.

The Salamander's face registered neither anger nor surprise.

"Did you expect me to submit to death? I would have thought that you knew me better than that." He chuckled with real humor, a sound as rich as brocaded silk. He paused as if delighting in a sound long unused and quite remarkable to him.

His guards called nervously to him.

"Take the perimeter," he told them softly. "Guard it well. Let none interfere." They fanned out surrounding the pair atop their mounts. Only the two standard-bearers with the enormous banners fluttering above their heads, the wings of a giant nocturnal bird of prey, stayed behind with their master.

"No, no," he said to Bonneduce the Last. "How unclever

you are not to have guessed. Only we survived. And how? Think! Like you I made a pact."

"With that thing. And with its power you flew across the ages like an animal, for that is all you really are. How many lives—"

"Candles snuffed out by an ungentle wind. They were all unimportant." He pulled on his reins, fighting for control of his ebon monster, the stench of blood a constant thing in its nostrils. "No, let me say rather, *less* important than myself, for I value this person above all others—"

"If dor-Sefrith were here—"

The Salamander's huge face darkened momentarily. "But he is not. He has been destroyed. Yes"—seeing the look on the other's face—"he is finally gone for all time. As he promised, The Dolman destroyed him, attacking him directly when he was otherwise occupied. That foray delayed The Dolman's arrival but it was worth it, I believe. No more tampering—"

The black beast reared high in the air, it's eyes rolling madly.

"Now it is but you and I. For you are the last of the race and you alone can tell Ronin—"

Bonneduce the Last had spurred his luma forward. He kept his features in careful repose but beneath the stone exterior he exulted. The Dolman must know of the coming of the Sunset Warrior, of who he had been, yet he had chosen not to inform his disciple.

"The end is nigh, Tokagé!" called Bonneduce the Last as he closed with the huge man. The Rhyalann was gone and its safety with it. He shrugged inwardly. It had been given to him, a sacred trust he could not refuse, just as he could not refuse the suffering of his quest. Not after the shame his lord had brought to his folk.

"The old name!" hissed the Salamander, his face twisting in rage for the first time. "On your knees, if you would use it, little man!" And he flung out his hand.

Bonneduce the Last saw them coming.

Suriken. Black metal stars.

His boots had already been freed from the prison of his stirrups.

He slid from the saddle.

There was time for nothing else.

His ears were filled with the buzzing as if from a swarm of angry bees. Two of the weapons buried themselves in his luma's head and it went down on its knees, toppling, and he had to roll, roll in the filth to avoid being crushed by its weight.

Over the sticky, slippery ground, spiked with fallen weapons. Hearing the booming laughter of Tokagé and, in his mind, the echoes reverberating along the vast corridors of Time, the long eons of his sorrowful existence, mocking all the good men whose blood he had spilled. Tokagé! The bones he had splintered, the tears of death he had caused. The unspeakable anguish.

Bonneduce the Last rose, climbing the mountains of the dead and the dying, his leg paining him now, his mind turning automatically away from the long-known, familiar physical agony. He tuned himself now to the grief of his long-dead people. Restless still. Crying out for retribution. Shamed by history. By Tokagé, their liege.

"I learned many things over the ages," Tokagé was saying to him. "I am no longer an animal, despite what you believe. I wish you to understand this before I kill you. It is evil's day, the cycle has come, as I knew it would. It is as simple as that. Who will be victorious—"

Bonneduce the Last came on, oblivious to the words flying at him, adrenalin pumping through his body, vibrating his sword arm. He heard only the cries of his shamed people calling to him over the interminable centuries. He felt only their torment. He meant only to end it.

"I would not wish this alliance," Tokagé continued, and his massive head turned briefly to look across the river, to the hissing charcoal pine forest, no more than a kilometer away. He turned back. "I do not love that hideous thing; no man could. It is annihilation. But what choice did I have? It was this or death—"

Bonneduce the Last felt the eyes of his people upon him, felt their strength bubbling inside him, and for the first time in long eons he felt what it was like to be alive. He marveled.

Now I am what I am, he thought.

"You would have made the same bargain," said Tokagé. "I know that. You have not stared death in the face. You have not felt its cold embrace, the slipping away of all consciousness, all volition—" The ebon beast reared again at Bonneduce the Last's approach. "I could not let go of life!" His eyes got small as a cunning look spread over his face. "And then I understood that it would be all right for I found that with each passing day I grew more powerful and secretly I began to leech more power away from him and soon, very soon, even he will not be able to stop me. Then can I end this servitude and destroy him!"

Somewhere in the back of his mind, Bonneduce the Last felt some last shred of compassion for this haunted man, driven by the unrelenting ghosts of power. Old associations, perhaps, he told himself. Then that too disappeared, engulfed by the red storm of his final avenging assault.

Carrying out the Salamander's directive, flogged mercilessly by their insect-eyed rikkagin, the squat warriors poured through the widening rent in the defenses of the army of man. They set a picket line of pikes which they moved outward, breaking the attempt at a counteroffensive.

Through the rent which they protected charged the plumed warriors, up the plain, toward the high walls of Kamado.

Screaming.

Moeru, seeing the foot soldiers routed, gathered up the few remaining cavalry about her and, wheeling, galloped downstream, searching for the Bujun.

They fought each other with long blades, as they had been taught eons ago, in the ancient manner, the thrusts and parries so swift that one began before the other ended, a constant flow of precisely directed energy.

"There is no one better than I, little one," said Tokagé. "Accept your fate. You shall die honorably, like a warrior."

"The time for talk is long past," said Bonneduce the last. "Your acts speak for themselves. There is nothing you can say to expiate your guilt."

"My guilt? I did only what I had to in order to survive—"

"You groveled like an animal—"

"And I lived, fool!"

"To survive is not enough. Life must have meaning."

"All that matters is that I am here now. And I will destroy you!"

She found Okami in the muddy shallows of the river, thrice wounded but battling still. He mobilized the Bujun battalions under his command and they moved off upriver in an attempt to enfilade the enemy breakthrough.

Up from the silty banks and across the littered plain rushed the Bujun, reaping a bloody harvest of all who stood in their path.

* * *

The thin round blade flicked out as they closed. A sixth finger, it was aimed for the jugular, but Tokagé countered with the *tokko*, the short metal weapon with a clawed trident at each end.

Tokagé jerked his wrist and the thin blade emanating from the inside of Bonneduce the Last's wrist snapped. Immediately he reversed the *tokko*, dragging it across the little man's chest.

Bonneduce the Last groaned inwardly with the pain. He reached up and pulled Tokagé down from his high saddle. The black beast leapt high in the air as the little man jabbed it with a powerful strike.

Into the mire of the grisly battlefield.

"Feel what it is like to be down here in the quagmire of death, Tokagé," Bonneduce the Last said.

Tokagé lurched, slipping across the curvature of a partially buried helm under his boot sole.

Bonneduce the Last attacked, a thin-bladed stiletto pushed forward.

In the instant of his attack he understood the nature of the other's ruse.

He ignored the blade which bloomed in Tokagé's fist, concentrating on what he knew he had to do.

He felt the cold metal like a fire as it pierced his armor and the flesh of his shoulder.

Perception narrowed as he consciously dulled the agony which swept through him as Tokagé's arm descended.

The point of his stiletto pierced Tokagé's right eye at the precise instant he felt the shock wave of the other's cruel blade.

A peculiar warmth suffused his body and, as he completed the strike, he had time to remember, a feeling denied him for many centuries. It was all he wished for.

Then Tokagé's blade swept relentlessly through his torso, splitting his spine.

He toppled over, his blood spilling out, mingling with the entrails, the bones, of the warriors piled beneath his body.

His eyes stared upward. The great black and crimson banners filled a hazy sky. Dimly he was aware of the prickle of the sleet against his upturned face. It filled him with a sudden, bright passion and, unaccountably, he wept.

Slowly, the banners seemed to settle over him like a shroud.

* * *

Dripping from the river's moisture, the Sunset Warrior climbed the high shore, shaking the encroaching enemy warriors from him almost as if they were drops of water.

Seizing the reins of Kiri's abandoned luma, he swung into the saddle and dug his boot heels into the foam-flecked flanks.

In a silver shower, he sped along the near bank, upriver to where the enemy had broken through the defenses and was pouring across the plain toward Kamado.

Onto the field of battle he plunged, screaming as he went, drawing *Aka-i-tsuchi*, and indeed his wake across the undulating plain was an explosion of blood and bones. He leapt barriers of broken bodies, barricades of war horses and fallen pikes. Corpses clung to him, their corded muscles twitching in death, their legs flapping like shredded banners against his steed's flanks, slowing him down. He hacked at their limbs, shedding them like great, frozen tears.

The fluttering of the Salamander's standards bloomed before him out of the driving sleet. He passed a ragged fence of waving pikes.

And then he caught sight of the huge frame clothed in ebon armor and ebon robes. He rode a black beast. As he watched, the Salamander bent to the side for a moment, reaching down to wipe his blade upon the tattered clothing of a warrior who had died upon his feet because there was no longer any space for his body to fall.

Perhaps he heard the insistent drumming of the Sunset Warrior's luma approaching, for the Salamander's huge head turned and his cruel obsidian eyes focused on the oncoming rider.

He spent no time in identifying the figure but wheeled his mount, calling to his guard. He took off over the plain toward the bank of the river, his ebon banners rippling in his wake.

The Sunset Warrior topped the last rise and sped across the shallow valley to the spot where the Salamander had stood. He missed Rikkagin Aerent atop the pile of the dead but he saw the still form of Bonneduce the Last and although he longed to overtake the Salamander now he knew that he could not.

Dismounting even as he drew back on the reins, he ran over the jellied earth. He knelt almost knee deep in the viscous slime and picked the small body off the ground.

"Oh, my friend, what has he done to you?"

There was no response and the Sunset Warrior felt his heart breaking. He had thought he was beyond all that. And at last he understood. As Ronin he had cut himself off from any more hurt after he killed K'reen. Because of that he had not seen the love that Matsu had for him. Worse he had not understood his own love for her until it was too late. To live was to feel. Thus he wept for Bonneduce the Last.

The little man opened his eyes. He felt the life leaking out of him yet was glad to see the strange, terrifyingly fierce face so close above him. He felt the enormous strength of the arms which held him tightly and was comforted. Only then did he feel the tears mingling with the sleet on his face.

"Do not mourn for me, old friend, there is no time." He closed his eyes, heard the harsh rustle of his own breathing. His lungs were beginning to fill up with his own fluids. "There is much to tell you before I die, so listen to me now. Your old nemesis, the Salamander, is known to me. When I was given the Rhyalann, sent on my quest, I thought all of my folk had perished." He coughed and the Sunset Warrior wiped the pink spittle from his dry lips. "He is Tokagé, my liege. It was he whose unquenchable thirst for power caused the creation of The Dolman. Yes. Yes. It is true." His voice was harsh and insistent. "For all these eons I thought him dead, destroyed by the very thing he had caused to be born. But I was wrong. He was too clever to die. He made a pact with The Dolman. It is his master now and it has made him immortal, given him great power." His head went slack and his eyelids fluttered as he fought for a few more moments of life. Time, he thought, you were always my enemy.

"My friend, there is a chance for you now. I know it. He has not been told what you have become. He calls you Ronin still. The Dolman has kept the knowledge from him. He believes he can win against that horror but even he does not understand what he unleashed. He cannot face that fact." He was wracked with coughs and he thought: Must hold on just a little longer. He clung to the Sunset Warrior like a child.

"Rikk-Rikkagin Aerent, did you see him?"

"No."

"Tokagé felled him near here. Find him. I do not think that he is dead. He tried to destroy Tokagé. Such a hero."

"I will find him."

"And Moeru?"

"Somewhere on the battlefield."

"No. No. She must be beside you—" He became agitated.

"Calm yourself, my friend."

"Tokagé told me. The Dolman attacked dor-Sefrith while

he was otherwise occupied. That is—is how he put it—"

"What does that—"

"The Dolman attacked him while the process of change—"

"Mine."

"Yes."

"I see, but—"

Bonneduce the Last's body convulsed, his entire frame shuddering as if a titanic struggle were taking place within him. The worn face drained of all color. The Sunset Warrior was drenched with his blood. And there was little left. Only this:

"Tokagé is dor-Sefrith's father." The voice was but a dry rattle. "The Dolman killed his son. As—as Tokagé wished."

The Sunset Warrior knelt in the chill quagmire holding the dead man. He got to his feet, slowly, slowly.

A shout came to him over the tumult of the battle and he spun about.

Moeru spurred her steel toward him. The smile on her face disappeared as she saw the small body he held. She reined in, her mount reared, and she patted its glistening hide. She was covered with blood and gore, her breastplate dark and running, her leggings sopping wet. Her hair flew from the confines of her dented helm.

"Okami also," she said.

He nodded.

"Rikkagin Aerent is wounded somewhere near. Can you spare someone?"

"Now perhaps yes."

She pointed downriver, toward the sea so many kilometers away.

"See there!" Her voice held a measure of excitement.

He peered through the sleet. Sailing up the river was a fleet of ships of a strange configuration all flying the same flag: black bars on a maroon field.

"It is Moichi!" Her voice a cry of delight. "His people come to join the Kai-feng!"

And the Sunset Warrior, feeling the enormous weight of the small body lying against his chest, thought: But still, too late for some.

The Dai-San

NOW he left them to it.

For him no longer the battle of man against man.

For him the Salamander and The Dolman.

For him the world had ceased to spin on its axis. The seasons were frozen, the sun invisible, the moon gone. For now the ultimate purpose of his life was before him.

All else fell away. A dream only.

Thus did he pursue the whipping banners of the rampant ebon lizard, tail in its open mouth, crimson flames licking at its body. And he recalled words from the ancient mythology of his world: *Thus the Salamander, rising from the living flames, eschews death to command, in league with Evil.*

Across the death-strewn plain he rode, pushing the luma past even its enormous limits. Its forelegs became battering rams as it flung aside the living and the dead alike, jumping piles of corpses black with buzzing furry flies, careening past death struggles, decapitations, disembowelings, past massacres and stalemates until at last it collapsed under him, tumbling with him down the slope of the near bank, greasy with mud and blood and entrails.

He leapt, uncoiling his powerful leg muscles, and hit the lapping water in a flat, economical dive, hurling himself outward, not down into the depths.

He surfaced nearly a third of the way across, shaking his head free of water, and kicked scissor-fashion with his legs, his limbs working in concert, establishing a rapid rhythm.

Came up out of the water, calling, calling, even as he launched himself up the steep incline of the far shore. And he heard the thunder of its hoofs and he loped across the hard ground to meet it.

He mounted his crimson luma in one wide sweep of his parted legs. It reared, snorting, and he spoke to it softly, crooning, and it took off after the rapidly disappearing banners.

Sang softly to it as it ran easily, effortlessly, over the wide field, away from the charcoal wood, and now its speed increased until they were fairly flying. And together they rejoiced in the passion of wind and sleet against their bodies.

Find her—Bring her.

Within the high yellow walls of Kamado, Hynd knew of Bonneduce the Last's passing. Rather than mourning, he felt only the warmth of their long years of friendship. He had known of the little man's vast torment and he was happy now that at last the pain had been stripped away, shed like the old and lifeless skin of a snake.

Find her—Bring her.

He prowled the narrow, deserted streets, past all the dark, dead gods, pillared as if crucified. Angrily, he sought an answer to a question beyond him.

Find her—Bring her.

The last thought glowing in his mind before the silken cord had been severed by Bonneduce the Last's death. A banner rippling against the skies of his mind.

Obviously he had meant Moeru. There was no doubt of that.

Abruptly he reined in, squinting ahead.

Six horsemen, including the two standard-bearers. And between them the coal-black creature upon whom sat—

He pulled hard on the reins. The luma leapt into the air, wheeling. He cursed himself for a fool as he dug his boot heels into his luma's gleaming flanks, heading back across the barren plain toward the verge of the ebon forest.

It was not the Salamander who rode that devilish thing, though the figure was fully as huge and was dressed in his black robes. The wind had shifted, coming directly at him from the party ahead, and he had caught the horrid stench of the thing which rode the monster.

Decoyed.

And now behind him, the fourth Makkon pounded its great malformed fists against the steaming coat of the creature upon whose back it rode. And it left the standard-bearers and the guards behind as it took off after the Sunset Warrior.

* * *

They both had seen the incompleteness that first moment when the Sunset Warrior had galloped into Kamado but there was nothing to say. Even if they could have told him—which, they both knew they could not—what was there to say? Dor-Sefrith was the only one and he was dead now.

At long last all the gods were gone, all the wise men used up, all the hosts of the mages dreaming their endless dreams.

We are left alone now to make our own decisions, thought Hynd. If we die, then it will be by our own hands. And if we live, then we will have earned all that we shall inherit. This world with its day and its night. Perhaps even the stars.

Down the refuse-strewn streets he ran, his round tail flying, and rats shrieked, scampering from his path. Out of the high gates and onto the vast field.

He knew now what he had to do. He wondered if the same could be said for the Sunset Warrior.

He left the panting luma at the edge of the dead forest and went in on foot.

Before the fire caused by the coming of The Dolman, the forest had been dense. In death it remained difficult to penetrate. Remarkably, none of the branches or trunks had been destroyed by the unnatural conflagration, only the foliage, so that now the wood had, more than ever, the appearance of a maze.

He ignored the muffled sounds behind him, keeping to an imaginary path that took him due north. Time and again, he was obliged to make circuitous detours. He did not use his sword or any other weapon for he was quite determined to give his foes no advantage whatsoever and this included any forewarning of his approach. The sounds of his cleaving the brittle branches would be heard a kilometer away. Now and then a thought threatened to intrude upon his consciousness or perhaps feeling was the more appropriate word. But his mind was narrowing as his concentration heightened and the wisp of intuition was thrust aside, losing itself on a sudden gust of wind.

At length he came to a clearing. The sleet had ceased but the day was darker now, oppressive and colder than ever. He peered up at the violent skies, watching for a moment the heavy amber clouds stretched across the world like the taut skin of a fevered animal. He thought briefly of Kukulkan, the lord of light, writhing in his domain far above the destruction encompassing the world. Here the sun did not exist.

He whirled even before he heard the crashing behind him. He drew *Aka-i-tsuchi*.

There was green mist among the trees, pale and opalescent, swirling, fuming, rolling into the tiny glade. Behind the mist, a dark, hulking shape, looming. Orange eyes like blazing beacons.

The fourth Makkon.

The Salamander's robes, torn and muddy, streamed open, fluttering to the earth. The reek of the Makkon scent filled the clearing. The long powerful tail whipped back and forth behind it, freeing itself from the last remnants of the ebon cloth. A wailing came from the curved beak.

This Makkon seemed taller than its brothers and perhaps it was older, though that concept might have been inimical to the creature. Its eyes were cold and alien and clever. Its outline pulsed, growing blurred here and there.

As it advanced, its arms swung out, and the movement was accompanied by a sound like that of scythes cutting through ripe wheat. And now the Sunset Warrior saw that where its brothers had possessed scaled, six-fingered claws, this one had hands fashioned from what appeared to be clear, cut quartz. But beneath the hard, glistening surface, lights of pastel reds and purples shot through the length of the curved fingers, magnified as if seen through the eye of a lens.

The gray beak, yellowed somewhat, opened spasmodically and the stiff triangular tongue fluttered again and again. The Makkon hurled its titanic bulk at him and he pivoted on his left leg, facing the charge with his left side. Slammed the flat of his sword across the shoulders of the thing.

As the massive frame hurtled past him, he heard the repeated sounds coming from the Makkon. Over and over it called and he believed now that it was the speech of man, garbled and tortured, as if the creature had spent long years learning one phrase and was now forcing it out of a larynx not meant to reproduce such syllables.

"I want them," said the Makkon.

It charged him again and he twisted, but this time it was ready, and more swiftly than it seemed possible for a thing of such bulk, it feinted, coming in under his guard. He felt a searing pain in his left arm. As if liquid ice were being injected into his veins.

The quartz hand had grasped him and the transparent talons had sunk into the inside of his arm just above the ending of the Makkon gauntlet. The living lights within the crystal skin lanced out of the tips of the hollow claws into his flesh. He jerked at the contact but could not break the grip. He swung his sword but his position was awkward and he had little leverage. The blow glanced, skittering off the pulsing hide. The hideous beak opened and a terrible howling broke from the Makkon's mouth.

"I want them."

He wrenched at his arm again, feeling the ice flowing into him. Pain raced through him and the blackened trees spun around him. He went to his knees, the strength abruptly deserting his legs. He dropped his useless sword.

"I want them."

The Makkon's other hand came down on the hide of the gauntlet and, with a raking motion, tried to peel it off his hand. He clenched his fist against the pressure and abruptly another memory hurled itself into the spotlight of his consciousness. Dor-Sefrith's green glazed brick house in the City of Ten Thousand Paths. Within the second story, an empty glass case with two imprints of things which resembled a man's hand. Larger. More fingers? Of course! The gauntlets had been the magus' doing. Had dor-Sefrith battled this Makkon? Had it been he who had cut the hands off it? He stared into the glowing, febrile eyes and knew.

Now the chill blackness threatened to engulf him and he cursed himself for his carelessness. He was in serious trouble, finished before he had even begun. He spiraled his mind inward.

The world turned upside down.

Hit the ground with the soles of his boots, allowing them to take the brunt of the velocity. He leaned forward and rolled. Free.

Because he had fought harder, pulling against the fury of the Makkon, building the strength within him, setting up the increasingly high stresses of the tug of war, digging his heels into the snow and ice, increasing the pressure, his teeth grinding, ignoring the encroaching blackness, feeling the answering response as the Makkon pulled harder against him. Reversed it then, using the thing's strength against him, entering when pulled, stepping through the move, slamming into the frame, then arching himself up and over the stumbling Makkon, the boiling amber sky the floor of his world for a long moment when the wind whistled through his hair and piled snow was a white barrier over his head.

The tearing almost wrenched his arm from its socket but

the talons left his flesh, their lights shooting into the air momentarily. Rolling across the hard ground, his high helm spinning into a snowdrift.

But the Makkon had already recovered and was upon him as he uncoiled, its transparent talons searching again for his flesh. He felt its humid terrible breath, choking him in viscous fumes, and he smashed his balled fist against the Makkon's skull. It staggered and fell over sideways, its long arms flailing dangerously but again it was a feint and one hand whipped in under his guard and crashed against his cheek. Immediately the whole side of his face went numb. Felt as if the cheekbone had shattered. Sight in that eye suddenly blurred and he lost depth perception. Something cold and slimy slithered around his neck. The Makkon's tail. It wrapped itself about his throat and the jeweled claw came for him, reaching for his eyes. It slashed. And at the same time he thrust the gauntlet up, smashing it into the underside of the Makkon's beak. It shattered and the creature howled in pain and rage. But the noose of the tail tightened, keeping the air in his lungs trapped, and as his system extracted the oxygen, manufacturing carbon dioxide, it became a poison. He was killing himself.

He fought one hand down to his side and drew his short blade. Its virgin metal whispered in the glade, bespeaking the mysteries of warfare, death, and destruction, and he thrust it up blindly, into the rent mouth. The hide had already been split and he searched for the broken flesh, sawing desperately with the blade. But the Makkon twisted, would not let the sword's point reach the vulnerable spot at the top of its palate. Viscous black fluid, Makkon's blood, gouted over him in a sickening wave and the creature's crystal talons sought purchase along his arms, opening the flesh, and time now narrowed into a few agonizingly short moments as the Sunset Warrior hacked at the flesh and the Makkon pumped its strange poison into his opened veins. Flesh ribboning and breath fouling.

The ice was a crimson tide leeching the strength from him, ten thousand flecks of shining death probing deep into him, and he ignored the rising agony and twisted, sight returning to his eye, depth perception critical now. He moved another centimeter to the left, concentrated his entire force upward from the sole of his boot, through his bent leg, straightening it, striking at the proper angle, the power thus magnified, totally awesome, crashing just under the Makkon's chin. It howled and the tail unwound, whiplike, but the talons remained embedded. Used the sword, thrusting mightily into the Makkon's mouth, feeling the blade breaching the roof, the sighing blade bisecting the creature's brain. It reared up, dragging itself over him in its last desperate attempt to outrun the shining sword, but he hung on, tenacious and relentless, increasing the force of the thrust until his muscles screamed for release from the enormous tension and, twisting, he heaved the massive body onto its back, sitting astride it and, using both hands, showing the orange eyes the sight of its own dead hands being used to kill it, jammed the blade all the way through the head, shattering the back of the skull in a burst of fury. The point buried itself in the white frost beneath them.

The great frame shuddered, spasming, and its ruined face turned into the snow as the Sunset Warrior pulled the short blade free.

He bathed the sword in the snow away from the corpse and, sheathing it, he retrieved *Aka-i-tsuchi* and his high helm. Transferring the long sword to his left hand momentarily, he set the helm back upon his head.

Above him the amber sky was darkening still although there was much time before the sunset. The day died and now he lived in perpetual twilight.

He quit the clearing and the sprawled body seeping its wastes blackly upon the whiteness of the forest's floor, plunging northward into the twisted, charred maze.

No birds sang here, or insects fluttering delicately amid the ribboning boles of the trees; no brush, no lichen, nothing save the endless trunks like makeshift grave markers set in the frozen, snow-covered ground.

He embarked upon an incline, the way becoming abruptly steep, the wood's floor littered with gray boulders around which the trees thrust themselves with tenacious fury as if in defiance of the force which exfoliated them.

Upward he climbed toward the ridge's high crest. He clambered through the snow and ice, using the blackened branches now to haul himself upward with increasing speed.

The ridge went on and on, stretching away from him on both sides in an undulating line, the end of the world. As he neared its crest, he saw the scarlet cloth billowing in the wet wind, the banners of the damned.

The lapis and sea-green jade of his ribbed armor gleamed as he lifted one hand to his high helm and carefully lowered its visor. And the world was finite now, seen through ebon bars, a prison of vengeance and death. The crimson banners beckoned to him.

He topped the rise, just to the east of the immense figure who stood astride the crest of the ridge garbed in a breastplate of carved obsidian. Over the heart a lizard of dusky red was set like a giant, malformed ruby. His crimson cloak flapped behind him.

Fat fleshed out the face so that the prominent cheekbones which Ronin would have considered alien were successfully hidden. Folds of skin cleverly cloaked the shape of the long almond eyes whose irises had been as bright as obsidian so that the Sunset Warrior wondered if he had seen some surgeon. Because now he saw beneath the layers of fat and flesh to the face's bone structure and he saw the ancestor of the Bujun. What had happened to the Salamander's right eye? It was a blackened hole over which a makeshift patch flapped ineffectually. Bonneduce the Last?

"Oh, Ronin, how foolish to have found me," said the Salamander, leaping at the Sunset Warrior. Their blades clashed once and parted. They stood facing each other.

"I see that your new friends have given you another sword," said the Salamander, "but it will do you no good. You were never my equal in anything." They eyed each other. "Do you still think your punishment so severe for your betrayal? Fidelity is a hard lesson but once learned it is salvation."

"Freidal is dead," said the Sunset Warrior, his voice muffled by the closed helm so that the Salamander could not make out its strange new tones.

"Well, I expected nothing less from my pupil. Was his death slow and agonizing? It should have been. The man was a sadist."

The Sunset Warrior laughed.

"You are amused?"

"K'reen." He just managed to say it.

"You defied me!" cried the Salamander. "I made you what you are. Only I knew what you could have been. You were mine to mold. You had no right to leave!"

Blue-white sparks flying, the echoing clang of metal against metal. The Sunset Warrior let *Aka-i-tsuchi* speak for him.

"I have his power now," said the Salamander. "See what your vengeance brings you? Only your own death!"

Their blades came together over and over in oblique strikes

as they moved along the humped back of the snaking ridge, a white scar along the gray and umber land.

"Your new weapons and armor do not fool me! I was told what to expect." His laugh bounded through the wood, sharp and distorted by the clogged air, the twisted trees like cracked mirrors sending off shards of reflections pulled out of shape.

He went against the fat man with short chopping arcs and the Salamander parried them all, standing his ground, then counterattacking with enormous swiftness, his blade a blur of living lightning, and now it was the Sunset Warrior's turn to parry all that was sent against him.

They hurled themselves at each other, battering, feinting, lunging. The Salamander moved to the right, his sword swinging out in a flat arc, the Sunset Warrior moved to counter as the blade hit the extreme edge of its parabolic arc and began to slash inward. But the Salamander's body moved the opposite way and the edge of his knee slammed into the Sunset Warrior's hip just below the protective lower edge of the ribbed breastplate.

The Salamander's booted foot reared into the air, blurred with momentum, a striking reptile, and the sole struck the Sunset Warrior on the point of his chin. He staggered under the force of the strike, felt the imminence of the killing blow as it headed for his unprotected neck. He knew the sequence, heard the soft whistle of the blade through the dense air on its way to cleave his head from his shoulders. He swayed, stood his ground, lifted his weaponless left hand, and almost languidly, allowed the Salamander's blade to strike the gleaming scales of the Makkon gauntlet. The sword edge slid harmlessly away.

He looked for it then, within the hard depths of the Salamander's eyes, and saw it, the first glint of an emotion long foreign to the big man. For just an instant it fluttered nakedly. Then it was gone, squeezed out by the flat glitter of the ebon pupils.

"If it is sorcery you wish," said the Salamander, "then it is sorcery you shall have."

As the Sunset Warrior advanced there was a dizzying swirl of crimson and the huge man was gone from the ridge. In his place stood his dusky-red namesake, a giant lizard, long forked tongue questing from its lipless mouth at one end of the wedge-shaped head.

Hissing, it leapt upon the Sunset Warrior, its jaws hinged wide, snapping at his face. The fangs dripped with dark venom. But he slashed sideways with *Aka-i-tsuchi*, sliced open its belly as if it were rice paper. He was engulfed by a warm wind of putrefaction.

The lizard was gone, not even its stretched corpse remained upon the ridge's crest.

"So you have disposed of my vassal," said the Salamander, returned in a billow of scarlet and onyx. He struck at the Sunset Warrior. "Still I have delayed you and the Makkon will be here shortly."

The Sunset Warrior struck downward, then across, obliquely, shearing through the Salamander's blade.

"The last Makkon is gone," he said.

Again that foreign emotion slid across the Salamander's visage.

"I do not believe you. You could not have slain it."

"The one with the crystal claws? But I have. It lies back, behind us, just another feast for the vultures."

"So, have I underestimated you?" As he spoke the Salamander drew from the folds of his billowing robe a tasselated black metal fan. Arcing up from its hilt the Sunset Warrior saw the pointed *jitte* and he set himself for the finality of this moment, for from Ronin's memory he knew that in all the Freehold there was none to stand against the Salamander when he chose to use the *gunsen*. In times gone by, his students would shudder at its appearance for he never opened it unless he wished to kill.

Now the *gunsen* fluttered open in the stifling air, the flight of a lethal insect. The black metal was dull in the uncertain light, the spiked *jitte* a constant threat even as a defensive weapon.

The Sunset Warrior attacked with his shorter sword, thrusting upward from below his hips, and the *gunsen* described its barely seen patterns. The *jitte* spiked his sword, locked to it near the narrow guard. The Salamander twisted his wrist and, turning, made a flicking movement with his other hand.

A moment before the Sunset Warrior had seen the glint of pale light off one of the honed points. He ducked. But the distance was the major factor, for and against. He had no time but the weapon could not gain much momentum.

The star-shaped suriken embedded itself in his armor at the junction of his right arm and shoulder. At the same instant, the Salamander twisted the *gunsen*, hooking away the Sunset Warrior's short sword. The *gunsen* blurred upward, smashing into his high helm. The visor was ripped away and, even as he slapped at the *gunsen* with his guantlet, bending one of its metal ribs, he watched the flat onyx eyes staring into his and at last he saw the fat face react. For it was not Ronin upon whom the Salamander now gazed but some strange alien creature whose countenance he found terribly frightening, and within those searing, singular eyes he found that which he could not imagine: his death.

He fell back as if stricken, calling upon his master for salvation. But the nightmare came after him. The Sunset Warrior used his legs, lashing out with immense force, so that he cracked the Salamander's obsidian breastplate.

"Why did it not tell me?" wailed the Salamander.

"The master deceiver had been deceived," said the Sunset Warrior. He used the edges of his hands now, pummeling the Salamander.

"Who are you?" cried the Salamander.

"He who comes to slay you."

"Tell me!"

"I am a friend of Bonneduce the Last. That is all you need to know," said the Sunset Warrior. "The eons have caught up with you at last. Chill take you! All the people you have killed, all the people you have caused to be slaughtered under your cursed banner, for your holy cause."

"Power!" screamed the Salamander. "You must give me more!" He called to the billowing amber clouds.

"Finished," said the Sunset Warrior. The one word, echoing within the twisted, nightmare forest, an epitaph.

And *Aka-i-tsuchi* was raised, came down upon the huge head with titanic force that was as much will as muscle. For Ronin. For the Hart. For all of Bonneduce the Last's folk. For K'reen.

The skull shattered.

But it was no longer the Salamander's. Nor was it Tokagé's. For the fat had already commenced to run like rivulets of wax down the rapidly atrophying musculature. The arms and legs bloated up as if filled with violent, bubbling fluid. The fat torso split apart, massing itself into another configuration, growing before him, horrifying in aspect though it had barely begun to form.

The Sunset Warrior stepped back, feeling the intense cold swirl about his ankles, knowing that at last the great battle had commenced, for here upon this last lonely ridge in the arcane

forest of charcoal, he gazed upon the still-forming shape of fear and annihilation.
The Dolman.

They moved with great deliberation into the blackened forest, a strange pair: a Bujun woman and a four-legged creature who was far more than an animal.
Hynd was concerned now. He did not know where he was leading her. But he was compelled as if through some atavistic homing instinct to cross the river, take them into the forest. He knew what lurked there. They all did. This did not bother him.
Something was wrong and he worried at it as a dog would a fresh, juicy bone, turning it around so that he could see all its faces, every angle. Still he could not understand it.
And then the thought came to him: Dor-Sefrith is gone, Bonneduce the Last is gone. What had they in mind?
Circling the massive broken body with the curious crystal hands, the ripped, blackened face, they commenced to climb the first gentle slopes of a wide-ranging ridge.

COME.
Echoes.
COME, WAVE-MAN.
Echoes upon echoes.
DEATH AWAITS, WARRIOR WITH NO NAME.
The words a physical assault.
THY MENTOR IS NO MORE. I HAVE SLAIN HIM.
Brain buzzing with reverberations.
THEE HAS NO POWER NOW. NICHIREN PASSES, DOR-SEFRITH PASSES. NOW IS THY TURN TO DIE. SOON ALL MEN. WE NEAR THE WALLS OF KAMADO.
Hallucinations beginning.
ONLY THE DOLMAN SURVIVES.
Flashes of pain.
COME WITH ME—INTO THE DEEP.
The twisted forest dissolving into a waving morass of copper kelp, fuzzy fronds filtering the purple light which spread over him in ever-widening ripples of dark and light, zebraed bands fluttering hypnotically away forever, replicated without end, a seashell world.
Outside.
Time lost in a fevered dream, caught on the lip of an incip-

ient sunrise, held motionless, halted in midflight. Impaled helplessly.

No one beside him.

Alone, within the jaws of annihilation.

And The Dolman in front of him, growing and glowing, writhing, hideous, a madness, the embodiment of fear, the nemesis of life itself.

It was not clear what The Dolman was.

Perhaps it had a multitude of tentacles, a spade-shaped tail, huge round eyes, lidless with double pupils, slit of a maw which pulsed.

Perhaps, too, it had an enormous beak and ridged skin. Was it horned? It had no teeth, yet its gaping mouth was far more abhorrent than if it was fanged.

Felt something rising within him, thought it was panic and chased it down, away into the unfiltered, unplumbed depths of his being.

He did not know how to fight it. He swung with *Aka-i-tsuchi* but the alien atmosphere was so thick that all momentum was dissipated.

It drew him toward it, saying:

IS THIS WHAT I HAVE FEARED?

Broke upon his mind like a violent storm, shaking his universe.

He was stunned.

Numb, he felt himself being pulled into its pulsing grasp and he felt death enwrap him.

Consciousness fled. He was impotent.

And soon he would be a lifeless husk, swaying on the tide, another bit of copper flotsam in the death sea.

Perhaps they heard a voice as they topped the long snaking crest of the forest ridge.

A calling.

It was snowing, the unnatural light lending the flakes a pink hue as if some vast animal bled upon them as they were driven downward through the thick, exhausted air.

The curling mist made them choke.

The ridge had no far side.

There was nothing but mist, green and opaque, encroaching upon the reality of the world as if eating it alive, the old flesh crumbling, dissolving in the oncoming tide.

Here, said Hynd in her mind.

Moeru and Hynd, staring at each other.

Silence, more complete than was possible on the world of man.

Still their eyes locked. Still their minds exerted their wills, seeing only what they wished to see.

Hynd prowled restlessly.

"What is happening?" whispered Moeru.

Something. Are you afraid?

"Yes."

Even he did not know the answer.

They heard it then, the calling.

Abruptly there was no air.

She turned to the mist, the woman, stepped quickly into it, out from the shallows into a darkness more complete than night.

Had it been a trick of the billowing mist or had two figures vanished into its solidity?

Hynd knew at last, and without a backward glance, he loped easily down the ridge back toward the Kai-feng across the wide river.

It came to him, crying on the lonely wind which whipped the slender pines atop the last hillock of his soul.

His body was taken, the tentacles, if such they were, lacerating his flesh, seeping into his bones, melting them.

Yet he held onto the last shreds of his existence knowing that he held the key.

What is it?

I have no name.

Stillness entering his soul as death crept higher.

And he let in the bright spark, the rain at the core of his being, because he had nothing left to lose and it was all now that was left for him. Whatever it held.

Salvation.

He called, understanding at last that he was the sorcerer now, accepting it. Karma. And more. He accepted who he was, opening the floodgates. At first he had thought to call the blacksmith, for he recognized that he had no anchor, thus no solidity. He was being destroyed, drowned in The Dolman because of this. The blacksmith was the anchor and he needed her and he had set his thoughts to the snowbound slopes of Fujiwara. But he had seen in his mind the cold forges, the empty house, and knew that she was not the answer. What then?

He called, the crying of gulls off a limitless shore, an end to drowning, an end to hiding himself from himself. He felt her close now, his final third, the last piece of dor-Sefrith's handiwork, balked by The Dolman's fierce attack at Haneda.

They would not come together.

Why?

He turned inward, ignoring annihilation.

And found the blacksmith within himself.

Then she entered him and he felt the bright sparks gyring about him, red, green, blue, and he touched them, one by one, in wonderment and delight, laughing, crying, his entire being alight with the knowledge that at last he was whole; that this is what The Dolman feared. There were no more masters, no more protectors—thus the Aegir's death—no more sages. An end to childhood.

Ronin, Setsoru, and now the Sunset Warrior caressed the facets of his final third. Red, green, blue. K'reen, Moeru, Matsu. Love, strength, trust. The merging of all his traits, all his power: the Dai-San.

Energy ran through him like a rushing river, endless, depthless, ageless. He thought of dor-Sefrith's last trick. The mage, knowing his defeat was imminent, had cast one final card: he created the blacksmith, using Matsu's essence pulled from the sleeping mind of the forming Sunset Warrior. As a signpost. And the Sunset Warrior had used it. Now his universe was infinite, the source of his power illuminated. Himself.

His great mailed fingers curled about the thick haft of *Aka-i-tsuchi*—Red Tidings—and he plunged its glowing tip into the heart of The Dolman. His intense kineticism lashed the being surrounding him like a cruel whip. Bolts of green and blue fire, hotter than the core of the sun, rippled like molten ribbon along the lavender edges of his slashing blade, rolling all along its length from hilt-guard to its double-edged tip, eating, eating ravenously. He heard a delicious humming which grew with a great heat until it filled all his world, matching the fierce beating of his heart. Exhilaration turned to ecstasy.

Perhaps then The Dolman screamed, realizing the proximity of its death.

Swirling, its life force gushed over him, spilling like a gurgling sewer from the enormous rents made by *Aka-i-tsuchi* as he struck downward at it again and again with unbridled fury. And now he inhaled its entire hideous history. Scene after scene of torment and destruction swept over him, each one more ghastly than the next. The taste of incalculable despair.

The atmosphere wavered as he labored. Then it bubbled as if blistering, boiling. The horizon buckled and heaved and he heard dimly the hoarse hissing of steam under immense pressure. There came an unbearable whining and then—

A soundless scar upon the fabric of the universe.

When Moichi saw the figure cross the river, he did not know what to make of it.

Day was done. A last pale streak of sunlight was being bludgeoned into the wet crimson snow.

Even with the aid of his folk, the army of man had been sorely pressed, forced to retreat into the shadows of Kamado's high walls. Defeat had been at hand for a seige now within the citadel would surely mean starvation and death.

And then, not long ago, so swiftly that none could say truly when it began, the tide of battle turned. The black, insect-eyed rikkagin who so cleverly directed the enemy began to lose control. Perhaps they went mad, for they sent their warriors careening insanely into each other. Entire platoons of the pike men were easily decoyed and slaughtered.

The Bujun came to the fore, having destroyed the remaining deathshead warriors, and now they sought out the insect-eyed rikkagin, killing them wholesale. Other soldiers who had for most of the long day feared the intervention of the Makkon and The Dolman saw now that these sorcerous creatures were not forthcoming and their superstitious fear fell away and they launched themselves upon their foes with enormous ferocity.

The Bujun and Moichi's folk led the counterattack and now only the last few pockets of enemy warriors remained, isolated and fast crumbling. All the sorcerous creatures were so much carrion.

The field was a mounded sea of corpses, a vast humped marsh of spilled blood and seeping entrails, shattered skulls and broken bones.

Moichi was sick with battle, weary beyond exhaustion. It went beyond his muscles into his soul. His clothes, under his armor, were sopping, so heavy with soaked up blood that he felt disfigured with the added weight. Where the blood had already dried, the cloth was so stiff that it might have been metal plate.

His gaze swept over the vast plain of death to the swirling

river, pearled and frothy, and at once he had seen the splashing, like a fount of liquid light.

And now he watched the tall figure stride up the near bank, swollen with bodies, bristling with fallen swords, water streaming from him, and he knew even before he saw that strange transfigured face that he beheld the last living legend of the sorcerous age of mankind. The only one to cross the barrier into the last dying days of this year, with the winter's chill still staining lovely, faraway Sha'angh'sei, jeweled snow hanging in the columnated gardens and on the flat roofs of the harttins of the city, the promise of spring already a thought held close in the minds of the kubaru who jammed the long wharves and slept their short dreamless sleeps upon the rocking tasstans.

The numinous figure stopped now and raised his great blue-green sword so that its long tip caught the last ray of sunlight breaking through the rents in the flying clouds at the rim of the horizon in the west. It fired all along the gleaming length until the light seemed to stretch upward into the very heart of heaven.

And Moichi, sheathing his blade, caked with blood and brains, ran out into the mounded field of the dead, out from the high blank walls of Kamado behind which fires had already begun, memorials for the dead, a razing against the Kai-feng, a celebration of the day of man, out from the dark loomings of the citadel's shadows, out into the light of a new age.

Out to meet the Dai-San.

About the Author

ERIC V. LUSTBADER is the author of *Zero, Shan Jian, Black Heart*, and *The Ninja*, all bestsellers. He lives in New York City and in Southampton, Long Island, with his wife, editor Victoria Schochet Lustbader.

Nariyuki no matsu.

Printed in the United States
by Baker & Taylor Publisher Services